YOU & ME: PART TWO

LISA SHELBY

ALSO BY LISA SHELBY

<u>Disregarded Heart</u>

A Grumpy / Sunshine, single dad contemporary romance.

The Between the Pines Series

Meet *The Crew* from Eastlyn in this series of standalone contemporary romance novels about found family.

<u>Raised On It</u>

<u>Bottle It Up</u>

Want to read Reece and Rachel's story? Sign-up for my newsletter and get their novella for FREE! <u>Click here for your copy of We Are Tonight!</u>

Blackbird

Standalone second chance contemporary romance.

The Gorgeous Duet

A steamy, suspenseful romance about breaking the rules and following your heart.

<u>Gorgeous: Book One</u>

<u>Gorgeous: Book Two</u>

The You & Me Series

Read this three-book series of sweet and sexy standalone novels filled with love, loss, secrets, and sass.

To my amazing husband,

You are the love of my life.
Thank you for making all of my dreams, that I never knew I had,
come true.
You will always be my more.

1

———

Jonathan
5 Years Later

nother Saturday night.

Another night of drinking at Kells.

Another night of Courtney hanging off me even when I don't act interested.

I don't know why I came out tonight because I'm just not feeling it. I usually love this place. Kells Irish Pub is our home away from home and I've spent many a night and many dollars in this place. This is the place that all of us cops go for special occasions; promotions, birthdays, retirements and the occasional wake.

I'm in a funk. If Mick hadn't let Devon know everybody was meeting up tonight, I'm sure I would be at home getting drunk alone. Instead, I'm here where it costs three times as much more to get to that same place. A place I seem to be seeking out a little more than I should these days.

I know that Devon can tell I'm not in a good place. It was his idea for me to move here to Portland after our time in the Corps was over. He knew that staying in Georgia wasn't a good idea for me and persuaded me to move here. I crashed with him until I was able to find my own place and he and Gabby are now a constant in my life. My family. They came by tonight and picked me up and made me come out with them. They didn't really give me a choice.

Now, here I am standing at the back of the bar with Courtney attached to me with no sign of letting go. If she would just step away for two minutes I would be out of here.

It's my own fault. I know that. I had been warned about her. She's what we call a *Badge Bunny*. She only dates cops and she's slowly but surely making her way through the single, and not so single, guys in the department. I, in a drunken stupor, not once... but twice fell into her vagina at the end of two hazy nights here at Kells. Don't ask me why because I cannot stand her. She is the opposite of everything I like in a woman. Fake tan, fake tits, fake hair, fake nails, fake eyelashes. and her personality is just as fake as the rest of her. She actually kind of repulses me but somehow she always seems to find me. She doesn't have my number and I have never asked for hers, but if I'm out...anywhere in this damn city...I swear to Jesus that woman is in the same place at the same time. It's getting really old.

I finally decide I've had enough and tell her that I'm gonna call it a night. Her response doesn't surprise me at all when she says, "Okay, let me just go tell my girlfriend we're leaving and I'll be ready to go."

"No, Courtney, I'm going home alone."

She looks confused.

"I've told you before Court, what happened before between the two of us was a mistake, a drunken mistake. Both. Times. I am not looking for anything from you and never will. I don't mean to sound like such a dick, but I don't want to lead you on."

Oh, that felt good. I know I sounded like an asshole, but my ability to give two shits has galloped off into the sunset along with my ability to give a fuck! I just want to find D and Gabby and let them know that I'm taking off. I find Devon standing at the bar talking with Mick and some of the other guys.

Just as I put my hand on D's shoulder to update him of my departure I feel something electric in the air and my head swivels to the door of the bar. In what feels like an out of body experience I see a girl who looks just like *my Gracie*. It's as though all the air has been sucked out of the room as I see her laughing and talking to somebody over her shoulder. Her hair is down and she has on a black sleeveless top that ties behind her neck. Not only is her hair down, but she has big curls in it that I don't remember seeing before. She is so beautiful. This can't be real, can it?

It's been over five years and I am still dreaming about the girl who broke my heart. I need to get a fucking grip. Maybe I should go to a therapist after all. It would get Devon, Liam, and Fiona off my back. Until this moment I thought I was doing okay, but I guess if I'm imagining her appearing in bars while I'm out and about in public...then maybe I do need some help.

Just when I think I've lost it I see Cami is the person she's laughing with as she comes up behind her along with another woman. I feel my knees nearly buckle and thank God my hand is on Devon's shoulder because that is the only thing holding me up right now. This cannot be happening.

"J, what is it? You okay, man? You look like you've seen a ghost."

When I don't answer Devon follows my line of sight and I hear "fuck" come out from under his breath, but I'm so mesmer-ized by the sight of her smiling face walking into this bar...*my bar*...that I don't hear anything else at all.

Walking through the bar she makes a beeline for Mick and jumps into his arms. He picks her up in a giant bear hug and then sets her on her feet. When he puts her down, their backs are to me and I watch as he leaves his arm around her shoulder and she puts her arm around his waist as he introduces her to people.

Mick?! Mickey fucking Jacobs?! He is such a man whore! Why the fuck is she with this asshole? I mean I know women say he's hot and he is a great cop and a good friend, but women are disposable to him. You have got to be fucking kidding me! I feel rage start to course through my body. I cannot believe *my Gracie* would be with somebody like him. What the fuck did I ever do to the universe to deserve this shit? I haven't been able to find anybody since she decided I wasn't worth the wait or the trust to share her problems with, and now here she is with this fuck wad!

Devon can feel me simmering next to him. Now his hand is on my shoulder as he says, "Dude, calm down. You don't want her to see you freaking out, do you? You look like you're about to blow a gasket."

"Fucking Mickey, Devon? Anybody but Mick, his blond, pretty boy ass, will just use her and then throw her to the curb."

Just as I say this Mick and Emily turn around and Mick heads straight for me. The minute she sees me and our eyes lock I see her gasp and she brings her hand over her mouth. Two more steps and she's standing right in front of me.

"Kelly, McCoy, I want you to meet my little sis! She just moved back home from California and..." he's distracted by somebody calling his name and says, "Sorry, Emmers, be right back."

Sister, he just said sister, right? Oh, thank Christ! I feel myself take a breath for the first time in what feels like several minutes.

While I stand there like an idiot, Devon helps out and jumps in and gives her a hug. I hear him say, "PDX, it's really good to see you."

"It's good to see you too, Devon." She says to him and I can hear a quiver to her voice while her shimmering eyes are locked on my mine.

He releases her and we lose eye contact.

"This is my girlfriend, Gabrielle, remember you guys talked that day in San Clemente?"

"Oh my goodness, this is Emily! *The* Emily!" Gabby says as she realizes who Devon is talking to. She hugs her and says, "It's so nice to finally meet you."

"Same here."

Those crystal blue eyes that haunt my dreams turn back to me. We just stare at each other for a beat. Then she whispers so that I can barely hear her, "Georgia..."

"Gracie..."

When I call her by the name that means so much to both of us, I see her eyes well up with tears and I can't take it. I take a step forward and pull her into a hug.

Bam!

There it is. Nothing has changed.

As I hug her that smell of vanilla and coconut from years ago hits me with full force and I am taken back in time.

"Good to see you," I say coldly and step away from her.

"Good to see you, too."

Mick returns completely oblivious and drags her away saying Riley, the bartender, is dying to see her.

Her eyes linger on mine as she turns to walk away and then my favorite shade of blue is gone again. I watch as she walks towards Riley, who comes out from behind the bar (something I've never seen him do) and kisses her on the cheek and a hug. My blood starts to boil.

Devon grabs me by the shoulders and turns me away from my view of her.

"Talk to me, J. You okay? You look pissed. You want me to take you home? Gabby and I can leave whenever you're ready. Just say the word."

Not answering any of his questions I turn around and she's still talking to Riley. Does she know every guy in this fucking place? I feel myself getting that feeling that I've felt too many times since the day she said goodbye to me. It's not a good feeling and it makes me feel like I am losing control just like I did that day.

I must sit in that jeep for twenty minutes before finally starting the engine. I just can't believe she's done this to me. I know she said she would, but I couldn't believe she actually did it after everything. I don't beg for anything and I was just begging for her phone number and she wouldn't even give me that. What the fuck was so wrong with me that she couldn't even give me her number or even her God! Damned! Last! Fucking! Name!

I feel a wave of anger come over me that I have never felt before. I flip a bitch in the middle of the road and head back to base. The thirty-minute drive takes me twenty as I speed through traffic. Thank God it's a holiday and there aren't a lot of cars on the road. When I get back to our room Matt is the only one there. He tries to ask me what's wrong, but I cannot be spoken to at this moment, and God help the person that gets in my way. I am on a fucking warpath right now as I pace back and forth in our tiny room. Finally needing to do something to release some of my anger I pick up the small desk chair next to me and yell "FUUUUUUCCCCCKKKKK!!!!!!" at the top of my lungs as I slam the chair into the ground and the wheels on the bottom bust off. Then I pick the chair up and throw it across the room.

"Dude, talk to me! What the hell happened? What can I do?" Matt yells, but his voice sounds far away because the rage pounding in my head is drowning him out.

I turn to Matt who is mere inches from me and yell right in his face. "There is nothing you can do for me, Matt! Not a God damned thing that anybody can do for me. Just leave me the fuck alone!"

If I had been in any other frame of mind, the look on Matt's face would have been enough to snap me out of my funk and beg for his forgiveness. But all I see is red, and I just keep throwing things and destroying our room in a rage like I have never experienced. It's a good thing we were pretty much packed to leave, and there isn't too much available for me to throw. I am out of control and Matt takes it all. He just stood in the corner and waited for me to finish my tantrum. At some point I slide my way down the wall and just sit on the ground with my back against it, heaving like a wild animal. Matt does the same and slides down the wall next to me and just sits there with me for I don't even know how long.

"She didn't even give us a chance, Matt. She said she loves me but she won't even try! What the fuck is so wrong with me that she can't even try?" I plead to him like he has the answers.

"Man, I am so sorry."

This is all he says. It's all he needs to say and thank God Matt was there. Who knows how far off the rails I would have gone. He's always the one who keeps me in check and is the calm, reliable one of the three of us. He's like the dad of our crew, and I know I don't need to worry about him telling anybody what just took place here in our room. Thank God Matt was here.

I have no idea how long we just sit and I breathe in and out and try to figure out how to breathe without her.

"Yeah, man I really need to get out of here. You guys don't have to leave though. I can just get an Uber."

"No, we'll take you home Jonathan. You go...we go," Gabby interjects.

"Let me run to the bathroom real quick," I say and turn to go.

~

As I leave the bathroom downstairs at Kells I instantly get a whiff of the strong smell that is coming from the cigar room. I don't smoke but I have spent lots of time in that room with the guys that do and for some reason, the smell gives me a small sense of calm. Calm is something I could really use right now.

Taking in one last breath, I lift my head to look up the stairs before heading up and there she is stopped three steps above me, looking scared to continue her journey to the bottom of the stairs.

"Hey," I say.

"Hey," she says back as she takes two more steps pressing her back to the wall. She's as far on the other side of the stairwell as she can get and is now one step higher than where I stand.

"So, Mick's your brother, huh?" I huff out sarcastically.

"Yep, you two work together, I hear?" She asks meekly and clearly to make polite conversation.

"We do," I say with my arms crossed not giving her anything.

"So, have you been in Portland long?"

She's trying to make conversation and I'm just making things awkward by being so cold. I know that I tell myself that I hate her. But it's just not true. Seeing her, right in front of me, clearly feeling uncomfortable in my presence makes me feel like an ass.

"Four years. Devon talked me into it," I say trying to lighten my tone and be nice.

Awkwardly, she says, "Oh. Well, that's great."

I have no idea why, but I just have to know if she's with him when I ask. "So, you know Riley?"

"Uh, I do. We went to school together, but I haven't seen him since I moved to California."

Thank Christ!

"You just visiting or do you live here too?"

"I just moved back into town this week. Alex came down and

made the drive with me and Cami this past weekend. I'll be staying with Mickey for a while."

Great, she'll be living in my neighborhood. That's just fucking karma for ya right there. And who the fuck is Alex?

"Cool."

My one-word answer makes her uncomfortable and she starts playing with her dragonfly necklace, just like she always did when she was nervous.

"You still have your necklace, I see," I say with a nod of my head in the direction of her hand on the necklace.

Her hand stops moving and she says so quietly that I can barely hear her. "You remember?"

"I remember everything about those nine days, Gracie. I always told you that there wasn't anything you did or said that I didn't remember. And I remember it all. Right up to the last minute."

2

———

Emily

Standing in the stairwell of Kells, it feels like my worst nightmare has come to life. I'm finally face to face with Jonathan again—just like he said we would be—and he hates me.

"I remember everything about those nine days, Gracie. I always told you that there wasn't anything you did or said that I didn't remember. And I remember it all. Right up to the last minute," he growls. This is not the way I had always dreamed this would go. No, this is right out of my nightmares. It's almost like I can hear disgust in his voice.

Not knowing what else to say I reply. "You do?"

He's now talking through his teeth like he's seething. He leans forward, just inches from my face, and says with all the barely contained rage that I can feel radiating off of his body. "It wasn't me that wanted to say goodbye and not try the long-distance thing. That was all you, sweetheart. I don't tell somebody I'm in love with them and then just leave them blowing in the wind. No...that would be the way you do things, sugar."

I just stare at him. Who is this person standing in front of me? Where is the Jonathan that I fell in love with? He looks like my Georgia and smells like my Georgia, but his eyes seem dark and he looks tired and seems so angry.

Then with so much venom I nearly jump from the sting of it he asks, "So, you still not available?"

Not answering him I just say, "I have to go!" and run up the stairs forgetting that I ever needed to use the bathroom. I resolve not to shed a tear in front of him or anybody in this bar.

I see Riley behind the bar once I am back upstairs and ask him if he's seen Cami and Alex. He points in Cami's direction with a concerned look on his face. I don't give him a chance to ask if I am okay, but I do ask him to call us a cab and I turn to find my best friend.

I find her talking to Devon and Gabby and it only takes one look for her to know I need to leave. She knows me better than anybody and with a quick goodbye to the happy couple and a text to Alex—who will get a ride home with her boyfriend that met her there—she and I are out the door. I hate that she was with Devon. I hate that he could see how upset I was and I am sure will tell Jonathan. This night just keeps getting better.

I manage to keep it together until we're in the cab, but the moment the door closes, the tears fall.

"He hates me, Cam. I knew he would and he does," I sob into my hands. Cami brings her arm around my shoulder and pulls me into her so she can hold on to me while I fall apart.

"Emily, he doesn't hate you. You were just the first bad thing in a string of worse things that happened to him, and I'm sure seeing you brought it all back to the surface for him," she says as she pulls away but keeps rubbing my back. I am so confused.

"What are you talking about, Cam?"

Her eyes fill with tears and I can tell that what she has to say isn't good. Cami is strong, but even this is hard for her.

"Well, Devon just told me that while they were in Afghanistan, Matt was killed in an IED explosion, and as their squad leader Jonathan takes the blame and still hasn't forgiven himself."

"Oh God! No! Not Matt...Oh God Cami...Poor Jonathan...Devon too. That's horrible." I have this instant need to turn the cab around and run back to him and hold him. But I think he made it pretty clear that's not what he would want.

"That's not all, sweetie. Two months later, Jonathan lost his mom. She had been sick when he was home, but she didn't tell him and he had no idea at all. It totally blindsided him and Devon says he hasn't been himself since. So you see, chica, he lost you, Matt and his mom in a matter of months. He doesn't hate you, you just remind him of the worst time in his life."

"Oh my God, Cami!" I feel like I can't breathe.

"I didn't mean that to sound so harsh, Em. I just want you to know that he doesn't hate you. If he didn't love you as much as he did, losing you wouldn't have been up there with losing Matt and his mom, but according to Devon it is."

I sit in the back of the cab and I sob. No wonder the Jonathan I knew was gone. His mom was his everything and he loved Matt like a brother. The fact that he couldn't save either of them has to be too much for him to even come to terms with. The fact that I could have anything to do with any of his pain is almost too much for me. My poor Georgia.

"Oh Cami, I feel so horrible for him. I wish there was something that I could do, but I don't think he even wants to speak to me. He was so cold and was practically seething with anger at me."

She continues to rub my back while I sob all the way to her apartment.

When we get to her place—that is covered in unpacked boxes from her recent move back home with me—we go straight to her room where she throws a nightshirt at me and insists I change. She puts me to bed and covers me up. She sits next to me on the side of the bed while I just lay there staring at the wall.

"Chica, I am sure this was not the reunion you had envisioned. I know you're hurting right now, but try not to take it personally. He's been through so much, sweetie. Seeing you tonight was just as much of a shock to him as I'm sure it was to you."

"Just the thought that I could have been a part of creating the version of him that I saw tonight is unbearable. I...I...I feel like I need to do something for him, anything. I wish I had been there for him. I was so selfish, Cam. I didn't even tell him my last name or give him my phone number. I wasn't there for him when he needed me most."

I sit up in the bed and throw the blankets off of me. I can't breathe. Before I know what I'm doing I start pacing the room.

"Em, stop."

I keep pacing.

Cami grabs me by the arms and yells into my face.

"Emily Grace Jacobs! Stop!"

I stop next to her bed and look my best friend in the face. The person that is always there for me. Some people go to priests. Some go to shrinks. I go to Cami.

"Em. Take a deep breath."

"I should have told him, Cam. I should have given him the choice. Maybe we could have at least been friends and then I could have been there for him when he needed me most. How could I have been so selfish?"

"Em, you were scared, you weren't selfish. You, yourself, were at the beginning of something life-changing and you had just been devastated by somebody else the week before. You were in self-preservation mode and it was easier to walk away from him than possibly endure any more rejection than you already had. I get it, chica, and I am so sorry it was a decision you ever had to make but it's not your fault. Even if you had said yes to trying to make it work, he still would have lost his mom and Matt."

I know she's right, but I still can't help but think that I'm to blame for him turning into the man that I saw tonight. He looked the same, and for the love of all that's Holy, he still smelled the same. But he was so cold and there was no light left behind his eyes. But I still felt *it*. I felt it in that first moment that our eyes locked onto each other. That electricity...that connection was still there.

"Cam, I still felt it. The moment I saw him I felt *it*. Even though he was cold and hurtful it didn't matter. The moment I touched him...Cam...it was overwhelming and just like it was five years ago. He hates me and I'm still in love with him."

Cami wipes the lone tear that is slowly making its way down my cheek and then hands me a much needed tissue.

"Honey, he's the love of your life. Of course, you're still in love with him."

"Cami, come on, that's a bit dramatic, don't you think?"

"Had you ever been in love before Jonathan?"

"No."

"How about since?"

"Cami, you know the answer to that question. Why are you doing this to me?" I whine like a petulant child and throw myself on the bed.

"Because it may have only been nine days, but Em, he was *the one*. The worst part of it is that you let him get away. Now, we know you can't go back in time and you aren't the same person he met in San Clemente five years ago but neither is he, Em. You've both been through a lot since then and that's bound to change you both."

She walks over to where I am and flops herself down on the

bed next to me. As we both lay on our backs staring at the ceiling, she grabs my hand and we lay there for a few silent minutes.

"You may not be the same girl you were when he met you but one thing I'm sure of is that I have watched you turn in to an amazing woman these last five years. You are so strong, Em. I am so proud of you. Maybe when you're ready...and he's ready...you guys can sit down and talk about things."

"Thanks, Cam, and I really do love your optimism, but if you had seen him tonight...well you would realize that there is no way he will ever feel like talking to me."

"Well, keep an open mind and if the opportunity presents itself and just remember, no regrets. Now let's get you to bed. You need to sleep and hopefully you'll feel better in the morning."

I know that she's right. The two of us have always vowed to live our life with no regrets, but right now I'm full of them.

I'm not sure how, but I do fall asleep. I dream of hazel eyes and dimples, cottages and walks on the beach.

3

———

Jonathan

I can't believe I am spending my Saturday morning in this ridiculous spin class. Most of all, I cannot believe I let D beat me at a game of freaking Horse. I mean seriously, when was the last time I played Horse and since when do I let D beat me at anything? He has a horrible jump shot and I always beat him in hoops. But here I am...so I guess I don't always win after all. Or maybe Horse is just not my game?

If I'm honest with myself though just being here is pretty damn cool. I could not be more proud of Devon for opening this place. *The Gym* is his baby and I don't mind supporting him in any way that I can. He saved for so long and found the perfect business partner, and just a little over a month ago they opened the doors to their very own fitness club simply called *The Gym.*

The name is actually pretty damn perfect if you ask me. Nobody ever says they're going to 24 *Hour Fitness,* they say they're going to the gym. Pretty ingenious. But that's Devon McCoy; he's smart and when he sets his mind to something he gets it done. Kinda like getting me out of the house. He knows that I've been in a funk since seeing Emily last Saturday night and being here will probably do me some good.

At least it's not Zumba. I should be grateful. Come to think of it I almost feel like Spin Class isn't such a bad debt to pay after all when Zumba could have been in the mix of punishments. Devon's better half, Gabby, is the instructor this morning and I hear the lights are turned down for most of the class. So, there are a couple pros right there. It'll be dark, Gabby is the instructor and it's not Zumba! Thank God for small miracles.

I made sure to get here early enough to snag a bike in the back of the room. As I get my bike set for my height and get situated I see Gabby walk over to the light switch to turn the lights down. Right as she turns the lights down the entire room lights up when Emily, Cami, and the same exotic looking brunette I saw with them at Kells, walk through the door. Talk about thanking God for small miracles.

The room is dark but I can still see them. Emily and Cami each hug Gabby and introduce her to their friend whiles she leads them to the three bikes she had saved for them up front.

God, she is just as beautiful as I remember. This morning with no make-up on and her hair up in a ponytail, she's perfect. I only got to see her with the light on for half a second but that's all I needed.

She's shaking hands with the person on the bike to her right and introducing herself. I can hear her voice and it is so soothing. As always, she's making those around her comfortable by introducing herself to the person next to her at Spin Class. Even at Spin Class, she goes that extra mile without even trying. I haven't said two words to the people on my left and right, but I'm an asshole so that's to be expected. God, I want to hate her but she makes it impossible.

Just as Gabby turns on her mic and starts to talk to the class,

I see Devon standing in the doorway of the room with a shit-eating grin on his face that is directed right at me.

That fucker! This was a set-up. He knew she would be here today and now I know why I'm not in Zumba class on this fine August morning. He's so going to pay for this. What. A. Dick.

I shouldn't be surprised he set this up though. He chewed my ass Saturday night because apparently Emily was pretty upset when she left. He asked me what I had said to shake her up and I was honest with him. It wasn't what I said but how I said it. I was cold. I was angry. He said that if I was trying to hurt her, I had succeeded and that I should probably apologize to her. I strongly disagreed with him since she's the one that tore my heart out of my chest, threw it on the ground and stomped it into the hot cement outside the Pier Side Inn five years ago.

To this Devon replied that there may have been a very good reason and that maybe I should try to find out what that was now that time has passed. I told him that when I asked her if she was still unavailable she just walked away, so clearly she isn't available so why bother? He then proceeded to tell me I was an idiot and said we were leaving. When he dropped me off at home he not so gently told me to get some sleep and snap the fuck out of my 'look how bad the world sucks' attitude. Come the light of day though, I realized he was right and I've been wishing I had handled the situation better. I knew I would see her again one day but it didn't go exactly how I had always dreamed it would go.

Before I realize it the class has started. The music is blasting through my eardrums and I'm cycling my ass off. It's hot, it's dark and it's loud but I could give a fuck because in front of me is one of the best views I have ever seen. That view comes complete with Emily in an outfit that looks similar to what she wore on our hike, the day I kissed her for the first time. That was one of the best days of my life but it feels like it was a hundred years ago. I know that I have always said that I knew I would see her again, but this just all seems like some fantasy come to life.

I mean...when I moved to Portland of course,I thought there was a chance I would see her, and I would be lying if I didn't admit to myself that I look for her on the street fifty times a day just hoping I'll bump into her. Then last week I finally do bump into her and what do I do? Jack it all up and treat her like shit. Looks like *I'm* the dick.

The thing is, I've spent the last five years thinking she must have been sick and dying. Why else would she have just walked away from what we'd found in each other in such a short period of time? Seeing her looking healthy, happy and still hot as fuck at Kells, sent me into a tailspin. I've been miserable for years and she couldn't look happier. That just pissed me right off.

I'm positioned perfectly so that I can stalk Emily from behind the entire forty-five minutes of class. She has no idea I'm even here. She's in black yoga pants that stop just below her knees and a work out tank that fits just right. I'm not even within touching distance and I feel that thing I feel whenever I'm around her. That buzz. That something special that is all her. I felt it Saturday night too but I was too drunk, shocked and pissed not to think it was a bad thing. I was too busy feeling sorry for myself and in a shit mood. So I ignored that thing she has about her and that electricity that we share between the two of us. I pushed her away.

Between my spectacular view and my thoughts running circles in my head, I'm shocked when class is suddenly over. I can't believe I am thinking this but I wish class would never end. When the lights come on and the stark reality that she is about to leave me again sets in. I panic!

Fuck! I can't let her go again!

I see her get off her bike and she, Cami and their friend head over to Gabby. While they chat she's standing on one foot while holding her other up behind her to stretch the front of her thighs. While she switches to the other leg she still has no idea I'm here but Gabby does. I love her for letting me handle this on my own and not letting Emily know I'm standing mere feet behind her. Emily starts to head out the door and Gabby gets my attention motioning with her head that I should follow. What she's really saying is '*Hey dumbass! Here's your chance to say you're sorry for being a total tool on Saturday night,*' and I hear you loud and clear, Gabs. It's time to go get the girl. Or at least time to go grovel to the girl and hope she gives me the time of day because the truth is I don't hate her. How could I? She's *my Gracie.*

May the luck of the Irish be with me today.

It took a couple of minutes to make my way through the sea of people and bikes and walk up to Gabby to get the look of confidence I needed from her. That look of support that silently told me that I could do this. I love that girl. Devon really is a lucky man.

When I finally make it to the doors to the parking lot, I see her saying goodbye to Cami and their friend and decide to wait until they're gone to avoid an audience.

As soon as Cami starts to back out I see Emily head towards her Jetta. The same Jetta she was driving five years ago. That means her car must be at least ten years old. The part of me that will always want to take care of her instantly starts to wonder if she's been getting the routine maintenance done on the car and if it's in need of an oil change. I can't help but worry that she isn't as safe as she could be.

Shit, am I going to stand here and wonder about the maintenance record of her car or grow a pair and approach her? I guess I better grow a pair...here goes nothing.

"Emily!" I shout across the lot just as she reaches out to open the car door.

She spins around and is shocked to see me. She instantly pulls on her ponytail to tighten it like she does when she's gearing up for something. That blush of hers that I love so much starts from her chest and goes right up to that perfect face of hers. She instantly takes two steps toward me and away from the car, but not in a run to jump in my arms way. More like a stay away from my property way. What the hell?

I catch up to her and breathlessly say, "Hi."

Between class, chasing after her and nerves I can barely breathe.

"Hi, Jonathan," she says with no affection in her tone.

"I saw you in spin class and thought I would try to catch you before you left."

"Well, it looks like you caught me."

Wow, it's cold out here in this August sun. I must have been an even bigger asshole than I remember last Saturday. She isn't being all warm and fuzzy, but she's talking to me. I'll take what I can get.

"Em, I just wanted to say that I am so sorry for being such a colossal jerk last Saturday night. I was shocked to see you and I had had a couple of drinks and wasn't really myself i So, like I said, I wanted to say I was sorry."

She takes a moment to think of her next words.

"Jonathan, I'm sure I probably deserve much worse than what happened Saturday night after the way I left things back in San Clemente. So, your apology is more than accepted."

I feel the breath I was holding rush from my chest.

Oh, thank you, baby Jesus! She forgives you. Now ask her out or something you ass-hat!

"So, I was thinking that maybe we could meet for coffee or something. Not a date or anything. Just to catch up?"

Please say yes! Please say yes! I silently pray to whatever God will hear my plea.

"I don't think that's such a good idea, but thank you for the offer."

Shit!

Fucking Alex!

"Are you with somebody?"

Please say no! Please say no! I once again beg the Gods above.

"No."

Thank God and everything that is holy! I feel like with that one-word answer, the course of my life has just changed and there is a light at the end of this long and treacherous tunnel. I know she didn't say she still loved me or wanted to run off and have my babies, but it's one less hurdle to get over. I don't think I realized until this very moment how much I still loved her. I feel like my heart just started beating again for the first time in five years. I can't get her to go to coffee with me but my heart is beating again and that's a start! I feel energized and ready to do everything in my power to get her to change her mind and say yes to having coffee with me. *Wait! If there isn't anybody else, then who the hell is Alex?*

"Who's Alex, then? I just assumed he was your boyfriend."

"Alex?"

"The other night...didn't you say that he came down to California and rode back with you and Cami?"

With a little giggle she says, "Jonathan, Alex is a girl. She's been friends with Cami and me since Jr. High. I can't believe I never told you about her. She's our other BFF. I just assumed you knew her. She just left with Cami."

Oh, thank Fuck!

"If there isn't somebody else then why can't two old friends meet for coffee and catch up?"

She's silent and staring down at the car keys in her hands.

"Emily?"

Still nothing. Shit, did I say something? This is not going well.

I take my forefinger and put it under her chin and slowly lift her beautiful blue eyes up to meet mine while I search her face for any clue that will tell me what is going through her head. "Emily, meet me for coffee. You pick the place and the time and I'll be there."

I remove my finger that is holding her chin up and instantly feel the loss of our connection. She looks at me with sad eyes, for what seems like forever, and then quietly she exhales. "Okay."

"Okay?"

Don't let her change her mind moron!

"Okay, it's settled then. I know it's August and a little warm for coffee but I guess we can get iced coffee if you want or a smoothie or something else. Whatever you want is fine by me."

Shut up! You're rambling! Just breathe, you idiot.

A small smile sneaks across those delicious lips of hers. At least I amuse her, it's better than nothing.

"Iced coffee is fine, Jonathan."

"Sounds good, what works for you?"

"Do you know Elka Bee's Coffee Haus, in Happy Valley?"

"I sure do."

"Is Wednesday okay?"

NO! That's not okay! That's four days away! I scream inside my head.

"Wednesday is perfect."

"Okay, I'll see you then," she says taking a step back to leave.

I don't want her to leave yet so I go for it and say, "Here, let me give you my number and you can just tell me what time works for you as it gets closer. What's your number and I'll send you a text so you have mine."

I break out into a cold sweat after I ask for her number. I mean really, what makes me think she'll give it to me now? We spent a week together and professed our love to each other and she never gave me her number. At this point what do I have to lose? It's worth a shot. I have to wipe my hands off on my shorts before I grab my phone out of my pocket. because my hands are so sweaty. I don't want to look like a total ass and drop my phone in front of her. Might as well try to keep the level of humiliation to the lowest level possible while I wait for her to shoot me down.

As I stream all the wishful thinking I have into my thumbs, I pull up a new contact and type *Gracie* into the name field and then hover over the phone number box waiting. I'm about to tell her that's it's okay and I understand, when she speaks. I can feel myself shaking as I enter her digits into my phone. Hoping to God she isn't messing with me and this is really her number because I am going to write it on my fridge, write on paper and file it away. Hell, I may buy a little black book just to put her number in it. I am not losing this bit of gold.

I quickly send her a text to make sure she isn't lying, and the relief I feel when I hear a ping from her bag is like a heavy weight being lifted from my chest. I watch as she pulls the phone from her bag and adds my number to her phone and then I hear my own ping. What I see on my phone brings the biggest smile to my face.

GRACIE

Got it, Georgia.

I must look like a fool but I can't help it. Just her three-word text has my heart practically pumping out of my chest. So, I send her another text but she starts to leave before she reads it.

"See you Wednesday, Jonathan." She says as she walks the two steps back towards her car.

"See you Wednesday, Em."

I make myself turn and walk back into the gym to get my stuff otherwise I know I'll just stand and stare while she drives away. I don't wanna scare her off.

I see Devon inside and he can tell just by looking at me that it went well. I'm too happy to talk about it so I just hold up my hand as I walk out the door. I jump in my truck and read her text:

GEORGIA

Thank you.

GRACIE

You're welcome, Georgia.

The use of her nickname for me is yet another glimmer of hope. I know it's foolish, but it is hope I'll feed off of to get me through the next four days until we meet for coffee.

I start my truck and take the first full breath that I've taken in five years.

4

Emily

You can do this Emily. It's just two old friends having coffee and catching up. It's not like you are going to have to go sit across from the love of your life whose heart you broke over five years ago and act like it's not at all awkward. No, that would be too painful for even you. That's why it's just two old friends meeting for coffee. No. Big. Deal. So you tried on everything you own to go get coffee, who doesn't? You can do this. You owe it to him to at least give him some of your time after the way you left things.

As luck would have it, the only parking spot is right in front of the little local coffee shop...and the little two-person table that Jonathan is already sitting at and...yep, he's seen me and has his hand up in a wave. Guess it's too late to put it in reverse and take off now that I have been spotted. I can't even take a moment to catch my breath because he's right there!

I. Can. Do. This. I tell myself.

As I get out of Justine, my trusty old Jetta—I must admit I named her after spending my week with Scarlett—I take the five steps it takes to get to Jonathan and I see he has a friend with him.

He gets up and awkwardly comes in for a hug. I lean to the right and he leans to the left so we clank our heads together. We both reach our arms up to take the hug high and that goes wrong too. This is just too funny and I can't help the giggle that bubbles out of me.

"Well, we're off to a great start," I say.

"Oh man, that was just terrible," he chuckles.

"Let's try again. I'm gonna go arms high and head to my right, got it?" I say with a smile on my face that I couldn't stop if I tried.

"Got it. I go arms low and my head to the right too."

Just to continue to lighten the awkward move I start to count and he joins in.

"1...2...3...hug!"

As we embrace we both hold on a little longer than we should. So long we are swaying a bit to the rhythm of both of our hearts that are beating a little faster and louder than normal. He feels like home.

Jonathan pulls away and says, "Well, that went a bit smoother than our first try, thank goodness."

"Yes, it did. But don't be rude, Jonathan," I say with my hands on my hips. I amuse myself while I watch the scared confusion that breaks out across his handsome face. "Introduce me to your friend here."

I can see the relief fill his body when he exhales a large breath and says, "Ah, yes. How could I forget my sweet girl... Emily, this is Frances or Frannie. Francis, this is Emily."

"Oh, Jonathan, she is so sweet!"

I bend down so I can properly introduce myself and give Frances—the cutest little dog I have ever seen—a proper hello.

A few scratches behind her ear and a few licks to my cheek and I tear myself away to tell Jonathan how adorable she is.

"Thanks. I rescued her about a year ago. I take her everywhere with me. Hope you don't mind me bringing a third wheel?"

"Of course not, she's awesome. What breed is she?"

"She's a mutt, but I'm sure there's a little shepherd and maybe even a little pitbull in there. Not 100% sure, but I love her just the way she is." He says and even though his words are sweet and there's a smile on his face he doesn't have that same sparkle in his eye that he did years ago.

"Uh, I hope you don't mind but I went ahead and ordered for you. One twenty-four ounce, iced, non-fat, white chocolate mocha, no whip and one of the best marionberry scones you will ever eat."

Breathe Emily...just because he remembers exactly how you like your coffee and what your favorite flavor pastry is, it doesn't mean anything. Keep breathing and say thank you.

"Thank you, Jonathan. It's perfect."

"No problem, I owed you for the other night. It doesn't make us even or anything, but I just want to say one more time how sorry I am."

I have no desire to talk about or think about that right now so I divert the conversation to something a bit more lighthearted.

"So, Frances huh? Is she named after somebody?"

"Nope, it's the name she had when I adopted her. She responded to it so well already that I just left it. Besides she an older girl so it fits."

"We've got Frank at Mickey's but he's nowhere as cute as her. Oh, man, does he snore and fart. He's a bulldog so there's just no getting around it."

"Oh, I've met Frank and you aren't kidding. He certainly leaves an impression." He chuckles.

"You have?" I ask surprised that he would know Mick that well.

"Yep, I've known your brother for four years now. I'm not sure why, but he brought Frank to a St. Paddy's party one year and then I helped him move into his place and saw Frank again then. There's been a BBQ or two as well. I can't believe Mickey Jacobs is your brother. What are the odds of that?" he asks, as if he's just as shocked as I am by the small world we find ourselves in.

I feel myself starting to get emotional at the fact that Jonathan has been so close to me all this time and I had no idea. I wonder if he knows?

"Life's pretty crazy isn't it?"

As always, he's reading my mind.

"It is...So, how did you end up in Portland?"

He takes a big inhale and slowly lets out the breath and shares his story with me.

"Wow, okay this is hard. Um, while we were in Afghanistan, I lost my mom. It turns out she'd been sick when I had been back to visit her the week before I met you, but she didn't tell me. She said she didn't want me worried or to take my mind off my missions. I was so angry, Em. How could she have not told me? She was all I had and she knew she was dying and she didn't let me be there for her."

I can't help but reach out and take his hand.

"I am so sorry for your loss, Jonathan. I know how much she meant to you, how much you loved her..." I say while holding back my unshed tears.

He squeezes my hand, then lets go to scrub his face with his hands and then runs them through his hair. I can tell he's trying to collect himself before he goes on. It's clear this is all still hard for him.

"They sent me home from the desert for a week to make arrangements and then I had to fly back after the funeral. I don't know what I would have done without Liam and his family being there to help me figure it all out."

"The Fanuas, right?"

"Wow, nice memory," he says with a little smile before he grows somber again. "Yep, Mr. and Mrs. F pretty much did everything. They knew mom was sick, but she made them promise not to tell me. I know they feel horrible about it now, but it's not their fault and I don't blame them at all. So, anyway I finished my tour and then came back to Camp Pendleton for the last couple of months, as planned, and then I got out and went back to Savannah. It was too hard to be there. Without my mom there it just didn't feel like home. I had the Fanuas and I had friends from high school, but being there just didn't feel like home. I had been saving money for years to buy my mom her dream house and now she wasn't there."

"Oh, Jonathan," I say because I don't know what else to say.

"So, after being home a month Devon could tell when we talked that I wasn't in a good place and he suggested I move out here. He offered me his spare room and I knew that Portland State had a really good Criminal Justice program so...I went for it. I didn't stay in his spare room long. I had my savings, so I got an apartment close to school at first and then after I knew the city better and had my group of friends I ended up moving out here to Happy Valley. I built my dream house and something my mom would have loved. It just felt right. The house may be too big for me and Frances, but I feel like in some way I kept my promise to my mom even though she isn't here to enjoy it."

"She would be so proud of you, Jonathan."

He looks a little embarrassed at my compliment and I can't

help but think how cute he is all embarrassed like this. It's nice to see him blush for a change, instead of me.

"Thanks, but I think she'd be more proud that I got my degree. I had gone to two years of community college before joining the Corps and then two years at PSU while working the road with Portland PD. So, I've been with the department for four years. The first two were crazy with school and work, but I got through it."

"I'm so happy for you, Georgia! Degree, check! Job, check! House, check! You are checkin' off all those life goals! Good for you and you're right. Your mom would be proud of you for getting your degree."

My phone buzzes and I glance down. It's a number I don't recognize. I don't answer it and let it go to voicemail.

"You can get that if you need to."

"It's an unknown number, so it's okay. Probably just a misdial."

"So, what's it like to have Mickey Jacobs as your big brother?"

With that, a light conversation starts and just like the old days we talk and talk and talk. I feel like I'm with the old Jonathan, minus a little bit of that light he had about him. I understand why that is now. I would love to have the magic wand that could change it all and add that light back to his beautiful, yet somber eyes of his. His light may be gone, but he's still just as attractive as ever. He still has that natural tan about him, and his short dark hair is a little longer now that he isn't sporting a military length. He's still in great shape, if not a little bigger. More built. He is a fine specimen, no doubt.

After some time, Frances starts to pant and Jonathan picks up her water bowl and excuses himself to go get her some more water.

While he's inside, I decide to check the voicemail of the unknown number and wish I hadn't. A voice I haven't heard in years fills my ears. Just as the message is ending, Jonathan is back and sitting across from me. He must be able to tell that the call has disturbed me because as soon as I put the phone down on the table he takes my hand in his.

"Em, you okay?"

The gentle touch of his hand is enough to calm me.

"It was my dad." I can hear the shake in my voice as I continue, "I haven't talked to him in years. He found out I moved back home and he wants to get together."

"What do you want?"

"I don't know, Jonathan. I just haven't been able to forgive him yet. Not only did he make my entire childhood a lie, but he just quit being our dad once he had a new family. I know I am twenty-six now and not that pre-teen kid he left but it's a little late for me," I say with a shrug.

With those soul-piercing hazel eyes of his, he makes sure he has my attention when he says, "Emily, you wait until you're ready. I do think that one day you'll probably need to see him and tell him how you feel and maybe let him explain, but do it when you're ready and do it for yourself. One thing I've learned is that life is short, Em. You never know from one day to the next what might happen."

"Jonathan, I heard about Matt...I am so sorry for your loss." I blurt out as I grip on to his hand even tighter to let him know that if he wants to talk, I'm here.

"Thanks, Em. Let's save that for another time though. Right now you and I are getting to know each other again and we're talking about you and your dad."

"You know what, can we not talk about my dad? I am sure you already know all about him. In fact, I'm sure you've met him if you hang around Kells."

"Shit, that's right. Mick being your brother means that Michael Jacobs Sr. is your dad. Could this world get any smaller? Em, I do know your dad. It's not from Kells though. My first year on the road I pulled him over for a DUII. At the time, I had no idea who he was and then later I found out he was Mick's dad. After that, Mick has made sure he doesn't get to keep a rolling tab at Kells anymore. He hasn't been seen around much since then. I was pretty new at the time and hadn't really started hanging out with the guys so I never saw your dad out and about. Only the time I arrested him. Sorry, Em. Not exactly the kind of catching up I had hoped to do with you today."

"That's okay, really it is. I'm so detached from him that it doesn't really faze me or surprise me, if I'm honest. I'm just grateful you were able to get him off the road before he hurt somebody or himself. So, thank you, Jonathan. Sincerely."

"Still, I'm sorry about things with your dad, Em."

I must change the subject! This is getting too depressing

"So, do you like being a police officer?"

"I do. It's not always the most fun, but I love to help people and I feel like I can actually make a difference in people's lives."

"I know I grew up around it, and my brother does it too but I just don't know how you guys do it. You go to work every day knowing that people hate you even though you're the first person they call when they need help. It just infuriates me."

"Well, at least I don't work at the DMV or for the cable company. Talk about people who go to work every day knowing they're hated," he says with a wink.

"Seriously, Jonathan...do you ever get scared?"

"I think I recall you asking me this question once before and just like then I'll tell you the truth...not really. We're trained to do our jobs and do them well. I trust the officers I work with to have my back and to make sure that we all go home to our loved ones at night. For me, that may not be a wife and kids but I know Frances is home waiting on me. I can't let her down now, can I?"

I know he's trying to keep things light-hearted but it isn't funny to me. He can tell so he tries a different approach.

"Em, my safety and the safety of the citizens and my fellow police officers is all that is on my mind out there. I know your brother is the same way. You don't have to worry about us, but it's very sweet that you do."

"Oh my gosh! I didn't even think about your sleep when I picked 9:30 to meet. Did you work night shift last night and you lost sleep to have coffee with me?"

"I did work last night but it was my Friday so I'll catch up later. Don't worry. Sacrificing a few hours of sleep to spend time with you and Frances is worth it."

"So, are you working four days a week, ten hours a day or are you one of those guys that work three twelves?"

"I'm lucky enough to work three twelves. It's really twelve and a half hour shifts, and then once a month you work an extra day to make up the difference. It makes for long days but it's nice to have four day weekends. So, I'm a Sunday, Monday, Tuesday guy. Doesn't Mick work Wednesday, Thursday, Friday? We work different precincts so I don't see him much, but we both lucked out and get part of the weekends off. Anyway, boring stuff, but at least you know when I am around if you want to get coffee again. What about you?"

"Me?"

"Your schedule?"

"Ha, oh that. At the moment I don't have much of a schedule, but school will be starting next week. I'll be a Teacher's Aide in the Special Education class for one of the high schools in the district. That's only part-time though. I'm also going to school to get my Masters in Special Education."

"Is that why you moved in with Mick?"

"That would be it. Ugh...I just couldn't afford California anymore. If I want to go to school and try to get it done in 20 months, I need to work part-time and not to mention I...well, anyway. It's just a lot and Mickey was nice enough to offer his place up. So, I finally sucked up my pride and did it. My mom offered too, but she's in a two-bedroom apartment and I don't want to invade her space. Mick's place is bigger and he's rarely home. It won't be forever."

"Sounds like a good plan. I'm proud of you, Em." He says with a lingering stare.

To break the stare, I pick up my phone and see the time and realize I have to go.

"Sorry, I have to get going but it was so nice catching up." As I bend down to give Frances some love I say, "And meeting this pretty little lady."

"It *was* really nice, Emily. I'd love to do it again sometime."

"Well, I'm sure that we'll bump into each other around town and maybe coffee again will work out sometime. I'll have to see what my schedule is like once my job and classes get started."

I turn to leave and take the few steps to the curb where Justine is parked and I turn back to see him watching me go. I step off the curb, and holding open her driver's side door I yell to Jonathan, "Justine!"

"Who's Justine, Em?"

That look of confusion on his face is pretty cute, I must say, but not as earth-shattering as the smile I get when I say, "You're lookin' at her. You once told me that you always name your cars and your guns. Well, I don't own a gun, but I do have a car that I have loved for years and since it's pretty obvious she's a girl...I couldn't name her Justin, so I went with Justine."

Now that I've backed out of the awkward little parking lot that Elka's is in and away from the handsome smiling man and his darling dog, I let the smile I've been holding back spread across my face. I let out a little shriek of delight at the fact that I had the last word and that it got the reaction it did. It was like I had given him some sort of gift with just the simple fact I remembered something from the time we were once together. That I had actually listened to him and acted on it. The fact of the matter is the joy on his face was gift enough to last me until Christmas.

On my drive to the house, I call Cami on my Bluetooth and tell her we have to talk, and like the best friend she is she says she'll meet me at my place in five!

Cami shows up just after I do and when she walks in she looks around and asks, "Are we the only ones here?"

"Yep!"

"Spill it, chica!"

"Oh my God, it was so great Cam! At the very beginning, it was awkward but then it felt like old times. Just like before. We were so comfortable with each other that we just talked and talked. The most important thing Cam...he doesn't hate me."

Just as my eyes start to swell with tears she grabs my hand and I repeat. "He doesn't hate me, Cam. He said he'd like to get together for coffee again."

"There isn't anybody on this planet that could hate you. You are the best person I know, and from what I remember Jonathan is a pretty smart guy, so of course he doesn't hate you."

"Now what?"

"Give him a chance, Em. Tell him."

"I know and I have nothing to hide. I am proud of everything that's happened in the last five years, and I've worked hard to keep my head above water. If we get together again I'll tell him, I promise. I just didn't want to remind him of how I had hurt him when things were going so well. I didn't want to dredge up the bad memories. Next time though, pinky swear."

I hold my pinky finger up, Cami does the same and we lock

them together and the promise is sealed. Now, when will that next time be?

"Listen, I have to get to my next showing so I have to run, but I am so happy it went well. Please give him a chance. He's been through a lot, and you may be just the person he needs in his life right now."

We hug it out and as she walks through the door she says, "Give kisses for me."

"Promise!"

As the door closes behind her I find myself alone in the house. I can't fight the childlike glee I feel with the simple knowledge that he doesn't seem to hate me and he wants to see me again!

I can't help it. I have had his phone number since Saturday and only used it once to tell him what time I could meet him for coffee. I dig my phone out of my purse and realize that I already have a text. And it's from him! I had forgotten that I had turned off the volume after my dad called. Ugh! I forgot about my dad, but he can wait for later.

I hold my breath as I open his text:

GEORGIA

It was so great to see you and Justine today.

GEORGIA

I mean it. It was really great to see you.

Gracie

Thank you. It was great to see you and Frances too. Thanks for the coffee. And the scone.

I figured it would be some time before I heard back from him so I walk to the kitchen, toss my phone on the counter, open the fridge and just stand there staring blankly. While in my far away la-la land I hear the ping of my phone. I throw the fridge door shut so hard all the contents inside rattle and I leap to the counter to grab my phone like somebody is going to beat me to it.

GEORGIA

Frances said it was nice to meet you too.

GRACIE

Maybe we can take Frank and Frances for a walk sometime?

Oh crap! Did I just ask him out? Crap! Crap! Crap!

GEORGIA

She would love that but I am not so sure…
Frank's owner is kind of a player and I hope the apple doesn't fall anywhere near that tree.

GEORGIA

Can you tell I'm a bit of an over-protective father?

GRACIE

'll make sure he's on this best behavior.

As if he knows we're talking about him Frank—named after Will Ferrell's Frank the Tank character in the movie *Old School* —saunters into the room looks at me, gives me a little snort and then plops himself on the cool kitchen floor.

GEORGIA

I'll give him one chance but if he steps one paw out of line they don't see each other again.

GRACIE

Understood.

GEORGIA

Hey, I have to run, but we'll talk soon and thanks again for agreeing to coffee.

You would think the high school quarterback had just asked me to prom, not that I had just gotten a handful of platonic text messages from the guy whose heart I broke. I am so giddy I can't even stand it! I'm bouncing around the house and singing a little JT to Frank, and not even caring if Mickey walked in and caught me. I haven't felt like this in years.

A few minutes go by and then I'm blessed with the sound of another ping!

GEORGIA

Just got an email from Mick that the crew is coming over Saturday for a BBQ. Some sort of housewarming party. You gonna be there?

Gracie

Well, this is the first I'm hearing about it but I'm sure I'll be there. I don't have any other plans for Saturday night.

GEORGIA

Good to know.

GRACIE

Are you making fun of me and my lack of a
social life?

GEORGIA

Nope, just happy to hear that you'll be there.

GRACIE

Me too.

5

____

Jonathan

I can't believe it's almost eight o'clock and I am just now on my way to Mick's! I've been looking forward to this for three days and then I get ordered to work overtime on my day off! I'm sure we were below minimums because everybody took the time off to be at Mick's BBQ. It's more like a housewarming, but dudes don't have housewarmings, so he's calling it a BBQ.

Since seeing Emily on Wednesday I've been living in my own little world. Spending time with her that day was like taking in air for the first time in years. Every text that we've exchanged in the last three days has started my heart beating again. I feel like the dark cloud that hasn't left me alone since she walked away from me that day is finally starting to lift a bit.

Our texts have been everything from the mundane about doing laundry or walking the dog, to moments that give me hope that she still feels even just a little bit of what I still feel for her. The conversation that gives me the most hope, but also scares the shit out of me, was from last night as we were saying goodnight.

. . .

> Gracie
>
> I really can't believe that you remembered exactly how I like my coffee...

GEORGIA

> I remember everything about you and about that week.

I got nervous when a few minutes went by before her next reply. Afraid I had scared her away already. Just as I pick up my phone to type some sort of apology, I hear the alert I'd been waiting for.

GRACIE

> You still a simple Americano guy?

She fucking remembers too. It's not just me! Now how do I play this? What the hell, I might as well go for it.

GEORGIA

> Yep and I still love chocolate ice cream...

Right now I am picturing that magnificent blush of hers slowly crossing her features as the memories of our week floods back to her. I hope I haven't crossed a line but it's killing me to know if she's pushing me into the friend zone or if I'm ever going to have a chance at something more with her. When five minutes have passed I realize I might have crossed that invisible line. I tell myself to wait another five minutes and if she doesn't reply I will.

With just a minute to spare she puts me out of my misery. I see the tiny bubbles start moving on my phone's screen that tells me she is in the process of writing me back. What I read next is not at all what I was expecting...

GRACIE

I'm ready to tell you what I couldn't in the past. I don't want to move forward with our friendship in any way without you knowing. I'm not the same person I was when we met, Jonathan and I want you to decide for yourself if you want to continue a friendship or anything else between the two of us. Do you think we can try to get some time to talk when you're here tomorrow night?

GEORGIA

Of course.

GRACIE

Ok, good. See you tomorrow. Goodnight.

GEORGIA

See you tomorrow.

I typed and re-typed my reply to her message and finally just decided to keep it simple. I want her to know how much it means to me that she trusts me enough to tell me whatever her big secret is. At the same time, it stirs up emotions that anger me and make me want to scream, why couldn't you have told me then?! Until I know what's going on I think simple is best.

Now, here I am driving like a maniac to get to her. The adrenaline that is coursing through my body is practically making me shake. I can't wait to see her but I'm scared to death to hear what she has to tell me. Our only communication today was when I texted to tell her I had gotten called in and that I would be late getting there. I hate that there were hours that I could have been with her that were wasted.

As I pull on to Mick's street, I can see that my theory was correct and that everybody and their brother took today off. There are cars lining both sides of the street. I find a spot about a block away and take a couple of breaths before I get out of my truck.

Walking down the sidewalk, I feel so amped that my hands are shaking and I have to put my hands in my shorts pockets to try to contain them. Just knowing that sometime tonight I will finally have the answers I've been needing has me going out of my mind. I have no idea what she's going to tell me or if it will change my mind about her like she said it would when we met, but I still have to know. I'm not sure if she knows how much her inability to trust her secrets with me all those years ago hurt me. I know I can't dwell on that right now so I shake it off and walk around the side of the house to the backyard where I can hear voices.

I walk through the yard and say my hellos, I grab a beer out of the cooler, open it up and toss the cap in the trash, all while my eyes are flying around the yard in search of her. I don't see her, but I do see Devon and Gabby.

I start to head towards them, but Mick stops me first with a handshake that turns into a bro hug. Bro, brah, brofus, dude... these are all words that sum up Mick. You would think he lived in a fraternity but nope, that's just Mick. He's a dude's dude and a player through and through. That's why seeing Emily with him at Kells filled me with instant rage. I was never so relieved to hear him say the word sister. Except that does mean that Mick is her brother, and I want more than friendship from Emily. Things could get ugly if not handled correctly.

"Bro! So glad you could make it! Sucks balls that you got called in on your day off, man. Glad you came by anyway."

"Of course, couldn't miss your first big shindig at the new place."

"Well, thanks for helping me move in, dude. Help yourself to whatever you want. What's mine is yours."

I don't think he's referring to his sister, but I thank him anyway.

Mick takes off to say goodbye to somebody, and I take another look around but still don't see Emily. I find Devon and Gabby again and head that way. They're talking as I approach them and with a nod of her head Gabby signals to D that I'm behind him and they instantly stop talking. As soon as Devon turns around, something seems off with him.

"Hey man, what's up?"

"Not much, J. Sucks you had to pull a shift today."

I can tell there's something that he's hiding from me and Gabby looks at me almost like she feels bad for me for some reason. What the Hell is going on here?

"Yeah, it does. So what's up?"

"Not much, just the usual crew here tonight."

"Not what I mean, D."

"What do you mean?"

"Come on man, I can read right through you. Something's not right and you aren't telling me what it is."

Gabby speaks up this time and says, "It's nothing bad, Jonathan. Emily was just looking for you. She wants to talk to you about something."

"Why does this not make me feel any better?"

"Just ignore him. Devon's already had a few too many beers and he's just being stupid," she says and gives me a hug. "Glad you're here, and I'm sure that Em will be back out in just a minute."

Just as she says that,the back slider door to the house opens and there she is. She is gorgeous as always and she doesn't even have to try. I noticed at *The Gym* the other day that her body hasn't changed much at all. She's a bit curvier, but in the best possible way. She isn't twenty-one anymore and it looks good on her. Tonight she's wearing those tight as hell skinny jeans that are rolled at the bottom—just like in California—with some flip flops and a dark blue t-shirt. Nothing fancy, but to me she is perfect. Intoxicating.

I've held so much hostility towards her these past years, but once I saw her again it all came back. That instant connection. It's like I was an addict who had been clean and sober, and the moment I saw her I fell right off the wagon and started imbibing again. I feel a calmness overtake me just knowing I'll be in the same room with her, but at the same time, I'm nervous as hell. What is she going to tell me? Will it be enough to make me understand how she could just walk away from us?

I start to make my way towards her and Devon pats me on the back and still has that strange look on his face. What. The. Hell? I feel like everybody knows what's going on but me.

"Hey there, Georgia, glad you could make it."

"Me too. Did I miss anything exciting?"

"Nope, no drunk cop stories to tell yet. I see you got a beer are you hungry? Can I get ya something?"

"I'm good right now. I'll get something in a bit."

Tell me now!

I hate this polite conversation and beating around the bush bullshit.

Right when I'm about to lean forward and ask her if she wants to go talk we're suddenly surrounded by people. It appears Emily was wrong and the drunk cop stories have begun. Eventually, we all find deck chairs to sit in and the beers start flowing. I notice Emily still doesn't seem to drink. She's been sipping on a Diet Coke all night. I notice her sneak away into the house a couple of times. She must be keeping her own personal stash of Diet Coke in the house. Lord knows you have to hide things with this crew because anything out in the open is fair game.

After a while, Emily seems to be in a deep conversation with MacKenzie Theissen and her girlfriend Liz, so I take this time to sneak away to the bathroom.

As I leave the bathroom I hear something coming out of the room just across the hall and notice there's a small light on and the door is cracked. On instinct, I take the two steps across the hall and peek my head into the door.

In the bed talking to her stuffed animals is the cutest little girl I have ever seen. She has big brown eyes and curly blond hair. She sees me and gasps and closes her eyes to pretend she's asleep.

"It's okay, I'm a friend of the person who owns this house. I won't tell anybody your awake if you don't want me to?"

The sweetest little voice I have ever heard whispers.

"You're friends with Uncle Mickey and Frank?"

Did she just say Uncle? What the...?

"Yep, I sure am. Mick's your uncle?" I ask as calmly as I can without hyperventilating.

"Yep," she whispers.

Shit...

"Who's your mommy?"

"My mommy is Emily. Do you know her too?"

My heart starts to beat out of my chest as I try to calculate how old she is.

"I do know your mommy, she's an old friend of mine."

"Cool."

"What's your name sweetheart?"

Still whispering she says, "My name is Ireland, what's yours?"

Did she say, Ireland? This cannot be happening. I just keep

hearing Emily telling me that she loved all things Irish back in California.

"It's nice to meet you, Ireland. My name is Jonathan."

"Hi, Jonafon."

I think she might be the cutest thing I have ever seen.

Trembling I take a couple of steps into her room but not far enough to frighten her.

"Ireland, how old you?"

"I'm four with a half."

My heart has jumped out of my body, I just know it has. I was never great at math but even I can do this math. Just as I feel I might have a God damned heart attack right here and now I feel a hand on my shoulder. I startle and turn around to see Cami holding what I think is a baby monitor in her hand just as Ireland says, "Sorry, Aunt Cami. I can't sleep. This is Jonafon, he's a friend of momma's and Uncle Mickey's."

Still with her hand on my shoulder, Cami says, "He's a friend of mine too, Ireland, and I'm glad you two could meet, but you need to go to sleep. I was supposed to be making sure you were sleeping tonight and I'm gonna get in trouble if you don't get to dreaming, little one."

"Okay, I'll try better, Aunt Cami."

Cami walks over to the bed and tucks her covers in around her and kisses her on the forehead. On her way back to the door she turns me around to leave with her.

"Bye, Jonafon. See you later," the cutest voice on the planet whispers.

"What the hell is going on, Cami? She's four and a half?"

I can barely breathe.

"Let Emily explain, Jonathan. Just listen to her. You may not like everything you hear and you may not understand it all but she's worth it. But I think you already know that though."

I see her look over my shoulder and give a nod of her head.

"I'm gonna let you two talk. I'll stay in here and listen for Ireland and you guys go out front where you can talk in private."

I still haven't turned to look at Emily, but I feel her as she gets closer and then walks past me and to the front door. She opens the door, walks out and leaves the door open behind her.

Cami gives me a push and says, "Go. She's worth it. They both are, Jonathan."

And with that Cami leaves me standing alone in the living room. I stand there for a beat because I'm just not sure I'm ready to hear what Emily has to tell me. I finally nut up and make myself go outside.

When I get to the front porch I see Emily sitting out in the middle of the big grassy front yard. She's just sitting there cross-legged, staring into the star-filled sky and playing with the dragonfly on her necklace like she always does when she gets nervous.

I walk out to join her but I just can't sit right now. I have too many questions and too many emotions raging through me and I have to keep moving so that I don't explode.

"I see you met Ireland?"

"She's four, Emily."

"She is."

"Fuck, Emily! Is she mine?"

Emily jumps up in an instant and is on her feet and standing right in front of me. Well, she's trying to but I won't stop pacing so she finally grabs me by the arms and stops me. I feel the connection as always but push it away. I'm too pissed at the moment to enjoy the feeling.

"Jonathan, no. She's not yours. I am so sorry that you

thought that. You must be so freaked out right now. She's not yours but every day I wish she was."

I bend over and put my hands on my knees and hang my head as I try to fill my lungs with air again. Oh, thank fuck! If she had kept my child away from me, I could never forgive her.

"I would never do that! I may have messed up plenty with us, Jonathan but I would never do that!" she practically screeches.

Shit! I said that out loud. I need to pull myself together.

"I am so confused, Em. Am I that bad at math?"

"No, you aren't. Let me explain, can we sit?"

I don't speak but I do sit my ass on the ground and she sits directly across from me. We're sitting in the dark, in the middle of Mick's front yard, but I can still see her face from the street lights. She's scared to death and I give her the minute she needs to gather herself enough to tell her story. I think I need the minute just as much as she does if I am telling the truth.

And then she begins...

"The week before I met you I had found out that I was pregnant. I hadn't even realized that I had missed a period yet but I had to go in for my drug test for the new job I was starting and when they called to say it was all good to go they congratulated me on my pregnancy. I was shocked. I couldn't believe it was true so that night Cami and I went and bought two packages of pregnancy tests. There are two in each box and Jonathan, I took all four tests because I had worked too hard to get where I was and I only had one year of school left. Then I was going to get my masters," she says as she hugs her knees to her chest.

"Jonathan, every one of those tests came back positive. I wanted to die. How could I have been so stupid? It wasn't like I slept around, in fact, it was quite the opposite. I was so busy studying I didn't really have time for guys but there was one guy that I did see from time to time. Harrison Flowers, you may have heard of him? He was a professional surfer and gone a lot. He would call when he was in town and we would hang out."

"I get it. I don't need details, Em. Keep going..." I say just in case she was going to go into any broken condom stories that I really don't want to picture.

"Sorry, I just don't want to leave anything out. I need it all out there. So, I found out on a Thursday and he called to hang out on Friday. When I met up with him I told him that I was five weeks pregnant and he said there was no way it was his because he had been on the road. It had only been two weeks since I had seen him last and about three weeks before that. Well, that's five weeks.

He lost it on me, Jonathan. We were at a party but had gone to a room to talk and he started calling me a whore and a slut and said that I was probably screwing every guy on campus when I wasn't with him, and there was no way it was his. Then he stormed out of the room and just left me there dazed and confused. I was so hurt and embarrassed. I was scared to death and I had no idea what I was going to do.

Cami and I left the party and I figured I would give him a day to cool off and try to talk to him again. I called and texted but he didn't reply the next day. I knew he would be leaving again in a few days, and we knew they were always throwing parties when they were home, so we showed up without an invitation and you know what he did? He pretended he didn't know me. Like I was some stranger. Even his friends, who knew we hung out, were confused and didn't know why he was being such an idiot. But I knew why. It was okay to ruin my life but his was too important for an unplanned pregnancy or at least that's how I looked at it then."

"What an asshole," is all I can get out at the moment. The thought that some dickhead could treat somebody like Emily like that infuriates me. It's probably a good thing I didn't know when we were in California because I may have paid him a little visit.

"That's a nice way to describe him. He made it pretty clear that he didn't want anything to do with me or Ireland. I tried again when she was born and he came to the hospital and saw her. But he wouldn't hold her and said he didn't want his name on the birth certificate."

She releases her legs from her chest, crosses them in front of her again and makes sure my eyes are on hers.

"Jonathan, I swear to you I wasn't sleeping around. There wasn't anybody but Harrison. I knew he wasn't the one and he was only around from time to time, so it was perfect for my busy schedule of school and work. I didn't love him. Hell, I don't even know if I liked him. I don't know how it happened, we always used protection but it happened.

I met you exactly one week later. At that point, I didn't know if I was going to keep the baby or not. I was so confused and scared and had so many decisions to make that I didn't know which way was up. That's why I told you I didn't date or do relationships. Between Harrison and my dad, I hadn't had the best of luck and really couldn't take any more rejection. I was some chick you met on vacation, and you were going away for nine months. Well, you would have come home and I could have very well had a baby. That wasn't fair to you, Jonathon. What was I supposed to say...I know we just met, and we've known each other a week, but want to be a dad to some other guy's baby? I would say that would be a little more than you bargained for."

"You should have given me that choice, Emily," I say coldly.

"I didn't know what choice I would have been giving you. Like I said, I didn't know what I was going to do. If I did tell you, and then didn't keep the baby, I would have felt like a slut for sleeping with you while pregnant with another man's child. And if I did keep the baby, I didn't want you to feel obligated because you had told me you loved me and I would have always wondered if you were only with me out of pity."

"I was in love with you for Christ's sake! I deserved to know!" I see her jump a bit and realize I just yelled that at her.

She whispers so low that I almost can't hear her when she says, "I was so ashamed. I went from being the good girl who never slept around to being knocked up at twenty-one with no baby daddy to speak of. I didn't want to see the look of disappointment or disgust on your face. Or to get rejected yet again."

I don't know what to say because I do understand where she's coming from, but I still wish I had known. I just stay quiet.

"The thing is Jonathan, it's because of you that I have her. If I hadn't gotten to spend a week surrounded by love and joy—to see that good men did exist out there in the universe—I don't know if I would have made the same decision. What I felt for you was so strong and that week with you made me feel whole. I was in such a dark place, and without even knowing it you pulled me out bit by bit. It started before I even saw you. It was your laugh. I heard you laugh and it shook me out of the haze I had been wallowing in. You woke me up, gave me hope and for a short time, love. You gave me strength and confidence. You will never know how that one week of my life changed me forever. I haven't felt that sense of wholeness again. Not since I walked away from you that day. Don't get me wrong. Ireland is amazing, and I could not love her more than I do or be more proud to be her mom, but the love I get from her is different than what you gave to me that week.

So, what I've wanted to say to you since December 1, 2010, is thank you. There wouldn't be Ireland without you. I thanked you silently the day she was born and I held her in my arms for the first time. I'm so glad that I finally get to thank you again in person."

I've been so entranced, hanging on her every word that I'm

just now noticing that she has tears streaming down her face. I lean forward and wipe her tears away with my thumbs, give her a kiss on the forehead, stand up and wipe the grass from my shorts. My mind is going a million miles an hour right now, but what I keep coming back to is that she didn't trust me enough or give me the option to stay or go. I can't talk about this anymore. I need a chance to think.

"Emily, I really appreciate you telling me everything and I really am sorry you had to go through all of this on your own, but I just don't know what to think. You were pregnant and didn't tell me. I was making love to you every night and you didn't tell me. I told you I loved you and you didn't tell me. We sat and had coffee for two hours and 'caught up' and you didn't mention the biggest thing in your life? This has been a lot of information and I really just can't talk about it anymore. I need to get out of here and just think. I can't fucking deal with this shit right now."

I run my hands through my hair so hard I'm sure I just ripped a chunk out, but my mind is so fried it wouldn't even register if I did. She's standing now, still crying, and I just stare at her for a beat then turn and head for my truck.

6

———

Emily

I didn't sleep at all last night. So many things were going through my head after talking with Jonathan. Should I have told him way back when? If I had told him would we even have happened? Would he still have wanted me to wait for him? Are those decisions I should have let him make? The hardest part... seeing his face when he thought for those few minutes that Ireland might be his. That is what is killing me. What's worse is that he thought I had kept her from him. His visceral reaction to thinking he could have been a father has me wondering if he would have wanted that role, or if the thought was something he couldn't even consider.

I understand he needs time to think, I really do, but I have so many questions for him now. To start with does he think I'm a slut because I was with him just weeks after Harrison? Does he think I didn't mean it when I told him that I loved him back then? And of course, I am back to thinking he hates me again. I just need to know where we stand and where we go from here.

I want to know all of this but at the same time, I don't even know what I want from him.

I know that I feel all the same things I felt before and that I love being around him. He is still drop-dead gorgeous and I miss his dimples that don't seem to make many appearances these days. I know I have missed him every day, but what do I want from him?

I have Ireland now, it's not just me.

I can't let her get attached to somebody if it's not the real deal, but at the same time, I don't want him to think that I expect him to be her fill-in dad. I don't need a man in my life to take care of me and my little girl. I have done that on my own for the past four and a half years. The problem is now that he's here I do feel like I need Jonathan in my life. I don't just need him in my life, I want him in my life. There may not even be a reason for me to wonder all these things because he may never want to see me again after last night.

Ireland and I are walking home from the park with Frank and I see that the driveway has filled up while we were gone. Mickey is hosting Sunday football at his place today. Seattle is playing the Rams and since this is Portland I have a feeling there will be a lot of Seahawk fans here today. Since Portland doesn't have a team most people root for the Hawks, but after all my years in California, I'm pulling for the Rams today.

I have no idea who all is here but I hope they can keep the foul language to a minimum with Ireland around. I feel so bad that I am cramping my brother's style and I hope he doesn't grow to regret having us stay with him.

We go in through the garage so I can throw away Franks bag-o-poop and come in from the laundry room and through the kitchen. I get stopped here by Shelley, Marnie and also Trish, who is Wesley's fiancé.

In the short time I've been back all of the ladies, and their husbands, have been incredibly welcoming. There's something to be said for the family that is created within a police department. It's a life that those not living it will ever understand. I may not be an officer, and I may not be married to one but I grew up with a dad in that line of work and now my brother is doing the same thing so, I get it. They have all offered to babysit, given me advice on day cares, the best stores in the area, where to eat and where not to eat...you name it and these ladies can fill you in. The best part is, so far, they don't seem too gossipy. But I am the newbie so things could change.

Ireland is still holding my hand as we chat about who brought what to eat, and Trisha and I confess that we really do love football and that we kinda wanna go watch.

"Mommy, if you go watch the game with Uncle Mickey can I too?"

"Only if you're quiet, sweetie. And you have to let your uncle watch the game."

"I pwomise, mommy."

"Ok, go ahead and I'll be right there."

After a few more minutes, Trisha and I go to see if there's anywhere to sit in the living room or if I need to grab a chair from the kitchen table. The first thing I see when I walk into the living room is the love seat that is filled with Jonathan and Courtney Sandberg. They aren't just sharing said 'love seat' but she is all up in his business sitting as close to him as she can without sitting on his lap. His arm is resting on the back of the chair behind her shoulders.

His eyes meet mine and he just looks at me and gives me a slight shake of the head as though he's trying to tell me it's not what it looks like.

I feel the burst of rage color my face as I try not to storm out of the room and pretend I don't care about what I'm seeing in front of me. That would be too easy though because this is exactly when Ireland sees Jonathan too. She walks up to him and leans on the arm of the love seat only inches away from him. "Hi, Jonafon."

"Hi, Ireland. What have you been up to?"

"Mommy and I took Frank to the park." She says for everybody to hear and then leans in his ear to whisper. She hasn't quite figured out that she isn't talking quiet enough because we can all hear her say, "He pooped in the grass and then Mommy had to use a bag to pick it up. It was so icky."

This gets some chuckles from the room and a, "Way to go Frank! Thanks for doing it on your walk with Emmers and not me! Score one for big brother!" from Mickey.

I just make a smart ass little sister face at him and shake my head.

"It is kinda icky but I have to do the same thing when my dog, Frances poops," Jonathan says sounding completely engaged in his conversation about dog poop with my little girl.

By now she's propped herself up on the arm of the love seat and is practically sitting in Jonathan's lap when she asks, "Oooohhh, you have a dog too? Her name is Frances?"

This has got to be annoying Jonathan and his date so I try to step in and save him.

"Baby girl, let's leave Jonathan and his friend alone. Come on."

Being the good girl she is she immediately starts to get down.

"Nah, she's not bothering me. In fact, here I'll show you a picture of Frances."

With his offer of Frances pictures, Ireland climbs up in his lap and Courtney has to move away from him as his arm comes down to get his phone out of his back pocket to show pictures to Ireland. Courtney seems put out, but Jonathan doesn't even give her a passing glance. He just focuses all his attention on Ireland.

I leave them to it and let him know that if she starts bothering him to send her to me. I calmly walk down the hallway and into the guest bathroom where I lock the door behind me.

I should be happy that he's so good with her, but in some ways, it breaks my heart thinking of what could have been.

I also shouldn't be so angry that he's here with badge bunny, Courtney. I have no claim to him and he's free to be with whoever he wants. But why her? Why bring her here today of all days?

I've only been back a short time and I've already heard all about her from my brother. According to Mickey she just seems to be everywhere they are, and he would bet his brand new house that she'll end up marrying some poor schlub from the department in the next year. I hate that Jonathan would want to be with somebody like her. But I guess he's a guy and they have needs that, from what I hear, she will take care of.

Seeing him with Ireland was almost harder on me than seeing him with that skank.

He seems to have gotten the same reaction from her that he did last night; one of familiarity and ease. She went to him and just climbed up in his lap and he let her get comfortable and lean back into his chest while he showed her pictures of his beloved dog. I mean how freaking amazing is that? Now, if only I was in Courtney's seat, it would be the picture I had always dreamed about. But nope, here I am hiding in the damn bathroom.

Enough! I will not hide from him.

I open the door and head to the kitchen to make myself a drink. I can't help but peek into the living room as I try to stealthily pass by without being noticed. Ireland is now on the floor sitting between Jonathan's feet playing with his phone. I can't even take the site of it so I just keep on walking to what is now an empty kitchen. I can see through the kitchen window that the ladies are out on the back deck. I open a cupboard and grab a glass and as I turn to get my diet coke and ice, Jonathan walks into the room. His eyes lock with mine and it's almost like he's daring me to look away.

"Hey, Em."

"Hey."

"She's awesome, Emily."

"Thanks," I say quietly looking down at the glass in my hand.

"I mean it, Em. She's freaking amazing. You've done such a great job."

And cue the tears. I spin back to the cupboard so he doesn't see the tears that I'm begging not to fall.

I can feel his body heat on my back and I hear him say just loud enough for me to hear. "I am so sorry for leaving last night, Em. My mind was whirling with so many crazy things and I needed to take it all in. Hell, for about five minutes I thought maybe I was a dad and then I wasn't. I mean I know she doesn't look like me, but the hair and eyes are so much like Mick that I thought maybe she just looked like her uncle? I was so relieved I wasn't her dad and disappointed at the same time. It was just a lot and I'm sorry."

I feel his hands on my hips as he slowly turns me around. We're only a couple of inches away from each other but I can't look at him and I just keep looking down at the empty glass in my hand. I don't have the strength to look at him.

"Em, I know we're just getting to know each other again, but I would really like to spend time with you and maybe see what happens. I understand why you wouldn't have told me about being pregnant back in San Clemente. I didn't at first, but when I put myself in your shoes, I get it, Em. I really do. Do I wish it had gone a different way, sure, but I do understand."

I finally look up into his eyes that have always seen me...the real me. I can see that he's being completely genuine and really does forgive me, or at least can appreciate why I made the decision that I did. I can't believe he still wants me. And did he say he was disappointed that Ireland wasn't his?

"What do ya say, Em?"

"Jonathan, I can't just *try* something again. My life is different now and I have a little girl to think of. I have work and school. I am not the same person I was back then, I'm a freaking single mom! I don't know that I have it in me to try again."

We're interrupted with shouts and curses from the living room and I hear the rustle of bodies moving around. Jonathan takes a couple steps away from me and leans against the kitchen sink

"Touchdown!" Mick yells as he saunters into the kitchen with his hands above his head. "You guys are missing all the fun! The Hawks are killing it."

Not feeling it, but mustering all the little sister sass that I can, I reply. "Sorry to break it to you big brother but I'm a Rams fan now. I'll be in there shortly and I'll be bringing them some luck. Sorry to say but your Hawks are going down."

"Did you seriously just say that you are a damn Rams fan, now?"

"That I did. The Chargers are really my team but any California team will do."

"Jesus, that California sun did some damage to your brain didn't it?"

He has the funniest look on his face. Like he's a cross between confused and sad for the loss of his little sister's ability to make sense.

"Your little sister is just fine big brother. Don't you worry about my brain damage. Any damage that's been done to my brain was done in my formative years by my big brother. Nice try thinking you can blame that on the California sun."

He doesn't say anything just walks past me to the fridge,

grabs a couple beers, and holds them in one hand. He needs the extra hand to pull on my ponytail as he walks past me.

"Truth."

"That's what I thought, Mickey. Love you, big bro."

"Love you too, Emmers."

Mick leaves the room and Jonathan and I just stand in silence...me leaning against the counter, and him against the sink.

He finally speaks and says, "That was so weird."

"What?"

"Mick, being a big brother and using the L-word."

A giggle slips out when I go to speak. "Mick is a lot of things. I know some of those things are a bit suspect but two of those things are being a great big brother and an even better uncle. He's a good guy, he just doesn't want anybody to know it."

"That's what I am afraid of, Em."

"Why would that be a bad thing?"

"Em, I told you that I want to try again. I know that means that Ireland comes as a bonus and that doesn't bother me in the least. I still feel it, Em, and I know you do too. What do you say? Dealing with Mick as your overprotective brother would be more than worth it if you gave us another chance."

He's saying all the words I wanted to hear but does he not remember the badge bunny waiting for him in the other room?

"What about Courtney? You seriously brought another woman to the house you know I'm living in the day after our talk. Then you come in here and say you want to try again with her sitting in the other room. You're kidding right?"

"Em, she didn't come here with me. I came here by myself. She has no shame and had only been there a minute before you walked in. I didn't want to cause a scene. She was doing what she always does; she attaches herself to whoever is available at that moment. Like I said, she has no shame."

"Well, clearly you seemed available because she was practically sitting on your lap in a room full of people."

"Emily, I don't give a shit about Courtney. I couldn't care less about the damn football game. I came here today to say that I was sorry for my reaction last night and that I want a do-over. I would love to get to know the new Emily *and* her adorable little girl."

As if on cue, Courtney walks in and walks up behind him and puts her hand on his shoulder.

"There you are. You left me out there all alone," she purrs.

"Court, you didn't come here with me. It isn't my job to keep you entertained. Go prey on someone else."

"So, that's how it's gonna be Johnny Boy? You gonna pretend that you've never used me as your prey?"

She's looking me straight in the eye, sending me a message, while his face turns red with rage.

"Courtney...Walk. Away." He is seething.

"I'll walk away Jonathan but you'll come back. You have before and you will again."

After releasing her talons from his shoulder she turns and struts out of the room as if she had accomplished whatever mission she had set for herself. I have to admit if she was hoping to put distance between Jonathan and I... mission accomplished.

Going into damage control mode Jonathan walks up to me and tries to grab my hands, but I pull away.

"Em, ignore her. I am not with her and I have no interest in her at all. She was a drunken mistake and that is all."

"See, I just don't have the energy to deal with drunken mistakes Jonathan. I have a little girl to take care of. I just moved here and am living with my brother. I have a new job starting this week and am studying for my master's. I just don't think I am in a place to start anything. Thank you so much for accepting the reasons why I didn't tell you about things in the past and thank you for your apology, but I think friends is all I can handle right now."

"If friends is all you can give, then I'll take it. It's not what I want, but I'll take it."

I hear stomping and my favorite sound in the world, Ireland's laugh, heading towards the kitchen and I step further away from Jonathan.

"Emily, look who I found in the living room crawling all over Uncle Mickey? Oh hey, Jonathan, how are you?"

What the Hell?

My mom knows him?

All these years the only man I have ever truly loved has been a part of my family's life and I had no idea?

"Hey, Ms. Jacobs. I'm good. How about yourself?"

"I'm great now that my girls are here in Oregon, where they belong! Hey Jonathan, do you think you could help me unload my car and bring in the goodies I made for you guys?"

"Sure thing. I'll go right now, is the car open?"

"It is, but I'll go with you. I just have to get this little monster off of me first."

While my mom detaches Ireland from her back Jonathan just gives me a weak smile and leaves the room. My mom gives me an odd look. That *'I'm your mom and I know everything'* look and follows after him.

I'm outside with all the other ladies when my mom comes out onto the back deck. She can tell I'm hiding. I love foot-ball and would usually be in there watching the game with my brother. But with my new *friend*, Jonathan, and his old friend, Courtney, in the same room, I think I'll pass this time.

My mom comes over and hugs me with a little extra squeeze and says, "You all good, Emmers?"

"I'm good, mom. How are you?"

"Nice try girly, but I know what I saw when I interrupted you in that kitchen. Ireland is fine with Mickey and everybody inside. Why don't you and I go chat?"

As she releases me from my hug, she puts her arm through mine and starts walking me off the back deck and to a little bench at the rear of the yard. It faces away from the house, but towards the beautiful view of Mt. Hood. She knows that nobody can hear us out here and there is privacy. She's so going to get me to talk. I always tell her everything in the end anyway, but I'm not sure I'm ready to talk about this.

"It wasn't anything mom, nothing worth talking about."

"Well, by the look on your face when I walked in, and his while he helped me bring the food in, I would say there was a whole lot more than just nothing going on."

Moms...how do they know everything? I think it's a gift and a curse but either way, their ability to know all is a real thing!

"Oh mom, it's a long story."

"I'm not going anywhere, sugar, and I am very interested in knowing how there is a long story about you and Jonathan when you just met."

"We didn't just meet, mom," I sigh before continuing. "Remember when I told you the story about my trip to San Clemente and the whirlwind romance I had, but it was the week after I found out I was pregnant, so I walked away?"

"Emily, no...It can't be...Jonathan is...he's...he's your Georgia, and you're his Gracie?"

As the tears start to fall, my mom puts her arm around me and just lets me cry.

"Well, it sounds like you remember that story."

"Of course I do, you were devastated. You fell in love with

him and if I remember correctly, he was head over heels in love with you."

"Mom, there was never anybody before him or after him that has even compared. I was so scared and I ruined everything before it even got going."

"Honey, he was leaving to go overseas, and you were scared and confused about what your future held. You did what you thought you had to do."

"I know, but still. There are so many 'what ifs' going through my mind. Seeing him play with Ireland earlier nearly killed me. She just instantly took to him and he's so good with her. Who knows if he would have wanted me back then if I had told him, but if he had...mom, Ireland's life would be so much better having him in it."

"And yours?"

"And mine. He told me today that he wanted to get to know me again. That he wanted to get to know Ireland. That he wanted us to try again."

"And what did you say?"

"I told him I didn't know if I could be more than friends with everything I had going on. And that Ireland comes first. He said if that was all I could give him, he would take it. But he agreed to one week before and it wasn't enough for him. What if he can't just be friends?"

"Do you still feel the same after all this time?"

"You mean do I still love him?"

She just nods her head and I nod back my answer. Saying it out loud isn't an option. We sit on the bench, on this beautiful day and look at our amazing view in silence. As I sit there, the reality that the love of my life is in that house with my daughter and my brother and knows my mother stabs me in the heart. A man I never thought I would see again is right here, right now and wants to try again, and I turned him away. Again. This is not how I imagined things going.

"Listen, I've gotten to know him here and there and he does seem like a nice guy. He is certainly a looker, but more than that he's a good man from what I can tell. He's been through a lot and seems a little closed off though. Be careful, but don't push him away. Take it slow for yourself and for Ireland, but don't hold yourself back from love. I know you won't let yourself say it out loud, but you still love him. It's obvious. Sweetie, you don't need to conquer this world alone. You will still be just as strong as you are today if you let somebody walk beside you. You, more than most, deserve to be loved and cared for. If he's offering to walk beside you maybe you should think about letting him. He didn't ask you to marry him, he just asked you to try. Ireland is gonna be five before you know it and you've been on your own since the day she was born."

I try to protest and tell her that I've had my family and friends beside me all this time, but she doesn't let me.

"Don't Emily. I know you're going to say that you have had Cami, Alex, all your other friends and Mick and me, but that's not the same as having a partner. You're still doing this on your own and have been since day one. I hope you know how proud I am of you."

"Thanks, mom, for everything."

"Honey, I'm always here for you and I am just so glad that both my girls are here, where they belong. I hope you know that if you ask me to help you in any way it is never a burden. Never. I will help you with Ireland any time I can and don't feel bad about it either, understood?"

"Understood."

I wipe my face, take a deep breath, and figure it's time to go rescue Mick from Ireland. Mom and I are walking arm and arm again across the big green yard when she stops and turns me towards her and looks me in the eye, making sure she has my attention.

"He's not your father, honey. I know that your father and I were poor examples of how a real relationship should be, but honey, it can be great when you find that one special person. It can be so much more than you ever dreamed of. Think about it, get settled, take it slow and then maybe, just maybe, let him in again when you're ready. If not, you might regret it the rest of your life and you don't do regrets if I am not mistaken?"

She gives me a wink and leads me back inside.

When we reach the family room Ireland is passed out on Mick, Cami is now sitting on the love seat in deep conversation with Jonathan, and Courtney is nowhere in sight. This I can live with.

I say goodbye to my mom and I go and gently peel my sweaty baby girl off of her big softie of an uncle. I make my way through the room and can feel the stares coming from the direction of the love seat. As I carry the second love of my life to her bed I try to take in the words my mom just shared with me about letting him in, but as I hold her in my arms I can't help but think of her getting hurt in the process. What if she gets attached and he leaves? Not only would it break my heart, but hers too. It's one thing to risk my heart but another to risk hers.

I purposely take a little longer than needed in her room covering her up and arranging her stuffed animals all around her before joining everybody back in the family room. There aren't any available seats, so I go sit on the floor in front of Cami's spot on the love seat so her legs are on either side of me. She gives my ponytail a tug and tips my head back to look at her and asks if I want her seat, but I tell her I'm good on the floor. I can feel his intoxicating buzz just fine from here thanks. I certainly don't need to be any closer.

Luckily it's already the 2nd half of the game because this is hella uncomfortable. The three of us stationed over here at the love seat are awkwardly silent while everybody else is throwing shade at each other and properly cheering and screaming at the TV.

With about ten minutes left in the game the Seahawks score a touchdown and the room goes crazy. Shortly after this outburst, I hear the familiar whimper of, "Momma."

"Baby girl is awake. Be back peeps," I say to whoever may be listening but to nobody specific.

"Let me go with you. I'm gonna head out in a few and I wanna say goodbye to that beautiful goddaughter of mine before I do."

Cami and I step inside Ireland's new room and she shuts the door behind us.

"Did you have a good nap, little lady?"

"I did, momma, but I's hot."

Her cheeks are bright red from being too warm.

"Well, you do have a bunch of stufties and blankets on you, no wonder. Come on let's get you out of there and brush that hair of yours."

As I get Ireland up and grab her brush from the nightstand, I finally look over at Cami who is standing with her arms crossed in front of her, tapping her foot and looking like she's waiting for something.

"What?"

"Just friends? You friend-zoned him?" she hisses at me with her hands on her hips. I feel like I'm being scolded and she's about to ground me.

"It's not so simple, Cam. I have a lot going on and seeing him with..." I nod my head towards my little girl. "There are two of us who will be hurt when Courtney or somebody else comes along and gets in the way. I can't do that to either of us, Cam."

"No regrets. Live today like it's your last and along the way kick some a...butt. That's all I have to say, Em."

With this reminder of how we always vowed to live our lives Cami leaves. It's not like her to just leave like that. She's genuinely pissed at me and my decision making.

"Mommy, what's regrets?"

"Oh baby, it just means not to ever do anything you might look back on when your older and wish you hadn't done it."

"Do you have any of those mommy?"

"I didn't think I did, baby girl, but I might be changing my mind. Let's get you up and go see who's still here."

When we get back out to the game it's over and the Seahawks have lost 31 to 34. Mickey seems upset and I'm sure has lost a bet or two today. He sees Ireland though and he can't help the smile that takes over his face.

"How was your nap, *I*? Come see me. I need a kiss to cheer me up."

"Why you sad, Uncle Mick?"

"The Seahawks lost and that means your mommy was right. I'm always sad when your mommy is right and I'm wrong. Now give me that kiss."

I just roll my eyes at him. She runs over to where he's standing and he picks her up and turns his face so his cheek is exposed for her to kiss. She wraps her arms around his neck and gives him a soft little peck like she always does.

Holding her tight but aiming his gaze at me he says, "See, I feel better already. I sure am glad you're here to take care of me and not all the way down in California."

I look at him and mouth, "Me too."

The crowd seems to have dispersed and only Emmett Martinez and Jonathan are left.

Emmett is single and pretty hot, I must admit, but with Jonathan in the room, nobody compares. When you take that handsome face, adorable dimples and warm eyes, not even Emmett can hold a candle to Jonathan.

I can tell he's struggling with how to handle wanting more but being friend-zoned. God, I am so stupid. I can't believe I am friend-zoning this beautiful man. Forget that. He's a beautiful person and for some reason, I feel the need to keep hurting him over and over, and in the process hurting myself. Hopefully, I'm making the right decision because I already feel regret seeping in.

"Well, I'm gonna go, guys. See you at work, Martinez. Thanks for having me over, Mick. It was good to see you again, Ireland. Take good care of that Uncle of yours, he needs all the help he can get."

"Bye, Jonafon, see you later."

"Later Dude, thanks for coming over. The door is always open so come over anytime and stay safe out there."

"You too, Mick."

He puts his hands in his front pockets and on a little shrug he says, "Later, Emily."

"Bye, Jonathan."

He walks out the door and I feel cold. Just having him in the room warms me up in a way that I only get around him. Even when things are awkward...I would rather be awkward with him in the room than to not have him near.

Shit! I messed up...again! I am so freaking stupid!

"I'm gonna head out too. Emily let's get that ride-a-long planned. You can come out whenever you want. I work the opposite side of the week than Mick, so you don't have to worry about big brother annoying you all night. Just let me know and we'll make it happen."

"I can't wait. How about next Saturday?"

"I'll be there so if it works for you it works for me. I work seven to seven-thirty. You can meet me there about fifteen minutes before roll call so we can get you a vest and sign the paperwork."

"I just need to be sure that night works for my mom so that Ireland can sleep over at her place, but it sounds like a plan. Let's just plan on me seeing you there at six forty-five."

Mickey's big brother instincts take over.

"Em, I don't know why you want to do this so bad, but if you insist on going you do everything Emmett tells you to and Emmett...you let anything happen to my baby sister, and I'll rip your balls off and shove them down your throat."

Completely unfazed by Mick he says, "Understood, Mick. See you next Saturday, Emily."

I know the moment he gives me the smile that goes along with his see you next Saturday line that he just made a big mistake.

"Oh and Emmett...keep your fucking hands to yourself."

Poor Emmett.

"Got it, Mick. You don't have anything to worry about. See you guys later."

Once we're alone I finally head to the kitchen to get Ireland her juice. Once she has her sippy cup and Mickey's iPad she heads back to the family room, plops herself on the couch and starts watching a movie. Mick and I start cleaning up and once we're out of Ireland's earshot, I have to reel my big brother in.

"Mickey, I appreciate you wanting to protect me, but if you are so worried about me going on a ride-a-long with Emmett then why won't you take me yourself?"

"Emmers, your safety is too important to me and I know that if you were with me I would only be thinking about you and your safety and I might not be focused on the job. I have to be focused on my job. I have to be alert and at the top of my game at all times and if anything happened out there because I wasn't focused, well...I just couldn't live with that."

"I get it, Mick but be nice to Emmett. It's not like we're going on a date or anything."

"Well, I need him focused too, so if he knows that you are off-limits that may keep you safer. I just need you and Emmett to come home at the end of the night."

"Okay."

He uses his arms to hop up on the kitchen counter and I can tell he wants to talk, so I do the same on the opposite counter, so we're directly across from one another.

"Emmers, is something going on between you and Kelly?"

Shit! Mickey cannot know about me and Jonathan. He would lose his shit!

"Nope, wasn't he here with Courtney?"

"Em, Courtney is the ultimate badge bunny. You look up the term in the dictionary and it will be her picture staring back at you. She wasn't even invited today and somehow she knew people would be here and she just showed up. That's what she does."

"They seemed pretty comfortable together."

"Well, I know he isn't interested in her. I think he got drunk once and ended up doing the walk of shame from her place, but trust me, that's happened to many of us. Soon enough she'll find that one cop dumb enough to actually want something from her, and she'll get that ring on her finger. But it won't be me, or Kelly, I can tell you that. Besides, Jonathan seemed a bit distracted by something else today."

"What was that?"

"That would be you and Ireland."

"Whatever, Mickey. You don't know what you're talking about. He was talking to Cami too."

"I saw that, but it wasn't the same thing. Emmers, you know

that I would prefer you not date one of my friends and especially not a cop. It's not that cops are bad guys; it's just a stressful
life. I know you know this and I don't have to tell you. We both
grew up in that life but it's not what I would wish for you. And
Jonathan…he's a really good guy and the type of guy I would
approve of but he's a cop and a friend. I'm not telling you who
you can or can't date but just be careful and know that if you do
go out with him, and it doesn't work, he will probably still be
around."

"Thanks, Mick. But I don't think you have to worry about
that," I say swinging my legs back and forth like a little kid up
here on my countertop perch.

"Em, I know dad reached out to you and you didn't call him
back. How long are you gonna shut him out?"

"So, you're talking to dad?" I ask incredulously.

"Yep, he's my dad. He fucked up and hurt mom and left us,
but he knows he let us down and he's trying. He would really
love to meet *I*."

"I just don't know how you can forgive him so easily. He
didn't make an effort until he knew I was back here and it would
be easy. He never made an effort to come meet his grand-
daughter when we were in California. Why does it always have
to be what he wants and what's easy for him?"

"I don't know, Em, and you don't have to see him if you don't
want to. Wait until you're ready, but it might be nice for Ireland
to have another grandparent in her life. And even though I
know you don't want to talk about it…she does have another
aunt in her life too. Just think about it."

"I'll think about it but I am not making any promises, Mick,"
I snap.

"I get it. So, how are you and *I* settling in? Do you need
anything?"

"Is her name so long that you can't say the whole thing,

Mick? You can really only bring yourself to speak one letter of her name?"

"Shut up, that's my name for her. Deal with it. Now, answer me. Do you need anything?"

"Nope, everything is great. Mick, I know I've thanked you but I hope you know how much I appreciate everything you're doing for me and Ireland. Who would have thought when we were kids that you would turn out to be such a great guy? Don't get me wrong you still annoy the hell out of me, but Mick, I couldn't do this without you right now. So thank you. Another thing...it's strange to talk to you about dating, but you're a good guy and whatever woman out there finally ties you down will be lucky to have you. I'm here anytime you want to talk about your dating life too, you know."

"I don't see that happening anytime soon, sis but thanks."

"I know that you like to *date* and I know that having your little sister and a four-year-old living with you is probably cramping your style. I promise that as soon as I can we'll be out of your hair."

"Emmers, I wish you would have moved back before *I* was ever born and I didn't have to miss everything that I missed with her. You are welcome to stay as long as you need. Let's just get you that master's degree and then we'll worry about all the rest."

I hop off my counter and Mickey hops off his and I walk up to him and put my arms around him.

"I love you, big brother."

"Love you too, Emmers."

7

———————

Jonathan

I can't get them out of my head. My beautiful Gracie and her cute as hell little girl are all I think about. It's been six days since I've seen them, but they're always on my mind. What would I have done if she had told me she was pregnant? Is she right, would I not have pursued her? I just can't imagine not being with her that week. The moment I saw her, she was everything. She still is everything. Fuck, I am such a pussy!

I can hear the guys around me in the locker room talking about Martinez having a ride-a-long tonight. Correction, a hot ride-a-long. She may be hot, but these guys don't know hot. Emily makes everybody else pale in comparison. Ride-a-longs are a pain in the ass and I avoid them at all costs. It's just one more thing to worry about in a job that already gives you plenty to worry about.

As I finish putting on my vest and making sure I have all my gear securely in place, I think back to Sunday at Mick's and how when not talking to me or Emily, Cami was on her phone the whole time, but Emily actually watched the game. She was interested. She is the sexiest woman I have ever met and all girl, but she can hang with the guys and be one of the boys just as easily as she can be a girly girl. She isn't a high maintenance girly girl either; she is fucking perfect! God, I cannot get her out of my head!

"See you at roll call, Kelly. You better hurry it up—you've only got a couple minutes."

"Thanks, Truman, I'm on my way."

When I close my locker door and head to roll call, I realize that I don't want to be friends with her. I want her to be my best friend and *my Gracie*. Why does she always get to make the decisions for the both of us? Why do I just give in to whatever she says? Why didn't I fight for more when she said no? I need to grow a pair, try again and make sure that I win the argument this time. She thought she was making the right decision last time and she was wrong.

History is not going to repeat itself if I can help it. Not this time.

I reach roll call and slip in at the last second and take the seat closest to the door right in front. I never slip in at the last second. I need to get my head out of my ass and focus. Now that I've made my decision to nut up and get the girl, I feel a bit calmer. I don't have a plan, but deciding to fight for her is enough to make me feel more myself.

Sergeant Callahan finishes briefing us on all the latest information from the streets of SE Portland, and we all get ready to head out to the lot to get our cars.

I walk out with Marnie Benson—who is the only grown-up on most shifts and keeps us all in line.

Finn Hardy is walking with us when Benson chimes in. "Hey Kelly, to what do we owe the honor of your presence?"

"Workin' on whorin' up some OT Benson. Can't let Hardy

here be the only one who gets to make all the money around this joint."

"Shut up, Kelly. You know I'm saving to buy a house and we don't all work your side of the week and have Saturday night's available to cover when everybody else takes weekends off. Besides, you probably only came in tonight because of the smokin' hot ride-a-along that Martinez has with him tonight."

"Jesus, it's like you guys haven't seen a real girl in years. You do know you're talking about Mickey Jacob's little sister right?" Benson states and I can hear the thumping of my heart in my ears.

"What did you say, Benson?" Both Finn and I say at the same time as we reach our squad cars.

"Yep, so you should watch your mouth there Hardy or Mick will kick your ass. You know Emily, don't you, Jonathan?"

"Uh, yeah I do. She's with Martinez?"

"Yeah, she *is* with Martinez," I hear Emmett say quietly under his voice as he slaps me on the back.

Fuck me!

I fight the urge to turn and take a swing at my friend. Instead, I decide to be mature about the whole thing and turn to give him some stink eye. And that's when I see Emily coming up behind us.

Surprised and looking nervous she says, "Hey Jonathan, I didn't think you worked on Saturdays?"

Sorry to ruin your plans with Martinez, sweetheart.

"I don't but they needed somebody to pull an OT shift so... here I am. I didn't know you were interested in a ride-a-long?"

"Always have been, but Mickey refused to take me. Emmett here over-heard us talking about it and offered. I can't wait!"

"Well, have fun. I'm sure I'll see you out there."

I know I should turn around and load my gear into my car, but she and I just stand there and stare a little too long before she quietly says, "See you out there."

Arranging my trunk and making sure I have everything I need for my shift, I'm trying not to stare at Emily at the car beside me, looking so cute in her 'bulletproof vest' that I know, isn't really bulletproof. It's not like you put these things on and you're suddenly superman with super-powers that prevent you from getting hurt. As cute as she looks, all I can think about is how I wish she wasn't out here. Not only because she's with a very single and very flirty Martinez, but also because it's not safe. I should be the one keeping her safe. Why the hell is she here?

Just as I'm closing the trunk to my car, I hear Martinez answer his phone. I can tell it's not a good conversation; something is wrong. As much as I don't want him around Emily, he's still my friend and I'm worried something bad has happened. I can't tell what though. He's answering in short clipped responses and not saying much.

"Yeah mom, I'm on my way," he says as he ends the call.

"Emmett, brother, what's wrong?" I ask.

"Jonathan, my dad...he's...he had a heart attack and they're taking him to the hospital. Right now. I gotta go." He turns to look at Emily and says, "Sorry Emily, but maybe another time?"

"Of course, go and don't worry about me. I hope your dad will be okay."

"Emmett, whatever you need just let me know. Go on and go. I'll call and check on things in a few hours if I don't hear from you."

I bring him in for a hug and say, "It's gonna be okay, Emmett. Be strong for your mom and your dad. You go take care of yours and we'll take care of you. Now go."

"Thanks, man."

I watch as he runs back into the building and hope that his dad truly will be okay, and if not, I just hope he makes it there in time to say goodbye. Not getting to say goodbye to mom, I know how important that is. Shit, I don't know if I'll ever get over not being with her at the end. There isn't a day that goes by that I don't think about it.

"Well, I guess I better go turn this vest back in. I'll see you later."

Her voice brings me back to the present, and the fact that the woman that has been on my mind every second of every day, is standing here with me. I guess there's no time like the present to man up and start the process of getting my girl back. I hate that Emmett's dad is sick, but they do say that things happen for a reason.

"No need for that, you can jump in with me."

She looks at me with apprehension on her face and starts to play with her necklace. "You sure?"

"Yep, I'll let the sergeant know when we get logged on and we'll be set. Let me just make room in the front seat for you and we can hit the road...unless you'd rather just ride in the back?"

"Ha, very funny, Georgia. I can wait for you to move things."

I fucking love it when she calls me that. It means she's comfortable and reminds me of Cali. Baby steps are what I need to take and I'll start with that.

"Here, let me just put this in the back and you can go ahead and get in. Just don't touch anything," I say only half-joking.

"What could I possibly break?" she says as she gets in the car. "Okay, you were right. There are lots of buttons and do-hickies in here that look they do something that I shouldn't make them do, so I will not touch a thing." She yells at me from her still open car door.

I join her in the car, start the engine and turn on my MDC. I explain to her that the MDC is the Mobile Data Computer and show her that this is where we see our lists of pending and active calls. It's also the system we use to run license plates. There's also an IM system on it so that officers can send messages to each other or the dispatchers. I let her know that she can run some plates for me later and her face lights up like Christmas morning.

I check my lights, sirens and set my radio volume and get ready to head out. I can't believe she's sitting in my patrol car with me. She's been all I have thought about for a week and somehow, on my day off, I happen to come to work and here she is. I know she once told me she wasn't sure if she believed in fate, but I sure as hell do.

We've been at it for a while and there have just been a couple of little stops here and there, but nothing too exciting. She asks lots of questions and I let her run plates on the MDC, but for the most part, things stay business-like and we don't discuss anything personal.

For me it's all personal. Sharing such a big part of my life with her is a big deal. Her interest in wanting to know about this world, *my world,* is a big deal to me. Having her so close to me brings me a calmness I haven't felt since I was with her in Mick's kitchen, before she friend-zoned me that is. Oh God and her smell. To have her smell all around me in my car is something that I wish I could bottle or put into one of those car fresheners that look like a tree. She smells better than any perfume out there.

I will not stay her friend.

Fuck the friend-zone!

I need much more than friends.

We stop at *Subway* to get a quick bite to eat and I squeeze into one of the tiny little booths they have there. With all my gear on it's not the most comfortable, but you get used to it and make it work.

"So, how's Ireland? Is she adjusting well to leaving California?"

"She seems to be doing great so far. She loves her new pre-school but luckily, she's only going for a few hours a day, since I only have part-time hours at the high school. She loves being close to my mom and Mickey, so she's a happy little girl. I'm pretty lucky, she's always been easy. I had an easy pregnancy and a fairly easy delivery. She was four weeks early and really tiny but she was a great baby. Now that she's a great big four your old, she's still pretty great."

"Well, look at her mom...she was born with pretty great genes."

"Shut up," she says as she throws a *Cheeto* at me.

"It's true, Em, she's pretty damn lucky to have you for a mom."

"Well, thanks but it hasn't been easy. I've had lots of help. That old saying 'it takes a village' is pretty true."

"Why didn't you move home to be with family when you had her?"

"Well, I didn't want to quit school. I had just started my new job working as an administrative assistant at an Occupational Therapist's office and the people there were great. It was like an instant family and just what I needed. Not only was I twenty-one, in college and pregnant but I started that job the day after leaving San Clemente and I wasn't exactly in the best headspace."

If it was even half as hard on you Gracie, as it was on me, then I know exactly what kind of headspace you were in.

"When they found out I was pregnant I thought for sure they would get rid of me, but they gave me enough hours to get health benefits and still go to school. Technically, it was illegal for the drug testing company to tell them I was pregnant but they couldn't have been better about it. It took me a little longer to finish school and I didn't graduate in the spring like everybody else, but I did finish by the next fall."

"Hit me," I say as I lift my hand.

She slaps my hand and says, "Thanks. I do deserve that one, don't I?"

A giggle bubbles out of her and I can't help but smile as she continues to talk. The high five was all I was willing to do or say because the last thing I want is for her to stop opening up to me.

"I have to confess walking around campus all big and fat was not fun. You don't see too many knocked up seniors walking from class to class. Let's just say my senior year wasn't everything I hoped and dreamed it would be. I got through it though."

"What did you do with Ireland while you were at school?"

I'm so impressed that she finished school with everything that she was dealing with at the time. What a badass!

"Well, that was the other reason I decided to stay in California. My position at the clinic was actually available because the woman that had previously had that position was retiring. She taught me her job and then a few months later she retired. She decided that she was bored and called me up at work one day and said that once the baby was here, and I was ready to go back to work and school, that she would love to babysit for me and free of charge."

"Whoa."

"I know. She was a lifesaver. Her name is Charlotte and Ireland absolutely adored her. The feeling was mutual. She refused to let me pay her, so I would have to get creative and find ways to pay her back in little ways here and there. I would save up what money I could to be sure that I could slip her a gift card or some sort of money on Valentine's Day, Mother's Day, President's Day—you name it. I did whatever I could to repay her because without her I don't know what Ireland and I would have done."

"Sounds like all that good you've always done for everybody else came back around to you, just like you deserve."

With her sandwich suspended in mid-air she asks, "What in the world are you talking about?"

"Emily, you have no idea the joy you bring to people. In just the nine days I spent with you in California I watched you bring smile after to smile to people's faces. There is a light in you that just reaches into people and lights them right up along with you. I've seen it happen to young and old. There was the older gentleman on the pier who you helped with his jacket. There was little Jacob and Buzzy Bear at Icon's, and there was the crying kid on our hike at the top of Patriots Hill. You calm people and you bring them joy, Em, that's just what you do. You don't even realize it, but you do."

"How do you remember all of that from so long ago? Until you just reminded me, I didn't remember any of those things. Well, that's a lie, little Jacob was pretty hard to forget. Still, your mind is like a steel trap!"

"I've said it before; I remember everything about you, Emily. I know you only want to be friends, but that doesn't mean that I've forgotten a damn thing."

"Jonathan..."

She starts to speak but I get a call on my radio about a drunk driver not too far from where we are.

"Sorry, Em, we gotta wrap this up and go. Got a call."

"No problem, I'm done. Is everything okay?"

"Sounds like a drunk driver not far from here."

We toss what was left of our meal in the bin next to the exit, jump in the car, and head out towards the last location the car was spotted.

"21-0-1 en route. What was the make of the car again?" I ask into the radio.

Dispatch replies that we are looking for a late model, blue, Toyota Camry. As we turn the corner onto Division Street Emily points it out and I pull up behind the car to run the plate. At the moment the car doesn't seem to be doing anything wrong, but that soon changes when the car runs a red light right in front of us.

"Shit!" I say as I turn on my lights and sirens. It takes some time for the car to finally pull over. When it does, I radio my location to dispatch.

"Em, I'm gonna need you to get out of the car and stand on the sidewalk at the rear of my car. That's the safest place for you to be. Just stay there okay?"

"No problem, Georgia."

God, if this woman only knew what she does to me!

"Thanks and please stay there."

I approach the car and see that it's a female driver in her late thirties and she has a young, teenage boy in the car with her. As I approach the car she still hasn't rolled down her window and her son has to get her attention and tell her to roll the window down.

"Ma'am, can you please hand me your license and registration?"

Again, her son has to get her attention and he ends up getting the registration out of the glove box and takes her license out of the wallet in her purse. Poor kid, this doesn't seem to be a first for him.

He hands the items to his mom who passes them to me. When she finally looks up at me, she isn't shy when she gives me a once over and then a big smile comes over her face as she hands the registration and ID over to me.

"Here you go, officer."

"Thank you, ma'am. Do you know why I pulled you over this evening?"

"Sorry to say I don't, sir," she slurs her reply.

"Well, ma'am you ran a red light back there. If you can just stay here I'll be right back."

I head back to the car and stand towards the back with Emily. She's quiet and just watches everything happen. I radio dispatch with the VIN of the car and her ID number. They let me know that she has a suspended license from a previous DUII. As I finish with dispatch, Benson drives up to serve as my back-up.

Just great, poor kid is gonna have to watch his mom get arrested tonight. I hate this part of my job.

I walk back to the driver's side window and ask that they both get out of the car. I ask her son to stand on the sidewalk on the side of the car. His mom gets out and as soon as she's standing in front of me I can smell the alcohol. She is beyond drunk. She's blasted out of her mind.

"Ma'am if you could come stand over here."

She meets me at the back of her car where my car lights are illuminating the situation now that the sun has almost completely set.

"Ma'am, how much have you had to drink tonight?"

She tries to step closer to me, and just as she's about to reach a hand out to touch me, I ask her to step back towards the car.

"Ma'am, please stay where you are and I'm going to ask you again...how much have you had to drink tonight?"

Slurring and wreaking of booze she answers. "Oh, just two glasses of wine. I'm fine."

I see her son sit down on the curb with his head hanging between his shoulders. He's placed himself between the back of his mom's car and the front of my patrol car. I'm sure he's been through this before and he looks tired, sad and alone.

I put his mom through a barrage of tests, and I look over to see that Emily has joined her son on the curb and is shaking his hand. She starts to talk to him and I can see his body language ease just a bit as some of his stress ebbs from his shoulders. I don't need a breathalyzer to know she's drunk, but we'll deal with that at the station.

I can see that Emily is rubbing her son's back and trying to comfort him. God, she is an amazing person. I should consider myself lucky to count her as a friend, but of course, I'm greedy and want more. Moments like this make my feelings for her even stronger than before.

It's at this moment that I know without a doubt I am still in love with her. She is and always has been *the one* for me. This is not the time to have a revelation, as I have a job to do. Besides, realizing I am still in love with her shouldn't be any kind of surprise to me. There hasn't been anybody that has even come close since her.

Come on, Kelly, focus for Christ's sake!

I have what I need, and it's time to head off to jail. Before we can head out we'll need to pat her down to make sure she doesn't have any weapons or drugs on her. Because she's a woman, Benson does the frisking, I hand-cuff her and go to put her in the back of my car.

As I put my hand on the top of her head to make sure she doesn't hit her head, she slurs, "Officer, you sure do smell nice. What kind of cologne is that?"

"Soap ma'am, just soap."

"Well, it smells awfully nice."

I hope Emily didn't hear that. Worse than that though is now telling this kid that his mom won't be going home with him.

"Hey Bud, Officer Benson can give you a lift if you like. Do you have grandparents or any family that we can call that you can stay with for the night?"

"I can call my grandma. I'm sure she can come get me."

"Why don't you give her a call and Officer Benson can take you to her? Do you have a phone or do you need to borrow mine?"

"Thank you, sir but I have my phone here. I'll call her now."

Emily stands to give him some privacy and walks over to Benson and I.

"His name is Jason and he's thirteen. He said he knew she shouldn't have driven, but she picked him up like this in front of his friends and he didn't know what to do. He was so embarrassed that he just wanted to get out of view of his friends. He's a really sweet kid."

"Thanks for keeping him distracted, Em, that was really nice of you. Although, I did tell you to stand on the sidewalk at the back of my squad car, not to sit on the curb up here, but still... thank you."

"No problem, he looked so alone and I just couldn't take it, so I came and sat with him. Sorry for breaking the rules." Oh how I would love to punish her for breaking those rules later, but we're just friends. So that won't be happening unless I pull up my big boy pants and prove to her that we can be more than friends.

Jason walks over and explains that his grandmother is expecting him and that if Benson can give him a lift to North Portland where she lives he would appreciate it.

Emily walks over and hugs him. Of course, that is what she does.

"You take care and keep up the good work in school. Things will get better kiddo even if you have to make that happen for yourself. You can do it."

"Thanks, Emily. It was really nice to meet you."

I thank Benson for taking him and as we walk back to my car we see Willy. He's a local transient who I've taken a liking too.

He's a nice old man who lost his family and all hope years ago. He doesn't cause any trouble and always does as I ask. He has just lost the ability to care about himself anymore.

"Evening, Officer Kelly. Who's this beauty you got along with ya tonight?"

"Hey Willy, this is my friend," I say begrudgingly. "Emily, this is Willy, Willy, this is Emily."

"Nice to meet you, young lady. Saw you there with that boy. That was very kind of you."

"It was my pleasure. Willy. He's such a sweetheart. It's nice to meet you too."

"So, Emily...how do you know Officer Kelly?"

"He's an old friend, Willy. How do you know him?"

"Old *friend* you say, do you? Hmmm...interesting...very interesting. He's an old friend of mine as well. He takes care of this old man and makes sure I stay out of trouble. He's one of the good ones, Emily."

"Okay, that's enough, you two. Emily, why don't you head back to the car and I'll be right there."

"Okay, bye Willy."

She gives him a wave and a smile that melts his heart, and mine.

"She's a keeper, Officer Kelly," Willy whispers to me.

"That she is, Willy...that she is. Hey, I have to head out but you okay? You need anything?"

"Nope, I'm fine but thanks for asking. If you do anything right now, it better be findin' a way to keep your hands on that pretty little thing. I think she's just what you're missing."

"You are a wise man and I think you just might be right. Gotta go, Willy. You stay safe out here and call me if you need anything."

As I walk back to the car I realize that I need to listen to Willy and not let her getaway again. I need to figure out how I plan to do that without running her off. She scares easily and her past isn't any help either.

Thankfully, the Fanuas are visiting next weekend and Liam and Mr. F can help me come up with a plan to get my girl back. But for now, let's go to jail and then write my DUII report. What a way to woo her; jail and report writing. That's some romantic shit right there.

After a trip to jail and processing my DUII I let Emily know that she should go. I have quite a bit of paperwork ahead of me as a DUII arrest is not just as simple as taking the person to jail, and there's no reason for her to sit around while I write. Besides, I don't think I could focus on my report if she was sitting right next to me while I tried to write.

I drive her to the station then walk her to her car. She seems reluctant to leave but it's late, and I'm sure she has to get up early with Ireland.

Knowing I can't stand here all night I finally break the silence and say, "It was great to see you, Em."

"Good to see you, too. Thanks so much for letting me tag along, it was great."

"No problem, I was glad to do it. Say hey to little Ireland for me."

"Will do. That will make her day."

Not knowing how to say goodbye but not wanting to let her go, I simply raise my hand and she knows exactly what I am looking for. A second later I get the slap to my hand that I was anticipating, and instead of grabbing her hand and pulling her into my arms I simply say, "Have a good night, Em. Drive safe." She shyly smiles, gets into Justine and drives away.

The only thing going through my head is *MORE!* I need more of her!

8

____

Emily

So far I have loved my time at my new job.

It's only part-time, but it works well as far as my Master's classes and being able to afford pre-school for Ireland goes. I'm working at Happy Valley High School and am assisting the SPED (special education) teacher, Heidi Colyer, for the first half of the school days.

The thing I love about the SPED group is that I get to spend time with all sorts of great kids. Some of the kids just have mild ADD and need additional assistance focusing and with organization. There are kids with behavioral issues that can be a bit of a handful but are still great. And some kids aren't neuro-typical and may be somewhere on the autism spectrum or have other challenges that require additional support. These kids usually have one-on-one time with specialized aides. I don't get much time with them but I love the time we do get to spend together.

All my kids are great, even the kids that have behavioral problems. When you get down to it, there's usually a reason for their behavior and sometimes in these smaller settings where the kids can get some one-on-one time with an adult, you can figure out what those things are and try to help them.

There are also some kids that you just click with and I already have a couple of those. Austin Gilbert and Jesse Miller are two such kids. They happen to be good friends and great kids. They've both had a rough start but they seem to have each other's backs and they have never been anything but respectful to myself and Mrs. Colyer. For some reason, I just get these two and I feel like I've helped them here and there. Their list of missing assignments seems to be dwindling, but the school year has just begun so only time will tell.

Today, when the boys arrive to class there's something odd going on between them. Jesse is keeping his head down and pretending to look at his work but is off somewhere in his head, while Austin is doing everything he can to get my attention without causing a scene.

"Hey guys, how was your weekend?" I ask as I approach their table and heed Austin's signals.

"Not too bad, Miss Jacobs. How about yours?" I get from Austin, but Jesse doesn't reply.

"It was good, thanks for asking. Either of you needs help with any of your classes?"

I can see Jesse just barely shake his head, but it's clear that Austin would like my attention.

Practically begging he asks, "Miss Jacobs, can we go over my English essay?"

"Sure, let's see what you have so far," I say as I take the seat next to him.

As Austin turns his notebook towards me I can hear my heart pounding in my head when I read the note that he has written for me.

Jesse's dad hurt him this weekend. He's not okay and needs help but he made me promise I wouldn't say anything to anybody but we have to help him. He has to get out of that house. He stays to protect his younger brother but it isn't safe for either of them. Check his arms.

I write 'ok' on the paper and my mind starts spinning with ideas of what to do. I know I have to play it cool so that Jesse doesn't notice anything is off, so I spend another couple of minutes with Austin and we do actually look at his English essay and then I leave him to work.

I walk around the class and check on a couple of other kids before I get to Jesse and once I reach him I take the open seat next to him.

"Hey Jess, you're pretty quiet today. Everything okay?"

"Yep."

"Why are you wearing such a heavy coat today? It's gotta be like ninety degrees outside."

"Dunno, just felt like it."

"Hey bud, can you look at me?" He's been hiding behind his long hair and I can tell he doesn't want me to see why.

"Jesse, you aren't yourself and you won't even look at me. What's going on?" I press on.

"Nothing, just leave me alone," he huffs.

He's getting frustrated with my insistence.

"Well, I won't do that but let's see what you have for homework that we can work on. Whatcha got?"

"Just some math, no big deal," he shrugs.

"Well, get it out of your backpack and let's take a look and make sure you understand what you guys are studying in class this week."

He just sits there, but once he realizes I'm not going anywhere he gets his binder out of his backpack and flops it on the table awkwardly.

On a heavy sigh, he says, "I don't have a pencil."

"Here, borrow mine," I say handing him mine.

Out of habit when he starts to write he pushes up his sleeves on his jacket and cringes. I can just barely see the burn on his forearm but it's enough to send a protective rage through me.

"Jesse, look at me," I order and all the sweetness has left my tone.

Still refusing to look at me and sounding exhausted, he pleads with me once more. "No Miss Jacobs, just leave it alone."

Standing from the table I announce, "Jesse is gonna help me run to get some supplies, Mrs. Colyer, We'll be right back. Austin, have her look at your essay when you're done if I'm not back in time."

Jesse doesn't move.

"Would you like me to cause a scene in front of the whole class or would you like to go sit in the Commons and talk to me?"

With that, he abruptly gets up and the screeching sound of his chair gets everybody's attention while he storms out of the classroom ahead of me. We don't say anything until we reach the Commons. He throws himself into a chair at the nearest table and I sit across from him.

Because we're out in the open and anybody that walks by can see and hear us he whispers, "Miss J, you don't understand. I can't let you get involved in this. I have to stay in my home with my brother and if they make me leave I won't be there to protect him."

He finally lifts his head to me and I can see that his left eye and temple are severely bruised. He lifts his jacket sleeve and shows me burn marks. I try my very best not to gasp out loud, but inside I am cursing and trying to catch my breath.

"Jesse, did your mom or dad do this to you?"

"My mom isn't around."

"So, it was your dad."

No reply.

"Are those cigarette burns, sweetie?"

With tear-filled eyes, this six-foot-plus boy who scares most of the other kids in school away with just a look pleads with me. "Listen, you can't take me away. Who will watch over William?"

"Jesse, let's see what we can do to help you. Let's go on up to the counselor's office and talk to somebody. As an employee, I have to report any abuse that I see, but hopefully, we can get both you and your brother somewhere safer."

"Do you really think we could both get out?"

"I can't make any promises, but I am sure there is always a chance, Jesse."

I cannot believe I am headed to happy hour after the day I've had. After a couple of hours in the office with Jesse and the authorities, I was an emotional mess and Cami thinks happy hour is just what I need.

I hope I did the right thing for Jesse and William. I just want them to be safe. The social worker from the Department of Human Services says that they've reached out to their Grandmother, and she's going to pick them both up and stay with them while things get figured out. They're issuing a warrant for his dad's arrest and hopefully, if Jesse continues to cooperate, his dad won't be coming home anytime soon. Thank goodness he's still 17 and not an adult yet or things may not be going as well as they are as far as getting the boys removed from the house together. I left him with our School Resource Officer, Officer Blackburn, and even though I knew he was in good hands, I hated to walk away from him.

After dropping Ireland off at my mom's and meeting at Cami's place, we hop in her car and head down to *The Observatory* to meet Alex. It's our favorite little spot, with the best drinks, and oh my God the oregano fry bread is to die for! I'm really not in the mood for this but I appreciate Cami trying to help. To be honest, I miss my best friends. I've lived with Cami for the last eight years and not seeing her every day has been more of an adjustment than I anticipated. She's my rock and I owe her so much. And I feel like I have years of catching up to do with Alex. I think I can manage a happy hour if it means time with the two of them.

I fill them in on the details of poor Jesse, and what a great friend Austin was. That he made sure that an adult saw what was happening, and got him help. reassures me that I made the right decision and that I deserve an adult beverage to celebrate.

Since I'm not much of a drinker, my plan is just to have one drink but Cami seems to have other plans. We manage to find three stools at the bar so we belly up and order our drinks. Our favorite adult beverage, here at *The Observatory,* is the Chelsey's Bellini. It's ridiculously sweet but sooo good. It's made with pear vodka, peach puree ,and champagne. One is all that's needed for this light-weight. I plan to sip slow and fill my tummy with fry bread.

We order our drinks and bread as we talk about Cami's new job in Real Estate, Alex and her job as an event planner, my Master's classes and job at the school. The bar is slowly getting louder and warmer. There is a group of guys that look like they just got off work and are looking to blow off some steam. As always, Cami zeroes right in on them.

"Hey chica, I bet I can get us some free drinks."

"I don't want any free drinks, but you go right ahead. I'm happy right here with my fry bread."

"Oh no, you're the one who had the shit day. You are drinking!"

"Cami, I have to go to work tomorrow and I have Ireland to take care of. I cannot get shitty."

"One shot won't kill you."

"Have you met me? I barely drink, let alone do shots. You go right ahead though, and I'll drive us home, but there is no way I am doing shots!"

"You know you can't stop her once she gets her mind set on something." Alex giggles as we watch Cami do what she does best.

Cami introduces herself to the guys and she's amazing to watch in action. She isn't overtly sexy, and she is far from a slut, but she is so damn cute that guys just fall under her spell. She promises nothing and still gets drinks everywhere we go. Tonight, she's in a professional yet sexy, tight, black sheath dress and with her heels giving her some height and helping her amazing legs stand out...these guys don't stand a chance.

She has a confidence about herself that I've never had. I haven't been out much in the last five years—my life has been more diapers and bottles than bars—and the time away hasn't done much for my self-esteem. I feel so much older than my 26 years and to be honest, I'm not really interested in meeting anybody.

Besides, I have the guy of my dreams wanting to try again and I friend-zoned him.

Not letting me down, Cami returns to my side with a big ole smile on her face and within a couple of minutes, there are three shots of fireball being placed in front of us. I push my shot towards Cami while she's turning towards the table of guys to wave her thanks, but she pushes it right back in front of me as soon as she turns back to me.

Damn!

"You deserve one night of letting loose. One shot with your girls, chica. It's just happy hour. We aren't going to stay out all night."

"If I take this one shot will you leave me alone?"

Cami crosses her heart and Alex says, "We promise to be nice, Em. Just have one shot to loosen you up a bit. You deserve it."

I hope doing this will get them off my back. If so...taking this shot may be worth it! I finally cave and pick up my shot glass.

"That's my girl! On three!" Cami hollers.

"1...2...3..." we all count down and slam down our shots. Damn, that stuff burns.

"Woo!!!! Damn, Cam, that's strong!"

We slap hands while I shake my head to try to get rid of what the fireball is doing to my brain because my brain...my brain is fuzzy already.

I'm such a lightweight! What was I thinking?

"I know, isn't it great?"

"No, I don't think great is the word that I would use. It's like fire!"

"Alex, why would you let her talk me into this? What kind of friend are you?"

"It's just one shot, Emmers. You'll be fine." Alex replies but Cami isn't having any of that.

"We'll have one more please!" she says raising her hand to get the attention of the bartender.

"Cami! No way! I have to work tomorrow!"

While waiting on the bartender she turns to me and says,

"So tell us about it." I just look at her confused. "Come on, Em. Talk to us about Jonathan. He told me at Mick's the other day that he wanted to try again but you weren't interested. Why?"

"Why does he always talk to you?" I don't know why it surprises me that they seem to be teaming up again after the plan they concocted back in San Clemente...but it does.

"Honey, you broke his heart that day. He's still crazy in love with you and he wants to get to know Ireland. He's such a good guy. You said you still loved him after seeing him at Kells and he's hella hot, so what's wrong with him? Do you not have feelings for him anymore?"

I can feel the *Fireball* warming my insides up and I'm already feeling tipsy, this must be why I suddenly become so free with my words.

"What is it, Em? Talk to us." Alex pleads ever so gently.

"There's nothing wrong with him, you guys. He's perfect and yes, I still have feelings for him. That stupid Badge Bunny, Courtney, just ruined it by throwing it in my face that she had been with him. It scared me and I instantly put my walls back up. I know it's been over five years and I don't expect him to have been celibate the entire time, but it just made me sick to think of him with her and I pushed him away."

"And friend-zoned him." Cami adds.

"Yep, I sure did," I say as I slam my hand down on the bar. "I just reacted and didn't think it through. But Cami, I do have a lot on my plate with raising a child, work and classes. Do I have time for more?"

"Do you still love him?"

Where is that next shot? I cannot have this conversation even a little bit sober.

"Here you go, ladies," the hipster bartender with a full beard, flannel shirt and suspenders say as he puts another shot of *Fireball* in front of us, but this time I can't slam it down fast enough.

"I'll take that as a yes, then?"

"Oh God, it burns Cami. No more!"

"That's why it's called Fireball, chica. Now, do you still love him?"

At that moment *Kings of Leon* starts playing in the background and one of my favorite memories of our time in California comes back to me....

It's Thursday evening and we'd spent the day at Universal Studios. Jonathan has built a fire for us on the beach, and we're listening to what is now 'our' album while we make s'mores. It is the perfect way to end a perfect day. As I'm trying to lick all the sticky marshmallow goodness off of my fingers, Jonathan comes over to assist. He puts each of my fingers in his mouth and makes sure that all the sticky goodness is now gone.

"You have a little something...right here. Looks like chocolate, don't mind if I do." He uses that amazing tongue of his to get the chocolate off of the corner of my mouth and then gives me a sexy, little smile. Everything he does makes my heart nearly flutter out of my chest.

"Come Around Sundown" is the perfect music for tonight. I've always loved Kings of Leon but this new album is...well, it's just perfect. It's set the mood for our week and we haven't stopped playing it. At this particular moment "The Face" comes on and Jonathan takes my hand and leads me a few feet from the fire. He holds me in his arms and we slow dance to 'our' music, on the beach, in the dark, in front of the fire. I think this might just be the most romantic moment of my life. There's no talking, no kissing—just my head on his chest as we sway to the music. The song ends and when "The Immortals" starts, and is a little peppier, he swings me out from him and then back into his chest. He starts trying to do some sort of funny swing dancing thing, but it doesn't work, and we both start to laugh. Before we know it, we're both just being the dorks that we are and acting a fool. We do every random dance we know and not very well. Jonathan

does do a mean sprinkler and my running man is usually pretty epic, but not in the sand. I fail miserably.

We're both out of breath from dancing and laughing our asses off when the next song comes on. It's a mellow tune that causes Jonathan to pull me back into his arms and we start swaying again. This time though there are words and kisses.

"This has been the best week of my life, Gracie."

"Mine too, Georgia."

"I wish we could just freeze time. I could stay here on this beach with you forever."

There are no words that would say it better than he just did, so I just kiss him to let him know how I feel.

"God, I do. I still love him. He's it for me. I know it now and I knew it then. Cami, you are so right…he's such a good man. You should see him on the streets at work. He's so respectful and kind to everyone he comes in contact with. There was this homeless man, named Willy, that he has a full on friendship with. He checks on him to make sure he doesn't need for anything. Do you think Mick is doing any of that?"

Alex surprisingly comes to my brother's aide. "I wouldn't imagine he is, but you never know. People are different at work than they are in their real life. Besides, you know better than anybody that Mick's frat boy image is just an act. Your brother is a good man, Em. It's nice to hear how great Jonathan is at work though." I just shrug, not wanting to talk about my big brother right now.

"Then there's Ireland. the two of them just clicked! She took to him so easily. Watching her in his lap was almost too much for me. It was like all my dreams coming true. She doesn't take to most men easily and she just took to him. He's all I think about! I can't believe he lives here and works with my brother and knows my mom! How did that happen?"

"Sweetie, it's loud in here but you don't have to shout. We can hear you just fine," she says with a grin.

Oh boy...I sure do feel all warm and fuzzy inside. My first drink and now two horrendously awful shots are hitting me quickly. I'm not sure there's enough fry bread to save me now.

"Cami, no more drinks for me. Let's share a mac and cheese and then I need to get my butt home."

"Deal."

"Wait, how are you gonna drive us home? You've had as much as I have."

"Nope, I've just had the Bellini. I didn't drink the shots. Those were all yours honey."

"You suck, Cam!"

"Oh hush, how else am I gonna get you to tell us how you really feel about him? Besides you're a cheap date."

She's right. I'm slumped and leaning my cheek on my right hand and my words have begun to slur just a tad while I try to get deep with Alex.

"Alex, he's so freaking hot and the sex...Alex...oh my God, the sex. There are just no words. I wonder if he's gotten better with age? Not sure how that's possible and I do not want to know who he might have practiced with, but God what I would do to have that man again. He is hot, sweet—remembered how I take my coffee after all these years—gorgeous, adorable, hot, strong and hung!" A little hiccup sneaks out at that last outburst and Alex just laughs at me. "Oh and don't forget he rescued the cutest dog ever and her name is Frances! He's hot and he rescues dogs, Alex!"

"Then why don't you tell him how you feel?"

"Alex, he doesn't need to be tied down with an instant family, and I have issues. You know that!"

Cami replies before Alex gets the chance. "You're stupid, that's what your issue is. Nothing will ever hold you back from your life more than your own insecurities, Em. I don't know how many times I have to tell you that, but you are both amazing and stupid at the same time. Hopefully, one day you'll wake up and realize how much you have to offer. Now eat your mac and cheese so you can sober up and we'll get you home and to bed."

"Love you, Cam."

"I know you do, Em," she says as she bumps my shoulder with hers. "And I love you right back."

Oh my God...my head is pounding...where the hell am I? What is going on?

It only takes a moment to realize I'm home—well, Mickey's home that I'm crashing in because I still don't have my life together—and that my head is pounding from the drinks that Cami made me partake in last night. We didn't stay out late, so I cannot believe I feel so crappy. I reach out for my phone and realize it is only three a.m. I also notice that there's a slew of text messages waiting for me and the one on top says it's from *Georgia.*

Oh no, Emily. What the hell have you done?

I drop the phone back on the bedside table scared to see what I wrote.

This cannot be happening!

I did not drunk text him. No way! That is just not me!

I don't get drunk, therefore I don't drunk text.

I get out of bed, get a glass of water and take something for the pounding in my head, while I pace my room. I just keep staring at my phone like it's about to jump up and bite me. I'm so anxious. I want to know what the messages say, but I'm too much of a chicken to pick up the phone and read it.

I distract myself and walk out into the hall and poke my

head in Ireland's room to see her sleeping soundly with all her stufties around her. She is an amazing little girl and I am so proud of her. I wouldn't change anything if it meant I didn't have her in my life. She's worth all the sacrifices I've made, but when I think about it, none of it was a sacrifice...because I have her.

I don't want to wake her up so I head back to my room, shut the door and pick up my phone. Let's see what kind of damage control I need to do. I make myself not read anything and go to the beginning and oh boy do I have a lot of scrolling to do. Looks like we were at it for a while.

GRACIE

I heard Kings of Leon tonight and it reminded me of dancing in the dark, on the beach, in front of the fire. That was fun.

GEORGIA

It was fun.

GRACIE

It wasn't a song from our album though.

GEORGIA

Where are you?

GRACIE

On my way home from happy hour with Cami and Alex. Cami made me go.

GRACIE

:(

GEORGIA

Ah, so you're drunk texting me, I hope somebody else is driving?

GEORGIA

I'll take the drunk texting as a compliment, I think?

GRACIE

Cami is driving.

GRACIE

California was great, wasn't it?

GEORGIA

It was. I think about it all the time.

GRACIE

Me too.

GEORGIA

Gracie...what's going on? Why are you texting me and not your other "friends"?

GRACIE

I don't know.

GRACIE

Hearing that song just reminded me of you and I am drunk.

GEORGIA

I thought you didn't drink?

GRACIE

I don't really and if I do I am a cheap date as you can see. I think you probably figured out why I didn't drink in Cali?

GEORGIA

Any other white lies from that week?

GRACIE

Just one...

GEORGIA

...

GRACIE

I actually love roller coasters! It's just all the signs said not to ride if you were pregnant and I didn't know what to do so I lied and said I didn't like them. I am so sorry but I swear the drinking and coasters are it! I really really love coasters.

GEORGIA

I think I can live with that. You're forgiven.

GRACIE

Thank you.

GEORGIA

Of course.

GRACIE

No I mean it.

GRACIE

Thank you.

GRACIE

For not hating me.

GEORGIA

I could never hate you. I understand everything now.

GEORGIA

Would you like to get coffee again sometime soon?

GEORGIA

Frances would love to see you again. She said we could even take Ireland to the park or something if you would rather do that?

GEORGIA:

Em, you still there?

GEORGIA

Sleep good, Gracie.

. . .

Gracie...he called me Gracie!

He forgives me and doesn't hate me!

I feel myself start to break out into a full sweat and must re-read it instantly and let the analysis begin. Steps must be retraced to make sure I didn't miss anything too embarrassing.

The first notable item is that this all started with the potential to go very bad when I mentioned dancing on the beach because what followed that dancing was very naughty. He didn't go there so that could mean he was being a gentleman because I was drunk, or he didn't want to remember the naughty times.

Second, I called it *our* album, so embarrassing! I can feel my cheeks getting hotter and hotter. This he didn't comment on, but was that because that album doesn't hold the same meaning for him or because he knew that I was drunk and didn't want to get too deep?

Third, he made it a point to call himself a friend and he did this in quotes. This could mean he's calling me out on friend-zoning him or does it mean something else? People usually drunk text their ex's or people they have a thing for. He is both to me, but maybe not in his mind?

Fourth, he called me out on my lies and forgave me. He forgave me for everything and I was passed out.

Fifth and the most important and notable item is that he called me Gracie. He knows what that means to me and he still called me Gracie.

I would say as far as drunk texting goes this wasn't too bad, but I am still mortified. Do I text him back and say I'm sorry? Well, not now, it's the middle of the night and I don't want to wake him up, but I would love to call and wake Cami up. She was clearly with me for some of this and I'm sure she was encouraging me. Some best friend I have. I could have confessed my undying love for him and she would have let me. Man, am I lucky it didn't go any worse than it did. Thank God for granting me this small miracle.

Now if this headache would go away and I wasn't so full of adrenaline I could go back to sleep. That would be a couple of miracles I could stand, but I don't see that happening in the next hour or so. I guess I'm up for the day. Today is going to suck...

9
———

Jonathan

I'm anxious...excited, but anxious.

What family I have left is going to be here, staying in my house that I am so proud of and that I was able to pay for free and clear thanks to my mom and my frugal four years in the Marine Corps. On top of the Fanuas coming to visit the other reason for my excitement—little girl giddiness, if I'm honest—is the fact that since Emily drunk texted me, we've continued to text. That was Monday night and now it's Thursday and we're still talking.

We aren't having deep conversations, it's just little things but it's something. It started with her apologizing for texting me when she was drunk. I wasn't sorry though, not at all. The hope that soared through me just knowing that she thought of me, of our album, and that my forgiveness meant so much to her, was something I couldn't put into words. As we texted, I told her not to feel bad and asked her how she felt that next morning. She wasn't feeling too hot so I decided I would text again in the afternoon to check on her and it went on from there. We're just saying hi and asking how each other's days are...for now. It's not a relationship but it's a start. Every text I get from her fills me with just a little more hope. Hope that I can get her to see how much more we could be.

My best friend Liam and his family are on their way from the airport. Liam texted me when they landed and said they were going to get their bags and rental car and be here shortly. I can't wait and I'm so amped that I can't sit still while I make sure the house is just right. I'm not the most organized or tidy person. I keep things clean but there isn't much organization involved. It works for me and Frances puts up with it. I feel like sharing the home that was always meant for my mom with her closest friends, is like sharing it with her. The nerves and excitement I'm feeling are a surprise, but they're my family and I haven't seen them in close to a year.

After about forty-five minutes of waiting there are finally headlights in my driveway and I race out to meet them. Fiona is the first one out of the Ford Focus rental car and she rushes to me, gives me a peck on the cheek, and throws her arms around me. Fiona may only be a little over five feet tall, but she's a sturdy woman and gives hugs that nearly take your breath away.

"Oh my, sweet boy, it is so darned good to see you. You look as handsome as ever!" She says with a spark in her shining green eyes.

"Thanks, Mrs. F. Let me help you with your bags and get you inside. Frances can't wait to meet all of you."

"Baby brother! How the hell are you?" Liam says as he unfolds himself out of the backseat.

"Are you ever going to let that two and a half months go? I'm good! How are you, man?"

"Not too bad. Glad to be here and can't wait to see what Portland has to offer, if you know what I mean?" He says with a wag of his brows.

Liam is good looking and knows it. He's just as tall as I am and he looks just like his dad—minus Mr. F's Buddha belly. Liam took after his dad's side of the family and his dark Samoan skin, brown eyes and black hair get him a lot of attention from the ladies. He looks exotic, I guess. That's what the girls always said when we were growing up. All I know is he has used this to his advantage and Liam Fanua always has a date. He's also a pain in the ass, but I love him like a brother!

"Still a dog."

"Woof!"

"Liam, you are just gross! Now move, so I can give my better big brother a hug!" Kate yells from behind him.

I give her a big squeeze and then ruffle her long brown hair like she hates and say, "How's my little sister these days? Anybody I need to beat away with a stick at the moment?"

"Nope, I have a boyfriend and he's amazing. No beating him off...wait...oh that sounded so bad! Shit! Sorry dad..." her light skin turns red with embarrassment but she recovers quickly. You have to if you want to survive in this family.

"In one ear and out the other, just like your mother always says. Bring it in, son," Mr. F says as he heads my way and in moments I'm enveloped in a hug so full of fatherly love that it almost chokes me up. I didn't realize how much I missed the four of them until they all finally got here.

"Hey Mr. F, it's so good to see you. Thanks for coming all the way out to Oregon to visit. It means a lot to have you guys here," I say with one last pat to his back and then he releases me.

"Of course, we couldn't wait to meet our first grandchild. Where is this Frances we've heard so much about?"

"Ha! Don't give me grief about grandkids when Liam is the oldest. He should be procreating first, but Frances is excited to meet you guys. She's a sweet old girl. Let's get your bags and head in."

After they get settled in their rooms, have had a tour and been introduced to their furry grandchild, we settle in. Since it's late for them with the time difference, I order some pizzas and we hang out and play a wicked game of *Catch Phrase*. We always play boys against girls and the guys just take turns sitting out each round. This is a game we've played for years. We've moved from the old school one, that is better in my humble opinion, to the new electronic version and it's amazing it's still in one piece after Kate has had her hands on it. She gets so fired up during the game that she practically throws it to the next person once she's done. She's nuts, but I love her.

It's crazy to see how Liam and Kate both take after their parents in the looks department. Kate looks just like her mom with light skin, green eyes, and brown hair. The only thing she did get from her dad is her height. At 5'9" she's tall for the women in Fiona's family. Kate is a younger, taller version of her mom just like Liam is of his dad.

After pizza, beer and five rounds of *Catch Phrase* the girls decide to call it a night. Robert, Liam and I head out to the back deck to sit around the fire pit and have another beer or two.

"So, J are you going to tell dad about Emily?"

"Emily? Who's Emily, son?" he says with a sly smile on his face. Just the thought of me possibly having a girlfriend seems to have perked him right up from that jet-lag.

"Well, not sure if Liam ever told you about the woman I met before my last deployment?"

"He did son, but I've never heard the story from you. Why don't you tell me about it?"

I spend the next thirty minutes telling our entire story from the first moment I saw her. Okay, I don't tell them *everything* but they get the picture. They understand that I instantly fell in love with her and that nothing has been the same since. I have gotten all the way up to where Courtney entered the room and I was given the 'let's just be friends' line.

For a few moments, the room is quiet. Then Mr. F leans forward and scoots to the edge of his chair and gets a very serious look on his face.

"Do you still love her or do you love the idea of her and what you had that week?"

"I love her, Mr. F. I've had a dark cloud hanging over me since she walked away, then I lost Matt and then Mom. The moment I saw her, the clouds started to fade away. Yes, she's beautiful but she is also kind and funny and seeing her with Ireland is amazing. As glad as I am that I didn't have a child out there that I didn't know about, seeing them together almost makes me wish I had been Ireland's dad. I know that sounds crazy, but it's true."

"You know, the fact that there is a child involved takes this to an entirely different level, right son?"

"I do know that, but I also know that she's *the one*."

"That's a big deal, Jonathan."

"It is. But she just wants to be friends."

"So, you're saying that she's 'the one' but you aren't going to fight to change her mind?"

"Of course I am, but I have to go about it the right way. She has trust issues and has been screwed over so many times. After living through what her father did to their family, and then Ireland's dad and his disgusting behavior, I get it. I know that I have to do what I can to make her see that I'm not them but I also don't want to scare her away. The fact that we're texting every day is just the first of many steps, I know, but it gives me hope."

"If you love her and you are really as okay as you say you are about Ireland, then you have to fight for her. Make her see the man we all know you are. It sounds like she knows it too and you haven't done anything to make her doubt you, but with her past, you're going to have to work extra hard. Sounds like she's worth it though, son."

"She is. They both are." I say with confidence.

"Well, that settles it then. You two can stay up and come up with the plan for 'Operation Get The Girl Back' but this old man is tired and hittin' the hay. I'll see you two in the morning."

"Night, Dad."

"Night, Mr. F and thanks for listening."

"Anytime, son. Night boys."

The next morning Robert is having his coffee and reading the paper in the kitchen, Kate is still asleep and Liam and I are getting ready to head out to *The Gym* when Fiona asks me to help her with something in her room.

When we reach my room, which I insisted they take while they're visiting, I ask, "Whatcha need, Mrs. F?"

"Have a seat, Jonathan," she says as she shuts the bedroom door.

I take a seat on the bed and she moves the little chair from the corner of the room over so that she's sitting directly across from me. She is scaring the hell out of me and I feel like she's about to give me some very bad news or I'm about to be scolded for something. I can't think of what I could have possibly done wrong in the time since they got here. This woman, who is all of five feet tall, has me feeling twelve again.

"Is everything okay, Mrs. F?" I ask cautiously.

"Everything is fine, sweetie." She takes one of my hands in both of hers and gives it a squeeze. "Jonathan, you know that I would never try to replace your mother. I don't ever want to over-step my role in your life, but I think you know that I think of you as my son and I love you just as much as I do those other two yahoos down the hall. You know that, right?"

I can barely breathe I am so filled with emotion. It takes everything I have to whisper. "I do."

If she only knew just how important she is to me.

"Good, now as you know I have to sleep with the window open no matter the weather—so please know I was not eavesdropping—but I did hear your conversation with Robert and Liam last night, about Emily."

I exhale the breath I was holding and with it the huge ball of anxiety that had been sitting in my chest. I let out a soft chuckle when I say, "You want to talk about my love life?" She nods her answer. "Thank God! I thought you had something serious to tell me."

"There's nothing more serious than love, my boy. From the sound of it, that's what you and Emily have but she may not be able to accept it yet?"

"I keep telling myself that we were only together nine days, and that was five years ago but I just know..."

"What do you know, Jonathan?"

"I know that she's *the one* and I love her. I'm sure that everybody thinks I'm nuts, but my time with her made me a better person; made me look at strangers differently because she treated everybody the same whether she knew them or not. She's an amazing person and she makes me better. I know that for sure."

"Jonathan, you were your mother's world. Her biggest wish for you was that you find somebody to love and that one day you would be whole and happy again. Your dad was the love of her life and she was his. Your momma would want you to find somebody that you love just as strong as she loved your daddy. I wish you had been able to see how wonderful they were together. It was a sight to see, Jonathan. They loved each other from the day they laid eyes on each other and nothing was going to get in their way."

"You know, I used to wonder why my mom never found anybody else. Why she never remarried, but I get it now. When you find the person you're supposed to be with nobody else compares, and that's how I have felt since the day she walked away from me." I look up to the ceiling and say, "I understand now, mom."

Fiona squeeze my hand and continues. "If you love her as much as you say you do, and she is worthy of your love, then you go and get her and her little girl."

"That's the plan, Mrs. F."

"You ready and willing to be an instant family and become this little girl's daddy if you fight for her?"

"I am."

Wow, I never really thought about that but by asking her to try it means the possibility of becoming somebody's daddy. That's kinda huge. I get why she wouldn't just jump in so easily and why just the sight of Courtney was enough to slow her down.

"You ready to lose them both if this doesn't work out?"

"I can't let that happen. It's not an option."

"But if it does it's gonna hurt twice as bad, kiddo."

"I can't let that happen."

"You think your momma would like her?" She asks with a small smile.

Smiling back, I assure her. "Momma would love her!"

Sitting back in her chair she asks, "So, whatcha gonna do?"

"Mrs. F, at the moment I am just going to go with baby steps. She just wants to be friends right now and as scared as she is of relationships she would probably move to New Zealand to get away from me if she heard me saying the "L" word. I don't even want to think about how bad she would freak out. I can't go full throttle or I am afraid I'll push her away. For now, friends, and we work our way to more from there."

"It sounds like your connection is pretty strong and I hope it doesn't take her as long as you think it might. It's good that you respect where she's coming from though. Remember she's a momma now and we are fierce when it comes to our babies, so you have an extra mountain to climb, but I know you'll make it to the top."

"Thank you. You don't know how much you guys mean to me and it means so much that you all flew out here to see the house. You know this should have been mom's house. I tried to have it built with all the things she had dreamed of. There are little things, like the big sink in the laundry room that always makes me think of her."

"Honey, the fact that after losing three people you loved in a matter of months, you didn't do what a lot of young people would have done and blow through your momma's life insurance and your savings that you worked so hard for. Honey, that's a big deal. And it's somethin' your momma would be so proud of. This house is beautiful and I hope that someday soon it's filled with your own family and all the love that you deserve."

She stands and pretends that she's getting rid of non-existent wrinkles in her shirt, picks up her little chair and returns it to the corner I put it in just for her. I can tell she needs this moment to collect herself so that the tears that were filling her eyes don't fall, and I give her that. Truth is, I need it just as bad as she does.

"Now, give me a hug and go get your work out on. I plan on hitting up as many food carts and yummy restaurants as possible while we're here so you are gonna need to burn some calories. I love you, kiddo. Now go on and get."

I give her one more little squeeze and a kiss on the cheek before I let her go.

"Love you too, Mrs. F. Thanks again."

It's Saturday night and we're all sitting around the fire pit in my back yard talking about the day. Devon and Gabby joined us today and the seven of us—well eight if you count Frances—had a great day. After stuffing ourselves Friday on food carts and late-night funky flavored ice cream at Salt and Straw, we decided to take it a bit easier on the calorie intake today.

We took the Fanuas to see Multnomah Falls since this is an obligatory must-see for first-timers to Portland. The drive through the Columbia River Gorge is beautiful and the falls are the bonus at the end of the forty-minute drive. After getting in all the mandated photos that Mrs. F and Kate insisted on we headed to Wachlella Falls Trailhead for a nice little two-mile hike. We spent the rest of the day hitting other local stand-outs, and taking in as much of the outdoors as possible. It's late September, but the weather is still great and we're trying to soak up every bit we can.

As I look at everybody important to me, outside of my work brothers, I am completely at peace...almost. There are two little ladies I would love to add to this group and then it would seem as though everything was right in the world. As if reading my mind, Liam decides it's time to bust my balls.

"So, Devon...did J tell you I met Emily yesterday?"

"No, he did not."

"Well, I did. She was coming out of spin class at *The Gym* when we got there."

"Told you, Devon, she is hooked! I knew once we got her there she would love it. Besides I teach the class, so you know she loves it." Gabby gives D a wink and then motions to Liam to carry on.

"Did you embarrass our boy?" he asks, hopefully.

"Nope, I was on my best behavior. Don't want to make things any harder for him. He can do that all on his own. Besides, I've heard about her for so long now that I was surprised to actually be meeting her. She really is a real person. Who knew?"

I flip him off from across the fire and he just shrugs.

"Dang, I'm sure that's not the way she would have wanted to meet you, Liam. All sweaty, no hair and make-up and a mess after working her butt off. Of course, she doesn't need hair and make-up. That girl always looks good. It's just not fair," Gabby says, speaking the truth.

Kate throws a marshmallow at her, from what's left of our roasting earlier, and says, "Who's talking? You are perfect! You could be Kelly Rowland's twin for God's sake! I don't want to hear it, Gabby!"

Before Gabby can reply Liam breaks in with, "She's not playin', D, you done good. I can't believe she liked you way back when you were just a scrawny little kid. You know how lucky you are, right?"

"Yes, I do Liam. Yes, I do." Devon answers leaning over and kisses Gabby on the cheek.

She mouths 'I love you' to him and his face lights up like it always does.

"Anyway, back to lover boy and Emily over here. Gabby, you're right she didn't need any make-up, but I could tell she was embarrassed. I haven't decided if it was meeting me all sweaty or seeing J for the first time in person since she drunk texted him. Of course, I think it's because she's in love with this idiot over here. I can't account for her taste in men but she seemed like a sweet girl in the few minutes I talked to her. What's your take, D?"

"She's a sweet girl, Liam, and I think she's crazy about this idiot over here too."

"Uh, guys. I'm sitting right here. You can stop talking about me like I'm not here," I interject to no avail. They just carry on. Even Fiona.

"Oh, I wish I had gone to *The Gym*. When Liam told me he got to meet Emily, I was so jealous."

"Honey, I think it's best that you didn't. If she's as frightened as the boy says she is about relationships...you would have scared her to death. You probably would have been taking her measurements so you could start on the wedding dress. The poor girl doesn't need all that."

"Amen, Daddy!" Kate chimes in.

Devon leans forward towards Liam and continues to pretend I'm not sitting right here.

"Liam, she's a sweet girl and I was there all those years ago and got to watch it from the start. I can tell you, this thing between them, it's the real deal. Now if we can just figure out how J can snap her out of keeping him in the friend-zone, and how he's gonna deal with her big brother, life will be sweet."

In unison Kate and Fiona ask, "Big Brother?"

D takes pleasure in filling them in...

"Oh, did he leave that out? Her big brother works with our boy here and is also a cop. He's not just a co-worker, but he is Mickey Freaking Jacobs. He's a bad man that you don't want to mess with. He's also very protective of Emily and Ireland. This could become a situation if he found out about our star-crossed lovers," he says leaning back in his chair with a look of satisfaction on his face.

"Wow, this just gets better and better dude," Liam says with a shake of his head.

"I still can't believe that her daughter is named Ireland...it's like it was meant to be or something." Kate says with a dreamy look on her face.

"Oh good God, she didn't name her after me! Her Grandmother's maiden name was Ireland! Enough about my non-existent love life people. Let's play a game or something. I can't take much more of this!"

"Spoil sport...as for the game how about *Would You Rather*?" Liam chimes in and we all groan at his suggestion.

The next morning the five of us get up early so we can get to Pine State Biscuits for breakfast as soon as they open. Then we take a whirlwind trip to the waterfront so that the Fanuas can visit the Saturday Market before they leave. It's a good thing we ate at Pine State first or we would have never gotten out of the Saturday Market in time with all the food options they have.

We make it back to the house by noon and when we walk in the door I see their packed suitcases waiting to be loaded into their rental car. My chest tightens at the thought of them leaving. I loved having them here and I'm starting to miss home for the first time since moving to Portland.

I help them load the car and Kate, Robert and Liam give me hugs, thanks for having them and see you laters. Liam and I both hate goodbyes so this works for both of us, and besides, we text so often it's like we talk all the time anyway.

Fiona stops me outside the closed passenger side door and takes one of my hands in hers and cups my cheek with the other. She has tears in her eyes, but she isn't letting them fall. This is something she seems to have perfected over her years of raising kids.

"Dear boy, your mother would be so proud of you. You have a good job that means something to you, you have a beautiful home, a beautiful heart and most importantly you are a good man. We love you so much and if you need anything, even just to talk, you know that we're all here for you."

"I know, Mrs. F."

Letting go of my hand and my cheek she pulls me in for a hug and whispers in my ear. "You stay safe out there, honey. Go get your girl and once you have her you better bring her home to meet me. Now give me a kiss and let this old lady go so I can cry in the car."

I kiss her on the cheek as I let her go.

"Love you, too. Safe flight home," I say quietly.

She nods, gets in and Robert reverses out of the drive to head to the airport.

Frances and I watch until we can no longer see their car.

10

Emily

It's been a week and Jesse still isn't back in class. I sure hope that I did the right thing. It worries me that he hasn't been back. It's been keeping me up at night that he hasn't returned and I don't know what to do. I'm a member of the staff here and it wouldn't be professional for me to reach out, but I am going to make a point to stop by the office today and see if they will tell me anything at all. I'm sure they won't as it's all confidential, but it's worth a try.

In the meantime, I need to focus on the kids that are here in class today, one of those kids being Austin. He seems to have a bit of hero worship going on since I helped Jesse. Some of these kids don't have the support that they need at home, so the fact that an adult actually took his concern to heart and acted upon it means a lot to him. I think it helps him to feel as though he has somebody on his side now, but I'm afraid that he's starting to feel a bit too close to me.

"Hey Austin, how's it going? Any missing assignments?"

"Nope, I'm all good Miss Jacobs."

"Good, need any help with math this week?"

"Nope, not so far."

"Hey, you heard from Jesse?"

"I haven't talked to him myself, but from what I hear he's ok. His dad's in jail and he was staying with his aunt, last I heard."

"What do you mean was?"

"I think he's back at his house with his little brother. He turned eighteen this weekend and I think it was cool for him to go home."

"Well, I'm glad to hear he's okay," I say to Austin, but it does concern me he and his brother are home alone.

Class is over in the blink of an eye and my day here at school is done. I don't stop by the office after all, now that I have a bit of an update from Austin. I decide to let it lie for the time being. I head to my car and notice there's a note under my windshield wiper.

Watch your back bitch!

What the hell?

A chill runs down my spine as I hold the note in my now clammy hand. I scan the school parking lot to see if there's anybody around, but I don't see anybody. I jump in my car and head out of the parking lot much faster than you are supposed to in a school zone, and I haul ass to Ireland's school. I know just giving her a squeeze will calm me down, and knowing she is okay is all I can think about.

I pull into the school parking lot, park haphazardly and rush from my car to the front doors of the building. At first, I don't see her playing in her usual spot over by the dollhouse, but after a quick look around, I see her in the back sitting on a teacher's lap. She looks lethargic and her cheeks are rosy.

"Hey baby girl, what's wrong?" I ask moving her hair off of her face.

"I don't feel good, momma," she whimpers.

I know when she calls me momma there's something wrong. I'm usually mom or mommy but when she's sick, tired or pouting she pulls out the momma card and it gets me every time.

"She had a temp of a hundred and one when we checked about five minutes ago. We knew you would be here any minute to pick her up so we hadn't texted you yet," her teacher explains.

"Wow, poor baby. Come here and let's get you home and feeling better," I say as I take her from the teacher's arms and into my own. I can instantly feel the heat radiating off of her.

"I know you know, but just a reminder that she won't be able to come back to school for twenty-four hours after her fever is gone." Turning her attention to Ireland she says, "You feel better, little one, and we'll see you later this week."

Shit! I'm going to have to miss work and I have class tonight! Thank God it's an online class and I don't have to go anywhere.

"Thanks, Beverly. Hopefully, she's better soon and just misses tomorrow."

Ireland is limp as I carry her to Justine and isn't much help as I get her snapped into her big girl booster seat. She's quiet all the way home and practically asleep by the time we get to Mickey's. I hate that we're at Mickey's and now not only does he have the two of us invading his space, but he has a sick child to put up with. I know he doesn't look at it that way, but I hate to be a burden to him or to anybody for that matter.

When I walk in the front door, Mickey's sitting on the couch, eating cereal and watching TV. When he sees that Ireland is not her usual self he instantly jumps up and asks if he can help. I tell him she has a fever and I don't want him to get sick either, but he tells me to shut up, takes her from me and carries her to her room. I bust out the Children's Tylenol and have her drink it down, then I get her in her jammies and sit with a cold, wet, washrag held to her forehead. I settle in for what I'm sure is going to be a long night, with a sick Ireland and class to get through. It's a glamorous life, I know, but somebody has to live it!

Ireland's fever finally broke around midnight on Monday night after she threw up all over her bed and herself. Mick got home from work shortly after while I had Ireland in the bath trying to clean her up. He came in and stripped her bed, started the wash and put clean bedding on her bed for me. He sure does have moments that just melt my heart. Once he settles down he's going to make himself a great dad and husband. It may be years from now, but he'll get there. It's just going to take the right woman.

It's now Wednesday and I'm sitting at my desk waiting for the bell to ring so that I can head home. Between taking care of my baby girl, class and not sleeping from worrying about life and where I'm headed, I am exhausted. Throw in the fact that every text from Jonathan makes my heart soar and butterflies dance around my insides and there is no sleep happening in my world. Fingers crossed Ireland will want to take a nap or at least watch a movie and I can crash next to her for a bit.

Ah, there it is, the gift that keeps on giving...the bell that says I get to go home. I gather all of my belongings, say goodbye to Heidi and I bail. I cannot get to my car, to the pre-school and to Mick's fast enough.

Before I even reach my car though, I stop in my tracks when

I see a piece of paper stuck under my wiper blade again. I look all around and don't see anybody, but I still approach my car on high alert. I look under the car and check the back seat before I grab the note and get inside.

Smart of you not to come to work yesterday bitch!

Once again I race out of the parking lot and to Ireland. I just don't understand why this is happening. Is this about Jesse? I don't know who else would want to threaten me. This just doesn't make sense.

Just as I reach the school my phone pings and tells me I have a text. I see it's from an unknown number and break out into a sweat when I read it.

UNKNOWN CALLER

You will get what you deserve - Just stay away

I drop the phone in my purse like it has some sort of disease and sit in my car trying not to panic. What the fuck?

Calm down, Emily. You have to walk into the school and get your daughter and not freak her out. Just breathe and get home to Mickey.

~

Mick looks like he's getting ready to head out to the gym when Ireland and I walk through the door.

"Uncle Mick!"

"Hey *I*, how was school today?"

She throws her backpack on the floor, runs to him and jumps in his arms.

"It was fun, we learned about our personal pace and if somebody is in your pace or doing something you don't like, the nice way to tell them to stop is to hold your hand up like this," she demonstrates by holding her hand up a few inches from his face. "And say pease stop!"

"Oh, so the next time you get in my personal *space* to give me one of your icky girl kisses, I just have to say *please* stop and you have to stop?"

"You don't love my kisses, Uncle Mick?"

She says as she looks down and her lower lip starts to come out but Mick is quick and starts to tickle her as he tells her, "Of course I do! I was just joking with you, silly!"

"I knew it!" she yells out between giggles.

"Mick..."

As I stand in a calm panic and watch all the cuteness in front of me, I can't help but whisper Mick's name. When I realize he can't hear me over the tickles and giggles I try again.

"Mick," I say a little louder.

He finally looks at me and I can tell that he can read my face and knows that something is wrong.

"Hey *I*, why don't you go to your room and pop in one of your movies so I can talk to your mom. I'll be there in just a little bit to check on you."

"Okay, Uncle Mick but you have to have one of my icky girl kisses first!"

She kisses her uncle on the cheek, he thanks her as he sets her feet on the ground and she scampers off to her room without a care in the world.

"Emmers, what's going on?" Mick asks.

I hand him the note and show him the text message without a saying a word.

"What the fuck, Em? When did this start?" he yells as his face turns red with anger.

"I found a note on my car on Monday, but Ireland was sick and I got so distracted with her and school that I forgot to tell you. Then when I left work today there was another note and then five minutes after I found this I got the text. I have no idea who would do this, Mick. The only thing I can think of is that I noticed some abuse on a student at work and I reported it, but the dad is in jail and there isn't a mom around so I'm not sure if it's his family or not."

"I want you to write down the name of the kid you reported and his dads name if you have it. I want to make sure he really is in jail. Could there be anybody else? A pissed off student? A jealous co-worker? Anybody at all that you could have pissed off?" He says while I watch him try to calm himself by opening and closing his now clenched fists.

"No Mick, I can't think of anybody else. It has to be somebody with my phone number...I just don't get it."

"Well, you are not going to work the rest of the week!" he orders.

"Yes, I am Mick!" I shout.

"No, you aren't Em!" he shouts back.

"Mick, if I don't go then they win and we'll never catch them."

"Shit! I'm supposed to leave Saturday morning for my hunting trip with the guys! I'm gonna call and cancel. There is no way I am leaving you two home alone," he says pacing and pulling his phone out of his shorts pocket.

"You are not going to cancel your trip. I'll have mom come over and we have Frank. It will be fine," I try to convince him as much as myself.

"Oh, mom will protect you? That is supposed to make me feel better? Leave all three of you home alone together for a week? I don't think so."

"Mick, you have an alarm on the house. Even if it's not monitored yet it will still make noise. Frank will bark if anybody gets near. I'll have Cami and Alex hang out and you can leave me numbers to any of the guys you trust that I can call if I get scared and need them to stop by and check things out."

"Anybody I would trust is going with me...wait...Kelly...I can have Kelly do drive-bys and check on you every day. You cool with that?"

Oh, big brother if you only knew....

"I'm cool with that, Mick."

11

———

Jonathan

Standing at Mick's front door I raise my hand to knock and my mind goes back to the frantic text I got from him a couple of days ago. It was telling me what some asshole is doing to Emily and if I would mind stopping by to check on her every day while he was off hunting. He also said that he had given her my number in case she needed anything. He would freak the fuck out if he knew that we already had each other's numbers and that I was in love with his little sister. I don't even want to think about that conversation.

When I read his message, the first thing I wanted to do was find whoever was doing this to her and kill the son of a bitch! There is nobody else I would want watching over her while Mick is gone. In fact, I don't plan on letting her out of my sight.

I know Mick told me to come by in the evening to check on her, but here it is ten o'clock in the morning and I'm already here knocking on the door. Mick texted me to say thanks when the guys hit the road, and I ran to my truck to get here as fast as I could. The thought of her and Ireland home alone with somebody out there threatening her brings out a possessive side I never even knew I had.

The sight I see when Emily opens the door is probably the best thing I have seen in five years.

In front of me stands Emily, with an embarrassed shade of pink coloring her make-up free skin, her hair is up in a mess on top of her head, and her long legs are on display in her short little boxer shorts. But the best part? The best part is that on top of those boxer shorts is my old USMC t-shirt. And if my eyes do not deceive me there isn't a bra on under that t-shirt.

She stole my t-shirt, has kept it all this time and still fucking wears it! There is a God!

"Hey," she barley squeaks out.

"Hey, Em. Mick told me he wanted me to check in on you while he was gone, so here I am." I'm trying my best to keep a straight face when all I want to do is give her shit about my shirt. It's so hard to keep my mouth shut and the smile off of my face.

"He just left like ten minutes ago. I don't need a babysitter but it's nice of you to come by."

She sounds irritated and I can tell she's trying to brush me off when I see a little head full of blond curls and big brown eyes sneak past Emily's leg. As soon as she sees me she jumps up and down in her footy pajamas.

"Jonafon! Mommy, Jonafon's here!"

Thank God for this kid because she grabs me by the hand and pulls me right past her mom and into the house. She takes me over to the family room table where her dolls appear to be having a party. I can see a stack of books and Emily's computer open on the kitchen table.

"Do you wanna play dolls with me?" Ireland asks. How could I ever say no to her?

"Baby girl, Jonathan doesn't want to play dolls," she says to Ireland and then turns her attention towards me. "Besides

I was just trying to get some studying done while she played, so see? We're all good." She's still trying to get rid of me.

She squirms a little bit as she tries to cover her bra-free chest with her arms crossed in front of her. I think she's hoping I won't notice the t-shirt she's wearing, but there is no way I would have missed that.

"I'm good. Why don't we play dolls and you do your studying for a bit?"

"Yeah!" My little partner in crime yells, affirming that my idea is better!

"No, you don't want to babysit," she says still fighting me.

"I won't be babysitting. I'll be hanging with my new friend just a few feet away from her momma. Sounds like fun to me."

Weakly she says, "Jonathan, you don't have to do this."

"I know but I want to," I assure her.

The thing is I really do want to. She is losing this battle so she may as well just wave the white flag now because I ain't goin' anywhere!

"You do not," she says as though I am pitying her.

"Come on Ireland, let's give your mom some peace and quiet and you can show me your room and we can play a game or something."

"Can we play dolls?" she pouts, not letting me get away with not playing dolls so easily.

This kid already has me wrapped around her little finger with those big brown eyes of hers. I am a goner and it looks like I will be playing dolls for the first time in my life.

"Sure we can, princess."

"Why you call me princess?" she questions me, sounding confused.

"Well, it says it right there on your pajamas," I point out.

Ireland looks down at her pink pajamas—that have a

princess crown on the front with the world *Princess* below it—and then gives me a little curtsy and a smile.

Yep, I'm a goner.

"Sorry, we thought we were just gonna have a lazy day at home and we haven't gotten dressed for the day yet."

"No worries at all. I like this look on both of you," I say with a smile. "Ireland, let's get your stuff and you lead the way."

As Ireland and I gather all of her things off the family room table I can feel how excited she is and how embarrassed her mom is. Walking past Emily with my arms full of dolls, I just can't resist when I lean in close and whisper, "Nice shirt."

Heading towards Ireland's room, with my back to Emily, I can't help the shit-eating grin spreading across my face.

This little girl is mesmerizing. She is smart, engaging, funny, and so sweet. She gets this all from her mother, of course. Spending time with Ireland, surrounded by all of her things I am struck by the fact that this is all Emily. She has raised Ireland all on her own as a young woman, working, going to school and with Cami as her only bit of family with her along the way. To see this kind little soul that she has created is awe-inspiring.

It's now around noon and after dolls, books and some coloring action Ireland is now settled on her bed watching Frozen while I sit on the floor leaning against the foot of her bed watching along with her. Well, watching may be an overstatement, I'm looking at the TV while thinking about the vision of Emily in my shirt and those boxers.

At some point, while we read one of several Dr. Seuss books, I saw Emily walk past the room and then when she came by again she was in knee-length yoga pants and a Portland Police

Department sweatshirt. It must be Mick's because she's swimming in it and it unfortunately, covers her ass.

As I stare at the TV in my own little world I feel something hit me in the face. I look down to my lap to see the offending item is one of my precious *Goldfish* crackers. I look up to see a smiling Emily in the doorway.

"You two want some lunch?" Ireland's momma asks leaning against the doorway. Shit, Emily is a momma. It's not what I always fantasized about, but I like this role on her. It fits.

I can tell Ireland already knows the answer when she asks, "Can I eat on my bed mommy?"

"No, but we can have a carpet picnic and you can eat on the floor here in your room. I'll be right back. Catch."

She throws the huge bag of Goldfish at me and leaves the doorway but she's back a minute later with plates balancing in her hands. Does she remember that these little crackers are my favorite or is it just a coincidence?

"Okay, here we go with our five-star lunch. How do we feel about pb&j's—one crunchy and two creamy—apple slices, cheese, blueberries and of course fishies?"

She remembers I like crunchy peanut butter! First the t-shirt, now the peanut butter and possibly even fishies! This day just keeps getting better!

"Fishies! They're my favorite snack, Jonafon."

"No, they're *my* favorite snack, Princess."

"They can be both of your favorites, but Ireland he did love them before you did. Before you were even born in fact," Emily says as she gives Ireland a little poke to the belly that makes her giggle.

Well, Fuck me! I guess she remembers. Looks like I'm not the only one with a good memory. Thank you, baby Jesus!

"So, you two having fun in here?" Emily asks.

"So much mommy!" Ireland answers with a mouthful of PB&J.

"Don't talk with your mouth full, baby girl."

Yep, I like this role on her. Emily gives good mom. She's a natural.

"Yep, we're having a great time. You getting through your schoolwork?"

"I'm plowing through it. I have hours left though. Please don't feel like you have to stay. I've got tomorrow too."

"Well, if you don't mind I'll stay here and hang with Ireland while you keep working?" I'm not really asking but I can play the part if she needs me to.

"Why do you want to do this?" she asks still sounding as puzzled as she did when I first arrived.

"What can I say, I'm a sucker for a pretty girl. You'd have to pry me away from this little princess. Now finish your lunch and go study."

With this, I have effectively ended the conversation.

12

Emily

How in the world am I supposed to study and focus on anything other than Jonathan in the other room with Ireland? I still can't figure out what he's doing here. Why does he want to spend his Saturday with a four-year-old and her single mom who sits in the other room studying? I know the image I've kept of him from years ago has been glorified with time. But now...the real him...the him that is actually here...that Jonathan is exceeding all of my dreams of him. I am so confused.

After giving myself an internal pep talk, hours have gone by and I was able to get a lot done. I told myself that I needed to get through this school work to make a better life for Ireland and that was what I needed to focus on. Not boys. I close my book and get up to go check on the new BFF's. When I get to her doorway, I see her fast asleep on her bed and Jonathan sitting in her tiny little bean bag chair playing a game on his phone.

"Bored yet?" I whisper.

"Nope," he whispers back.

"You can head home now. I got all my studying done," I say as I motion for him to join me with a nod of my head.

He gets up and walks out of the room, and I follow him into the kitchen. He helps himself to a glass of water and drinks it down before replying to my statement about him leaving.

"I was thinking, I could run home real quick, feed Frances, take her for a little walk and then come back with some pizzas and we could have a movie night."

"Jonathan, what are you doing?"

"Just keeping you safe. We still need to talk about these threats, Em. We'll do that later though. So, I'll head out and be back in an hour or so, sound good?"

"Jonathan, I don't need a babysitter. You don't have to hang out just because my big brother asked you to check on me."

"This has nothing to do with Mick. I want to spend time with you and I won't be able to function if I know you two are here alone. So let me do this, okay?"

"Okay."

Jonathan should be back any minute and I'm one frazzled woman. I don't know what to do with myself. As soon as Jonathan left I finally hopped into the shower, put on real clothes, did my hair and added a touch of make-up.

I cannot believe that he caught me wearing his shirt. I saw the moment it connected in his brain and how he tried to hide his smile, but of course, couldn't keep it hidden. I was mortified and waiting for the smart ass comments to start flying my way, but he didn't make it a big deal. He made his little comment to acknowledge that he noticed but didn't accuse me of stealing or any other embarrassing thing he could have come up with.

I still can't believe he spent his day off sitting in Ireland's room playing with her and just hanging out while she napped. What guy does that? I know he said he wanted to try and that he wanted to get to know Ireland too, but he's actually doing it. I guess his words weren't hollow pick-up lines and he meant them. It also looks like he isn't taking no for an answer, but he also isn't making any moves. Is this all just a friendly gesture or does this mean he's still trying for more? Do I want more?

Emily, don't be stupid...of course, you want more. Now, what are you going to do about it?

"Mommy, do you think Jonafon will like my dress?" Ireland asks as she does a twirl in her Princess Elsa dress.

She is so sweet and kind and I don't want her heart to get broken this early. Do I subject her to also falling in love with Jonathan knowing full well that he could leave one day and leave us both broken-hearted?

I don't get to answer the thought in my head because there's a knock on the door. I take one final glance at myself and decide my skinny jeans and a loose sweater will have to do...

I check the peep-hole and there he is with pizza just like he promised. Taking a calming breath, I unlock the door and open it to dimples. I haven't seen much of his elusive dimples since seeing him again, and I must say it is quite a panty-dropping sight.

"Sorry sir, but we didn't order any pizza," I play with him to hide my nerves.

"I know you didn't ma'am but I did. You see there are these two really cute girls that I'm trying to impress. I thought I could win them over with pizza."

I don't reply because in my head all I can think is that he just said I was cute and he was trying to impress me. Well, me and my four-year-old but still...cue butterflies....

"I drove all the way to Sparky's to pick it up and I got two kinds just to be safe. Do you think my plan will work?"

I lean on the door and shake my head. "You really are too much, you know that?"

"Ah, you love it and you know it. Now let me in woman!" he jokes as he pushes past me.

He's right, I do love it. I love all of it. His protectiveness, kindness, humor, dimples, everything about him really.

"You gonna stand there all day or are you going to join us?"

I turn to see him standing by the kitchen table grinning ear to ear.

"Sorry, I was lost in my thoughts there for a minute."

Not taking his eyes off of mine he says, "Trust me, I understand. It's been happening to me a lot lately, too."

I close and lock the door and meet him in the kitchen to get plates and drinks. Out of the corner of my eye, I see Ireland is doing a little twirl for Jonathan and asking if he likes her princess dress. I can't help but roll my eyes.

"I love it Ireland. You look pretty in anything though. You don't need to dress up to impress me, but I do like it. Have I seen a dress like this in a movie before? Maybe earlier today?"

"Yes!!! You remembered! My dress is just the same as Elsa's!" she squeals.

"That's right it is." Whispering he says, "Don't tell Elsa but I think it's even prettier on you."

"Oh, you are really working it, Georgia. She's only four, you know that, right?"

"It's never too early to build her self-esteem, especially if I speak the truth."

"I think her self-esteem is pretty dang good if you ask me." All I can do is shake my head as I fix Ireland a plate of cheese pizza and then one for myself.

"It is and that's all because of you, Em. She's awesome... you've done a great job." His tone is now serious and sincere.

He comes to stand next to me to make up his plate. I will not get choked up while eating pizza, but he sure is making it hard with comments like that. He wasn't kidding when he said he was trying to win us over and it looks like he is giving 110% effort at impressing us. Standing this close to him isn't hurting anything either.

A quiet 'thank you' is all I can get out.

All of a sudden I see my little angel trying to strip in the middle of the living room floor.

"Ireland, what are you doing?" I ask hurrying in her direction as she struggles with her dress.

"I don't want to get nuffin' on my dress. These are spensive mommy."

"Let's run to your room real quick and we'll get you changed into something else."

After a quick change, pizza and a movie—where Ireland sat pressed up against Jonathan's side the entire time—it's time to wind down and clean up. After I pick up the pizza boxes and plates it's time for me to get my mom face on.

Pointing my finger in the direction of the hall I get Ireland's attention.

"Okay, bath time baby girl."

"No, what about Jonafon?"

She is working this just as much as he is! Ugh! She's acting like she is never going to see him again. Truthfully, this is a worry of mine too.

He's looking at me like he's asking if it's okay, but I can tell he's already made his decision. These two are quite a little team. God help me!

"How about I go take Frank for a little walk while you're in the bath and I'll say goodnight to you before you go to bed. Sound good?"

Ireland, of course, siding with Jonathan, squeals yet again. "That sounds awesome!"

Ireland walks up to a snoring Frank and tells him to be good on his walk and then grabs my hand and leads me away.

"His leash is on the hook in the laundry room. Thanks again for everything, Jonathan," I say in resignation.

"My pleasure."

He turns to get the leash and I head towards the bathroom where Ireland is already stripped down to her birthday suit.

"What are you doing? I haven't even run the water yet, silly girl."

"I want to be done before Jonafon gets back," she says jumping up and down with excitement.

Looks like I'm not the only one that has it bad. He is a smart one. He knows exactly what he is doing by winning over Ireland, the key to my heart. He definitely has the upper hand at the moment but I think I'm okay with that. He was patient once before and it looks like he's willing to go even further this time. The truth is, I want him to win us over. I want him. Shit. This is not good. Am I up for this?

Just as I am drying Ireland off I hear the front door and Jonathan yells, "We're back!"

"Oh, mommy! They're back! Hurry!" she says giddy to see him again.

I know just how you feel baby girl. I feel exactly the same.

"We'll be out in just a minute." I yell back.

The moment Ireland's princess nightgown is on she's out the door and running to find Jonathan.

"Come back here little lady, you still have teeth to brush!" I yell after her.

I pick up her clothes, hang up her wet towel and turn to go find my missing child just as Jonathan crowds the doorway with Ireland over his shoulders—just like I was once when he carried me out of that bar in San Clemente.

"Looking for this?"

"As a matter of fact, I am. Thanks so much for the delivery service," I quip.

He puts her down and she steps up on her step stool in front of the sink and I hand her a very pink princess toothbrush already covered in toothpaste and she starts brushing. I figured Jonathan would have left by now, but he's still standing there watching us go through our nighttime routine. Ireland has a huge grin on her face the entire time she brushes. She tries to finish a little too fast so I stop her from hopping off her stool and help her finish.

"Okay, say goodnight baby girl. It's off to bed for you."

She sticks out her lower lip out and looks down at her feet while she hugs my leg. Suddenly shy she pops her little head out from behind me and says, "Goodnight."

"Don't look sad, I'll be back tomorrow."

"You will?" Ireland and I ask in unison.

"I was planning on it so don't you worry about bedtime. You'll see me tomorrow."

Ireland grabs his hand and leads him to her bedroom. She's up to something. She hates going to bed and can think of a million things to delay the process each night. Tonight, she's walking toward her favorite stack of books and hands one to Jonathan and then crawls up into her bed.

"No, Jonathan doesn't need to read you a story. Let's let him go home and I'll read to you in a minute."

"Ah, pease mommy?"

She's begging me and in front of him. She really is too smart for her own good, and if this is any indication, she's going to have her way with many male hearts along the way. I don't want to even think about that!

"I don't mind if it's okay with your momma?"

"Okay, but only one Ireland. Jonathan, do not let her talk you into book after book because she'll do it. Trust me on this one."

Then I fake whisper so they can both hear me, "It's a trap!"

He chuckles, kneels on the side of her bed, opens up the classic *Where the Wild Things Are* and starts to read. She stops him though. She pats the side of her bed asking him to sit on the bed with her. He looks to me for permission and I nod my approval. Once he's settled with his arm around her and with her pressed into his side once again, he starts to read.

I step out into the hallway to catch my breath. The sight of them together like that is just too much. I've had dreams with this same scenario. I wish so badly that her father hadn't rejected us both, but he did, and I am doing my best to make up for it. Moments like this though, these moments make me realize that no matter how much I try to make up for the loss of her father I can't. The thought breaks my heart.

My poor baby girl.

Ireland fell asleep half-way through the book but he finished it like a trooper. After we detached her from Jonathan without waking her up we quietly creep out of her room and shut the door. He follows me down the hall and then we awkwardly stand in the middle of the family room not saying anything. In the middle of the screaming silence Frank farts so loud he wakes himself up and that is all it takes for the both of us to start laughing and break the silence.

"How about a drink? Got any wine or anything else around this place?"

"Uh, I do have some wine if you want some."

I know I am looking at him suspiciously but I really did think he would be leaving now. I can't believe he's been here since 10 am.

"Let's do it. Let's have some wine and maybe watch a movie but without the G rating."

Shit, what will happen when we're alone with wine and a movie? Double Shit!

Heading towards the kitchen I cannot believe I say, "Sure, let's see what we have."

After we're settled on the couch—not close enough to touch but not far away from one another either—he pick up the remote and we search for a movie we both want to see on Netflix.

"So, how's the new job going?"

"Not too bad. I wish I was working more hours, but I like it. Mick is being really cool about it and won't let me pay rent. So, with Justine being paid off."

My reference to the fact that I named my car after meeting him earns me a smile.

"And with no rent or utilities I just have preschool and my schooling to pay for and most of my check goes to that. I would love more hours but then that would just cost more in daycare, so until I finish school and can get a full-time teaching job I'm staying here with Mick. I hate that he's giving up his privacy for us, but I also know how lucky I am to have him and my mom."

"How did you do it on your own down in California all these years?"

"Well, I had Cami for a roommate and free day are. I told you about Charlotte and how she watched Ireland every day. For free. Free Jonathan...what would I have done if she hadn't been there and watched my little girl for free? Honestly, you said that Ireland is so great, and she is, but it is just as much because of Cami and Charlotte as it is me. I couldn't have done it without either of them. So, financially things were a challenge, but because of the amazing support in my life we managed."

I feel the tears coming so I take a sip of my wine to try and calm the emotions that are hovering on the surface. Jonathan's face has been serious while he listens to me tell him another piece of my story and it's making me feel even more on edge.

"It's called karma, Emily. Just like I told you before. You put out enough good for all of us and that is why the good came back around to you. You deserve every good thing that has come your way. You deserve more if you ask me."

"You're exaggerating, but thank you."

We continue to talk about my job and how much I love the kids I work with and how I can't wait to do it full-time and have my own classes. He talks about his job and how much he loves it but that there are lots of challenges. We talk about the climate around the view of the police in our country. We talk for what feels like forever and then he asks the question I know he has been dying to ask me all day.

"Who do you think is doing this to you? The threats? Who would want to scare you like this?"

I fill him in on the situation with Jesse and that this is the only possible thing that I can think of. He asks if I would mind if he looked into and if I would share the same info I already gave to Mick.

"I already gave it to Mick, but if you really want to dig a little deeper you can."

I go into the kitchen to get a sticky note and write down Jesse's name and his father's information.

"This is all I have, thanks for looking into it."

As I hand him the sticky note, he takes it but keeps a hold of my hand, moves the sticky note to his other hand and puts it on the table. Before I know what's happening he pulls me back down to the couch, but this time right next to him so my legs are over his. Still holding my hand that now has its fingers inter-twined with his, he leans in a couple of inches from my face and scans every inch of my face with those magnificent eyes of his.

His gaze finally meets mine. "Gracie...I'm going to kiss you now."

I just continue to look at him...

"That okay with you?"

I nod and the moment my head starts to move his lips find mine; feather-soft at first as he dips his foot in the pool to check the temperature. He takes his time and then gently bites my lower lip. I softly moan as he growls lightly and sends a shiver of lust down my spine.

"I have dreamed about this for years. I can't believe you're here, in my arms," he whispers against my lips.

As if this proclamation was what he needed to say before he could really let loose, he lets go of my hand and cups my face in his hands just like I remember. He kisses me harder and our tongues start their exploration of each other. Before I know it we've changed positions and he's above me with a leg on either side of me. You can hear us both breathing heavily as if we will never get enough of each other. He lowers himself onto me but is sure to keep most of his weight on his arms. He breaks our kiss and trails his glorious mouth down my neck. He has me squirming as I feel his excitement pressed between my legs. He then trails his lips and tongue back up my neck to my ear and whispers. "I missed you, Gracie."

I glide my fingers up his back wishing I was touching his skin and bring my hands to his head where I guide his lips back to mine. A few moments later he pulls back and sits up. The excitement I was just feeling against my core is now visible and has me yearning for more. I remember what's under those shorts, but I wouldn't mind a reminder of what I've been missing.

"Emily, I am so sorry. I know you said that you just wanted to be friends and I'm trying. I really am. But you can't deny that it's still there. That connection between the two of us...it's still there."

"It is."

"I'm sorry if I crossed a line."

"You didn't, I wanted it just as badly as you did. I did say I wanted to be friends. I have Ireland, school, class, threats...I just don't know if I have enough to give. I also don't want to hurt Ireland. If we try this and you leave or it doesn't work out, it's not just me that's left behind to heal."

I can tell that he doesn't like my last statement but he checks himself before saying, "I don't want to be an added stress to your life, Em. I know you have a lot going on but I'd like to be there to help you. I know you pride yourself on your independence and I don't want to take any of that away. I would just love to be there for you and Ireland, but you're already talking about when I leave. That's not me, Em."

Yep, I pissed him off.

"I know, but it's what I know."

"Emily, I think we should call it a night. I am going to sleep on the couch, after drinking that entire bottle of wine by myself, and you go to bed and think about what you can give and if you want to really try this. Just know that I'm all in but I don't want to add stress to your life. Now please go to bed before I jump you again."

He's saying everything that I know to be true and everything I want to hear and all I can do is stand here staring at him. I can't move and I can't speak.

"Em?"

I jump at the sound of his voice and reply on auto-pilot. "Let me go get you a pillow and a blanket. I'll be right back."

In a haze of lust and with his admissions of wanting to try floating around my head, I walk in a daze to my room to grab a pillow and the extra blanket at the end of my bed and walk them back out to him.

He stands as I reach him and he grabs my face in his hands, closes his eyes, sighs, and kisses my forehead.

"Goodnight, Gracie."

"Night, Georgia."

13

———

Jonathan

I'm surrounded by my favorite scent of vanilla and coconut—and whatever it is that makes Emily always smell like vacation—as I start to wake up. But I'm not ready to open my eyes and leave my little dreamland. As I lay here in-between sleep and being awake, her scent surrounds me and the instant replay I have going on in my mind. On a constant loop, I keep reliving having her in my arms last night. I know I have to be patient and go slow, but it's hard when all I want to do is throw her down and ravish her. Keeping my eyes closed and hidden from the morning sun starting to peek through the blinds, I think back to last night on this very same couch with her in my arms and her lips on mine. I'm afraid if I open my eyes I'll be back at home alone in my bed and everything from last night will end up being just a dream that will disappear.

Tap. Tap. Tap.

I feel a tiny little finger tapping me on the nose and am assured that I'm not at home alone in my bed and last night was thankfully not a dream. The smell of vacation is from the pillow

I slept with that must be right off of Emily's bed. And I have a feeling the tap on my nose is from a cute as hell little blond. I think I'm in Heaven.

"Good morning, Jonafon," Ireland whispers into my ear.

I'm lying on my side facing her and I open one eye and whisper back, "Good morning, Princess."

"You slept over?"

"I did."

I sure hope this is an okay conversation for me to be having with her?

"Did the Wild Things make you sleepy too?"

"They did."

"Well, if you stay over again tonight you can use one of my stufties to sleep with so you aren't all by yourself out here on the couch," she says as we both continue to whisper to each other. This little girl and her big brown eyes and her sweet little smile are quite something to wake up to. She is something else.

"Ah, thanks, sweetie. Is your momma still asleep?"

"Yep, just me and Frank are up and now you!" she says loudly and then pops her adorable little hand over her mouth realizing she didn't whisper that time.

"Shall we get up, let Frank out and then make your momma breakfast?"

"Oh yes, let's make breakfast!"

"Okay, let me get up and get dressed and then we'll go brush our teeth and get breakfast started. But let's be sure to be quiet so we don't wake up your mom okay?"

"Okay!" She runs off down the hall as I throw on my cargo shorts from yesterday and meet her in the bathroom. I use my finger to bush while she uses her pink toothbrush and we whisper as we brush and rinse. She giggles at my improvised brushing method and I can't help but think how adorable she is and that I know exactly where she gets it.

We head to the kitchen and gather eggs, bacon and some pancake mix since Ireland has informed me she does not eat eggs. Duly noted.

We have the bacon cooking when the most adorable sight—next to the little blond helping me cook—I have ever seen walks into the room. Emily walks into the room with her hair all a mess wearing a baggy t-shirt and those damn yoga pants. She is rubbing her eyes and looks confused.

"What is going on out here you two?"

"Mommy, we're making you breakfast!"

"You are?"

"Yep, bacon and eggs but Jonafon is making me pancakes 'cause I don't like the icky eggs."

"What can I do to help?" she asks still looking confused.

"Not a thing, there's a pot of coffee on if you want some. I can pour it for you and you can take your time waking up. Food should be done here pretty soon. Sorry if we woke you up."

Emily shuffles into the kitchen, gets a coffee cup out of the cupboard and pours herself a cup. As she sips her coffee, she walks over to me and steals a piece of bacon off the plate on the counter and says thank you.

"Mommy, Jonafon did a sleepover!"

"He did," Emily confirms apprehensively looking at me.

"Can he stay over again tonight? I pwomised him he could borrow a stuftie tonight if he sleeps over again."

"We'll see, sweetie," Emily says to Ireland. She's looking at me but I can't read her face. I don't know if she's trying to tell me something or not.

"How do you like your eggs?"

"Scrambled please," they both say together. It's cute to see Ireland answer for her momma.

"Comin' right up."

As I finish cooking, the girls set the table—Emily still not able to comprehend that I'm still here, cooking her breakfast and Ireland bouncing with glee to have me here—and then we all settle in at the kitchen table and eat up. Ireland talks the entire time. There is a lot that she's talking about that's going way over my head but I just play along. At one point Emily catches my eye and mouths 'sorry' to me but I give her a wink back because there is nothing to be sorry about. I haven't felt this light in years.

Emily helps me clean up the table and then I kick her out of the kitchen.

"I got this. You go finish your coffee and figure out what we're going to do today."

"You don't have to stay, Jonathan, you can get back to your own life. We don't want to keep you."

She really doesn't get why I'm still here.

"Darlin' there is no place I would rather be."

I love the hint of pink that lands on her cheeks after my comment. Just knowing I affect her is all I need to strengthen my hope that we can have more.

Skeptically she asks, "You sure?"

"Yep," I say to her and then louder to them both I say, "So ladies what are we going to do today?"

"Let's go to the zoo!" Ireland yells jumping up and down.

"Baby Girl, we really shouldn't be out spending money. Let's just have another movie day here."

Not this again, Gracie.

She starts to fidget with her necklace and it's clear she's

uncomfortable. I guess I need to make things clear like I did back in the day.

"I know it's been a while, and maybe you have forgotten, so I won't take offense this time. I will, however, remind you about something we talked about a long time ago."

"What's that, Georgia?" she says with just a touch of sass and I love it. Bring it, little lady. I'll win this battle too!

I dry my hands off after putting the last dish in the dishwasher and walk over to where she's sitting at the kitchen table. I grab the chair next to her that's currently home to her sock covered feet, and turn it so that she has to put her feet on the ground in front of her. I face the chair towards her so that I'm sitting just inches away from her with my legs on either side of hers. My hands wrap around her legs and my thumbs rub back and forth just above her knee. Simply touching her makes me feel like anything is possible. Here goes nothing.

"When you are with me, you don't pay. If I offer to take you somewhere, I will pay. I don't want you to offer to pay or ever even think about paying me back."

She tries to open her mouth to speak, but I simply shake my head slowly telling her now is not the time to protest.

Quieter, so Ireland can't hear me, I lean in even closer and say, "Again, I know you know this but like I said it's been a while so I think a reminder is in order. I take care of what is mine and before you freak out...I know you aren't really mine. But when you are with me and we go places, you and Ireland are mine and I will take care of things. No talk of feeling obligated to me and no expectations, understood?"

She nods her understanding.

"Good, now I'm going to go home so that I can take care of Frances, take a shower and then I'll be back. You ladies get ready for the zoo!"

I stand and get ready to leave while Ireland jumps all around the room singing about going to the zoo. Emily continues to sit motionless, seemingly in shock. I wish I knew what was going on in that pretty little head of hers but I learned long ago—growing up with just me and my mom—that women are a mystery we men will never completely understand. No matter what she's thinking I hope she is starting to understand that I meant what I said last night. I am *all in*. The ball may be in her court, but I'm certainly going to be playing some offense to get her to come around.

14

———

Emily

Jonathan leaves and only a few seconds later I hear a knock at the front door. I walk over and throw it open to see Jonathan standing there with his arms crossed over his chest not looking too happy.

"Lock the door behind me, Emily," he says gruffly.

"Okay," I reply while I stand there and stare at him like he is a crazy person and he looks at me as though he's about to ground me.

"Now shut the door and lock it. I'm not going to move from this spot until I hear you lock the door."

I shut the door, lock it and then giggle as I hear him yell, "Thank you."

It appears Jonathan is making a point to push his way back into my life and that both excites me and scares the hell out of me. I feel so torn. One part of me is soaring and beyond happy that the love of my life is here and wants to try again, but the other part of me is scared as hell and doesn't want it to go any further so that Ireland and I don't have to deal with the aftermath.

I haven't been able to think like a rational human being since our kiss on the couch last night. It was just as good as I remembered, if not better. Feeling his thickness press into me filled me with a lust I have never felt with anybody but him. It was as if he wanted me to feel what I was doing to him to prove to me that he still felt the same way.

And now...we're going to the zoo. I am taking my daughter to the zoo with Jonathan Kelly. Who would have thought this would ever happen? It is happening though and I should probably get in the shower so that he doesn't find me still standing in this same spot daydreaming about him when he gets back.

"Ireland, grab your crayons and a coloring book. I need to get in the shower and we both need to get dressed."

I don't like the thought of Ireland in the house by herself while I'm in the shower, so when we're home alone I have her come into the bathroom with me. We lock the door and she colors on the floor. We have some of our best chats while I am in the shower. It may be overprotective, but she is all I have and it's what I need to do to stay sane when half the time I feel my sanity is slowly slipping away from me.

While I wash my hair, I take this time to talk to my sweet little girl happily coloring on the fluffy bath mat that I luckily brought with me from California. Mick's new house is great, but he sure doesn't have much as far as decor and it helps that I did have a few things to add here and there.

"Ireland, sweetie, please make sure you aren't asking Jonathan to stay the night again or to stay for dinner and things like that, okay?"

"Why? He's our friend."

"I know baby girl, but we don't want him to feel like he has to. He is our friend, but we don't want to ask him to stay the night or take us places just in case he's just doing it to be nice."

"But mommy, he asked us to go to the zoo."

How do you explain to your daughter at such a young age not to get attached or to expect people to stick around?

"He did, you're right. Just...don't invite him to stay over or to stay longer unless he offers okay?"

"Okay, mommy. I really like him though. He's fun and he calls me Princess."

"He is fun," I agree with her.

And he loves to use nicknames sweetheart. Be careful because he will steal your heart with that nickname. Been there...done that...

"Can I wear a princess dress to the zoo today?"

"No, it's too cold for that. You'll need a little jacket or sweatshirt and comfy shoes so that won't really go with your princess dresses. Let me just get dried off and I'll lay your clothes out for you and you can get dressed while I get ready. Don't forget to make your bed too, little one."

After getting out of the shower Ireland and I both get ready. She is so excited that she's bouncing all over the place. I need to find a way to calm this girl down or she is going to be a little too hyper for Jonathan and he may rethink his plans for the day.

"Baby girl, let's take Frank out for a quick walk before we go."

"Ok, can we stay by the house though so we can see when Jonafon gets back? We don't want to make him wait."

"Sure baby."

Yep, she's a goner.

By the time Jonathan gets back and we hit the road for the zoo, it's noon. Jonathan seems just as excited as Ireland does about our little outing. He tells us he hasn't been since he was a kid and can't wait for Ireland to show him around. Man, does he knowsall the right things to say and do. If he is still the same guy I met years ago, then I'm pretty sure he is sincere. He does want more than just to get into my pants but he's just too good to be true and That. Scares. Me.

Ireland has been talking and singing the entire trip but when we're about to drive through the tunnel she reminds us all to hold our breaths and we get about thirty-seconds of quiet.

"What?"

"We started this about a year ago, it's our thing. We hold our breath as long as we can when we drive through a tunnel." I lean towards him and whisper, "It gives you a moment of silence, enjoy it."

"I see. Okay well, we're almost there, Princess. Here we go... 1...2...3..."

And just like that Jonathan joins in our little tradition and doesn't bat an eye at our crazy little ritual.

"Woo hoo! Did you do it Jonafon? Could you hold your breath the whole time?" she asks the moment the truck is back in the daylight.

"I did, how about you?"

"I did and now that we are out of the tunnel that means we're almost there!"

"How often have you been here in the couple of months you've been back?"

"Just once, but clearly it made an impact," I say turning to look at my adorable daughter in the backseat.

Ireland in her seat, looking like she and the booster seat are born to be in his truck. She's giddy and about to bounce right out of her seat with excitement.

The zoo is packed, but that's not surprising. It's the beginning of October and Portlanders know that this sunny weather that we're still having won't last long. It's time to get all the fun outdoor things done before the rain arrives. The fact that it's already 12:30 doesn't help either. The only time this lot isn't full is in the morning before the gates open and there will still be a line full of people waiting to get in. *The Oregon Zoo* is worth the wait and price of admission though. I grew up coming here and love that I get to see it again through a child's eyes by bringing my own daughter back to a place I loved so much growing up. I can't wait to bring her to *Zoo Lights* at Christmastime and to *Concerts On the Lawn* in the summertime.

We finally find parking and make our way to the line. The line moves quickly and just as he made it clear he would, Jonathan pays and hands us our tickets for entry and the train. When we first walk in the gates Ireland runs right to the Big Bear in front of the gift shop and begs us to take her picture. Jonathan pushes me to go with her and we take our picture with the ten-foot black bear. As we're stepping away an older woman offers to let Jonathan step in with us and she'll take our picture. He jumps at the chance and runs over to us, picks up my baby girl with one arm and puts his other around my shoulder and pulls me into him.

The woman takes the picture and then just as we start to step away I feel his lips on my temple as he gives me a quick, yet innocent kiss. Just as fast as it happens, his arm leaves my shoulder and he sets Ireland down and goes to retrieve his phone from the kind lady that took our picture. I feel his lips on my temple the rest of the afternoon. It's as if he's branded me and deep down I want nothing more than to be branded his.

We spend the next few hours hitting every single exhibit the zoo has to offer. We spend the longest time at Ireland's favorite spots. She seems to love all the same spots that I grew up loving. Our number one place that we spend the longest amount of time is with orangutans. They love to hang out by the glass and play with buttons or their toes or just roll around like they know they are entertaining us. Ireland has no shame and pushes her way to the front of the glass and kneels down to be face to face with Inji. She's a female orangutan who loves to wear t-shirts. She takes them off and puts them back on and she's often hanging out here where the people are rather than roaming the fairly new and large enclosure. She is spectacular and we could both sit and hang out with her all day. Thank goodness Jonathan is here to keep us moving because I think the two of us would have sat there all afternoon.

The only other places that Ireland and I need his prompting to leave are the Polar Bears and the Harbor Seals. Both are so playful and engaging and it's so hard to leave them. I just know they are going to do something even more amazing as soon as we walk away. I may actually be worse than Ireland when it comes to walking away.

We did find Jonathan's weakness and surprisingly it's the otter exhibit. Apparently, he has always loved otters and even used it as his camp name when he worked as a counselor at a summer camp the summer after high school. I can't even imagine having a counselor that looked like Jonathan. I bet he was a big hit with all the little girls that summer. The thing is he doesn't even seem to realize it. I mean he has to know he's attractive but he doesn't act like Mick or other guys I know that think they are God's gift to women. At least I've never seen that side of him.

After we pry Jonathan away from the otters, we stop for a little snack and share some kettle corn that smelled too good to resist. Jonathan pays again, and it takes everything I have to hold back and not offer to pay. By the look on his face and the wink that he sends my way when I say thank you, he can tell how hard this is on me.

After we finish our little snack break we start to head towards the elephants and when Ireland asks us to swing her I realize she's been walking in between us all day with each of us holding her hands. I'm sure we look like a little family and boy do I wish that the illusion was real. The sight of us walking along like this warms my heart and breaks it at the same time.

"Swing me!" Ireland asks jumping up and down and swinging her arms.

"Okay, on the count of three," Jonathan says.

Together we all count.

"One...two...three...swing!"

Ireland jumps and Jonathan and I swing her between us over and over again, all the way to elephants.

"It's stinky in here," Ireland whispers later from atop Jonathan's shoulders when we enter the indoor enclosure.

"It is, but look how close they are." Jonathan whispers back while he takes her off his shoulders so she can get right up against the glass.

Still whispering she says, "So cool."

And it is... the elephants are cool, the zoo is cool, my baby girl is cool and being here with Jonathan is very cool.

By the time we reach the top of the hill that Ireland insisted on walking up to view the outdoor enclosure, I can see that she's starting to fade. She's coming down from her zoo and kettle corn high. By the time we're done with the elephants, she has asked to be carried. Jonathan doesn't hesitate and picks her up and she instantly puts her arms around his neck, her cheek on his shoulder and she settles in. She is so comfortable with him and he seems to be with her that it is almost overwhelming at times. This would be one of the times. I have to force myself to look straight ahead and not at the beautiful man carrying my sleepy daughter.

We decide it's time to go and head for the parking lot. Ireland is barely awake when we buckle her in and head home. By the time we reach the tunnel, her little blond curls are bobbing up and down as her head hangs forward in a deep sleep.

The ride home is a quiet one and I and can't help but feel that there is something bigger happening here today. It's like the cab of the truck is thick with unsaid words and feelings and you can hear both of our minds whirring through the scenarios of what's going to happen next. Or maybe that's just me and I am hoping that he's as anxious as I am.

We make it home with Ireland still asleep. Jonathan pulls into the driveway, turns the truck off and removes his seatbelt from its lock and turns his body to face me. He doesn't say anything but leans his head back against the window with his eyes locked on mine.

"Thank you for a great day, Jonathan," I whisper so we don't wake Ireland.

Jonathan whispers back. "No, thank you for including me. I hadn't been to the zoo since I was a kid and I had a great time. She's an amazing girl, Emily. It was fun to experience the day with both of you." He takes a look behind us at Ireland hunched over in her seat. "We should probably get her out of the truck or her little neck is going to be sore. How does she sleep like that?"

"I have no idea how she does it. I would be aching for days if I slept like that. She seems pretty durable though. She never even says a word about it but yes, let's get her inside."

Jonathan unbuckles my baby girl from her seat and lifts her into his arms. Watching him with her it's clear he's a natural at this whole kid thing and will make a terrific dad one day.

He follows me to the front door and stands behind me as I unlock it. We get into the house and head straight to Ireland's room. It's 6 and she is still out for the count as I remove her coat and shoes, cover her with a blanket and surround her with her favorite stufties. Jonathan turns on her nightlight and walks out of the room. I follow behind him and gently shut the door.

As soon as my hand is off the door handle, Jonathan pulls me to him and grabs my ass as a way to lift me off my feet and my legs naturally go around his waist. He gently and quietly pushes me against the wall. The moment my back touches it, his warm lips devour mine. Even though he isn't rushed he's still kissing me like a starved man eating his first meal in weeks.

I'm grateful for several things in this moment. I'm grateful that Jonathan was clearly feeling the same thing I was amid the silence in the truck on the ride home. I'm grateful that Ireland didn't wake up when the truck engine stopped, like she usually does, and I'm grateful that my brother isn't a decorator and there isn't anything hanging on the hall wall to get in the way of what Jonathan is doing to me.

As Jonathan uses the wall as leverage his hands leave my ass and work their way up my body. One hand stops and cups my breast while the other tangles in my hair and pulls me even closer to him. All the while my hands make their way up his strong arms and over his broad shoulders, but in the end, both hands are grabbing his hair and pulling him to me frantically. We silently kiss for what seems like forever before Jonathan pulls away and leans his forehead against mine and says, "I have wanted to do that all day."

"I've wanted you to do that all day," I say practically out of breath.

"My God woman, what you do to me," he growls.

He just stares at me for another moment and then with both hands grabbing my ass again pulls us away from the wall and starts walking down the hallway to the kitchen. He sets me on the counter and is standing in front of me with my legs now hanging to the side of him with his hands on the counter on either side of my hips.

"How about some dinner? You hungry?"

And just like that our make-out session is over, much to my dismay.

15

Jonathan

Stopping that kiss in the hall and bringing her to the kitchen and not to her bed, was one of the hardest things I have ever done.

I've never wanted anybody as much as I wanted her in that hallway, but I want so much more than just a trip to her bed. I want to be the man she needs me to be. I want everything from her and I know she isn't ready to take things all the way, but I needed a taste. Spending the day with the two of them was better than I could have ever imagined. The day felt so right. So many times I nearly took her in my arms to steal the kiss that I had just taken. Everything in me wanted to rip the clothes from her body and take her right there against the wall. Thankfully my big head won the battle and took control of the situation.

Now here we are in the kitchen sipping wine and making spaghetti and I'm just fine with that. I want to soak up every moment that I can spend with her. We talk about our day and all of Ireland's entertaining moments at the zoo while we cook. As she gets plates and silverware out for us, Emily tells me about her usual Sunday routine of laundry, Downton Abbey and The Walking Dead.

"It's an exciting and glamorous life I lead. My Sunday night ritual is proof of that if you ask me."

I can't help but chuckle. She is just too freaking adorable.

"It sounds pretty good to me."

"Well, try not to be too jealous while I go poke my head in to check on Ireland. I'll be right back."

I bring our dinner of salad, spaghetti and garlic bread to the table and top off our glasses of wine. Just as I finish she's back.

"She's still out and I am starving! I can't wait to dig in to our masterpiece of a meal here," she says as she takes her seat at the table.

Dig in and eat is just what she does. I could just sit back and watch her for hours. Apparently, that's exactly what I'm doing without realizing it.

"What?"

"What do you mean?"

"Why are you sitting there just staring at me? Do you not like it?" she says with a full mouth of spaghetti.

I realize I'm sitting back in my chair with one arm over the chair next to me and my glass of wine in my other hand, just sitting back and watching her eat. She must think I'm some sort of weirdo with a strange food fetish or something.

"Sorry, I didn't even realize that I was staring. I must have been lost in thought there for a minute."

I place my wine glass on the table and start eating. It only takes a minute for the awkward moment to end and for our conversation to pick up again. While we're cleaning up after dinner, Emily squeals and does a little jump as she turns to me with glee in her eyes.

"Hey, how about some dessert? I know I don't need any more food after eating half of the loaf of bread myself, but I need something sweet." She opens the freezer and pokes around.

"Not sure we have anything other than vanilla ice cream, but that works for me if it works for you?"

Standing right behind her so we are just barely touching I say, "Come on now, Em, you know I like ice cream, but vanilla isn't my favorite flavor now is it? My fondest memories of ice cream are of you and chocolate."

She slowly turns around with the carton of ice cream in her hand. The blush I love to see brightens her cheeks and makes my heart skip a beat. I take the carton of ice cream out of her hands and set it on the counter. Sliding my hand into her hair, I gently tilt her head back and expose her neck. The passionate whimper that comes from deep inside her the moment my lips touch her makes me hard in an instant. Her hands run up my chest and then back down again as they journey towards my waistband.

I hate myself for what I am about to do, but I grab her hand and stop her from going any further. I lean my forehead against hers still holding her head in my hand and whisper to her.

"No, Em. I hate telling you no because there is nothing that I want more than to take you on this kitchen floor right now, but no. I need to know that if we go further you are ready; that you are 100% in. I am not going to mess this up by moving too fast. You mean too much to me to take the chance of messing up whatever possibility we may have."

Once again I find myself putting it all out there for her. It wasn't planned, but I can't seem to ever follow any plan when it comes to this woman.

"Okay."

"Okay?"

"Yep."

"Can I sleep on the couch again? No expectations and no

hidden agenda. I just don't want to leave the two of you here alone, and I kinda want to see what all this Downton Abbey hype is all about."

"Okay."

~

After getting another one-word answer from her I pull back so I can look her in the eye.

"So, when does your show start?"

She looks over my shoulder at the time on the microwave and says, "We still have two hours since it doesn't come on until nine."

"Cool, so we can get the laundry going before your show starts then. Sounds like your Sunday schedule will stay intact."

"Yep...wait...don't you work tonight? Shit Jonathan, you're late!"

Time to fess up Kelly. She's going to think you are a fucking stalker, but you just have to rip the band-aid off and tell her.

"Nope, not late."

"What do you mean?"

I casually grab the ice cream off the counter and put it back in the freezer. I can feel her staring a hole through my back waiting on my explanation.

"We'll get this out when the show is on. Don't want it to melt while you sort out the laundry."

"I thought you worked Sunday through Tuesday?"

"I do."

"So, aren't you late?"

"Nope, I took the next few days off."

"You what?"

"Yep, I have more time than I could ever use and they've been on me about taking time off before I lose it. I have plenty to do during the day while you're at work and Ireland is at school. So, I can help you with drop-off and pick-up if it helps? The two of us can hang out while you study. I mean if you're cool with that?"

Shit! She is freaking out. She hasn't said a word and is just standing there staring at me. Shit! I need to calm her down.

"No expectations, Em, I swear. I'm gonna stay on the couch and remember, I'm just doing what Mick asked and watching over the two of you while he's gone. He's gone until Saturday and there is no way I can let the two of you be on your own that long. It will also give me time to look into who is threatening you. So, I'm gonna run home and grab some things and Frances. You good with that?"

Not giving her a chance to reply I kiss her forehead and grab my keys off the counter and head for the door.

"Be right back, text me if you need me to pick anything up on my way back."

And with that, I'm out the door!

16

————

Emily

Wait!
What the hell is happening?

Did he just say that he was leaving to pack a bag, get his dog and he would be right back?

And I agreed to it?

How did we get here?

What happened to just being friends?

Now he's taking the week off of work and basically moving in.

How...when...what?

I am so confused, scared, pissed and excited all at the same time.

How is he doing this? He's working his way into our lives without us even noticing. On the surface, it's great but deep down I am shitting myself. This is too much too fast. My emotions are so up and down that I can't keep up with them.

I run to my purse and grab my phone and call Cami but she

doesn't answer. I send her a 911 text letting her know that I need to talk to her ASAP!

I call Alex next. Just like Cami, she's always there for me and if anybody can talk me down, she can. She answers and before she can even get hello out I'm rambling about the zoo and dinner and him wanting to watch Downton Abbey and bringing his dog over and sleeping on the couch and...and...

"Emily...sweetie...breathe..."

"Alex, what do I do?"

"First, breathe."

"Alex."

"Emily, I know that I wasn't there when you two met in California. But from everything that you and Cami have both told me, he sounds like a great guy."

"Hi is."

"Well, it also seems pretty clear he's still in love with you."

"Alex..."

"He's offering to sleep on the couch, and to be honest, it makes me feel better to know that you two aren't home alone. Give him a chance, Emily. But most importantly give yourself a chance. You deserve happiness, a chance at love and to be taken care of. You've always put everybody else first, and it looks like he's putting you first. There's nothing wrong with that, you know."

"What about Ireland?"

"I'm not saying run off and get married, but let him in, Em. Let him love you and let yourself love him. And before you say it, I know you're scared, but don't let the people of your past prevent your future."

Knock...knock...knock...

"Alex, he's back, I have to go."

"Breathe, Em."

"Thank you so much for listening and for the pep talk. I

know you're right, I just don't know if I can let myself believe it. Love you to pieces, lady. Drinks after Mick gets back, deal?"

"Love you too, Em. Don't forget to breathe and you've got a deal on the drinks. Go get him, girl!"

After texting Cami to tell her to ignore my 911 message, I slip my phone into the back pocket of my jeans. I check the peephole to make sure it really is him—because let's be honest he wasn't gone very long. It's almost like he was already packed or something. Shit, he was already packed! Shit, shit, shit, shit!

He knocks again and I nearly jump out of my skin.

I unlock the door and open it. There he is. The man I spend my nights dreaming about with a duffel bag and his adorable dog. I am so screwed.

"You gonna let us in?"

He asks this sarcastically, but I can sense that he's a little nervous too and this makes me feel a bit better. So glad it's not just me.

"Oh, sorry about that, come on in."

Moving aside and let the two of them in. As I shut the door, I hear Frank and Frances getting to know each other and Jonathan's bag hit the ground.

I turn around and see the most magnificent man I have ever laid eyes on. He's standing with his hands in his pockets and his head slightly tilted. My hands are trembling and my heart is beating a thunderous cadence in my chest.

"What's wrong?"

"Nothing. Why would you ask if something was wrong?"

"Because I can tell. You're freaking out just a little bit aren't you?"

"Well, this is moving pretty fast isn't it?"

"Listen, Emily, I don't know exactly what's happening here, but I do know that I am feeling more myself than I have in the past five years. Meeting you changed me forever and made me see how happy life truly could be. After watching you walk away, losing Matt and then my mom. Em, part of me died over there."

"Georgia, I'm so…"

He shakes his head not wanting me interrupt him. "

"I have felt empty for so long now but every second that I'm with you…I feel like that empty part of me is slowly filling back up. *You* are bringing me back to life."

That was not what I expected to hear come out of those perfect lips, and I know he can see it on my overwhelmed face. He closes the space between us, takes my hands in his and rubs his thumb soothingly over the back of my hand.

"I'm not asking anything from you. Okay, that's a lie. I am asking you to have an open mind and think about giving us a shot. But right now, all I am asking is to spend more time with you and Ireland. I've been given another week, Emily, and I don't plan on wasting it."

I lose my breath.

Another week.

"Please believe that I don't have some dastardly plan to get you in bed and that sex is what this is all about. I won't lie though; I meant what I said. I want to try again. My feelings for you haven't gone anywhere, and they're getting stronger every day. I'm not going to let another week with you go by without trying my best to stop you from walking away this time."

And just like that, he silences me.

He's right.

We've been given another week.

I had all the reasons in my mind why this was a bad idea. But after hearing him share his feelings and knowing that he still feels what I feel, well…that's what silences me. I don't know what to say. He's so good at telling me he's feeling while I fall mute. I feel like I can never get out what I truly want to say, yet he says it all with perfect clarity.

"Thank you," I manage to say.

"For what?" He asks with another adorable tilt to his head.

"For being able to tell me how you feel. I wish I could give the same back to you, but I'm just not ready, Jonathan."

"I know that, baby, and I'll wait as long as you need me to. I'm not going anywhere."

He kisses me on the forehead and with a squeeze of my hands, he lets me go. He kicks his bag to the side of the couch out of view and then bends down to give both dogs some attention as they lay there already comfortable with each other.

"These guys have met before so I knew there wouldn't be a problem. How about Ireland? Is she still asleep?"

And just like that he steps away from the serious conversation we were just having—well, that he was having while I stood gawking at him—and makes things normal without letting the situation stay awkward for too long. He is a natural at that.

"Yep, she sure is. Once she's out she is a really hard sleeper. It was so nice when she was a baby. I cannot even imagine how much harder things would have been if she wasn't a good sleeper. This doesn't mean she isn't going to wake up in the middle of the night. I am half tempted to get her up and make her go to the bathroom, but then she might wake up and not go back to sleep. You do not want to see her in the morning without enough sleep. She's not so cute when she hasn't had enough sleep."

"Well, you're the expert, so whatever you decide, momma. Now, pretend I'm not here and get that laundry going before Downton is on. I can't wait to see what all the madness is about!"

17

———

Jonathan

Downton Abbey was actually pretty good.

The most entertaining part of the whole experience was watching Emily and how into it she got. Even though I promised not to ask any questions, and I didn't, she would still pause the show to explain who Anna and Mr. Bates were, or why Lady Mary was scared to fall in love with the race car driver. As always, she was fucking adorable.

Another reason I loved Downton Abbey was because of my *Goldfish*. Before the show started, Emily got her snacks together and she pulled out that big old bag of fishies—as I now call them—and poured a huge helping into a bowl. She slid it across the kitchen counter for me with a smile and asked me if they were still my favorite. The day before, I wondered if it was just coincidence that she threw one of the crackers at me, but now knowing that she remembers, she gives me another slice of hope.

The other slice of hope is the fact she never stopped touching me in some manner the entire duration of the show.

Most of the time, I had my legs propped up on the table while she was against the arm of the chair with her legs on my lap. It felt so natural and so comfortable; like we had spent years together, but we haven't even had weeks.

She stands to get up and stretches her arms up above her head. I can't help but notice the lift of her breasts or the bit of skin that peaks out at me when the hem of her shirt rises. I know she has no idea what she's doing, but I feel like she is slowly torturing me to death.

"Well, thanks for watching my show with me," she yawns. "I am exhausted. We'll have to catch up on *The Walking Dead* tomorrow night, if that's cool with you? 5:45 will be here before you know it."

You gotta love a girl who watches *Downton Abbey* and *The Walking Dead* and loves them equally. That is just so fucking hot!

She's about to leave the room for the night, and I suddenly have this surge of panic that I don't want her to go. She starts to take her first step to leave but I grab her hand and pull her gently to me. I cup her beautiful fucking face in my hands, give her a soft kiss and whisper against her lips. "Night, Gracie."

She puts her hands over mine that are still on her face and stays there for a moment with her eyes closed. It's as if she is etching this moment into her mind to keep forever. I understand how she feels, because that is how I feel every second that I spend with her.

She finally opens her eyes and this time she leans forward on her toes, and softly kisses me and says, "Night, Georgia."

With that, she takes my hands off her face, kisses the palm of each of my hands, turns and leaves the room.

Hearing her nickname for me leaves me with a smile and a throbbing dick. Sleeping on the couch also means that she leaves me with no way to take care of the later. Just to hear the name Georgia whispered on her lips makes me hard, but for those same lips to touch even just my hands is enough to make me hard as steel. I hope I know what I'm doing by staying here because she may just be the death of me.

I use the half-bath in the hallway to brush my teeth and change into a t-shirt and shorts to sleep in. I can't go commando here like I do at home, so a t-shirt and shorts it is. I'm just getting comfortable surrounded by the smell of vacation—of Emily—when I hear her call Frank from down the hall.

"Frank, come on boy, let's go to bed."

She's whispering; as if she thinks I could possibly be asleep already.

When he doesn't appear for her, she walks down to the edge of the hallway in her SDSU college t-shirt and another pair of boxers that make her long legs look even longer. It's dark, but I can see her just fine with the tiny bit of moonlight coming in through the window. What I wouldn't give to have those legs wrapped around me right about now.

In a vicious whisper, Emily tells Frank just what she thinks of him.

"Fine! Traitor!"

In a huff, she walks away. I swear I can hear her pouting until her bedroom door clicks shut.

I can't help but laugh. She is so damn cute!

"Frances, I think I am falling into like with her. I mean serious like. I don't just love her, but I like her a hell of a lot too. I may end up feeling just like I did last time. Then again, I might not. I think it's worth the risk, old girl. How about you?"

We're walking hand in hand on a California beach with the waves gently crashing over our feet. Holding her hand and having her near me is enough to calm all the fear and anxiety I feel in my everyday life.

Fear that I will lose somebody else that I care about.

Fear that I will let another person that I care about down.

Fear that I will lose her again.

When I'm here, in *our place*, with her hand in mine, all of that fear goes away.

Tonight the dream feels more vivid than ever. I can smell her all around me, and the little things about her that were starting to fade over the years are back in HD and stereo. I can hear her laugh again, the way she calls me Georgia, or the look in her eyes when I tell her how I feel. Only there isn't any fear, just love and trust pouring back from her.

Something new is happening in tonight's dream though. In the distance, I hear a low cry almost like a whimper. I can feel the panic start to rise in my chest as I hear her comforting words say, "It's okay, baby. We'll take care of this. Shhh..."

My eyes fly open in confusion and just like that I am back on Mick's couch and see light coming from down the hall. I can hear Ireland crying.

"Sorry, momma."

Rushing down the hall on high alert—because the thought of Ireland unhappy unsettles me in a way that is new to me—I reach her room and see that Frances and Frank have beaten me there. They seem just as concerned about the situation as I do.

Emily has stripped her out of her clothes and Ireland is standing in the middle of her room naked and crying. I quickly turn my back so that Ireland isn't uncomfortable.

"Everything okay?"

"We just had a little accident. I should have woken her up and made her go to the bathroom. It's my fault and she's still half asleep. I'm just going to get her cleaned up and change her sheets. Go on back to bed, we got this."

It's clear that she's used to doing everything on her own. It doesn't even occur to her that she has another person here that can help her.

Watching her with Ireland the last couple of days has been awe-inspiring. She is such a good momma she doesn't even think about asking for help. I know that staying here with Mick isn't easy for her. I'm glad to see that she has the self-worth to want to better herself by getting her masters, even if that means taking help from her big brother so that she and Ireland have a better life.

God, I want to be a part of that better life and would give anything to be there to support her through it all. If only she'll let me.

"Why don't you go get her cleaned up and I'll strip the bed?" I offer.

As she walks Ireland past me and into the bathroom, she looks over her shoulder and mouths her thanks to me. While the girls are cleaning up and getting Ireland into some clean pajamas, I strip her bed, take the sheets to the laundry room, and start the wash. It feels good to be able to help, even in this small way.

When I return, Ireland is curled up in her pink bean-bag chair and Emily is scrubbing the bed. I ask where the clean sheets are and she directs me to the linen closet down the hall. Being pink, and therefore hard to miss, I manage to find them quickly. I deliver the sheets to Ireland's room, and Emily and I quickly make the bed together.

Ireland has fallen back asleep so I pick her up, carry her to her bed and we tuck her in. I wish I could decipher the feeling I get carrying this sleeping beauty to her bed. It feels like I've known this little one her whole life. It just feels natural to take care of her.

Once Emily's turned her light off and closed her door, I follow her to the bathroom where we wash our hands and Emily splashes cold water on her face. She seems unsure of herself as we walk back out into the hall and she lets out an exasperated sigh as she presses her back to the wall.

"See what a glamorous life I lead, Jonathan? You sure you really want to be spending time with a single mom whose wild nights consist of Downton Abbey followed up with changing a wet bed in the middle of the night?"

"I think you're pretty lucky to fill your days *and nights* with that amazing little girl in there. Even if that means changing a wet bed in the middle of the night. Seems like a pretty good life to me. And yes, I am sure I want to try again and I know that includes that little Princess in there."

"Jonathan..."

I cut her off by pressing a soft kiss to her lips to stop her from saying whatever doubtful words were about to come out of her mouth.

"Go back to bed, Gracie."

Pink blossoms over her cheeks—as they did early tonight when I called her Gracie—and I turn to walk away leaving her leaning against the wall. Hopefully, she's getting it through her head that I really do want to try, with or without wet beds in the middle of the night.

I land back on the couch and the moment my head hits the pillow, she's all around me again. Not sure I will get back to my beach again tonight, but I'm here with her in the same house and that is still a great place to be. We may not be holding hands yet, but I'll get her back on that beach, if it's the last thing I do.

18

Emily

5:45 a.m. comes faster than I would have liked.

After lying in bed thinking about Jonathan out on the couch, Ireland's wet bed and then trying to fall back to sleep after Jonathan's words in the hallway, there wasn't much sleep to be had. I turn my alarm off, stick my feet into my slippers, and throw on my robe. I point myself in the direction of the shower that will hopefully wake me the hell up!

The moment I open my bedroom door I can smell the freshly brewed coffee coming from the kitchen.

I shuffle down the hall towards the kitchen to find a sight that I could get used to waking up to. Before me is a barefoot, Jonathan, still in his sleep shorts and t-shirt from the night before with slightly messed hair, a sexy as hell five o'clock shadow and a cup of coffee in his hand that he's holding out to me.

"Morning, Sunshine. Coffee?"

"Why are you up so early? Are you one of those crazy

morning people?" I ask as I greedily take the cup from his hands and bring it to my lips. So good.

"Nope, I'm a night-shifter remember?"

"Then why in the world are you up with coffee and a smile? You seem like one of those crazy, happy the moment I get up morning people."

"You said you were getting up at 5:45 so I made sure I was up before you to get the coffee going."

"Some vacation this is for you."

"I don't mind at all. Besides I want to drive you in this morning."

"What do you mean?"

Does he think I need a chauffeur now too?

"Well, I figured I would go with you to drop off Ireland at the school so you could introduce me, and they could add me to the list of people who can pick her up. That way if you have things you need to do and need her to be picked up, I can help."

My mouth hangs open in shock.

"Now, what do you normally eat for breakfast? I know you didn't really do breakfast in the past but that could have changed. What'll it be? I can get it going while you jump in the shower." He says this almost as if he's excited at the prospect of making me breakfast.

"Jonathan, you don't have to become my manny. It's very kind of you, but you don't have to do all of this. You don't have to make coffee, cook, do pre-school pick up..." as I am speaking I see the folded sheets on the table from last night's wake up call. "...And apparently do laundry too. You're making me feel horrible."

"I don't want you to feel horrible. Especially when it's making me feel so good to be able to help you and take a tiny bit off your plate. I'll feel useless if you don't let me help, and if I feel useless I'll get bored and when I get bored, I get annoying.

More annoying than usual. I guess it's your choice, but I'm not going anywhere. And I am driving you to work and Ireland to school. So, I think you might as well let me help."

I'm still too hung up on his first sentence to laugh at his cute little joke about being annoying. Of course, I heard him, but the first part is what stuck.

I have to know so I ask, "It makes you feel good to help us out? Why?"

"Emily, I don't think you're ready to hear all the reasons why. The last thing I want is to scare you away." He tucks a stray hair behind my ear with sincerity and fear in his eyes that I am not used to seeing. "I don't want you to walk away again."

Finally, being honest myself, I set my coffee cup down, stretch up on my toes, put my arms around his neck and rest my head on his shoulder nuzzling into the soft skin under his five o'clock shadow. As his arms come around me we just hold each other in silence before I whisper into his neck.

"Thank you for the last couple of days, and thank you for wanting to give us another chance. Just so you know...I don't want to walk away again either, Georgia."

I can feel the tension fall from his body. "Thank Christ," he says lightly before kissing me on the top of my head.

Stepping away from our warm comfortable hug—that I could have stayed wrapped in all day—he hands me my coffee, spins me around, pats me on the ass and says, "Go get ready for work, baby."

I let out a little squeal and head to the bathroom as ordered.

On my way, I can't help but think about how much I love to hear him call me baby. I can remember the first time he did that in California. It still sends tingles through my body and gets me a little hot and bothered.

When he calls me baby, it's sexy.

When he calls me Gracie, it's his way of telling me how special I am to him.

Both give me an incredible feeling but in two completely different ways. One is sexy and the other is sweet. I love them both.

I can't help the extra pep in my step as I go through my morning routine. After getting dressed, I step out of my room and hear conversation and giggles coming from the kitchen. I follow the sweet sound and see an even sweeter picture. Ireland is sitting on the barstool in her nightgown with her little bare feet swinging as she eats what seems to be a bowl of oatmeal. She hates oatmeal. It's like he has magical powers and I can't help but wonder what else he might have up his sleeves.

Walking up behind my blond beauty I ask, "What do we have here?"

"Hi, mommy. Jonafon and I are having oatmeal for breakfast."

"I see that. How is it?" I question knowing that she won't eat it for me.

"It's nummy, mommy. It's got apples in it."

I walk over to Jonathan and lift my hand to him. He knows what I want and gives it to me with a slap of the hand and a confused look.

"I'll tell you later," I mouth to him.

"What about you? Can I make you anything?"

"Thanks, Georgia but I'm okay. I'm just gonna fix myself an English muffin and some OJ and I'll be set."

"Well, if you like English muffins then you will love the Kelly McMuffin. I must say it's my breakfast specialty. Maybe one day if you're lucky I'll make you one."

"That good huh?"

"That good."

After breakfast, I get Ireland dressed and ready for school

while Jonathan lets the dogs out and takes a shower. I'm in Ireland's room directly across from the bathroom when the door opens and out walks a shirtless Jonathan. His jeans hang low enough to see that he still has that V shape that disappears into his perfectly fitting jeans. He's drying his hair with his towel and doesn't notice me gawking as he walks down the hall to the living room where he must have left his shirt. Just seeing his bare skin does something to me.

He was in amazing shape during our time together all those years ago, but now he is seemingly perfect. He's still lean, but a bit thicker to go with all that cut muscle. Simply put...he looks like a man. He's aging nicely. Very nicely indeed.

Ireland comes bounding into my face and says, "I'm ready, mommy!"

I shake my head to clear myself of my lustful thoughts and follow her out to the family room. Jonathan unfortunately now has a shirt covering his bare chest and is tying his boots.

"You pretty ladies ready?"

"Yep, all ready Jonafon," Ireland says proudly. She hooks her thumbs in her backpack straps and sways back and forth while she waits for him. If only she got ready for me like this every morning. So far, having Georgia around has its benefits.

Jonathan throws a red plaid flannel on over his white t-shirt, leaving it unbuttoned but rolling the sleeves up his forearms. Put that together with his jeans and hot as fuck work boots and he is quite the sight. I'm not so sure I want him to come into the school for drop off. All those teachers are going to have heart failure when they see him. God-forbid even one of his dimples makes an appearance while he's there because none of those women will stand a chance.

Ireland is in her seat—still in the back of his truck—and is talking a mile a minute telling Jonathan all about her new school. She is so excited to show it to him that she's practically jumping out of her seat. Thank goodness she's strapped into that thing because she might just bounce right out of it.

We get to school and Jonathan lets them make a copy of his ID and they add him to the list of adults that are allowed to leave with Ireland. When I think about the fact that her list has me, Mick, my Mom, Cami, Alex and now Jonathan. I realize that she is a pretty lucky girl to have so many cool people to take care of her. Once again this just proves that it really does take a village.

As expected, all the teachers at school are completely charmed by Jonathan. It's a struggle to get him out of there as Ireland walks him around to show him everything!

Once we're finally out of the school we head to the high school campus. Jonathan pulls up to an empty spot near the front and puts the truck in park.

"Listen, Carter Blackburn, the school resource officer, is fully aware of what's going on. He's going to be around if you need him. I'm going to text you his number and I want you to program it into your phone. You know that I'm just a phone call away. If anything happens or even if you just have a gut feeling that something is off, you call me and I'll be here. Got it?"

"Got it, Georgia. Thanks for worrying about me, but I'll be fine." I assure him.

He hops out of the truck and walks around the front to open my door and help me out.

"Just call me if you need anything. Otherwise, I'll be here at 11:45 to pick you up," he says putting one hand on the back of my head and gently pulling my head closer to his and placing one of his sweet kisses on my forehead.

I feel myself float into the building and turn to look over my shoulder to see him still there waiting to make sure I make it into the building safe and sound. I give him a little wave and he lifts his hand in reply.

Wouldn't it be great to start every day like this?

I continue to float my way through the halls of the school, into the office to check my mailbox, and then head toward my classroom. I always get in early and get things powered on and ready for class so that Heidi doesn't have to worry about anything before the bell rings.

I unlock the door and flip the light on and see that there's an envelope on the floor. I add it to my pile of mail, power on all the computers and the overhead projector. As I log into my email, I remember the envelope.

I dig it out from under the other stack of papers I had picked up in the mailroom and nearly drop it when I see the writing on the front.

E. Jacobs

I know this writing and I know this is not good. This means that whoever this is knows what car I drive, my name and what classroom I'm in. What the hell have I done to somebody out there for them to want to scare me like this? I don't want to open it, especially alone. Knowing that somebody was in the school after or before hours to place this letter here is disconcerting, to say the least.

I follow my first instinct and call Jonathan.

He answers on the first ring. "Hey baby, everything okay?"

This time his baby is a comfort and that is all I want to feel right now. I don't want to feel the sick feeling that I have in the pit of my stomach.

"Jonathan…there was a note left under the door of my classroom."

"What's it say, baby?"

He sounds calm but I can hear the anger he's fighting hard to hide.

"I don't know. I haven't opened it yet. It just says E. Jacobs on the outside of the envelope."

"Okay, I want you to open it and tell me what it says. I'm right here, baby, and I'm turning the truck around and headed back to you."

I can hear the wheels of his truck screech as he turns around to come back to me.

I open the envelope slowly making sure I don't rip it, and when I unfold the paper a picture falls out. The moment I see the picture, tears fill my eyes and I feel as though my throat's closing up.

I try to speak, but I have to try again and I barely get the words out. "Oh my God Jonathan...there's a picture...it's the three of us walking at the zoo with Ireland in the middle of us. They've seen her, Jonathan. This can't be happening. Not my baby girl"

"Baby, I need you to take a deep breath and keep talking to me. Did they draw anything on the front or back of the picture?"

"No."

"Okay, was there anything else in the envelope?"

"Yes, there's a letter."

"Read that to me, darlin'."

Hope you, Ireland and your boyfriend had fun at the zoo!

Stay away from my family if you want me to stay away from yours.

"Oh my God, they know her name! Jonathan, they know her name!"

I suddenly notice that the halls are getting louder and the bell is about to ring. There will be students in the room any minute.

"What do I do, Jonathan? The bell is about to ring and Heidi isn't here yet."

"Just stay calm and try to act like nothing is wrong. I'm calling Blackburn right now and I'll be there in five minutes. Hang in there, baby. I'm on my way and we'll figure this thing out. Why don't you take a picture of the letter and the picture and send it to me, okay?"

"Okay, I will. But, Jonathan don't disrupt class. I don't want the students to know that anything's wrong. Just come in as soon as first period is over, okay?"

"Okay, but I'll be with Blackburn or right outside your door."

The bell rings and the first few students start to trickle in.

"I have to go, class is starting. Thank you and see you after class. Thank you so much, Jonathan."

"On my way, Gracie."

I hang up my phone, take the picture and send it to Jonathan. I throw the picture and the letter in my purse and put my purse in my desk drawer. I can feel myself shaking, but I've stopped the tears from falling. Taking deep breaths to try to appear normal, I get up and go check in with my kids.

The bell rings and Austin walks in with Heidi right on his heels, and she closes the door behind her.

"Hey, Miss J. How was your weekend?"

"It was good. How was yours, Austin?"

"Not too bad. Just hung out with Kayla all weekend and actually did a little studying."

"That's great, Austin. What did you study? Please tell me it was math?" I ask him, trying to stay engaged. He's a great kid so it's easy to fall into conversation with him.

"I did. Math and Spanish. I've narrowed down the sections I

need to go over with you today if we have time. I have my math test next period so I would love to have it fresh in my head."

"No problem, we'll make sure to find time. Hey, how are things at home Austin? I know things were pretty rough last week."

"You know, it's been better. Dad is still drinking a lot and I walked in the other day and he had just hit mom and split her lip open, but when I jumped in between the two of them he just walked away. He still has never touched me, but he hits mom sometimes when I'm not there."

"Austin, I am so sorry. Your mom still won't press charges or leave?"

"Nope, I've begged her to and she just won't do it. I told her I would leave with her and for some reason, she won't leave. I don't understand why he'll hit her and not me. I could take it so much better than her."

I rip the corner of a piece of paper off and write my number on it and give it to him.

"Listen, I'm not supposed to do this so please don't tell anybody that I gave this to you, but this is my number and I want you to program it into your phone. If you ever have an emergency, and you and your mom need help, you call me okay?"

"Thanks, Miss. J. I appreciate it, but to be honest I already have it. Jesse said you gave it to him and he wanted me to have it in case my dad ever did touch me. Sorry, please don't be mad at him. We just don't have too many adults that we can count on and he wanted me to have it just in case."

Shit, I could get in so much trouble if any of the staff or parents found out that I gave my number out. I need to be more careful.

"Of course I'm not mad. But again, please don't tell anybody because I could get into a lot of trouble or even lose my job, okay?"

"Promise."

"Okay, now let's get that math out and see what we need to go over."

As Austin gets his homework, I look up and through the glass on the classroom door, I see Jonathan talking with Officer Blackburn. The sick feeling in the pit of my stomach eases just a bit knowing he's here.

~

I'm barely holding it together when the bell rings and the students gather their things to move on to their next class.

"See you later, Miss J. Thanks for everything."

"Have a good day, Austin."

As soon as the class is clear of students Jonathan walks in. The moment his eyes meet mine I feel a tear glide down my cheek. He wastes no time getting to me and pulling me into his arms.

"I'm here, darlin'. You aren't alone. You don't have to deal with any of this alone."

His words are exactly what I needed to hear, and I feel some of the weight lift off of my chest. He gives me a little squeeze along with one of his comforting kisses to the top of the head.

"Where is it, sweetheart?"

"What?"

"The note and the picture."

"Oh crap, duh, sorry."

I go get the note out of my purse and hand it to him. By this time Heidi can see that there's something going on. We pull her to the front corner of the room and fill her in on what's been happening including this latest threat that now involves my daughter.

"Emily, I am so sorry. I had no idea. Do you think it's Jesse's family?" Heidi asks as she pulls me into a hug and then holds me by my shoulders. "Go home if you need to, but be sure that you go talk to Principal Utz and make sure that he's up to speed on the situation, okay?"

"I have no idea if it's Jesse's family, but I do know that I don't want to leave. I don't want to show any signs of them getting to me. It's important to me that I stay, if that's okay with you?"

"Of course, you do what feels right to you, but please go see Mr. Utz right now and fill him in."

"Jonathan Kelly, Mrs. Colyer, nice to meet you. I'm a Portland police officer and Officer Blackburn and I are on top of this. We'll take her to the office right now."

"Nice to meet you, Officer Kelly. Thank you for helping Emily out with all of this."

"Of course, we're gonna head over to the office and I'll have her back soon."

Jonathan ushers me out with his hand on the small of my back and we meet up with Officer Blackburn in the hall to make our way to the office.

The principal is in a meeting, so we have to wait in the office until he's available. I can't help but fidget. I have one hand worrying my necklace while one leg bounces up and down. Jonathan puts his hand on my leg and strokes his hand up my thigh and then back down to my knee, over and over. Eventually, my leg stops bouncing and I grab his hand in mine.

I turn to look at him. To take more strength from him. He holds my stare; telling me it's going to be okay without any words. He's such a calming force and makes the constant anxiety that I feel seem to slip away.

How did I get through these past years without him?

At the moment, he may not be taking away all of my anxiety but he does make me feel like I'll get through it and that there is a light at the end of the tunnel. He feeds my soul every time he looks at me.

Principal Utz opens his door and calls us in. We go over the details of the threats and show him the latest letter. We also bring up Jesse Miller and the fact that this started just after I reported his abuse. He makes arrangements with Officer Blackburn to view the videos from the few cameras that are spread out throughout the school. It's a quick conversation and before you know it we're leaving his office and I'm heading back to class.

Jonathan makes me promise to not go anywhere in the school without Blackburn and to text him if I need him. Thankfully, I only have an hour and a half left in my workday. Jonathan says he's going to take care of a couple things and will be back to pick me up.

I feel the loss of his calming force when he waves goodbye. I head back to class with Officer Blackburn and pray that I can keep it together for the next hour and a half.

19

Jonathan

I can feel myself raging as I walk out of the school. I couldn't even touch her when I left because I knew that I wouldn't leave without her if I did. The thought of leaving her at that school knowing that somebody is messing with her is one of the hardest things I have ever done. Thank God she only has an hour and a half left and then she'll be with me again. I may go out of my fucking mind otherwise.

Once I get in my truck I pull out my phone and pull up the info I had gathered on Saturday. While Emily was studying and Ireland was watching her movie, I was emailing back and forth with my favorite records clerk at work getting as much info on the Jesse Miller situation as possible. I program his address into my phone and point my truck in the direction of his house.

I'm sure it's not Jesse, but it just makes sense that this is connected to Emily reporting his abuse. I know this is against the rules and I shouldn't be using my resources at work to solve a problem in my personal life, let alone be going to his house when I am off duty, but fuck it. I have to get to the bottom of this. Emily has enough to deal with and doesn't need this shit.

I pull up to the nondescript single-story apartment complex, park in front of apartment four and turn the truck off. I get out and head up to the door and knock. It only takes a minute for the door to swing open and there stands a burly, unkept teenage boy who I can only assume is Jesse.

"Hi, I'm Officer Kelly with the Portland Police Department. Are your parents home?"

"Uh, no it's just me."

"Are you Jesse Miller?"

"Yes. Am I in trouble officer?"

"No, you aren't in trouble, bud. I'm just checking in on you for a friend of mine, Emily Jacobs. She's a Teaching Assistant at the high school and she wanted me to check on you."

I watch to see if any emotions flash across his face at the mention of her name. All I see is the relief that I'm just here to do a welfare check and not because he's in trouble.

"Oh, Miss J is the best. Tell her thanks for checking on me. I really appreciate everything she did for me that day."

"She's worried that you haven't been back to class. Is everything okay?"

"Uh, well things are okay I guess."

"Talk to me. What's going on? Can I help with anything?"

"Well, I don't think there is anything that you can do for me, sir. My dad is in jail and it doesn't look like he will be out anytime soon. My mom took off years ago. I have a little brother and I know if we look for help they will probably separate us. I can't let that happen, so I'm trying to find a job that I can work during the day while he's at school and somehow not lose our apartment. My brother has already been through too much and I can't let him be taken off to foster care."

"So, you don't have any family that can help out or that you can go stay with?"

"My grandma was here with us but I turned eighteen last week, so she left the day after. I have an aunt and some cousins nearby but they don't really have room for us. I don't know what else to do, sir. I know that Children's Services thinks my grandma is still here, and I'm probably breaking the law, but I just can't lose him to the system."

Poor kid, he's doing the best he can and trying to keep his tiny little family together. I can appreciate that, but he needs to finish school if he wants to keep them together in the long run.

"I'm sorry to hear that, Jesse. I want you to take my card and if there is anything I can do, or if you need help please don't hesitate to give me a call. We need to figure out a way to get you back in school. I'll update Miss Jacobs on how you're doing and we'll see if we can come up with something."

He apprehensively takes the card from me and I can tell that he's wondering if I have ulterior motives.

"Really, Jesse, if you need anything at all. A friend of Miss Jacobs is a friend of mine, so call me if you need anything."

"Thank you, sir."

I turn toward my truck and hear the door to the apartment four shut behind me. I don't know what I expected from my visit, but I just needed to come here to talk to him myself and try to get a vibe on things. I can't help but wonder if I should have mentioned the threats to Emily, but I didn't want to add to his worries. I saw the look on his face when he talked about her. It's the same look most people get when they talk about her; a look of fondness and thankfulness to have her in their life. I know the feeling. I suspect that if he did know something he would have told me, but I could be wrong.

Back to the drawing board, I guess. It doesn't sound like he has any family that he's that close with or else they would be stepping in, and clearly, if they aren't stepping in they wouldn't be issuing threats would they? Who is doing this?

All I know is that I am itching with frustration not having Emily and Ireland in my presence. I have never felt the fierce need to protect anybody like I do these two.

GEORGIA

Hey, you cool with me picking Ireland up a little early?

GRACIE

Uh...sure is everything okay?

How do I tell her that I just need to have one of them with me so that I don't lose my fucking mind? I don't.

GEORGIA

Everything is good. Just thought I could take her for a snack and then come pick you up. It really will only be 30 mins early.

GRACIE

Sure. She will love it.

Oh, thank Christ. I drive as fast as I can to Ireland's school that we just left a few hours ago. It feels like forever after seeing the picture and knowing that whoever this is knows her name. I should probably look into the fact that it could be somebody at the school. Not sure how Emily could have hurt anybody's family, but right now I will search any avenue that I can to figure this out.

I arrive at the school within minutes and when I walk in, I see Ireland sitting and listening to storytime with all the other kids. I sign her out and head to where the kids are gathered. As soon as she sees me her mouth drops open, her eyes go wide and she gasps! I put my finger up to my mouth to remind her to stay quiet and she instantly pops her cute little hand over her mouth. She gets up from her spot on the floor and runs over to me and jumps in my arms.

The fact that she is so comfortable with me—and has been since the first time I met her—is something that I can't wrap my brain around. I feel like I've known her for her entire life...if only that were true. I cannot even imagine how adorable she was as a baby because she is the cutest kid I've ever seen. Her big brown eyes do me in every time she looks at me and it's like she knows I'll do whatever she asks.

"Why you pick me up, Jonafon?" Ireland asks as I strap her into her little booster seat in the back seat of my truck. I never thought I would see one of those in the back of my truck, but it's a nice accessory if you ask me.

"I just wanted to see you and I thought we could go get a snack and pick your momma up together. Sound like a plan?"

"Sounds like a great plan!"

"I was thinking we could run up to Elka's and grab a scone?"

"Yuck, I don't like scones, Jonafon. What else?"

"Well, they have lots of different treats there so we'll find you something, I promise."

"Okay, deal."

After getting our treats at Elka's, we head to the high school to pick Emily up. I put the tailgate down and Ireland and I sit with our legs swinging, eating our treats and waiting for Em.

Not too long after, she walks out of the building and my heart soars when I see her face light up when she sees us waiting for her. These two have turned me into a damn ball of mush and there is no denying it.

Shit J, these two own you already.

I hand Emily her scone and Ireland shows her what's left of

her flower-shaped cookie. I pick Ireland up off the tailgate and get her settled into her booster seat. On the drive home, she tells her mom all about me coming to get her and our trip to Elka's. You would have thought I had taken her to Disneyland she is so excited.

Shit, Disneyland with Ireland. That is something that needs to happen.

"Wow, sounds like you two have had some fun. Don't get used to it, baby girl. We won't have Jonathan around forever to come pick you up for trips to Elka's. Don't get too spoiled."

Are you fucking kidding me right now?

I really cannot believe after all the feelings I have conveyed to her over the last few days that she would have the balls to say something like that to Ireland, of all people, and with me sitting right here in the truck next to her! You have got to be fucking kidding me. The moment the words came out of her mouth, it felt like she had taken a knife and shoved it right through my heart.

"Where is Jonafon going?"

"I'm not going anywhere, Princess." I grunt out with a clear edge to my voice.

If Ireland weren't in the truck with us I would pull this mother fucker over and deal with this, but she is in the truck and so I just keep on driving.

"Jonathan?" Emily quietly asks for my attention from the passenger seat.

I can't even look at her as I grip the steering wheel so hard my knuckles are turning white. I can feel a twitching in my jaw.

"Jonathan, what's wrong? What did I say?"

"You said we wouldn't have Jonafon forever, mommy. I think that made him mad."

Gotta love four-year-olds keepin' it real. How is it that Ireland knows exactly what's going on and Emily doesn't? I mean, what the fuck?

"Oh my God! Jonathan! No, I didn't mean that how it sounded at all!"

I'm still pissed, but I can feel the ticking in my jaw ease as she looks over her shoulder to explain what she meant to Ireland.

"Baby girl, I just meant that Jonathan won't always be on vacation and be able to just come and get you whenever he wants. He has a job and usually sleeps during the day. He just happens to have time off this week to spend with us. It doesn't mean that Jonathan isn't going to stay our friend for a long time or that you won't see him. This week is just special. Do you understand?"

"Yes, mommy," Ireland replies but sounds a bit sad at the realization that this isn't her new norm.

I know that she asked Ireland if she was the one that understood her explanation, but I can feel her stare at me as I look straight ahead out the windshield of the truck. I know that she's really asking me the question.

Do I understand?

I do, but I also caught the fact that she called me their friend.

I don't know what I expect her to call me, especially to a four-year-old, but it stung a little. She knows I want more, so yeah, it stings. I get it though. I do. We're just getting to know each other again and we haven't defined anything at all...yet...so I guess friends is what we are at the moment.

"Jonathan?"

Yep, just like I thought, she was asking me for confirmation that I understood what she meant. And if I pull my head out of my ass I would realize that I do get it. I've just spent the last five years pissed at her. It's really easy to fall back into that feeling and stay there if I'm not careful. I realize in this moment that the constant feeling of anger has dissipated a little bit every day that I've had Emily back in my life. Who am I kidding? I can't stay pissed at her. She's my Gracie.

"I get it, Em. Thanks for the explanation. I needed that after today. It's not even noon yet and it's been a pretty emotional day. I overreacted. Sorry."

"You don't need to be sorry for your reaction. I'm sorry for not thinking about the way it sounded when I said it. You've made it more than clear that you don't want to walk away. I didn't mean for what I said to sound like it did."

She reaches across the cab of the truck and takes my hand in hers and gives it a squeeze. She doesn't let go until we pull into Mick's driveway. As always, her touch is what I need. By the time we walk through the front door, I feel like I'm back to myself again.

The girls set upon their after school routine while I walk the dogs. Frannie and Frank seem to have found a groove already and there might even be a little bit of puppy love going on here. Frank better keep his paws off my girl though. No dog of Mick's will be getting his groove on with my sweet little Frannie.

Once lunch is out of the way and Ireland is settled, Emily finds me in the kitchen filling a glass with ice from the fridge and then pouring *Diet Doke* over it. It's an addiction and I know it's not good for me, but after the lack of sleep last night I need all the caffeine help I can get.

"Want some?"

She shakes her head and I see a tear fall down her face. It's then that I realize that she's been holding herself together for Ireland, and that she needs this moment to break down for a beat.

I put my glass down and walk towards her. "Come here, Gracie."

I pull her into me and I wrap my arms around her. Her arms

come around my waist and I can feel her balling my shirt up in her hands as she holds on for dear life. I can't believe on a day like today I was so sensitive to what she said in the truck. I am such a dick.

She isn't sobbing out loud, but the tears don't stop, and I can feel my shirt dampening with each tear that falls. It's seems as though she has perfected crying in silence over the years, trying to hide her pain and worry from her precious little girl because she's a great mom and that's what moms do. I don't say a word and I don't let go. I need to let her take whatever time she needs, and we'll talk once she's ready.

After several minutes of holding her and letting her get it all out, she steps back but stays in my arms. "Thank you, I needed that. I'm good now in fact...I think I'm better than your shirt. Sorry," she says as she tries to wipe the dampness off with her hands just to give herself something to do.

"No need to be sorry. It's been a crazy day and you're allowed to get some of that crazy out. You ready to talk about it?"

She takes my drink off the counter where I left it, takes a sip, nods her answer, hands me my drink and heads to the family room where she flops down on the couch. She sits with her back against the arm of the chair, and I tap her legs as a signal for her to lift her legs. I sit next to her and she puts her legs over my lap.

"So, I heard back from Blackburn. He said that there aren't any cameras in your hallway, but they checked all the camera angles in the main hall that leads to your room and there weren't any adults that didn't belong. It was just the appropriate students and maybe their friends. He didn't see anything odd, but I'm still gonna take a look myself tomorrow."

"Okay."

"Okay?" I ask to make sure she's good to go on.

"Yep, so where did you go after you left the school?"

"Well...I um...shit. Listen, I know it wasn't policy and I

shouldn't have gone, but I went to Jesse Miller's apartment to talk to him."

"You what?" She says as her bloodshot eyes open wide.

"Let me explain. I know it sounds bad, and I swear I didn't even tell him about what was going on with you. I just wanted to go to his place to see what family might be with him. I don't know why, but I had this need to go there myself. I identified myself as an officer, told him I was a friend of yours and was checking on him for you. I don't know what I thought would come of my visit, but I needed to do it for me since he's the only link we can come up with in this whole mess."

"Okay, and what did you find out? How is he?"

"Poor kid is all on his own and trying to get a job so he can support himself and his younger brother. As soon as he turned eighteen last week, his grandma left them on their own. He has an aunt and some cousins that don't have room for him, so he's on his own with his brother for now. I left him my card and let him know that if he needed anything he could call."

"Shit! We have to find a place for him. This is all my fault, Jonathan." Her voice trails off as she speaks the end of her statement.

"Sweetheart, this is not your fault. Not only are you required to report abuse in your line of work, but you got him out of a violent situation and maybe even saved his life. You have enough of your own shit going on to worry about him too. I gave him my info and I promise I will keep checking on them. I told him you wanted to see him back at school if possible. It was clear you mean a lot to him."

"There has to be something we can do for him. I could move into Ireland's room and Jesse and his brother could have my room. Wait...I could probably lose my job if I did that! Shit! This is a kid's life we're talking about though. Shit! Shit! Shit!"

Now, she's up and off the couch, pacing the room. She's

fidgeting with restless energy. She pulls her hair up and into a messy bun then she pulls that out and lets it fall. Two-seconds later it's in a ponytail high up on her head and then it's back down again. Where do these hairbands even come from? Watching her is amazing and exhausting all at once. She cares so much about this kid that she isn't even thinking about her own situation.

"Emily, come here," I say using my forefinger to summon her to me.

She comes back to the couch and sits next to me, facing me with her knees pulled up to her chest while she worries her necklace.

"Sweetheart, do you have class today or any homework you need to get done? I can take care of Ireland if she needs anything."

"No class today. I have a paper I should be working on but there's no way I can focus on that right now. My brain hurts trying to figure out who's doing this to me, how to protect my baby girl and how to help Jesse."

"Why don't you take some time off work until we figure this out? Just focus on school and Ireland."

"I can't take care of Ireland if I don't have a job. You have no idea how lucky I am to have a part-time job that includes benefits. I have to have benefits, Jonathan. You just never know what could happen, and I can't lose this job. Besides, I won't let these bastards win. Fuck them if they think they'll scare me away from my job."

That's my girl.

20

Emily

It's Tuesday morning and I'm sitting at my desk staring blankly at my computer as I wait for the students to start arriving. I should be getting my day organized and checking my emails, but I can't stop daydreaming about yesterday and how great Jonathan was.

He took care of me all night. He slept next to me and just held me. He didn't make any moves, and I didn't feel any pressure from him. He simply held me and took care of me all night long.

The more time I spend with him the more I realize he isn't just this hot guy that I had a whirlwind romance with.

He's an amazing man. Genuine. Thoughtful. Kind.

Last night he cooked dinner, took care of the dogs, read Ireland her bedtime story and then took care of me the rest of the night. He could have taken advantage of my emotional day, and tried to push things further in my vulnerable state, but he didn't. Instead, he rubbed my shoulders and then slept on the top of the bed covers with my head on his chest. He rubbed my head and stroked my hair until I fell asleep, just like he did every night that we shared a bed in California.

The last thing I recall before falling asleep was him kissing the top of my head and saying, "Goodnight, Gracie." The next thing I know, my phone is buzzing with the sound of my alarm and I'm still in his arms. I reach over and slap the alarm off, but he quickly pulls me back into our spooning position and puts his nose in my hair and takes a long sniff.

"God, I love the way you smell."

I love his morning voice. His voice is already deep and sexy as hell, but add the rasp that comes with him just waking up and my panties practically fall right off.

Before I've had a chance to respond to him, he pulls my hair to the side exposing my neck and kisses me gently.

"I'll go get the coffee started and you hop in the shower. Want me to make you anything for breakfast?" He says as he gets out of bed still fully clothed from the night before. It looks like he slept with just the throw blanket I keep on the edge of my bed. He stayed on top of those covers all night. Damn.

"I'll just have some cereal when Ireland has hers. Thanks for getting the coffee started and thanks for last night...for everything really. Not sure how I would have gotten through yesterday without you."

"I'm glad I could be there when you needed me, but there really isn't a thank you needed. I would have been losing my mind if I wasn't able to help, so it was more for me than for you," he says with a wink. "Now get up, beautiful, and get in the shower."

I never knew that little things like eating breakfast together or talking over a cup of coffee each morning could mean so much, but they do. Who knew there were really good men like him out there? I guess I did, but I never thought I would find him again. Now, it looks like it's up to me to decide if I am going to walk away again, or take the risk of a broken heart and being let down.

Alex, Cami and I always say no regrets. I think it's time I start actually living my life to match our motto. Let's face it, today could be my last so I might as well start kicking some ass.

The bell rings and snaps me out of my thoughts of the beautiful man that I am so in love with that I can't even find the words to tell him. I don't even have the balls to tell myself half the time. I was able to admit it to Cami with two shots in me but sober in the light of day and I can't get it out.

"Hey, Miss Jacobs," Austin says as he walks in and puts his backpack on his desk. He looks over his shoulder and signals to the cute little brunette waiting in the doorway to class. Miss J, I want you to meet my girlfriend, Kayla."

Kayla walks into the classroom and puts her arm through Austin's arm, but doesn't say anything in the way of a greeting. She seems shy, but totally in love with Austin. It's very sweet to see them together.

I put my hand out and say, "Nice to meet you. I've heard a lot about you from Austin and it's nice to finally put a face to the name."

At the sound of me saying that Austin has talked to me about her, her face lights up with pride. She shakes my hand and says, "Me too."

We all stand there quietly after our handshake, so I remind the kids that class is about to start.

"Well, Austin class is about to start so we should probably get things settled and ready to go."

"Sounds good, Miss J. I'll be right back."

He walks Kayla to the hall outside the door that leads to the main hallway and gives her a kiss goodbye. She looks at me over his shoulder, gives me a little wave and a smile and walks away.

"So glad she could finally meet you. I've told her all about you and how you helped Jesse. She thinks it's cool there's a teacher around here who actually cares about all of us misfit toys."

It makes me feel good to see a kid like Austin so happy. Ah, young love.

"There are lots of teachers that care, Austin, you just haven't given them all a chance."

He simply shrugs, gets his things out of his bag and settles into his chair.

"She's really sweet, Austin. Thanks for introducing us. You guys must balance each other out because she seemed really quiet and then there is you." I joke.

He gives a little chuckle and says, "She's just a little shy. Who knows, maybe she was star struck? You are my favorite teacher, after all. Okay, you're the only teacher I like, but that's kinda saying something. She was glad to meet you, trust me. She's *the one*, Miss J. We're already talking about getting married when we graduate. I'm glad you finally met her."

After the couple of classes that I have in the morning and some one-on-one math work with Austin, I do a little work in the office making some copies and getting some things done for Heidi. Busy work, but I'll take it. I know I'm lucky to be assisting in the SPED program here, and I want to soak up as much as I can from her while I have the opportunity.

I pop into the staff lounge to rinse out my coffee cup real quick. Before I head out, Coach Barnes enters the room. He does his usual flirty hello, but then leans against the counter and says he's heard what's going on with the threats, and to let him know if I need anything. I thank him, but I'm a little embarrassed. I wonder who said something. As far as I know, only Heidi, Blackburn and the principal are aware. I hate to think that the staff is talking about me. This is not the way I want to get noticed at work.

I return to the classroom, organize all the paperwork I just copied for Heidi and get her set up for her next class. I gather my things and head out the door to where Jonathan should be waiting for me since he won't let me drive myself to work. I know that he's worried and being overprotective, but at some point, he will have to go back to work and he won't be able to drive me every day. If I'm being honest with myself though, I love it. I love every minute with him and I plan on enjoying every minute with him that I can. Time to start living today like it's my last!

I walk out the school doors and there they are; my two favorite people. I can't contain the smile that spreads across my face at just the sight of the two of them together. Ireland is in the truck with the window down while Jonathan stands on the outside of the truck with his shoulder leaning against the door. They're clearly in deep conversation. Ireland sees me and starts smiling which causes Jonathan to turn around and there they are...those dimples. What a great feeling to know that Ireland and I have brought those dimples out to say hi again.

I think we're helping him just as much as he's helping us. I see that light in his eyes slowly coming back, and I feel it inside me as well. He was the light in my darkness when I met him all those years ago, and today we seem to be the light in his darkness too.

21

Jonathan

It's the little things in life that really matter. One of those things is bringing a smile to one adorable four-year-olds face. Seeing her reaction to me picking her up yesterday has had me itching for the same thing again today.

As I pull my truck into a spot in front of Ireland's school, I'm shocked at just how truly excited I am to pick her up. I guess knowing somebody is equally as happy to see you will have that effect on you. It's kind of addictive.

When I get there I sign in at the desk so that I can check Ireland out. The moment she sees me, she comes running towards me with her blonde curls bouncing around her perfect little face. She hugs my leg real quick, then heads to her cubby to get her hoodie and backpack, and comes running back to me.

After losing Shell, and then my mom, I have felt like a shadow of myself. I've spent years barely getting through my days without feeling anything. No real joy, anger, love or fear. Not having a sense of fear in my line of work just isn't safe, and I can see now that some of the situations I've put myself in at work were because I didn't have that fear or care that anything might happen to me. This little one and her momma, though… they make me care…make me want to be safe.

As we walk to the truck with her tiny little hand in mine I say, "So Princess, you ready to go get your mommy?"

"Yep."

When I buckle her into her seat, she's right there face to face with me and I see a look I've never seen on her face; one of concern and maybe apprehension.

Searching the perfect little features of her face I cautiously ask, "Is something wrong, Ireland?"

"No," she whispers.

"You know you can tell me anything, Princess." I try again.

She just looks at me unsure but doesn't speak. I give her space like I know her mom sometimes needs and she waits until I am in the driver's seat to speak. It's almost like not being face to face is easier for her.

"Mommy seems sad. I was finkin' we could get her a yummy and that might make her feel better."

"You think that will do the trick?"

"Yes, and I know just what she loves, Jonafon!" she says with confidence.

"A cake pop?"

"Yes! Pink and sprinkles! How did you know?"

Yep, when it comes to Emily my brain is a steel trap. I haven't forgotten a thing. While I'm happy that I still know her as well as I once did, I'm more concerned that this sweet little thing thinks her momma is sad and needs to be cheered up.

"Sweetheart, why do you think your momma is sad?" I ask as I pull out of the parking lot.

"Because at bedtime she squeezed me extra-long and I fink hers was crying when she left me at school today."

Shit!

"Okay, then I think you're right Princess. She needs a cake pop!"

She is young, yet so wise. It's clear that this mother and daughter are close, and that Emily clearly can't keep much from Ireland no matter how hard she tries. There is no way to explain to Ireland what is going on because it would scare her to death, and I'm sure Emily feels helpless in this situation. Threatening notes and pictures just aren't things you share with your four-year-old, and I don't think it's my job to tell her. I'll leave that to her momma. When I find out who is doing this, I am going to tear them limb from fucking limb.

Not sure how I missed the tears this morning, but I did wait in the truck while she dropped Ireland off. She must have gathered herself before coming back out of the building. Emily is strong, but she isn't invincible. Even tough momma's like Emily can only take so much.

Ireland is in the cab of the truck but unbuckled while I lean my shoulder against the truck door and gab with her through the window. This kid never stops talking. She talked all the way to Starbucks but got silent when we went through the drive-thru to order our cake pops. As soon as we had cake pops in hand, she started up again and hasn't stopped since.

She's told me about her favorite teachers, favorite kids, least-favorite kids and who doesn't wash their hands after they go to the bathroom. I know that today they started working on their Thanksgiving play they'll be performing next month and that she gets to be a pilgrim. She says the show is top secret though and that is all she can tell me. She did ask me if I would come to watch her in it, and I told her I would love to! It's the truth, I really can't wait!

Ireland has a cake pop in each hand and I have one as well. I can tell the moment that Emily walks out of the school doors because Ireland's eyes light up. She puts her cake pops behind her back and whispers. "Mommy's comin', Jonafon!"

I take this as my cue and hide my cake pop behind my back as well. When Emily gets within a couple of feet of us Ireland yells. "Surprise, mommy!" and holds both of her cake pop filled hands out the open window.

"For me? Both of them?"

"We got one for each of us, but you can have mine mommy."

Emily taps Ireland on the nose and says, "One is all I need, baby girl. Thank you. This is just what I needed."

She then turns her attention to me and says simply, "Thank you."

I shyly pull my cake pop out from behind my back and Emily takes one of Ireland's. I bring my cake pop towards them and say, "Cheers, ladies." We all tip our cake pops together until they touch and the girls say cheers back to me. After we all take our first bites, I can't help myself when I moan.

"Damn, these things are good!" I'm savoring each bite of my tiny dessert when I hear Ireland call me out.

"Mommy, Jonafon said a bad word."

"He did, but he'll try to be careful in the future, right, Georgia?"

"Right, Gracie. Sorry about that, Princess."

I walk around to the driver's side of the truck while Emily buckles Ireland back in, and then joins me in the front of the cab finishing her cake pop. Once again, Ireland waits until both Emily and I are in front of the truck's cab before she asks her question.

"Momma, why you call him Georgia and he calls you Gracie?"

Emily's cheeks turn an adorable shade of pink, but she looks me in the eye and smiles while she says, "Baby girl, those are nicknames. Kind of like how I call you Baby Girl and Uncle Mick calls you *I*. When I met Jonathan a long time ago, before you were born, he told me he was from the state of Georgia. So when we became friends way back then, I gave him the nickname of Georgia. He calls me Gracie..."

I interrupt her because I want to take this one. "I call your momma Gracie because it's my way of letting her know how special she is to me. When I met your momma she told me a story about your great-grandparents and that story was about how her grandpa called her grandma Gracie to make her feel special. I want your mom to know she is just as special to me as her grandma was to her grandpa. I call you Princess because you have reminded me of a princess since the first time I met you. And you just happen to be the cutest little princess I have ever met!"

"Oh, okay," Ireland says simple as that. I look at her in my rearview mirror and I see a smile break out across her adorable face when she confesses. "I like it when you call me Princess."

"I like it when your momma calls me Georgia so I know just how you feel, little one."

Emily doesn't speak but she does lean over and take my hand and doesn't let go until we reach our next destination. That's enough for me.

~

The rest of the afternoon is filled with all sorts of little things. Boring, mundane things that all of us need to do on a daily basis, but having this dynamic duo with me sure makes it all that much more enjoyable.

We left the school and went grocery shopping. The only hiccup we had was Emily fighting me in the line at the checkout over me paying for the cartful. I don't know how many times I have to tell her that I take care of what's mine, but I remind her again. I think she only relents out of embarrassment and not wanting to cause more of a scene than we already have. The checker was clearly entertained by our little argument.

After the store, we head home and put groceries away. I take Frank and Frances on a walk and Emily has a small lunch waiting. While Emily does some studying, Ireland drags me to her room where we have a princess party. I'm sitting on the floor with a teacup in front of me and a tiara on my head while I pretend to eat finger sandwiches and drink tea. I mean that's what any civilized princess would do. The truth is, if it keeps Ireland content so that Emily can study, then I will do what it takes.

When the princess party has wrapped, Ireland sets herself up with a movie in her room. It is amazing how tech-savvy she is. She didn't need any help at all. She is so much like her momma...strong and independent. While Emily grades some placement tests, and Ireland watches a movie, I start to prep for dinner.

After our dinner of chicken stir-fry, Emily takes Ireland off to the bath and I clean up the kitchen and listen to ESPN in the background. As I'm cleaning it hits me that I'm in Mick's house. Fucking Mick. He's going to kill me when he finds out I am in love with his sister. You know what, Fuck Mick...I knew Emily before I knew him.

Just as I am about to sit down on the couch to watch the latest scores for the day, Ireland comes out in her adorable footy pajamas and drags me to her room. Emily is pulling back the covers and waiting for her to hop in.

"Can you both read me a story?"

Emily looks at me to silently ask if I mind and I give her a little nod.

"Two short ones, how's that?"

Already knowing what she wants Ireland gives us her instructions. "Okay, but Jonafon has to read *Five Little Monkeys Jumping On the Bed* and you read *Goodnight Moon,* mommy."

Even I know we're getting off lucky because those are both really short. Even though reading to her isn't a chore I wouldn't mind a little alone time with her momma.

Two books, kisses for Ireland, her stufties and one drink of water, and Emily and I head out of Ireland's room. Before I even realize what's happening my back is against the wall and this time it's Emily that's attacking me. She doesn't start off gentle either. It feels like she has been waiting all day for this make-out session against Mick's empty wall. It's like the moment was finally hers to take and she is fucking taking it. I am certainly not going to stop her.

Her hands are in my hair and she gives a little tug which causes me to growl. She whimpers into my mouth as she pushes herself closer to me. My hands are all over her, I can't seem to settle on one spot. I just keep roaming all over her back, through her hair and grabbing that amazing ass of hers.

She pulls her lips from mine and kisses her way down my neck, then back up to my ear lobe where she takes a tiny nibble then whispers into my ear.

"Thank you...for everything."

I start to speak, but she presses a finger to my lips. I silence myself immediately.

"Please don't sleep on the couch tonight. I can't remember the last time I slept as good as I did in your arms last night."

"I slept well too." She lets me reply this time. "Only I do remember the last time I slept that well, and it was with you a million years ago. You sure you want me to sleep in your room with you?"

"Please?"

"Whatever you need, baby."

Once I've given her the answer she was looking for she asks me to wait just one minute and runs into the bathroom. She leaves the door open behind her but is back before I can figure out what she's doing.

She joins me in the hall and takes me by the hand leading me to her room. I feel like I'm in a dream; a dream that I don't want to wake from even if by sleep she means *just sleep*. That is fine by me because this is the first time she has made the first move and truly said what she wants. If just sleeping curled up in each other's arms is what she needs, then that is what I will give her. Would I love more, of course, but just sleeping next to her last night on top of the covers was heaven, and I'll take more of that piece of heaven any day.

Once we're in her room she shuts the door behind us but her eyes never leave mine, and she is still holding my hand. She takes a few steps backward and then drops my hand. Without any hesitation, she reaches for the hem her shirt and brings her shirt over her head and drops it to the floor. She is standing before me in her pink lace bra and jeans. As if that couldn't be any sexier she reaches into her back pocket and pulls out a condom and drops it on her bedside table to make her intentions clear.

Is this really happening?

Is this my Gracie? Being this bold and taking what she wants?

As if answering my internal question, she unbuttons her jeans and then bends over pushing them to the floor and stepping out of them, revealing her matching pink, lace panties. The amazing view in front of me leaves me speechless. I am awestruck by her beauty. I'm still finding it hard to believe that my dreams—that have haunted my sleep at night for years—seem to finally be coming true.

"Jonathan?" I hear her ask me, confused, and then I see her cross her arms in front of her stomach and a look of insecurity crosses her gorgeous face.

I snap out of my awe-inspired gawking and give her a small shake of my head, there will be no hiding from me tonight, or ever, if I have my way. I take her hands in mine and interlock our fingers together and look at every inch of perfection she is offering to me.

"You are so beautiful, baby. You have nothing to hide from me."

I let go of our hands and fill mine with her beautiful face. As I speak the words, "I'm gonna kiss you now, Gracie," she is already nodding her head. She knew what I was going to say and she wants me to kiss her as badly as I need to kiss her.

We stand in each other's arms and I kiss her with all the tenderness that I hope to convey to her. I want her to know what this means to me. What she means to me, and I don't want to rush this in any way. I pull her further into my embrace and slide my hands up the soft skin of her back. God, I've missed the feel of her skin and I need to touch her everywhere. As my hands roam, one tangles in her soft waves to pull her even deeper into our kiss. My other hand trails back down her back and to her perfect ass.

She pulls back a moment later and for a split second. I worry she's changing her mind. She quickly reassures me by pulling my t-shirt over my head and then it's her turn to take her time gazing at me. Her fingers leave a trail of heat behind them as she slowly drags them down my neck and to the tattoo over my heart. She takes a moment and traces over my tattoo and then brings those beautiful oceans of blue up to my eyes. I can feel her understanding and what it means to me. She then leans forward and kisses the center of my chest. Her fingers start their way down my stomach to my pants that are now almost uncomfortable from trying to contain the raging hard-on I have for her.

Her gaze has been following her fingers and as her fingers pass the button of my jeans, her hand gently rubs me through them, she brings her eyes back up to mine and gets a sly little smile on her face that says she's happy she can still do this to me. If only she knew I have been in a state of a partial hard on every minute that I'm alone with her. She is the sexiest fucking woman I have ever known, whether she's standing before me as she is now or she is fully dressed. She just does it for me like nobody else, and I can't wait to show her how she makes me feel.

After her little tease, she moves back to the waistband of my jeans and starts unbuttoning them for me. She's moving in slow-motion though, and I can't help but help her out after she has the button and zipper undone. I pull the jeans down as fast as I can and step out of them. I take my socks off in a split second and all that is left are my black boxer briefs.

She does her own assessment of me, just like I did of her, but she doesn't speak. She steps closer to me, stands on her tiptoes, gently brushes her lips to mine, and I feel her fingers reach into the front of my boxers. Fuck, if the soft touch of her hand feels this good with just a couple of slow strokes, I may not last long once I'm actually inside her. While her hand continues its gentle assault, I reach behind her back and unhook her bra. She lets go of me so that her bra straps fall down each arm and her bra falls to the ground. She uses her foot to kick it across the floor and then she climbs on to the middle of the bed and lies down with her hair fanned out on the pillows beneath her. She looks like an angel. *My angel.*

I move to the foot of the bed and crawl to her. I spread her legs so that I can settle in between them. I hover over her and lose myself in her mesmerizing, blue eyes. There are no words spoken and I don't think any are needed—because this moment for me is perfect just as it is. I lean forward, bring my lips to hers, and as I kiss her I hear the slightest little moan escape her lips— I think this is my absolute favorite sound—and I feel her move her hips underneath me. My girl is impatient. This is going to be fun...because I don't plan on rushing a thing.

I remove my lips from hers and kiss a trail down her neck to her chest. One of her perfectly hard nipples is just begging for me to take it. Without any further hesitation, I take her nipple in my mouth and twirl my tongue around it and give it a little nibble. After I've given the first the attention it deserves, I give her other hardened nipple the same well-earned attention.

My tongue slowly moves down her stomach and I make sure to go around her belly button. I can feel her tense a little as I reach her lower stomach and I simply hum, "Perfect," against her skin as I continue. I know she's worried about the tiny, barely-there, marks that are now on her perfect body. But they are the result of carrying Ireland, they are hers, and they gave her that beautiful girl across the hall. To me they are beautiful.

I've now reached her lace panties and I kiss my way down the center of them and find she is just as drenched with desire as I am hard. I look up at her as she squirms under my mouth and see her with her head tipped back and her back arched with pleasure. I hook the sides of the fabric with my fingers, and even though I want to rip them off her body, I gently pull them down her legs and add them to the rest of our clothes that litter her bedroom floor.

I look at her flushed and spread out before me and I don't know how to fully express to her how perfect she is to me. I crawl back over her, bring my lips to her ear and whisper, "You are exquisite. More beautiful than how I remembered you in my dreams all of these years. I can't wait to taste you, and then I cannot wait to make love to you. God, I've missed you, Gracie." I take a gentle bite of her earlobe and can tell her breathing has picked up after hearing my lust-filled words.

As I work my way back down her body, I cup one of her perfect breasts—that fills my hand as though it was made just for me— and I work the other with my mouth. I keep working my way back down to where I left her when I removed her panties. Once there I settle in, push gently on her thighs to spread her legs and she puts her feet flat on the bed next to my head. Finally, I take my first taste and I nearly come right then and there. I tease her with my tongue, and as I drag it down her center she grabs my hair and tries to pull my face closer. I drag my tongue back up to her swollen nub, and slide a finger inside and hear her gasp. I look up and see pure lust and want on her face as I increase the pace of my finger and my tongue. A moment later, I give her what I know she wants as I slip another finger into her warmth, and I can instantly feel her tighten around me. She's already close.

I pull my mouth from her so I can watch her come apart. I keep my fingers working at their slow pace, and when I look up I find her watching me with rapt attention while her hands fist the sheets below her. She finds my eyes and I keep her gaze locked on mine as I return my mouth to her. I don't increase the speed of my fingers, but keep it slow and steady. With my eyes on hers, it's all she needs. Within just a few seconds she's pulsing around my fingers and breaks our gaze to throw her head back and moan as quietly as she can. To feel her come apart for me is still the best feeling I have ever had. I help her ride her orgasm through to the end and remove my soaked hand. I give her a moment to catch her breath while I stand and remove my boxers...my boxers that are no longer able to contain me as I push out of the top of my waistband.

It doesn't take her but a second to notice that I'm now just as naked as her. She quickly sits up on her knees as she beckons me with her forefinger and a naughty little smile. I meet here in the middle of the bed on my knees as well. We join in a kiss, but all too soon she breaks it, pushes me down on to the pillows, and gives me the same sweet torture that I just gave her.

She starts at my neck and follows the same path her soft fingers left earlier, but this time she follows it all the way down and takes me deep into her mouth. She pulls me back out and then licks a circle around the top of my head. With her hand at the base of my thickness, she starts to take me to the place I just took her. Using all the strength I can muster...I stop her. I cannot let this happen. I need to be inside her. I will not come in her mouth our first time together again. No way in hell!

I gently push her off of me and it's clear she knows that I don't want to finish that way. With a small, yet sexy smile on her face, she reaches for the foil packet on the bedside table. I quickly snatch it from her hand and tear the packet open with my teeth. I can't slide it on fast enough. The moment it's on, I'm back on top of her but holding most of my weight on my forearms.

I put my forehead to hers and ask one last time, just to be sure. "Are you sure?"

"More than sure."

With her answer still on her lips, I crash my mouth into hers as I slowly and gently push my way into her warm perfection. She is so fucking tight. I know I have to take my time to let her body adjust to me so after slowly working my way in and out a couple of times, she gives me the signal I'm waiting for. Her legs wrap around my back and she uses her feet to push on my ass; her way of telling me she wants more. Just like that, we start moving in sync like no time has passed at all. We're both silent, and never take our eyes off of each other. I can feel her start to tighten and pulse around me, and I know she's about to come again. We continue to watch each other as we both fall apart in each other's arms.

22

———

Emily

Waking up in his arms is like waking up in a dream. I would love nothing more than to wake up to his warmth every day for the rest of my life. If only life were that simple...

As I lay in the arms of the only man I have ever loved, I think back to the night before and how gentle and loving he was. He didn't rush anything and he made sure that he satisfied me before even thinking about himself. It was amazing to feel how in sync we still were and just how natural and right being with him still felt. Looking into his eyes as he made love to me made all the anxiety of the last couple of days melt away. He and I together seem to be a magic elixir.

I'm brought out of my memories of the previous night when I feel a kiss to the top of my head and "Good morning, baby," is whispered into my hair.

God, how I love the way his voice sounds first thing in the morning. It's too bad my alarm is about to go off and I don't have more time on my hands. If he keeps talking I may never make it to work.

"Morning. Hey...um...we need to be sure we're up before Ireland. We don't want to confuse her."

"What do you mean, confuse her?"

Leave it to me to ruin the moment.

"Well, I don't want her to think this is the new normal or to try to explain to her what grown-up boy/girl sleepovers are just yet. I also don't want to have to ask her to keep a secret from her Uncle."

As if he only heard the first part of my explanation he says, "Do you not want this to become your new normal?"

I can tell he's upset, and I try to reassure him when I say, "Jonathan, this is Mick's house and our sleepovers won't be happening once he gets back."

I can see his face cloud over, and any residual joy from the night before vanishes.

"Hey, don't think about what happens after this week. Let's enjoy the time we do have before Mick gets back."

"Sure...yea...okay...whatever," he says in frustration as he throws back the covers and starts to jolt out of the bed.

I grab his hand before he's completely out of the bed and say, "Jonathan, don't be mad that I don't want to confuse her. I haven't had to navigate these waters before, and I'm not sure know how to handle it."

"What do you mean?" he asks still standing, naked in all his glory.

"I just haven't really dated much...well...at all."

"You mean since us?" He says as he moves his finger between the two of us.

I am so embarrassed. He must think I'm such a loser, but I have to be honest with him if I want this to work, and I do. I just don't know how to do it, so I just let it all out.

"Yep. I know how pathetic that sounds, but I was a twenty-one-year-old who was pregnant with a baby by a man who pretended he didn't know her, and I had just left you. I was a mess after San Clemente. I could barely function, to tell you the truth. The next thing I know I'm a pregnant college senior, and then Ireland was here. I've been a working, single parent all this time and there wasn't time or anybody worthy enough to bring around my baby girl. So...no. I haven't been with anybody since you. Lame, I know."

Embarrassed, I cover my face with his now abandoned pillow.

I feel my butt leave the mattress as I am bounced into the air. He's jumped back into bed, thrown the pillow covering my face to the floor and is on top of me. His dimples are out in full force.

"You have just made me the happiest man alive. All this time I have imagined you with other people, or in a relationship with someone else, and it has always made me sick to even think about. To know that nobody else has had what I had last night doesn't make you a loser. But it does make *me* happier than you will ever know."

His lips have now found mine and just as I forget that I need to get up so Ireland doesn't catch us, my alarm goes off and he pulls his lips from mine. With a shit-eating grin still on his face, he rolls off of me and jumps up from the bed with an extra little spring in his step.

"I'll go get the coffee started while you jump in the shower."

He ends his sentence with a smack to my bare ass, pulls on his clothes and leaves the room happier than I recall ever seeing him.

～

Today has been such a great day, apart for the moment that I saw the hurt that I inflicted flash across Jonathan's face. I didn't mean to hurt him, but I am trying to be completely honest with him. The truth is, after a week of playing house, what then? We won't be having sleepovers every night because I have Ireland. I need to keep things based in reality so that I don't mess this up again.

The news that I hadn't been with anybody since our time together in California seemed to get him over my other comment rather quickly. He was like a kid on Christmas and seemed giddy at finding out this little tidbit of information. What I thought would be embarrassing turned out to be just what he needed to hear. I know that it helped to ease his mind, but it wasn't enough to take away my other comment about wanting this to be our new normal if the intense kiss that he left me with when he dropped me off is any indication. His goodbye kiss almost felt desperate, like he was trying to convey his feelings for me with this one kiss.

As I gather my things, I walk past Officer Blackburn who's waiting to walk me to the front door of the school where he knows that Jonathan will be waiting. If only Jonathan could be waiting every day. The reality is he will have to go back to work once Mick is back, but I don't want to think about that right now.

Officer Blackburn does his daily check-in with me as he walks me out. "How's it going, Emily? Anything new today?"

"Nope, nothing today and if I haven't said it, thank you. I know that getting stuck on my detail takes you away from your other duties around the school. I hope you aren't bored to death?"

"Nah, it's no problem. We'll get this figured out soon and you can stop having me as your shadow. Until then, it's no problem at all. You just be sure you tell me everything that could be a threat or even a clue, and we'll follow up on all of it."

"I promise," I assure him.

"Well, here you are. Looks like Kelly is out there waiting for you as usual. You guys have a good afternoon."

"Thanks. You too, Carter."

I can see him smile at the fact that I used his first name when most everybody in the department uses last names. Comes with the job, I guess. He's probably surprised that I even knew his first name.

Carter opens the door for me and I see the new norm that I wish could become my reality. Not just for this week, but every week.

Ireland and Jonathan are waiting for me again, and as per usual my heart skips a beat at the sight. The thought that I may be hurting this amazing man, who is so beautiful inside and out, is not something that I can even fathom. I would be happy spending all of the rest of my days just making him happy, but I have a little girl to think of, and we can't just move into a relationship like other people do. We have other factors to consider. I still plan on doing whatever I can to make him happy. To let him in. I just hope I'm able to do that as fast as he wants so he doesn't walk away.

Please don't walk away...

23

Jonathan

We're cooking dinner while Ireland sits on one of the barstools at the kitchen island. This little girl is something else. She carries on conversations with us just like she's an adult and our equal. She's very mature for her age, and I'm more and more impressed with her every day.

While we cook I can't help but notice that Emily seems different then she has been the rest of the week. After picking her up at the school, she was the one that reached across the cab of the truck to take my hand in hers, and she didn't let go until we got out of the truck.

Now, as we move around each other in the kitchen she's touching me more than before. If she stands next to me she has her hands lightly moving up and down my back or is touching me in some way. I'm not complaining at all, but I do tread lightly as her comment from this morning is still running around my head. I'll take what she's giving though.

The three of us seem to work together well, as we navigate our dinner routine smoothly. The only time that anything seems odd is when Emily gets a text that she doesn't comment on or reply to. I've seen her do that once or twice, but she never says anything, and I don't want to pry. Well, I do want to pry, but I know that she would tell me if she wanted me to know, so I leave it alone for now.

After getting Ireland off to bed, Emily and I are sitting on the couch hand in hand, with her legs on my lap watching TV. At least she seems to be watching. I am blindly staring at the TV while my mind is running a million miles an hour with all of the things I want to say and want to ask her. Next to me, Emily seems unaffected as she laughs along with the show she's watching. She doesn't seem to be losing her ever-loving mind like I am.

Thirty minutes later I can't take it anymore; this feeling of not knowing where we stand. Feeling like we're in some kind of limbo is too much for me. I mean, I already know she's mine, but I need her to know that too. Shit, I want the whole world to know it!

I turn my body toward her and she has to move her legs off of me. She tucks them underneath her and we're both facing each other now. I need to see her eyes for this.

"Gracie...do you only want this to last two more days?"

Silence. She just stares at me. She doesn't say a word. God, she makes this all so damn hard.

"Because I want more...lots more. I don't want just another damn week, Em. I want endless weeks. I don't think I can take another week that just ends..."

More silence.

Could I be alone in this? Am I the only one of us that wants more?

Still, without a word, she climbs onto my lap. She looks me in the eyes and then slowly closes hers when she softly brings her lips up to caress mine. After several minutes of her kisses and her rubbing herself on my—growing harder by the minute —cock, I can't take it any longer and I stand up with her attached to me. Her legs naturally come around my waist and I carry her to the bedroom. It's not the answer I was looking for, but I'll take it...for now.

I'm dreaming about the morning in California when Emily woke me with a special wakeup call. Only in this dream, it isn't her hand that's waking me up, but that sweet little mouth of hers. Fuck, if this isn't the best dream I've ever had. It feels so real that I feel myself growing harder and harder until I slightly wake and move my hand down to try to adjust myself, but I'm met with a roadblock. An amazing roadblock, one in the form of Emily's beautiful head while she takes me into her mouth.

When she realizes I'm now fully awake she pops me from her mouth and gets a devilish smile on her face and says, "Morning, Georgia."

"Morning, baby. Whatcha doin'?" I ask not able to hide my smile.

"Just wanted to give you something to think about while I'm at work today."

"Oh baby, I'm always thinking about you. You don't have to do this."

"Trust me I do. I was dreaming about tasting you, and I need to have you in my mouth. Now sit back and let me enjoy this."

With that, she wakes me up in the most glorious of ways and starts my day off with a fucking bang.

I spend the rest of my morning floating around them as they

rush to get ready. I help with breakfast and taking care of the dogs. I love feeling the organized chaos of their morning routine. I'm learning to love all of the domestic routines that come with these two lovely little ladies. It's a feeling and a routine I never knew I wanted, but I do and I hate that it's about to end.

24

Emily

It's Friday, our last full day and night together before Mick comes home. I'm sitting in my classroom impatiently watching the seconds tick by so that I can get out the door to Jonathan. The last two days have been so great. Last night was another night of exploring each other for hours and lounging in each other's arms. He didn't bring up the discussion of our status again. Instead, he peppered my body in kisses and brought me to amazing highs over and over and over again.

I swear the clock has frozen in time, because the bell just will not ring. How can this class not be over yet? I already have all of my things gathered and am ready to bail the moment I hear the shrill sound of class being over. I feel like a senior on the last day of school; counting down the last seconds of high school and then cheering as the clock strikes that golden hour.

No cheering today, but I do bolt the moment the bell sounds and nearly run over Officer Blackburn. He has a hard time keeping up with me as I navigate down the hall. The kids are just sauntering about, without a care in the world. Not caring at all that I have only a matter of hours left to spend in fake domestic bliss with Jonathan. In my mind, I shove past them all and they go sprawling to the ground as I make my way through the halls and to the doors. I'm losing it, but I don't care. I cannot get out of this building and out the front doors fast enough.

With Officer Blackburn only steps behind me, I finally push my way out to the front doors with a little wave to him over my shoulder and I scan the parking lot for Jonathan's truck. I don't see it. Where is he? I feel my heart start to sink and wonder if he forgot to pick me up?

Walking down the steps, I hear a car horn and see him pulling up in Matt's jeep. *Our jeep.* My heart skips a beat and I freeze mid-step. It's only when I see him jump out and walk around to open the passenger side door for me that I move my feet in his direction.

"How?"

"Later, baby," he says stealing a quick kiss.

I get into the car and so many memories start flashing back through my mind. I also notice, as he walks around the front of the jeep, that he isn't in his usual t-shirt attire. He has on a white button down shirt with rolled sleeves, dark jeans, and not his usual heavy boot, but more of a dress shoe. What is happening here?

He hops back into Scarlett and gives me a wink and a smile. As I'm about to ask where Ireland is, he explains that she's with Cami and that we're in no rush today.

"Where are we going?"

In reply to my question, he just smiles and turns on the stereo and Justin Timberlake comes blaring out of speakers just like the last time we were in Scarlett.

～

For October, it's a beautiful day but not warm enough to take the top down on the jeep. Jonathan holds my hand the entire journey but doesn't say much. I cannot figure out what he's up to just yet, but I have a feeling I will soon enough. He seems so pleased with himself right now, and it's kind of cute. I don't want to ruin anything for him so I don't ask too many questions.

It's mid-day, so the traffic is light, and in a little over thirty minutes we're over the bridge and in Vancouver. As Jonathan navigates through the streets he finally speaks.

"Here we are."

I pull my eyes from his devastatingly handsome face and look to see that he's pulling into the parking lot of a restaurant called *Beaches*. I get it now...Scarlett...JT on the stereo... he's wearing almost exactly what he wore the night we went to dinner...and now a restaurant called *Beaches*. He's trying to recreate our time in California. Shit, he's good.

"I know it's not the actual beach, but I didn't know if you would want to be that far away from Ireland, so I figured we could fake it. It's not the fanciest restaurant, but the beach reminds me of you. I thought it was fitting."

"Jonathan, it's perfect," I lean across the front of the jeep, and give him a quick kiss on the cheek before I reach for my door handle.

"Wait! I'll get it!" He says, almost sounding panicked.

Wow, chivalry really isn't dead. He runs around the front of Scarlett and opens my door for me. This service includes a little bow to go along with the hand he's holding out to me.

"Milady."

With a little giggle, I take his hand, thank him and hop out. As we walk towards the door of the restaurant, I can't help but look over my shoulder at Scarlett and say, "It sure is good to see her."

Jonathan gives my hand a squeeze and leads me into the

restaurant. They have our table ready for us, and we're led to our window seat with a gorgeous view of the Columbia River. The restaurant is fairly casual and decked out with a beach theme complete with starfish and seashells for decoration. It's a cute place, and I've never been here, so I can't help the smile that's on my face as we take our seats.

Lunch is great, but not anything like the dinner we had at Carbonara's in California. But who cares? I can't believe he's doing all of this to set the mood and take us back to when we met. If only he knew that our time together is forever etched into my memory. I don't need any reminders. I could never forget our time together. But I do love that he's gone to so much trouble, and I'm having a great time.

When our server comes back he offers us a dessert menu, but Jonathan says no thank you and that we have other plans.

We do? What in the world is he up to?

After lunch, he takes my hand, and we walk out of the parking lot and down the street. It's a cute little street, lined with little shops on the street level and condos above. I can't imagine how great those views must be with the river and the mountains in the distance.

As we walk past the storefronts, the wind is starting to pick up a bit so he wraps his arm around my shoulder and pulls me into him. I put my arm around his waist and we cuddle tight to one another. I'm sure we look like one of those annoyingly in love couples that have always made me a little sick. I think I get it now because this doesn't feel sick at all.

Soon he's opening the door to a small ice cream shop, and when I look up at him he just gives me a wink. I start to look at the list of flavors when I hear Jonathan order a chocolate cone and a vanilla caramel swirl cone. I spin around to look at him with my mouth hanging open. He has a smart ass 'yep, that just happened' grin on his face. A grin that also says, oh yes, I thought of everything. They aren't the same desserts we had in California, but they are the same flavors, and he knows exactly what he's doing.

He pays for our cones, hands me mine and leads me to the door. When we leave the shop and start to head back to the *Beaches* parking lot the wind is howling and it's even colder. The ice cream certainly isn't helping things. We jog as quickly as we can without losing our ice cream and find sanctuary inside Scarlett.

I can see the disappointment on his face when he says, "I had planned on taking you for a walk down along the water, but we can just eat these in here if that works for you?"

"Of course, this is all so great, Jonathan. Thank you so much for everything. This was so thoughtful of you."

"My pleasure, baby," he says and a smirk pulls up on one side of his mouth and I can tell he has another question for me. "You still don't like chocolate ice cream, huh?"

"Nope."

He angles his body so that he's leaning against the jeep door and I do the same so that we're facing each other.

"Really? I have this memory of you saying that it wasn't so bad once? Am I not remembering correctly?"

He's trying to embarrass me. He thinks the memory of me kissing him, after he made a mess of me, with his precious chocolate ice cream, is something I would be embarrassed of. Quite the opposite. It's actually a very fond memory. One I have thought about many times over the years.

"No, your memory serves you correctly, but I was not of sound mind at the time. Doesn't count," I say unfazed and take another lick of my cone.

Still trying to embarrass me he tries again. "And what was it that caused you to not be of sound mind at that particular moment?" I know that he thinks I will turn a thousand shades of red and turn shy at his question, but I don't feel shy around him anymore. Nobody makes me feel more myself than he does.

"You, Georgia. You had just given me one of the best orgasms of my life and I was a bit incoherent. Is that what you're looking for? Confirmation that you rocked my world that night? I think you know you did?"

He takes a lick of his ice cream, and then leans over to me, pulls me to him and gives me my first real kiss since he picked me up from work. Once again, I can taste the offending chocolate ice cream, but mixed with the taste of him and his expert tongue, it's more than tolerable. "How about now?" He asks, as he pulls away and leans back against the door looking oh so proud of himself.

I shrug my shoulders and reply. "It was okay. Not too bad."

"I guess I'll have to rock your world later and ask you again."

He sounds determined.

"I guess you will."

I can't wait!

We're both finishing our cones and he explains that he has another spot to take me to. As we drive along the river, the view just gets better and better. It feels so good to be alone with him. I love Ireland, but it's great to just focus on each other and not worry about what we say or do in front of her. This is some much needed adult time for me and I'm sure for Jonathan too. This kid thing is brand new for him.

A short time later, Jonathan pulls down a little road that leads down to the river's edge where there is a No Trespassing sign posted. He assures me we are fine, and that he cleared it with a friend that works for Vancouver Police as he puts the jeep in park.

We sit in silence for what seems like forever, but I can tell that he's working his way up to talk about something. By the way he's rubbing circles on the back of my hand, and the fact that the pace has picked up, he almost seems panicked. I can tell this isn't going to be an easy conversation. I squeeze his hand, and he starts to speak.

"We lost Matt about three months into our tour in Afghanistan."

He takes a second to collect himself. I take the time as well. I know he doesn't ever talk about what happened with Matt to anybody, not even Devon. This is a big deal for him. I just wait and let him know that I'm here for him by putting my hand on top of his. I lightly rub my fingers back and forth over the back of his hand to try and help calm him. Eventually, he's ready and starts again with his voice low.

"We lost Matt about three months into our tour in Afghanistan. We were on a mission in the Helmund Province when we were attacked. We got out of our Humvee and within our first few steps away from our vehicles, we were under fire. The first shot that we heard hit Matt, and he was gone instantly. He was standing two feet in front of me, and I watched him take the hit and then fall to the ground. I had grabbed him before he hit the ground and I pulled him back to the Humvee, but he was already gone. His damn helmet was too big. He hated to tighten it too tight, so it was tipped back and he was shot right here." He points to the low part of the center of his forehead while looking out the windshield. "I see that moment in my daydreams and in my nightmares. It's always with me."

I have no idea what to say to that so I just say, "It wasn't your fault, Jonathan."

Still looking straight ahead out the windshield he replies to my useless comment.

"But it was, Em. I was his squad leader and I led him into harm's way. I know that I was just following orders, but I had a bad feeling that day. I should have listened to my gut and done things differently, and maybe he would still be here driving

Scarlett instead of me. You know when his parents were in California visiting him that week, he had written them a letter in case anything happened to him. And in that fucking letter, he said that he wanted me to have Scarlett. Can you believe that shit? He left me his pride and joy. This is the first time I've had her out of my garage. It was just too hard before."

He finally brings his shining eyes to mine.

"My mom, Em..."

I reach up and cup his cheek in my hand and rub my thumb back and forth to try to soothe him. I don't know what else to do. I just want to take away his pain. To think I was part of his pain during the toughest part of his life is almost too much for me to live with.

"I'm so sorry, baby. I wish I had been there for you. You went through so much. I wish I could take your pain away for you."

He takes my hand from his face and holds it in his lap, and stares at me for what seems like an eternity. I hold his gaze, letting him know I'm here for him now, and I see him take a deep breath and then exhale. He opens his mouth to speak, but then he closes it as if he's changed his mind.

"It's okay Jonathan, you can tell me anything. If you want to tell me how shitty I was for not telling you the truth, and giving you a chance so that I could be there to help you through it all, then do it. I deserve it."

He shakes his head and looks down at our hands in his lap. He takes a deep inhale and I steel myself for what he says in reply.

"You did get me through it. Just knowing you were out there somewhere, and that there was something as good as you still out in the world stopped me from giving up. I would lay awake at night and recount all of my memories of our time together. That would be the only way I could close my eyes without seeing the nightmare of Matt getting shot, and watching them lower my mom into the ground. I know it sounds crazy, but you did get me through all of it, and I think deep down I knew I would see you again. Knowing in my heart that I would see you again was what kept me from going further into the hole I was in. I always told myself to think about accidentally running into you one day, and how much of a mess would I want you to see me in. I'm functioning because of the hope I had of seeing you again."

I'm stunned silent at his confession. He lifts his head and his eyes connect with mine again. He brings our interlaced hands up and kisses the back of mine before setting it back down.

"You know if it wasn't for my mom, I wouldn't have met you," he confesses with a half-hearted smile.

"What?" I ask confused.

"Yep, my mom knew she was sick when I went home that week before I met you. She was starting her chemo and didn't want me there or to know that she was sick. She told me she wanted me to go back to Cali with the guys and to have fun for her since she had to go back to work. She changed my flight without telling me and acted like it was a gift she was giving me."

Watching him relive all of this is heartbreaking. He's dealt with so much and all I want to do is make it all better for him.

"I was so mad when I found out that she already knew, and that I was there with her and she never told me. She sent me away instead of letting me be there to help take care of her, like I should have. I had so much fucking anger and resentment towards her until Liam pointed out that she didn't just send me away, but she sent me to you. That's how I was able to forgive her. I'm not saying that if I had known I was going to meet you, I still wouldn't have picked staying home with my mom to take care of her, but I wasn't given the chance to pick. My mom chose for me."

"Jonathan…"

"No, let me finish. I'm not angry any more because I figured something out. All my mom wanted was for me to be happy. She got to talk to me more than once that week that I was with you. She got to hear me happier than I had ever been. You and me, baby, we brought her happiness that week. I never did tell her that we weren't going to try the long-distance thing because she was so happy that I had found 'the one'. I wasn't ready to burst her bubble, so I let her think we were still talking when I left."

I start to speak but he stops me by bringing his finger to my lips.

"See, Em, I didn't tell her because I didn't want her to hurt for me, and she didn't tell me she was sick for the same reason. She didn't want me to go fight for my country with the worry of her being sick on my mind. She knew it would overwhelm my every thought, and that would be dangerous. She knew me well enough to know that she was keeping me safe by not telling me. Do I wish I could have said goodbye, or that I would have done things differently while I was home for that last week? Of course. But as much as I try to tell myself that I should have been there for her, or that it wasn't my fault that Matt died, I still feel like I let two of the people I cared about the most down."

He's silent long enough for me to know that he's done sharing.

Squeezing his hand, I say, "Thank you for sharing all of this with me, Jonathan. You have no idea how much it means to me that you would trust me enough to share your story with me. I hope you know I am always here for you if you ever want to talk about anything. You don't have to keep any of it from me."

"Thanks, baby." I can feel his hand start to shake in mine. "It's been really hard because when it comes to Matt, I know that I have Devon to talk to, but I can't help but feel that I let him down that day too, and I think I am afraid of what he'll say if I ever do bring it up. Then when I'm around the Fanuas and my mom comes up...well, I feel guilt around them as well. They took care of her in my absence. Fiona never left her side at the end. It should have been me, and I can't help but feel that they feel the same way."

"Jonathan, I know for a fact that Devon doesn't blame you, and I'm sure that your mom had explained to Fiona that she hadn't told you. They knew that you would have been there had you known or had been able to be. You have to give yourself a break, baby. Nobody blames you but yourself, and you need to let that go. Try to forgive yourself. You're a good man, and you don't deserve the guilt you're putting on yourself."

A lone tear escapes and runs down his face. It's more than I can stand so I crawl into his lap and hold him while he comes to terms with the fact that it isn't all his fault. That he is, in fact, a good man. We're in quite a tight space, and it's not comfortable in any way to be jammed in between the sterling wheel and this beautiful man, but it's worth it to give him what he needs right now.

I whisper into his hair. "I hope you know how lucky they were to have you in their lives. Just knowing you made them better people, and I know this is true because you made me a better person in only a week's time. Imagine what they got from you in the years they had with you. You are beautiful inside and out, Georgia. Don't you ever forget that."

He doesn't speak he just squeezes me even tighter to him, and we stay that way until he's ready. He can take as long as he needs. He deserves it.

The sky is now darkening and we're headed in the direction of home. I'm confused when he doesn't turn to go towards Mick's neighborhood but drives out a little further to a less congested area of Happy Valley. He turns down a road that leads to a beautiful home on what looks to be several acres.

"Where are we?"

He replies by leaning in front of me to open the glove box, pulling out a garage door opener and pressing the button to open the garage. It's then that I see his truck parked on the side of the house. He's brought me to his home.

I am flooded with emotions. It's a feeling of excitement, fear and calm all at once. I'm so excited to be in his space and see where he lives, yet afraid that I'm still not as ready for all of this as he is. The feeling of calm is stronger than the fear though, because in the back of my mind I know I'm going to give him the more that he wants.

How one person can have all of these emotions at once is beyond me, but it is possible because it's happening to me right now.

Maybe I'm losing my mind?

If I am going crazy, this is the best possible way to go that I can imagine.

He parks Scarlett on the empty side of the garage, and I notice that the other side is full of moving boxes.

"I thought you'd been here a couple of years. Have you not finished unpacking yet?"

"Those are from my mom's place. Still not ready to go through it all, but I will soon," he answers with a shrug.

He walks me through the house and explains that he had spent his years in the Marine Corps saving his money so that he would have a down payment to buy his mom a house. They had always rented apartments and he'd always dreamed of buying her a home. It turns out that all of his life, well after his dad died, his mother had been making small monthly payments to a life insurance plan. She wanted to know that when she passed, he was left enough money to take care of himself, and with her policy, she did just that. With her life insurance, he was able to pay for his house in cash and tuck all his savings from his years in the military away.

"I would rather have my mom with me, but it feels good to have had the opportunity to be in this kind of a place financially so early on in my career. I owe all of this to my mom."

I wrap my arms around him and tuck myself into his side. I make sure he knows that his mom knows just how well he has done.

"Jonathan, you have to know how proud she is of you. She knows how great you've done and she's proud. I know she is."

He kisses me on the temple and says, "Thank you, baby."

His house is large but all one level. He has a gourmet kitchen that is right out of a magazine. There's a huge island and room for several bodies in the kitchen together at once. This is the perfect kitchen for entertaining. The kitchen faces a great room that has a wall of floor to ceiling windows that he says have a great view of Mt. Hood. It's too dark right now to see anything past the amazing deck—with a built-in fire pit that the back lights are shining on.

This place is amazing.

There's a butler pantry in the kitchen that leads to the formal dining room and living room. These two rooms are empty, and it's clear he hasn't had a reason to furnish them just yet. We pass back through the kitchen and past the front entry, that has a coat closet as well as a half bath, and head down a wide hallway.

Everything about the craftsmanship of this house is perfect. The wainscoting and dark wood floors are all of the best quality. He had this built exactly as he had envisioned it. It's perfect.

Down the hallway, there are three doors on each side as well as one with French doors at the end of the hall. The first door on the right side of the hall is the laundry room. It. Is. Amazing. My mouth hangs open in awe at how perfect this room is. It's a dream laundry room with new front loading appliances, tons of beautiful cabinets and a huge country style sink. He just gives me a little chuckle when I tell him I could live in this room.

Across from the laundry room is an empty spare bedroom as is the door next to that one but they are connected by a Jack and Jill bathroom. The second door on the right is a beautifully designed bathroom and the room next to that houses what he says is his "office". It does have a desk with stacks of paper all over it, as well as other random things shoved here and there. This looks more like a catch-all to me, but the desk does give the illusion of an office.

Next to the Jack and Jill bedrooms is another empty room that currently just has exercise equipment in it and isn't being used as a bedroom. At the end of the hallway is the set of French doors that lead to the primary bedroom.

This room is more Jonathan than any other in the house. The room is huge with a fireplace at one end of the room, and a huge king-sized bed with a dark brown leather headboard at the other end. All of the furnishings are dark wood and the bedding is a simple beige. Under the window, there's a dog bed for Frances. I have a feeling she sleeps on the bed with him more than she does on her bed on the floor though. She seems spoiled to say the least. The space is very manly, but also beautiful...very Jonathan.

Since we walked through the French doors of the bedroom he hasn't spoken. He walked into the room, turned on the fireplace and then just one low lit lamp. He plays with his phone and *Kings of Leon* starts quietly playing out of the little speaker on his dresser. He walks me through to the massive on suite bathroom that has a shower for two as well as a huge soaking tub. This house is what dreams are made of and I tell him so. It's big, but not too big, and so well made and well thought out. It's perfect...just like Jonathan.

Now that my tour is done, he walks me back to the bedroom and we stand next to the bed. He takes me in his arms and as *our* album plays we silently dance in the dark. We may not be on the beach, but we have the fireplace to set the mood. He missed a thing. The song ends and without speaking, he slowly undresses me, then himself, and we spend the next few hours making the sweetest love I have ever known. This night has been pure bliss.

I lay on my side next to him with one hand holding my head up as my other swirls over his new tattoos. Over his heart in small, intricate, cursive writing is his mom's name, *Caroline*. Over on the bicep not already covered in his family crest, he now has a memorial to Matt. It is beautiful, yet somber. It's a picture of a pair of a Marines boots with a rifle leaning against them and a helmet balanced on the top of it. There are also dog tags hanging down the rifle. It's such a nice memorial, but heartbreaking at the same time.

Jonathan breaks the silence and finally communicates what this day was all about to him.

"Baby, I am going to ask you the same thing I did a little over five years ago. Do you want to make this work? You and Me? And yes, I know that means Ireland is a part of this, too. To me, she is just an added bonus to an already perfect package. It doesn't scare me away, Emily, not in the least. I'm putting it out there again and leaving it up to you. I want more, Gracie."

Of course, I want him, but it doesn't seem like it can be that easy, can it? The fact that the one and only man I have ever loved has walked back into my life, and is offering himself up to me again just, seems too easy. Besides that, how will I put myself back together again when he leaves?

As if reading my mind, he speaks again after my silence doesn't give him the answer he's looking for.

"Gracie, I know you have been hurt and let down by men in your past, but baby, I'm not them. I know you watched your dad cheat on your mom, and then uproot your family by leaving, and it turned your world upside down. I can't imagine how hard it was to watch him pick a new family over you, Mick and your mom. I know watching your mom's heartbreak had to be unbearable, but baby, I'm not him. I'm also not that asshole that is missing out on a life with the most perfect little girl I have ever met. It's his loss, and please don't get me started on him because if I do I just may punch my fist through a wall, and I like my walls just the way they are."

I can't help but chuckle at his last statement and to be honest, I agree with him, I like his walls just the way they are too.

There is only one concern he hasn't addressed.

"What about Mick? He's gonna kill you when he finds out that he asked you to watch over me and we've been having 'sleepovers' every night."

"You let me worry about Mick. Besides, I think he cares about your happiness more than anything else, and I have no problem proving to him that I can make you and Ireland happy." He pushes a stray hair behind my ear and searches my face for answers. He brings his pleading eyes back to mine and it's obvious he's scared to ask his next question. "Emily, is Mick your problem or is that just an excuse you're telling yourself because you're too scared to say yes?"

I nod my head to answer him and in a flash, he's on top of me. His dimples are out in full force as he gently lays on me without putting all his weight down. He closes his eyes, and his face gets serious as he takes some cleansing breathes and says, "I cannot believe I am going to do this, but you leave me no choice...brace yourself, baby."

He messes with his phone, and one of my favorite JT songs

begins to play. He brings his lips to mine and gives them a gentle kiss, but as soon as the lyrics begin he moves those amazing lips to my ear and starts to sing quietly. He sings about healing my heart, and for me to stop acting like falling in love with him would be such a bad thing. He tells me he wants all of my nights and my mornings too. He also promises not to fill my head with broken promises.

He finally pulls back from my ear so that I can see his face. His face that is now gloriously beat red with embarrassment, and I have to say it is the sweetest thing anybody has ever done for me. It was so romantic, just like the rest of the day and night has been. It was perfect, just like him, and when he starts to break into the chorus again, I can't help but put my hand over his mouth and shush him.

"Yes, Georgia...Yes...You and me. Let's give it shot." I am still covering his mouth but I can see the relief in his eyes and feel it in his body. "Can we keep it quiet for now, just until I can talk to Mick? I feel like I owe him an explanation."

I release my hand from his mouth and he brings his lips to mine and our tongue dances together for just a brief moment. He ends the kiss and brings his forehead to mine.

"If that is what you need then yes, we can wait to tell other people until you talk to Mick, but I need you to know that you are mine. From this moment on you are mine, and I am yours, Gracie. It's been that way since the first time I laid eyes on you so there's no need to fight it."

He lays back down and brings me and the blankets with him. I'm tucked into his side, and I can tell that there are three little words he wants to say but is too scared to. They're on the tip of my tongue as well, but for now, knowing he's mine and I am his is enough.

25

———

Jonathan

It feels like I'm breathing again for the first time in what feels like forever. Hearing the word 'yes' come out of her mouth felt like a ton of bricks had been lifted off of my chest. I think part of what lifted that weight was also talking to her about Matt and Mom. At first, I felt like such a pussy for falling apart in her arms, but she soothed me and was there for me. She is slowly making me whole again.

I couldn't have been more honest with her last night. When I told her that the fact that Ireland comes with being with Emily is an added bonus. It just means having two of them to spoil and love. Love. That is what this is and I was so close to telling her last night, but I wasn't sure if she was ready to hear it. I know that deep down she knows that I still love her...that I am in love with her...but I still think hearing it would make it all a little too real for her.

Getting to sleep with her in my arms, and wake to her beautiful smile and that sexy morning voice of hers these last few days has been fan-fucking-tastic. Having to give that up is going to kill me. Mick came home this morning and that means our adult sleepovers will be coming to an end. Emily better talk to him soon because with the way Ireland likes to talk about anything and everything...he's going to find out sooner rather than later that I was at his place a little more than I'm sure he expected while he was gone. I don't think he's going to be thrilled about that.

This morning Emily had me take her to Cami's where Ireland, Frances, and Frank had stayed the night before. Frances and I went home and Cami was going to take Emily, Ireland and Frank home later.

I owe Cami for all of her help with yesterday. When I called her she jumped right in and didn't hesitate to do whatever I needed to give us our night together. She's a character, that one. Her last words to me on the phone after I called to make sure that pick up for Ireland went smoothly was, "Get some!" She's just like one of the guys, and the best friend Emily could ever hope for.

Now with the girls all sorted, I have time to kill until five o'clock when I pick Emily and Cami up to go to Wesley and Trisha's wedding. It worked out great that she was already planning to go, but she was already bringing Cami as her plus one, so I'll be arriving with two dates this evening. If Alex weren't the event planner for the reception, I'm sure I would have three dates tonight. Cheryl, Emily's mom, will be taking Ireland, and we'll have another date night tonight. I love spending time with Ireland, but time alone with Emily is nothing I will ever complain about.

I try to pass the time today by going to *The Gym,* running errands and taking Frances to the dog park. I can't help but feel like I am walking on air. Like all the puzzle pieces of my life are finally coming together. I feel like an idiot walking around with a constant smile on my face. I may be whipped already, but I don't give two shits. I've got my girls and that's all that matters.

Luckily for me, Mick is in the wedding so I don't have to worry about any confrontation with him today. When I get to the house to pick the girls up, Cami answers the door all dressed and ready to go in a mid-length dark pink dress.

"Hey Jonathan, come on in. Em is still finishing up."

"Thanks, Cami. You look lovely this evening," I say as I walk past her and into the living room. Frank comes up to greet me, but I try not to let him get too close so that I don't get white fur all over my dark grey suit.

"You don't look too bad yourself. You want something to drink?"

"Nope, I'm good. Thanks though."

A few moments of awkward silence fall over us, but Cami breaks it. "Thank you, Jonathan. You're bringing my girl back to life again."

"It's her that's bringing me back to the surface, Cami. It's all her," I assure her.

"I know you want to think that, but she has just been getting through life doing what she feels is right, but not truly living or loving. Don't get me wrong, she loves Ireland and her family, but that light that she always had has been pretty dim these past few years. She has that light back in her eyes now, Jonathan and that's because of you. So, thank you."

"It's my pleasure, Cami. All I want is to make Emily and Ireland as happy as I possibly can."

"I know that, but be gentle with her heart because she will scare easily. I know I don't have to tell you this, but after all the bullshit she went through with her dad and then Harrison, it won't take much for her to run. I wish that weren't the case, but it is, so just go easy on her. It's still there, what you had before. You just don't want to push too hard at first. Be patient, and she'll get there."

"I know, Cami. I'm trying to go as slow as I can, but I've waited for what feels like forever to have her back in my life. I'm so ready to just jump in and just go for it that I find I have to pull myself back and reign it in at times so that I don't push her too hard. I think we're in a good place. We just have to get past her fear of what Mick's gonna do, and I think we'll be okay."

"Mick is going to shit, you know that, right?"

"Yep, I do. But I don't care, Cami. He can hate me all he wants, but deep down I know he loves his sister and he wants her to be happy. I have to hope that will out-weigh any anger he may have, but I'm not going to count my chickens on that one just yet."

I hear the bedroom door down the hall open up, and I turn to see Emily walk into the room and then I don't see anything else. She is stunning. She is in a simple black dress with short capped sleeves that is somewhat tight at the top but then flares out a bit at the bottom. Her hair is down, like I like it, but she has big waves in it and it looks fuller than normal. My eyes travel down her perfect body to her legs. Those fucking legs that seem to go on forever in this short dress and three-inch heels. Whoa... this dress is short. Not slutty short, but sexy and classy all at once. I can't help but imagine her naked with nothing more than those damn black heels on. I need to get those thoughts out of my head if I don't want to have an awkward moment right here in front of Cami.

There are no words that can express how proud I will feel to have her on my arm tonight, but I'm not so sure how excited I am for all of the other pervs I work with to see so much of her. All I keep hearing over and over in my head is MINE. The possessiveness I feel over her is out of this world. It's a feeling that takes over my whole being when I'm around her. All I want to do is claim her and protect her from everything bad in this world.

Cami clears her throat from behind me and I snap out of my open-mouth gawking to tell Emily how beautiful she is. She thanks me and then I walk up to her and give her a soft kiss on her painted red lips. I see the pink that I love color her cheeks as I take her hand and ask her if she's ready to go.

26

———

Emily

The vows were beautiful, the bride looks gorgeous, the cake was delicious and the speeches were appropriate. The fact that Mick gave one of those speeches, and it was appropriate, is a bigger feat than pulling off the wedding itself.

I don't know why I didn't talk to Mick earlier today when I saw him at the house. I had the chance but didn't because I am such a freaking chicken. The longer I take to tell him the worse it will be for all of us. Besides, how long do I think I can keep Ireland quiet? The fact that Mick was busy unpacking from hunting, and then having to head out to be with Wesley on his wedding day was my excuse. I was distracting Ireland with getting ready to go to my mom's. This is the only reason Ireland didn't tell him all about her week. I did manage to fill him in on the latest threats from earlier in the week and that Jonathan was a big help, but that is where I left it.

Now, he's busy with all of his wedding duties and trying to hook up with some Amber chick, that Alex is setting him up with. Not sure why Alex would set somebody up with Mick, she must not like this Amber girl too much. I keep telling myself he's busy and I'll talk to him later. Man, I need to grow the hell up and tell my big brother about Jonathan. Time to stop with all of the lame excuses.

I think all of this as I adjust my dress and leave the stall I'm in. At the same time, I hear voices coming from the lounge area of the bathroom. Washing my hands, I can hear Courtney and her merry band of whores talking up a storm, but I don't pay much attention until I hear Jonathan's name. This hotel bathroom is so big that she has no idea I'm in here. To tell you the truth, I don't think it would matter to her one little bit if she knew I could hear her.

One of her merry little whores says, "Jonathan Kelly is looking fine tonight. I thought he was your latest mission, Court. Looks like he's here with Emily Jacobs. They seem pretty close."

"Oh please, she's a single mom with baggage and Mick will never let that shit happen. He's mine. I just need to remind him of that. I think he's forgotten how good a night with me can be. By the end of the night, though, I'll make sure he remembers."

On that note, I dry my hands, touch up my lipstick and then saunter my way through the sea of skanks in the lounge. They all look shocked, except for Courtney. I just wave over my shoulder at them as I pass by and say, "Have a nice night, ladies."

When I arrive back to the table dancing is in full effect. Jonathan doesn't even let me sit down before dragging me out on the dance floor.

The first song that we dance to is slow, and at first, he holds me without pressing our bodies together. I can tell he's trying to be a gentleman and be as discreet as possible. When the next song comes on it is another slow one, and I can't help but press in closer to him and lay my head on his shoulder. It's the most natural thing for me to do. I feel like I can't get close enough to him. I would crawl inside him if I could. He just brings me such comfort and calm. I don't think I will ever get enough.

After the second slow song, the Sister Sledge classic, *We Are Family* comes on, Cami joins us and now everybody is on the floor. We're all having a great time, but I lose sight of Jonathan by the time the song ends.

When the next song starts and it's *Somebody* by Natalie La Rosa, I squeal like Ireland does when she gets a new toy. I see Jonathan, who looks like he was about to head back to our table, stop in his tracks, turn around and head back my way with a huge smile on his face. He knows this is my favorite song and he's not gonna leave me hanging. As he shakes his ass back across the dance floor to me I turn back around to dance with Cami. A second before I feel his hands on me, her eyes sparkle and she gets a silly grin on her face.

I feel his hands on my hips as he starts to sway in time to the slow—but not too slow—sexy rhythm of the song. My body just naturally sways with him. The song is sultry and sexy, and our movements match the song. I can't help myself when I press against Jonathan's hard body, dragging my hands up around his neck and into his hair as we continue swaying in unison to the music.

With him still behind me and his hands on my hips, it's as though we're the only two people in the room, and the song is being played just for us. I pull myself away from his hardness to do a little circle in front of him while I continue to shake my ass to the music. After my flirty little spin, I put my arms around his neck and straddle one of his legs. I know he can feel the heat I'm radiating on his leg while we move together. Pressed against him like this I can feel just how hard he is, and it's clear we're both having the same effect on each other. It's that electricity...that connection that we have. It's always there whether we're touching or not. It feels so good to finally be acting on it. I am so happy to be here with him. He's like a drug, and I have a serious problem, only I don't want an intervention. I never want this high to end.

We keep up our dancing and are in our own little world when the song ends. He gives me a little peck on the lips, and then as soon as we start to step away I realize that we have an audience, and we weren't as alone as we felt.

The first person I see is Courtney. She's surrounded by her merry band of whores and her mouth is hanging open. I think she realizes her prediction from a little earlier just might not come to fruition after all. At least I hope she does. She would be an idiot not to see that. That's right, skank! I say in my head as we pass by Court and Co.

I'm feeling a little proud of myself as we walk off the dance floor hand in hand. I feel confident. At least I do until the moment I see Mick across the room.

He is seething.

I drop Jonathan's hand and speed off across the room in the direction of my big brother. I use the few seconds it takes to get to him to clear my head, and face the realization of what we just did on that dance floor in front of not only Mick but all of his friends and coworkers.

Shit! What was I thinking?

I brace myself, worrying my necklace as I approach Mick's table. The few people that were sitting with him when I first spotted him have left the table, and it's just he and I when I approach him.

"So, Emmers…is there something you wanna tell me?" Mick seethes. I expected his anger, but it shocks me.

Shocked as I am, I play dumb and say, "Mick, we were just dancing. Not sure what you mean?"

"I'm not stupid, Em. And if that was just a dance...in public...
at a wedding...then I'm going to kill Kelly right here and now,
but I think there was more to it than that. Are you guys together,
Em?"

The moment I've been dreading is here and I feel myself
panic. I can't breathe. I don't know why this is so hard for me,
but in the next moment when I could finally break down my last
barrier and move on with my life, I fuck it up, just like I
always do.

"What? No, Mick! You know I don't do relationships. He's
just some fun, for now. He's a nice guy and I deserve some fun,
don't I?"

Mick looks over my head just as I hear Jonathan practically
spit, "Fuck this!" from behind me.

I still and freeze on the spot that I'm standing; too scared to
turn around and see the hurt on his face. Hurt on the face of the
man who has offered himself to me and my daughter, and has
declared that I am his and he is mine. Two minutes ago I
couldn't have been closer to him, and with this one false statement, I have ruined it all.

"I think somebody else may have had a different answer to
my question, Emmers," Mick says with a look of anger and pity
all rolled up into one.

I slowly turn and see Jonathan's back retreating through the
exit doors. With tears in my eyes, I take off after him as fast as I
can in these stupid ass shoes I'm wearing.

I finally catch up to him in the parking garage just as he's
opening the driver's side door of his truck. I yell his name, and
he turns to look at me with nothing but rage etched across his
face. It's a look I've never seen on his face before, and one I hope
I never see again.

Once he sees me he yells from across the garage. "I cannot
believe I did this to myself again. I should have fucking known

better. I have never been anything but honest with you. I let you in, and I don't let anybody in! I have always been honest with you and thought it was clear that I needed that in return. Just last night you lied to me and let me believe I had a chance at happiness. I cannot believe I fucking did this to myself again. My bad, Em. I knew better, didn't I?"

He slams the truck door and leaves me standing in the parking garage alone and desperate to take back the last five minutes of my life. What the fuck have I done?

27

Emily

I wake up to a tapping on my head and a sweet little voice.

"Mommy, I'm home," Ireland whispers as she continues to tap me on the forehead.

"Hey, baby girl," I say with closed eyes. Why is she home so dang early?

I open my eyes and lift my head to the doorway of my room where my mom is leaning against the door frame.

"Rough night?"

"Miserable night, but not what you think. What time is it?"

"It's eleven o'clock."

"Crap, I am so sorry. I was up all night. Mom...I am so stupid...I messed up."

"Ireland, sweetie why don't you go in your room for a minute while I talk to your mom."

"Okay, Grandma."

Ireland leaves the room, and my mom comes and sits next to me on my bed. My phone is plugged in and lying on the bed next to me. I tried to call Jonathan all night long. I texted him letting him know how sorry I was, and that I didn't mean what I said to Mick. That I knew what a bitch I was. I sent another text letting him know that I had told Mick everything, starting with meeting in San Clemente, and up to the moment that I ruined everything.

"Talk to me, Emily. What's happened?"

I fill my mom in on everything since we last talked at Mick's BBQ. She doesn't speak, just listens. When I finish my story, she pushes some of my wild hair behind my ear and gives me a little smile.

"You did mess up, Emily. I can't imagine how bad hearing those words must have hurt him. He needs some time to cool off, but I am sure he'll talk to you, sweetie. You two have too much history to throw it all away. You need to show some humility and explain it all to him once he's ready to listen."

My mom ends up sticking around and makes lunch for Ireland, Mick and myself. She and I watch a movie with Ireland, but I just sit and think about Jonathan. After spending every day of the last week with him, I miss him terribly. Not only do I have the guilt of hurting him, but I miss him.

It's Sunday. I know that he's going back to work tonight, and there's still no word from him. I am checking my phone incessantly, but he still hasn't returned my calls or texts from the night before. I've tried to leave him alone today but knowing he'll be leaving for work in a couple of hours I have to try one more time.

GRACIE

Please talk to me. I am so sorry. Mick knows everything.

GRACIE

Miss you.

After dinner, my mom heads home. Mick has gone out, and I still haven't heard anything from Jonathan. I go through the motions of Ireland's bath and bed routine for the night. I get her tucked in and her story read but I'm not really there. I'm just trying to get through what's left of the day without breaking down.

The last thing I want to do is to try and explain to Ireland why I'm upset. How do you tell your little girl that because you were too immature to deal with your own feelings, you might have lost the best man you or she have ever known?

You don't, because she will want to reason with it, and there is no reason for my behavior, except cowardice. Plain and simple. I was a coward. I hurt him. Now we are both paying the price.

After I leave Ireland's room for the night I go to check my phone, grabbing it off my bedside table and preparing myself for more disappointment. My heart nearly stops when I turn the phone over in my hand and I see that I have a text from him.

GEORGIA

Elka's at 1 pm tomorrow?

GEORGIA

Miss you too.

Oh, thank God! My hands are shaking as I text him. I know he's already at work, but I need to respond. I don't want to let another minute go by.

GRACIE

Thank you and I'll see you there at 1 pm.

An hour or so after replying to his text—and feeling like I can breathe just a little bit again—I'm in the bathroom drying my just washed face and getting ready for bed when I hear Mick say my name and knock on the door. He has his own bathroom so why the hell is he bugging me?

Maybe Ireland woke up?

Crap, not tonight.

I'm emotionally exhausted and really don't want to deal with a nightmare or wet bed. I take a deep breath, and let him know I'll be right out.

Only a few seconds pass when Mick speaks again in a low, calm voice that worries me. "Emmers, you almost done in there? I need to talk to you."

I open the door as I continue to apply my nighttime moisturizer and with a bit of sass and irritation, snap. "Geez, Mick! What do you want?"

I can tell the moment I see his face that something is very wrong. I know in an instant that I don't want to hear the words that are about to come out of his mouth.

"Emmers, there was a shooting at work. Bob Truman was shot and killed and, Em, Jonathan was hit, too. It's not looking great, so we need to get you to the hospital right away okay? I called mom and she's on her way over. She's gonna come stay with Ireland while you and I head to the hospital."

I don't know how long I just stand there in shock, and all I hear is the beating of my heart as it thuds through my body. The loud pulsing is all-consuming as I stand there staring at my brother, but not really even seeing his face.

This cannot be happening.

Not now.

Not ever.

No. I refuse to believe this is happening.

In shock, I walk past Mick and into my room where I change my clothes and get my shoes on. I quietly go into Ireland's room and stare down at my baby girl, and vow to do anything in my power to always protect her to the best of my abilities. I give her a gentle kiss on the forehead and then quietly leave her room. I join Mick in the living room while we wait for my mom to arrive. We don't speak, we quietly wait in silence.

28

Jonathan

B*eep...beep...beep...*

What the hell is that noise? I'm in some sort of dream that has this incessant beeping noise that just won't end. It's hot, it's dark and I have a raging fucking headache. I feel like I'm walking through a fog that's too thick to penetrate, and I can't seem to get out of it. I'm trying to find Emily. I can hear her voice in the distance, but I can't get through the fog to find her.

Why won't my eyes open? I feel like I'm fading, and the dream and Emily's voice are slipping away.

Beep...beep...beep...

.   .   .

The fog is back. My head is still throbbing, and I can hear her voice again. I'm trying hard to get through the fog to get to her, but I just can't get through it. I need to get to her. We have so much to talk about. Why can't I reach her? Why am I trying to get through this fog with my damn eyes closed? Why can't I open my fucking eyes?!

Open your eyes, you idiot! For Christ's sake, open your damn eyes!

I'm tired and the dream is starting to fade again.

I never do find her.

Beep...beep...beep...

I can hear Emily again, and this time I can hear Devon too. I need to wake the hell up. I need to get out of this damn fog. They sound closer than before. I hear her telling him how stupid she is and that she'll never forgive herself. Devon is reassuring her and telling her that I'm going to be okay and that the two of us will figure our shit out once I'm awake. This isn't a dream after all, what's happened to me? Why can't I wake up?

Beep...beep...beep...

It's quiet except for the loud beep that will not stop echoing in my damn head. My head still hurts like a son-of-a-bitch and my neck feels hot as hell. It doesn't hurt like the back of my head does though. It almost feels like it's on fire. It's so quiet that Emily and Devon must have left. How long have I been asleep? Did she give up on me? Did she leave again?

I give it everything I have and finally feel my eyes start to slowly peel open. What I see when my eyes finally do open makes the effort worth it and takes my breath away. Sleeping soundly curled up in a small chair right next to my bed is my sweet Gracie. She didn't leave...she's still here...she didn't fucking leave. Everything hurts, but the relief I feel seeing her here, curled up in that chair makes me feel like I might just be okay.

The feeling is somewhat short-lived when I try to speak her name.

Shit that hurts.

What the hell happened to me?

Every time I try to say her name I feel like I'm trying to speak through a throat full of gravel. I know that I can do this. I need to see her open those beautiful blue eyes of hers; those eyes that reach into my soul and take away all my pain. I need her to comfort me like nothing and nobody else can.

I try once, twice and then on the third try, I finally get her name out loud enough to cause her to stir. When she does finally open those captivating pools of blue and it sinks in that I'm awake she gasps and is out of the chair and holding my hand in a flash. Tears are streaming down her face, and she keeps kissing my hand, scanning my face for what I don't know, and saying how sorry she is over and over.

"Oh my God, let me call the nurse."

"Emily," I grunt out.

"No baby, don't talk. Just take it easy, and wait until they come in and check you out."

I nod my head to let her know I will obey, and I don't miss that she called me baby. Fuck that feels good.

It's all I've ever wanted.

Just to be hers and for her to be mine.

I don't take my eyes off of her. She holds my gaze and my hand, and her tears keep streaming down her face.

"It's so good to see those eyes that go with that handsome face of yours. It's been two days, but it feels like two years. I got you, baby, you're going to be fine," she says still holding my hand as the nurse comes in and starts to check me out. She's an older, round woman who looks like somebody who gives great hugs.

"Good evening, sir. Well, I guess it's good morning now. How are you doin' Mr. Kelly? I'm Nurse Jackson and I've been looking after you." I instantly feel comfortable with her, she has that mama bear thing about her.

"My throat and my head hurt." I manage to grunt out.

"Well, that's not a surprise," says a man's voice from behind Nurse Jackson.

A short, grey-haired man with a comb-over steps into view, and pushes his glasses up on his nose with his forefinger. He leans over in front of me and lifts each eyelid while flashing his little light in each of my eyes.

"You had a close call, Officer Kelly. You were shot. Do you remember the shooting?"

"No, I don't really remember much. I know it happened fast. Truman called for backup. When I got there the passenger got out of the car with a gun in his hand. I heard a bang and then that's it."

Fuck that hurt! My throat is killing me!

Seeing the grimace on my face the doctor says, "I know that hurt, Officer Kelly, so let's try not to talk too much more if you can help it. We had a tube down your throat during surgery, and that's probably why it hurts so bad. Nurse Jackson, can you bring Officer Kelly some ice water, please?"

As if she was expecting his request, she is right there with a beige plastic cup of water complete with a straw. I start to try to lift myself to drink, but Nurse Jackson gently pushes on my shoulder, shakes her head and brings the straw to my lips.

Emily is still holding my hand on the other side of the bed.

She's squeezing it so hard I think she may break it, but you couldn't pay me to ask her to let it go.

Once I have my water down, Nurse Jackson moves out of the way, and the doctor moves back in so he's right in my face and pushes his glasses up again.

"Officer Kelly, my name is Dr. Green and I performed surgery on you last night. You were shot in the head on the right side, just behind your ear, and the bullet left your body through your neck. You are a very lucky man, and most certainly have a guardian angel looking out for you."

Make that two. I think to myself.

"The bullet didn't hit any vital organs or any major veins or arteries. During your surgery, we made sure that all of the bullet fragments were taken out and that we closed up the entry and exit wounds. We're going to need to keep you here for a few days to monitor you, but if you take it easy I think you will heal just fine in no time."

Wow, I was shot.

I am in a state of shock at hearing that news. It all happened so fast that I don't even really remember getting hit. I remember turning to yell at Truman, but I don't remember getting hit.

"Do you have any questions for me?"

I hear him ask the question, but I'm still lying here trying to imagine how it is that I don't remember getting shot. Shouldn't I remember something like that?

"Okay, well it's a lot to take in, but if you do come up with any questions just let Nurse Jackson know, and she can page me. Or press the call button and somebody can come get me. You take care now, and we'll step out and give you a moment with your girlfriend before we let anybody else in. If you don't want guests, you just let us know and we can keep visitors out for you."

Girlfriend? Did he just say, my girlfriend?

Once we're alone Emily asks, "Are you okay?"

I start to open my mouth to answer her, but she stops me and starts rambling. But it's a ramble I will never forget as long as I live.

"Wait, don't say anything. I need to get this out before you have a chance to kick me out. So, please just listen to me. Please hear me when I tell you that you are so much more to me than a good time. I know what you heard me tell Mick, but that was bullshit. Jonathan, I don't know why I said it, well I do. I was scared and stupid and didn't want to deal with Mick yet. I told him everything, Jonathan. I told him our entire story from the first day I met you until now. He gets that I am completely in love with you and that he will just have to deal with it. I may not have fought for you before, but, honey I am here and I am fighting for you now. I beg you to forgive me. You are the last person on earth I would ever want to hurt. You mean so much to me, and I will do everything in my power to never hurt you again. I'm not perfect. I will make mistakes. But will you forgive me? Can there still be a you and me?"

I am awe-struck by this phenomenal woman standing before me. My scared little Gracie just told me she loved me. At least I am pretty sure that's what I heard.

"Emily?"

"Yeah?"

She looks scared to death as she replies.

"Did you just say that you loved me?"

Her face lights up with the most beautiful smile I have ever seen.

"I did! I love you! I know this is the worst place to say it, and it is so selfish of me with everything you have going on right now, but I couldn't go another minute without you knowing. I'm in love with you, and last night was just another reminder that life is short, and Ireland and I don't want to miss another minute with you. That is if you still want me...us?"

"I really can't believe you, Emily. Do you really think there is a chance in Hell that I wouldn't want you? I have been in love with you since the first time I laid eyes on you. You're it for me. You always have been. I love you right down to your bones, baby."

My beautiful Gracie stands before me with tears streaming down her face.

"So, you forgive me?"

It hurts like hell but, I need to be perfectly clear how I feel for her right here and right now. No more pussy-footing around. I just need to keep it short and sweet, but crystal fucking clear.

"Gracie, I love you and I forgive you. You are mine and I am yours. And I want the whole world to know it. No more hiding. If we dance in the dark again—and I hope we do—it's not because we're keeping our love a secret. So, I hope it's clear, and I mean crystal clear, that we belong to each other and nothing is going to come between us again." She gives me a nod as tears continue to stream down her face. With one last scratchy sentence, I seal the deal. "Now, come give me a kiss."

29

Emily

I find myself nearly skipping through the hospital's doors when I return after Jonathan sent me home to clean up.

He loves me!

Jonathan Kelly loves me and forgives me!

I cannot believe how lucky I am to have him walk back into my life. Not only did he walk back into my life, but he fought for me. He had to shake sense into me, but he did it. Even after I let him down he's forgiven me, and he's mine. I've been his since I walked away from him years ago, but now he's mine as well. Now it's time to get him on the road to recovery and home as soon as possible so I can help him get back on his feet.

He didn't want any visitors when he woke up in the middle of the night last night. His throat hurt, he was exhausted and he wanted some alone time with me before others started invading our space. Of course, there were nurses and doctors coming in and out of the room, but our eyes rarely left each other's even when they were talking to him or checking his vitals. He finally sent me home early this morning so that I could get cleaned up. After only being gone a couple of hours, I feel like I haven't seen him in days and can't wait to get back to him.

As I walk off the elevator and enter the waiting room, there is still a big crowd of people, *our people.*

I'm realizing more and more now, that my entire life the police department has been my family, and they are Jonathan's family too. As a kid, I didn't appreciate the family that comes with your father being a police officer. As scary as the job is, I'm so glad that Mick and Jonathan both have such a big support system; people that would do anything from help you move to give their life for you. I didn't think I wanted this life after watching my parents' marriage crumble, but now it's something I plan to embrace and appreciate.

I notice as I get closer to the group—many of whom were here when I left—that they all seem a bit more down than they did when I left. Mick sees me, and heads my way, he also lets out a big breath like he's preparing himself for the conversation he's about to have with me. My heart rate picks up speed and I can feel myself start to panic.

"What Mick? What's happened? Tell me he's okay? He was fine when I left!" I ramble as he approaches me. I can feel eyes watching me but trying not to be obvious. What the hell is going on?

"Emmers, he's okay. He uh…just doesn't want any visitors."

"What do you mean, Mick? What are you not telling me?"

I can tell that he's trying to be quiet and not cause a scene. I'm the one raising my voice, but I am so confused.

What is he trying to say?

As I wait for him to answer, he takes me by the arm and we move to the back of the room away from everybody else.

"Em, they finally told him about Bob not making it and he isn't taking it too well."

"Oh my God, he has to be so upset right now. I need to get back to him. He needs me, Mick."

"Em, he doesn't want any visitors."

"I heard you, but that doesn't mean me," I say incredulously.

Mick just stands there staring at me and I finally figure it out.

"Mick, does it mean me?"

Hesitantly, he nods his head to confirm that I too am not wanted in Jonathan's room.

"I don't understand, Mick. Just two hours ago we finally said 'I love you' to each other and now he doesn't want to see me?"

"It's not you, he doesn't want to see anybody. Devon is the only person he'll let in, and he's in there with him now. He gave strict instructions to the hospital staff and the officer standing watch outside his room. He's been through a lot. He's coming to terms with the fact that Bob died when he was supposed to be his back-up. That would be hard for any of us to deal with. It's not you, sweetie."

I can't believe he doesn't want to see me. I hear what Mick is saying, and I appreciate that he's upset and suffering, but I want to help him through this. I want to comfort him and make sure he knows it's not his fault. I want to be there for him when he needs me most.

The high I was feeling when I walked through the front doors of the hospital has vanished, and I feel like my heart is being torn in two.

I need to pull myself together. Time. I just need to give him some time. I can do that. I'll wait as long as he needs me to. With this mantra running through my head, I thank Mick, give him a hug and return to the group that is still gathered to support Jonathan. I give my hellos and thank yous for their support and find an open chair where I sit and wait with everybody else.

About an hour later Devon comes out of the room and addresses the group.

"Hey everybody. Um...so, J says he still doesn't want visitors right now. He knows you're all out here, and he really appreciates it, but he wants everybody to go home, get some rest and get back to your lives. Again, he appreciates you all being here, but he just isn't up for visitors right now."

Most leave but Devon, Mick, Chaplin Tom and I stick around.

"Devon, thank you so much for being there for him. He's lucky to have a friend like you," I say as I give Devon a hug and then turn to head towards Jonathan's room. Devon grabs me by the wrist to stop me and says, "I'm sorry, PDX, but J really doesn't want *any* visitors. I am so sorry. It kills me to say it, but he doesn't want to see you right now."

He can see the tears in my eyes before they start to fall and pulls me into a strong hug. "He feels like this is Shell all over again, and isn't doing so well. He doesn't want you to see him like this. It's a lot for him to handle, and he has a lot of guilt right now. He's been through so much already, and I think this might be a bit of a setback for him."

I wait all day.

I've been told more than once by the nursing staff that he still doesn't want to see me, but I stay strong and stay there because when he's ready to see me I want to be here.

Somehow I've fallen asleep on the miserable bench in the waiting room when I feel a tap on my shoulder. Nurse Jackson is back and she gives me a sweet smile before she says, "Darlin', it's after visiting hours and he still doesn't want to see anybody. I am so sorry, but you should go home and get some rest."

The entire day has gone by and he still doesn't want to see me. I should get home to Ireland and give my mom a break for a bit, but leaving feels so wrong. I won't quit on him though. I've waited five years to tell him that I love him. I am not going to give up now that we're back together where we both know we belong.

"How's he doin', Nurse Jackson?" I ask as I stretch my aching neck.

"He'll be okay, Miss Emily but he needs to get some rest and so do you."

"Yes, ma'am, I'll go. Will you please tell him I was here and that I'll be back in the morning?"

"I sure will. You get some sleep and I'll let him know."

"Thanks."

Against everything in me that's telling me to stay I get up, grab my purse and reluctantly head to the elevators. I sit in my car for several minutes just staring up at the building that the love of my life is in, wondering how the hell I can help him if he won't let me in. I hope he knows that I'm not quitting on him, and I won't let him quit on me either. I will come back every day until he lets me into that damn room.

It's now noon on day four after Jonathan's shooting and I'm still sitting in the waiting room. I'm still texting him every day and he's still not returning my texts. He still won't let anybody but Devon in to see him.

This morning when I arrived and the nurses wouldn't let me in, I took up my spot in the waiting room and began my wait. Alex came and sat with me for a while but then had to leave for work. Not too long after, Devon came out of Jonathan's room looking horrible.

He plops down in the seat next to me and weakly offers up. "Hey PDX."

"Hey, Devon. You okay?"

"I don't know, Em. I'm worried about our boy, and I don't know what to do to get him through this. I am at a complete loss."

He leans forward with his elbows on his knees and hangs his head looking completely overwhelmed.

"I know that *you* are the thing that will snap him out of it. You're his missing piece, Emily. You make him whole. I know that sounds crazy because it hasn't been that long that you guys have been back in each other's lives, but I saw it. I saw the old J returning. You were bringing him back to life. He's been in love with you for years. He finally has you and he's pushing you away. If I could just get you in that room. Emily, I know you're what he needs."

"I just don't understand, Devon. He told me he loved me and he wanted to shout it out to the world that I was his. I leave for two hours and now he won't let me be there for him. I know he's going through a lot, but I just don't get why I can't be there for him." I say, hoping I don't sound as desperate as I feel.

Devon sits back up in his seat and rubs his face with his hands. After a beat, he puts his arm around my shoulder and pulls me into his side.

"I know it's confusing. He's just going through a lot. Losing Bob is bringing back all of the guilt, loss, and lack of feeling in control that he felt when we lost Matt, and his mom for that matter. He's blaming himself for all of it. I don't want to speak too much for him, so I will leave it at that, but just know it doesn't mean he doesn't love you. He just doesn't know how to deal with it all. Survivor's guilt is a real thing and I have seen him go through it before. He'll get through it. He just needs us to be patient and not to give up on him."

"Devon, thanks again for everything. I don't know what I would do if you weren't here to update me. You have to be exhausted and overwhelmed. I wish I could take some of that off of you. If there's anything I can do just let me know." I look him in the eye and speak with conviction. "Devon, I promise you that I won't give up on him."

"I know you won't, girl, and yes I am tired but I'm doin' fine. Better than our boy in there." He says as he stands and lifts his arms over his head and stretches.

"Listen, I have to go to work for a while. I'll call the Fanuas on my way and update them. I'll come back tonight. You should probably head home, Emily. He knows you're out here and he feels really bad about that. He knows that you aren't with Ireland if you're here."

Standing, I give him a hug. "Thanks, but I'll stay...in case he changes his mind. Between school, mom, Cami, Alex and Mick, Ireland is covered. I'll just stay a little while longer."

After Devon takes his leave, I head to the vending machine down the hall and grab some reinforcements to get me through the day. I return to what I now think of as my chair in the waiting room. Maybe I'll start up a new trashy romance novel and take my mind off of Jonathan just down the hall.

He's so close but feels a million miles away right now.

As I pull out my Kindle, out falls the picture that Ireland made for him. I had forgotten all about it. Looking at the picture of Frank, Frances, Jonathan, Ireland and myself at the park, I can't help but tear up over the hopes and dreams that I feel wrapped up in this picture.

Hopefully, Ireland will remind him that he has more to fight for this time around. It will also remind him that I'm out here waiting for him. Ready to fight alongside him whenever he's ready.

I walk over to Tommy a.k.a. Officer Buford who I've known most of my life, and he takes the picture. His expression is one of pity. I'm too tired and too stubborn to care that I'm probably making a fool of myself by staying around, but it's the only way I can stay sane right now. I'm right where I need to be. Tommy promises to make sure that Jonathan gets his picture, and I head back to my chair. I really hate this chair, but if this is as close as I can get to him then this chair will just have to do.

I sit with my Kindle in my hand, but all I can think about is how close I was to him when I gave Tommy the picture. He was just on the other side of the door. I wonder if he heard me talking to Tommy? I'm starting to feel lost without him, but I don't know how that can be when he has only been back in my life for such a short time. I think Devon may be right. We are each other's missing pieces. We do need each other to feel complete. I guess when you find *the one* that's the way it is, and there isn't anything you can do about it. Two weeks or twenty years, love is love and *the one* is *the one*. What are you gonna do?

It's about eight o'clock, and Ireland has just gone down for the night when my phone alerts me that I have a text.

GEORGIA

Tell Ireland that I said thanks for the picture.

GRACIE

I will.

GRACIE

Can I see you tomorrow?

GEORGIA

No. Going home tomorrow.

GRACIE

That's great news! Can I bring you anything?

GEORGIA

No, thanks. Go back to work Emily. I'll be fine.

GRACIE

Well, if you aren't going to be at the hospital I'll go back to work, but I can stop by after and bring you lunch.

GEORGIA

No thanks.

He doesn't realize he is breaking my heart with every denial he gives me. Or maybe he does. Maybe he doesn't care. I'm trying to remember everything that Devon told me this morning. Mick and Cami have tried to remind me over and over as well that I haven't done anything wrong. I just have to give him time. I feel like I need to bust down his door and tell him to go screw himself and his request not to see me! I don't bust down his door though. Instead...I text him back.

GRACIE

Let me know if you change your mind or you need anything at all. I'm not going anywhere, Georgia. I'll be here when you're ready. You and me, remember?

No reply.

Not that night.

Not the next day.

Not the next week.

30

Jonathan

It's Sunday. I've been home since Friday, but I still cannot bear to see anybody. I don't want to see Devon, but I know I have to. He won't leave me alone and will just break the damn door down if I don't let him in. I just sit in the same spot on my couch, day in and day out. I only get up to piss and get more alcohol. Thank God I had a case of beer in the garage to get me through after I ran out of the hard stuff.

The thought of seeing anybody—knowing that Truman died on my watch—is not something that I could stomach right now. I don't want to see the look of disappointment or pity that will surely cloud their faces. I don't want to hear them tell me it's not my fault when we all know it is. I was his back up, and yet again I let one of my own down. I am a sorry excuse for a man. I know that, and I'm sure everybody else does too.

My recurring nightmare is to see any of those expressions cross Emily's face. I fought so hard to get her back only to realize that I don't deserve her. She deserves somebody who doesn't let everybody around him down, time and time again. Those girls, Emily and Ireland, they have become my everything, but I just can't be around them. I am no good for them, and there is no way I can let them see me in my current state. I feel empty without them in my life every day. But if I am any kind of man at all, I will let them go.

The problem is that Emily won't let go. She is a woman on a mission and won't give up. She has this determined resolve and is texting me every day like everything is normal. Sharing her day with me, giving me cute messages from Ireland, and checking to see if I need anything. I can't bring myself to reply, but I sit and read her messages over and over. It's like my own form of torture.

If I reply it will only give her hope. I can't do that. It's not good to be close to me because I tend to lose those that I care about. If anything ever happened to either of my girls, I don't know what I would do or how I could live without them in the world. The best thing for me to do is just stay away, and as hard as it is, not answer her texts.

I smell like shit!

I mean I am fucking disgusting.

No, a fucking nightmare is what I am.

I've been home for a week and can't remember the last time I took a shower. Even Frances won't come near me. If it wasn't for her, and the fact that she needs to be fed, watered and let out I may not have made it through this week. Devon should just come take her. I'm not fit to take care of her and even she is disgusted with me. I can see it in her eyes. She thinks I'm pathetic and she's right. I am.

Every bottle of alcohol in the house house been consumed and am officially out of my pain pills. I'm even out of the few sleeping pills I had on hand to get me through my crazy hours as a cop. A fucking cop. Who the hell am I kidding? I have no damn business protecting and serving anybody.

I could be back to work by now if only I could stop wallowing in my own misery long enough to give a shit. Nope, I'm in the same spot I've been in for days, thinking I may actually have to leave the house soon to re-stock on some cheap booze.

My phone has been dead for days, and Devon has pretty much given up on me. He hasn't come by in a couple days, but that's fine by me. I don't need him riding my ass. I'm not ready. Not sure I ever will be. I don't want to talk it out. I don't want to do anything but drown out my self-induced sorrows. It seems he's finally leaving me the fuck alone though. Thank Christ!

I haven't had a drink since sometime last night and I think it's late afternoon by now. I hate feeling sober because it means I can feel again. I don't want to feel.

There's a sudden pounding on the door and Frances starts barking like crazy. She's probably hoping whoever is on the other side of the door is here to rescue her from the monstrosity that I've become. I hear Devon yelling on the other side of the door, but I still don't make a move to get up and let him in.

Finally, Devon uses the key I gave him when I moved in and bursts through the door.

"Dude, why aren't you answering your phone?"

I have no answer for him. I just lift my head and watch him as he paces the floor. He looks desperate.

"Wake the fuck up, Irish!"

He's shouting and Devon doesn't shout.

"What the fuck do you want, D?"

Still yelling, he stops his pacing and stands in front of me fuming.

"What do I want? I want you to snap out of your goddamned pity party and wake the fuck up! Emily and Ireland need you, asshole!"

I start to tell him that they don't need me when he interrupts me.

"Just shut the fuck up, Irish. The bullshit has started again and it's serious this time. Emily is terrified, dude. She needs you. YOU. NEED. TO. WAKE. THE. FUCK. UP!"

His words are starting to sink in, and *I'm* starting to feel anxious. I've never seen him like this. He is pissed, scared and frustrated. It must be serious.

What the fuck is wrong?

My girls...no!

This cannot be happening.

Not my girls!

"What do you mean it's started again? Why is she terrified, D?"

Devon calms down and sounds very somber when he replies.

"J, whoever this is, that is messing with your girl? They've been in Mick's house. They were in Ireland's room, man. They fucked up her things."

That is all it takes. It's like somebody has flipped a switch and the surge of adrenaline and anger that I feel shooting through my body brings me back to life.

What the fuck is wrong with me? I thought by being away from them I was protecting them, but I was wrong. They need me with them to keep them safe. I was too busy feeling sorry for myself and not doing what I was put on this earth to do. Take care of those two girls. Nothing else matters.

Devon can see me waking up out of my masochistic funk and says, "Go get in the shower, Irish. You fucking stink."

"Thank you, D, for everything."

"I got you. Now go get yourself together. Your girl needs you."

I run down the hall to take my first shower in days and wake myself up so I can get myself back to where I belong.

31

———

Emily

"Chica? Why don't you let me take her and lay her down in the other room?" Cami asks from beside me on my mom's couch.

I know she's trying to help, but I just can't seem to let her go. Ireland is fast asleep in my arms after falling asleep in the car on the way here. We were on our way home after a big day of running errands when Mick called and told me to come to moms instead. I can't stop replaying the phone call in my head on a constant loop.

"Hey, Mick, what's up? Did you think of something you needed me to pick up while I'm out?"

"Emmers, where are you right now?"

"We're in the car about five minutes from home. Why?"

"Sis, I need you to head to mom's."

"Why? Mick, did something happen?"

He sounds somber when he says, "Mom's fine, but I don't want you and Ireland at the house right now."

"Mick, is everything okay? You don't sound okay."

"*Emmers...they got in the house.*"

"*What do you mean? Who got in the house, Mick?*"

I don't understand him. It's like he's talking in code.

"*Whoever is messing with you, Em. Em...I came home and Frank was sitting on the front porch because the front door had been left open. I went into the house and nothing was taken, but when I got to Ireland's room...Em...they messed up Ireland's room. It's bad.*"

I feel like I've been punched in the gut and all the air in my lungs escapes me. I can't breathe.

On a whisper, I manage to say, "What?"

"*I am so sorry. I hadn't gotten to turning on that alarm system yet, sis. When I find who did this I am going to make them wish they were never born. Trust that, Em. This is going to end now,*" *He hisses.*

"*How do you know it's the same person who's been threatening me?*"

"*Em, they left a note in your room. It's the same person. It says basically the same thing all of those damn text messages from the last week have been saying. Now, go to mom's because I don't want you guys to see this. I have detectives on their way over. We'll get things cleaned up as best we can before you come back. Where did you get Ireland's bedding? I'll see if I can replace it with the same thing so it isn't so obvious to her.*"

I can't even reply to him. It's so bad that he has to replace Ireland's bedding. What have I done that is so wrong that my baby girl deserves this?

"*Em, you there?*"

Shit!

I need to snap out of this.

I have a little girl to take care of. If the last week or so of my life is any indication, I'm on my own in this world except for Mick, Mom, Alex, and Cami. I need to get my head right and work with Mick and do whatever he says.

"*Yeah Mick, I'm here. Her bedding is from Target and I think it's one they always have in stock, but I can go get it. You don't have to do anything else. It's my fault your house was broken in to. I don't know what's going on, Mick, but I am so sorry."*

"Stop it, Em. This is not your fault and that will be the last time I hear you talk like that. Listen, get to mom's and I'll call Cami and have her meet you there, okay? We're gonna figure this out, sis. I won't rest until we do. Detectives are here, so I got to go. Love you, sis, and call me if you need anything or if you get any more messages, okay?"

"Okay, Mick. Thanks."

That was an hour ago.

Now, here I sit, perched on the edge of my mom's couch with Ireland draped across my lap. I can't seem to sit back and relax into the couch. I'm sitting on the edge feeling like I'll need to jump up and protect my baby girl at any moment.

Cami's gently rubbing her hand up and down my back and trying to soothe me with reassuring words. I think she's worried because I haven't said anything in the last hour. Nor have I cried or had much emotion at all. I'm just holding Ireland and staring blankly ahead.

I know that my silence is freaking Mom and Cami out. I heard Cami on the phone updating Alex, and I could hear the worry in her voice. But I can't speak. I feel like if I talk I might lose it. But I am a mom and I don't get to lose it. I have a little girl in my arms that needs me to keep it together.

Cami has been there for me every day since Jonathan's shooting. She helped Mom and Mick with Ireland and then when Jonathan rejected me. Every day she has been there for me. She has let me cry on her shoulder, scream and rage over how angry I was that he was shutting me out, and most of all she has simply listened. In addition to my relationship woes, she's been there through all of the threats that have started since I went back to work. She has been here every step of the way, just like she has been since that fateful day in elementary school.

Turns out, her deciding we were going to be best friends, was the best decision anybody ever made for me.

There's a gentle knock on the door, and it startles all of us.

"Hey, it's okay. Mick probably just sent somebody over to ask some questions or to guard you or something. Don't worry. You're safe here," Cami says as she continues to rub calming strokes across my back.

Devon enters the room and my heart instantly stops. No. Not now. Please tell me he isn't here with bad news. Please tell me that Jonathan is okay. I can hear my mom whispering with somebody in the hall, and I assume that Gabby must have come with him.

"Devon, what is it? Is he okay? What's wrong?"

He just looks at me, then takes a step to the side. Jonathan walks in behind him, followed by my relieved looking mom. The moment I see him, all the tears I've been holding in come flooding out and I burst into silent sobs.

Everything that happened this past week and a half comes crashing down on me in one fell swoop. From the scene at the wedding to Jonathan's shooting, the high of Jonathan loving me, to his rejection mere hours later, to the radio silence that followed, the threats and now the break in.

Seeing him here and walking towards me causes my dam to break and the tears won't stop. I knew I was stressed, but I had no idea how much I was truly holding in. I have always done my best in life to not need anybody, but I need him. I know this now.

I feel Cami get up from beside me as Jonathan comes down to his knees in front of me. He takes my face in his hands, like I love so much, and leans his forehead against mine. He whispers my sweet nickname that I have come to love and crave from him. I close my eyes and revel in the wonder of him being here.

After what seems like barely a second and hours all at the

same time, he releases me and puts his hand on Ireland's head and simply stares at her for a moment.

"Baby, we're gonna have Cami take this sweet little princess into the other room, okay?"

I just nod my head, still not ready to speak. The tears have stopped, and I'm slowly starting to feel stable with Jonathan in my presence, but I'm still not okay.

He stands. Cami approaches us and gives Jonathan a hug and thanks him for coming. She bends down and as she takes Ireland from my arms she whispers in my ear. "I knew he'd snap out of it. He's here and he loves you. He just needed time. It's gonna be okay, chica. It's. Gonna. Be. Okay."

She stands with Ireland in her arms, and she and my mom leave the room. Devon must be outside because I don't see him anymore, and it seems we're now alone.

He's on his knees in front of me and is as close to me as he can get. His body is pressed against my legs and his hands are rubbing up and down my arms as if he is trying to warm me.

"Talk to me, baby. Devon gave me the basics, but I need you to tell me what's been going on? I'm here now, honey and I am so sorry for everything. We'll talk about all that later, but right now I need you to fill me in and tell me everything you can."

32

Jonathan

God, even in the shittiest of situations, being near her and being able to touch her again is everything.

She is my everything, and I cannot believe that I shut her out.

I am a selfish bastard.

I really am.

Emily is always so strong and determined. To see her look so defeated and in so much pain was something I have never seen before, and I hope to never see again.

I haven't been there for her.

It's almost too much for me to bear.

Not only did I break her heart because I shut her out, but she had finally trusted me enough to love me and let me love her back. But I was so involved in my own self-pity that I wasn't there for her when she needed me most. I couldn't even be bothered to answer my phone or return a text.

Enough.

This selfish bastard routine is over and it's time to take care of my girls. Right now I need to focus on finding the piece of shit that is doing this to them, and then I will try my damnedest to earn back her trust and love. For now, I have to figure this shit out.

It has to be somebody at the school. As soon as Blackburn was out on watch, the notes on the car and in the classroom stopped. She had gotten one strange text before the shooting, but the entire week she was out of school—waiting on my sorry ass to let her in—there were no threats. But they started again the day she went back to school. It has to be somebody at school that would have her number. We are going to have to interview everybody that she has given her number to.

All of this is running through my head as I pull up to Mick's house. There are several city cars here, and I'm relieved to see that everybody is taking this seriously.

Getting out of my truck, I bend my neck to avoid hitting my head and get a twinge of pain from my injury. I had forgotten all about it. Even though I'm healing just fine, the pain is still there and I still have stitches. No more pain killers though, and no drinking for a while either. It's time to deal with the pain, and not hide from it.

As I walk towards the house, I have a feeling of dread come over me. Not only do I not want to see the damage that was done to Ireland's room but I know I'm about to face Mick. After what I did to his sister this may not go so well. I deserve whatever he dishes out though.

The pain in my neck is nothing compared to what I feel when I enter Ireland's room. As I stand in the room where I have read bedtime stories, had tea parties, worn tiaras and tutus while playing princess, I am filled with a rage that has my heart beating so loudly that I can't even hear myself think.

Thud...thud...thud...

Everything feels like it's in slow motion as I look at her pink bedding cut to shreds. Somebody has taken a knife and literally shredded her blankets and pillows. There are feathers everywhere and her things are scattered all over the room. They have chosen one of her stufties to decapitate. Leaning against the body of that stuffed bear is a picture of Emily walking Ireland into school.

WHAT! THE! FUCK!

Rage. I am filled with rage.

Whoever this fucker is has been following Emily and Ireland. They know where she works, where Ireland goes to school, where they live and they have Emily's phone number. What the hell is going on?!

I have to get out of this room before I lose it. I cross the hall to Emily's room. Mick is standing there with Detective Noah Caldwell looking at something on the bed.

"What is it, Mick?"

Mick turns around and motions for me to join them. When I have full view of the bed, the scene isn't anything dramatic. There is just a simple note that says,

Leave mine alone and I'll leave yours alone.

"Mick, what the hell is going on? Who would want to do this to her?"

"Fuck if I know, man."

Mick leaves the room and I follow him. He stops in the kitchen, grabs a coke for himself and hands one to me as well.

Leaning against the counter on the other side of the kitchen, I have a direct view of the refrigerator, and I can see a new picture that has been added to the gallery of Ireland art that covers the appliance. This new picture says *Happy Birthday*

Mommy on it. Then I see the wilting bouquet of balloons tied to a dining room table chair, and I realize on top of everything else I missed her fucking birthday.

The woman I love was heartbroken, because of me, on her birthday.

"Don't worry about it, man. She understands and she's resilient as shit. You've been through a lot and nobody expects you to get over everything overnight."

This is her brother, and I can't let him let me get away with it that easily. I need to talk to him because if I'm lucky, he just might be my family one day.

"Thanks, Mick, but I still feel like a dick. The guilt took over, man, and it reminded me of losing my friend Matt over in Afghanistan, and not being there when my mom died. It's no excuse, and I know that I have a lot of work to do to earn back her trust. I swear I won't check out again, man. This was a huge wake-up call. Believe me when I say that I am in love with your sister. All I want to do is take care of her and Ireland and make them happy. I have been in love with her for years, and I'll do anything not to lose her again. I know you probably want to kick my ass right now, but there isn't anything you can say to keep me away from her."

Mick crosses the kitchen and holds his hand out to me. He waits until I reach mine out to shake his before he says, "Good. As long as we're all on the same page, and that Emmers and *I* are taken care of and happy, that's all that matters. Now let's figure this shit out."

33

Emily

"Listen, Austin, thanks for stopping by before class starts. I am so sorry to bring you into this, but some strange stuff has been happening to me lately and the principal needs to talk to anybody that I might work closely with. There might be a police officer in the room as well, and I know that might make you uncomfortable, and I'm sorry about that."

"No problem, Miss J. Of course, I'll talk to them. Are you okay?"

He is such a sweet kid. I hate that he has to be involved in this.

"I'm fine, Austin. Thank you for asking. If it's all right with you Officer Blackburn is gonna walk you down to the office to talk to Principal Utz?"

"Sure thing. I'll see you later, Miss J and let me know if you need anything. After what you did for Jesse and how you take care of all of us, I got your back."

I walk him to the classroom door where Officer Blackburn is

waiting and I thank him once more. This is so embarrassing. I hate involving other people in my problems and I certainly don't want Austin to think that I suspect he could be involved in this in any way. He's a kid who struggles and he has a rough family life, but he's a good kid.

I take a deep breath and prepare to endure even more embarrassment as I leave the classroom to head to the office and the library for Heidi. I know that the word is out and everybody knows what's happening. Many of my co-workers are being brought in and questioned. I feel horrible. Stupid. Naive. These are not feelings I'm accustomed to. I don't feel uncomfortable in my own skin.

The one positive about today was that Jesse was back in class. It sounds like some family friends have stepped up and taken him and his brother in. Things are starting to look up for them. He seemed glad to be at school, and that is all that any teacher can ever hope for. I needed to see his face to help me get through all the unpleasantness that surrounding me.

Sitting in the passenger seat of Mick's over-zealous monster of a truck, I am completely exhausted and it's only 11:30 am. The roller coaster that my emotions have been on since the Samson's wedding has me on edge, and I'm hanging on by a thread. Now that Jonathan's back, I should be happy, but there is still so much to say and so much going on with trying to figure out who's creating this nightmare. I am exhausted.

Mick insisted on picking me up and taking me to my mom's where Ireland spent her day. It was decided that I needed to go to school and keep my routine to try and draw out whoever is trying to destroy my sanity, but it wasn't safe enough to let Ireland go to school.

Mick and Jonathan haven't shared many details, but I know that Ireland's room was the target of the break-in. The thought that this person would stalk me enough to know where I live and break into my personal space has rocked me. The fact that they are involving Ireland has me shook to the core, and I'm barely functioning.

I also hate being such a pain in the ass to everybody around me. Mick took time off work to help figure all this out and fix Ireland's room up as best he can. My mom has taken time off of work to help with Ireland. Jonathan is now spending his time on the case, and I am not even sure exactly where we stand. Not to mention all of the staff at school and even some students are being questioned.

I hate this!

This is complete bullshit! I just don't understand what the hell is going on, and what I have unknowingly done to be on this side of somebody's hate. A hate so strong they would break into my home and threaten my child. None of this makes any sense.

The thought that this could be somebody that I see every day at work is unfathomable to me. I usually only see the good in people, and I am not naturally skeptical of others, but I feel as though this entire situation is changing me. I try not to show it, but I am second guessing everybody I talk to at work. Trying to listen closely to see if they say anything that could be suspicious at all. I hate the feeling of not being able to trust those around me, and the dread that I feel in the pit of my stomach is constant. I can barely eat and my sleeping is sporadic. I tend to wake up in a sweaty panic most nights.

When we get to my mom's, Mick walks me in and then says he has to head out to follow up on some things. He's still not telling me much and it's making me feel like a child. At this very moment in time, I don't have the energy to fight him for more information, so I just let it go.

The only energy I have left is for the little girl that just came running to me and jumped in my arms. I cannot believe how big she's getting. Pretty soon I won't be able to carry her around like this, and I know I need to enjoy every moment that I have with her at this age.

I'm so glad that she isn't old enough to understand more than she does right now. I can tell that she knows that something is off, and I know she wants to be home with all of her things, but she doesn't know enough to be scared.

Like I am.

All the time.

At the moment, she's just so excited to be around her Grandma and see more of Uncle Mick. She thinks this is all fun and games.

She does ask for some of her things so shortly after Mick leaves, I text him and ask him to bring a laundry list of things back to mom's later that night. Mick says he's on it and acts like it doesn't bother him, but I hate that he is having to go out of his way again.

I wish he would just let me in the house to get her stuff myself. That is impossible though since he won't even let me drive right now. When he comes back later tonight, I will make a point of getting more information about the break-in and when I can go back to the house.

I love my mom, but she lives in a two-bedroom apartment and doesn't have room for us. Ireland needs the normalcy of being around her things and not living out of her backpack.

But, if it's not safe I will not put her in harm's way.

Sitting here on the couch in my mom's place, I feel trapped. Even though I'm not alone, I sure do feel it.

Jonathan came back last night after his first visit and he played with Ireland. After bath time, he read her a story. By the time he was finished with her, I was falling asleep out here on the couch. When he found me nearly passed out, he didn't say a word. He just scooped me up, sat down on the couch and held me in his lap.

When he first sat down, he took my chin and tilted my head up so that my eyes met his and he whispered. "I am so sorry, Gracie," and then he brought his lips to mine and gave me the softest of kisses. I could feel some of my anxiety melt away, just from the warmth of his lips on mine.

He then told me to rest and gently guided my head to his shoulder. My face naturally nuzzled into the crook of his neck. He kissed me on the top of my head and then just held me. The comfort his hold brought me and being surrounded by his smell was all I needed to fall into a deep slumber; a sleep that I hadn't had in weeks.

He held me for hours and I didn't wake up again until I felt him tucking me into the couch. The apartment was dark, and I could only see the silhouette of him as he stood above me.

"I'll be back tomorrow, baby. You get some rest and let Mick drive you. Make sure Ireland stays home with your mom, okay?"

"Okay, but Jonathan where are you going?"

"I have to go help Mick and the guys try to figure all this out, baby. I want nothing more than to spend all night with you in my arms, but I won't be able to rest again until we know what's going on. Just do what Mick tells you and we'll do everything we can to get your world back to normal as soon as possible."

"Okay."

With that, he kissed my forehead and left. Needless to say, it took quite some time to fall back to sleep without his arms around me.

Now I'm sitting where he left me wondering why I haven't

heard from him today. I am so confused. He says I'll see him today, but I haven't heard a thing from him. I know he's been through a lot, and he needs time, but where is he?

I'm shook out of my wallowing when there is a knock on the door, and it scares me half to death. The glass of water I've been holding, but not drinking, spills all over my hand and I get up and curse as I walk to the door and wipe my hand on my pants.

Since when have I been a person that is jumpy and scared of everything? I hate what this is doing to me. I am not this person and I refuse to let all of this change me. It is some bullshit that a knock on the door—one I am expecting—scares the ever loving shit out of me.

This has to end.

Even though I'm sure it's Mick, I still check the peephole and am very pleased to see that it's not Mick. It is one handsome looking man from Georgia holding our bags. If only his face looked a little lighter. He looks like he is carrying the weight of the world on his shoulders, and I'd do anything to help ease that load for him. The problem is that I am part of the reason for that weight being so heavy. Again, I am a pain in the ass.

I open the door and say, "Hey."

"Hey," he says, as we stand in the doorway holding each other's gaze. After a long moment, he says, "Mick wanted me to bring over some of your things."

He looks exhausted.

"Oh, thanks for that. Come on in."

The moment the door shuts, Ireland comes running to see who has arrived. The smile that spreads across her face is one so authentic and real that it nearly breaks my heart when she yells, "Jonafon!".

She is just as in love with him as I am.

He drops the bags and squats down so that she can jump

into his arms and she wraps her arms around his neck to give him a hug. I notice that her right arm is resting on his stitches, and I reach over and move her arm.

"Baby girl, be careful! Jonathan has a boo-boo and we have to be careful with him." I then turn my attention to him and catch him watching me.

"How are you doin', Georgia? I can't believe I didn't ask yesterday. Things were so crazy and then I just fell asleep on you. I'm so sorry I didn't ask."

"Hey, it's all good. Don't worry at all. I am healing just fine except for some headaches here and there. I'm on schedule with my recovery and will be back to work soon."

"I'm glad you're doing okay. What are you doing for the headaches?"

"Nothing right now. It's not too bad though. Please don't worry. That's my job anyway; to worry about you two."

Before I can protest and tell him that I don't want that to be his job—he doesn't need any more stress in his life right now— he tickles Ireland and says, "Don't tell me it's not my job, Emily, or Ireland here will get more tickles!"

Ireland screams and laughs at the same time while Jonathan goes in for the tickle and I hold my hands up and say, "Okay, I give up. I won't say anything. Just don't tickle the poor princess to death!"

"Princess? Did you say, Princess?" Jonathan stops his tickling and gets a very serious look on his face. He puts Ireland on her feet and then takes a bow in front of her and says, "Please forgive me, Princess. I should know better than to tickle the Princess of Happy Valley. Do forgive me?"

She giggles but loves when they play princess and says, "You are forgiven, Sir Jonafon."

In mock relief, he thanks her for her kindness and gives her the backpack that's filled with all of the things she requested. She thanks him, but suddenly has no interest in all of the things she had wanted from her room.

She takes Jonathan by the hand and pulls him to the couch. He follows her lead and takes a seat. She then proceeds to climb all over him while she chats about school, and how excited she is that next month it will be her turn to bring the class goldfish home for Thanksgiving week. A quick look of puzzlement crosses his face but is gone almost as fast as it arrived.

On the topic of the class goldfish, the conversation about snack foods begins as he reminds her that fishies are the best snacks ever. She disagrees and says that *Teddy Grahams* are the best. He agrees that they are in the top five, but that the number one will always be *Goldfish*.

They go on and on like this for what seems like forever, just like they always do. I never thought I would be jealous of my daughter, but at the moment, when I'm feeling so unsure of where things stand between the two of us, I do feel a twinge of jealousy. I hate to feel it, but she is getting all of his attention, and I feel like I'm left floundering with all of my emotions about to bubble over.

Finally, I try to come to his rescue and mine.

"Baby girl, let's give Jonathan a break. Tell him thank you for bringing our things over for Uncle Mick, but he probably needs to get going now."

He looks up at me, and I feel the blush flooding my cheeks. I hope that he can't read my mind, and that he didn't hear the sharpness that came out in my tone. It wasn't intentional, but I heard it. I just hope he didn't.

While they were having the chat of their life, my mom came home and has just walked back into the room when Jonathan stands form the couch and addresses her.

"Hey Cheryl, do you mind if I borrow Emily for a little bit?"

"I don't mind a bit, Jonathan," mom replies.

"Is it okay if we leave Ireland with you while we go for a walk?"

"Of course not, you two take your time. Ireland and I are gonna have a little snack and start a movie."

He turns his attention to me and asks. "Do you mind if I steal you for a little bit?"

Suddenly, I feel scared to death but in a totally different way. I can tell he wants to talk, but after he basically just sat here and ignored me I'm wondering what he wants to talk about. I want nothing more than to be alone with him, but I'm afraid to hear what he has to say.

"Sure, let me go grab my coat and we can go for a walk?"

"Sounds good."

I walk over to Ireland, give her a high-five and tell her to listen to her grandmother. Jonathan is right behind me and helps me slip my hoodie on. Always the gentleman, he opens the door for me.

As soon as we're outside and the door is shut, he pulls me into a huge hug and he holds me so tight I can barely breathe. After several minutes of holding each other without speaking, he releases me and then cups my face like he always does before a kiss.

As I am preparing to feel his lips on mine, he surprises me when he says, "I want nothing more than to kiss you until you can't breathe, but we need to talk first. I have some things I need to say."

He lets go of my cheeks, takes me by the hand and we start walking. We don't say anything for quite some time. He leads us across the street to a little park, and we find a somewhat private picnic table to stop at. We both sit on the top of the table and

Jonathan takes my hand in his. We turn to face each other and I give him my full attention. I don't speak because I can tell this is something that he feels he needs to do, and so I let him guide us through this.

He looks to the side and exhales a big breath before returning his eyes to mine. Even with the uncertainty that is on his face, he is still the most beautiful man I have ever encountered, and I cannot believe I'm fortunate enough to have him in my life. He squeezes my hand and begins.

"Emily, I am so sorry. I am so sorry for pushing you away. I was a mess. Hell, I probably still am, but I thought I was doing what was best for you and Ireland. When I found out that Bob was killed on that call, everything that happened with Matt came rushing back, and with that came all the feelings about not being there for my mom. Bob was yet another person that I let down."

He rubs his hand over his face, but I give him the beat he needs to take so he can continue.

"Knowing I was going to have to face his wife and look into her eyes knowing that she knew it was my fault that her husband wasn't here anymore, was more than I could handle. I was drowning in guilt and self-pity. I kept telling myself that I didn't deserve you in my life. That if I let you in I clearly wouldn't be able to take care of you like you deserved to be. I seem to let down everybody I care about."

I try to step in and speak, but he doesn't give me the chance before he continues.

"I know I was wrong to push you away without an explanation, but I was a mess. You had finally made all my dreams come true, told me you loved me, and what do I do to thank you? I push you away and then drink myself into oblivion. I told myself that if I truly loved you I would remove myself from your life. I would do anything for you, even if that meant walking away from you. I was wrong. I can't walk away from you. The thought that I wasn't with you when you were being terrorized by this scumbag is something I will never forgive myself for. I would give my life for you and Ireland. I hope you know that?"

He asks the question but doesn't really want an answer, because he keeps going.

"I know that I don't deserve your forgiveness, but I know I was wrong. I also know that when I'm without you, I'm miserable. You are it for me, Emily, I just want *you*. I don't care about anything else but you and Ireland. I love you so much and I am so sorry."

By the time he's done talking he's no longer looking at me. He's looking down at our joined hands. I can tell he feels almost worthless over all of this, and it is breaking my heart. It's my turn to make sure things are clear from my end for a change.

"Are you done?" I say with all the confidence I can muster.

His eyes pop up to mine, clearly surprised by my reaction.

With a nod of his head ,he tells me he's done talking, but he looks a little scared to hear what I have to say.

"Good, it's my turn now," I say locking eyes with him. I want to be sure he hears what I have to say. "These last couple of weeks you may have been a mess, but guess what, Jonathan? You're my mess. Isn't that what we said?"

He nods, but he looks like he doesn't quite understand what I'm saying.

"I'm yours and you're mine. You are my mess and it's my job to help you get through the tough times. You have been helping me get through all of this crap going on with me, and it's my job to do the same for you. You have made me see myself for the very first time, and to realize I *do* deserve to be loved and cared for. By you."

He lifts our hands and kisses the back of mine.

"You have made me trust somebody besides myself for the first time in a very long time, baby. You say you're a mess but I think you are a kind, amazing, funny mess that makes me and my little girl feel safe, cared for and most of all happy." With a wink and a careful smile, I add. "You aren't too bad to look at either."

I see the first smile I've seen since our words of love in the hospital, and I can see some of that weight lift off of his shoulders as I continue.

"Let me be there for you like you're always there for me. Next time don't walk away from us. You and me, remember? Life is always going to throw us curveballs, and it will be hard, but you can't walk away."

His eyes grow big. Yes, I've called him out but I'm not finished.

"Honey, what you have been through is more than anyone person should have to deal with, but let me help you when you feel it's all too much. I love you, Jonathan, like I have never loved anybody else. I need to know that you aren't going to walk away. That is something that I can't live in fear of. I have always built up my walls to avoid being left because I have always thought that I wasn't enough. You make me feel like I'm enough, Georgia. We can get through anything as long as we walk through it together. Promise me that if we do this you aren't going to walk away again."

I can tell that this isn't what he was expecting. Was he expecting my rejection? I hate that he really thought I would quit on him or us. I can see in his eyes that he didn't expect the words that I have just given him. I see my words slowly sink in and his face starts to relax.

"Gracie, I need to kiss you...now."

With the words on his lips, he leans forward, and in the way he knows I love, he gently strokes his thumb over my cheek. With his big hands engulfing my face, he finally kisses me! He starts gentle, but within seconds the gentle is gone. We are both kissing each other with a fierceness that is unlike anything we've experienced before.

Without even realizing it, my legs are wrapped around his waist and I am in his lap. After a while, we both need to come up for air, and while we gather ourselves he places small kisses on the corners of my mouth, my forehead, my chin, my nose, and both cheeks.

I have never felt so cherished.

"Baby, I promise you I will never walk away again. I will never hurt you again as long as I live. I don't know if I am worthy of your love or your forgiveness, but it makes me feel like more of a man than I have ever felt to know that you are giving me both. I love you so damn much, Gracie. I love you so much it scares the shit out of me. I don't ever want to let go of us."

"Don't let go then."

And there it is...one of those precious dimples pops out and I feel like all is right in the world again.

"I don't plan on it."

We sit on our bench and watch the October sun set. We lean on each other like we should have been doing these last couple of weeks.

We continue to talk, and Jonathan says that he finally realizes that he needs to see somebody about losing his mom and Matt, and also about this recent shooting. He plans on making an appointment to talk to somebody in the morning. He also says that he thinks he should apologize to Ireland for being MIA these last couple weeks, but I tell him to stop beating himself up and that she's four. She knew he had been hurt and was recovering.

Although it does mean a lot that he would think to offer this to her, there is no need to confuse her when she really had no idea that there was anything wrong to begin with.

We finally head back to my mom's once the moon is shining above us and we get home in time for Ireland's bedtime routine. We've both agreed that we have to take things slow and not jump right into sleep-overs again. We need to show respect to my mom and then Mick once we're back at his place. It's something that I know is important, but it's hard when all I want is to fall asleep in his arms every night. But knowing he's out there, that he's mine, and if all goes well he will never walk away again, is enough for now.

After Ireland is in bed and Jonathan has gone for the night, I finally take the time to unzip the bag he brought me from Mick's. As I unzip the bag, I catch a glimpse of colorful ribbon. I reach in to find that there are several little gift bags with what looks to be a card on the very top. I take the envelope out and it isn't a card but a handwritten note from Jonathan that says...

Gracie, I am so sorry that I missed your birthday.
I just want you to know that you are perfect to me.
I know you don't need a man by your side to make you strong, but I
sure hope to have you by my side so you can make me stronger.
You are the smartest person I have ever met.
You have a compassionate heart.
You are independent and capable.
Your smile lights up every room and you make everybody around you
feel better just by being in your presence.
You have a grace about you that I cannot explain in words.
You are such a good momma and such a great friend.
You are beautiful inside and out.
You are perfect.

Happy birthday to the most perfect woman I know.
All my love,
Georgia

Once I gather myself and wipe away the tears, I reach into the bag and pull out the first of many gift bags.

Wrapped in plastic, to keep them fresh, is a bouquet of a dozen birthday cake cake pops! They're put together like a bouquet of flowers with ribbon tying them together. He had to have gone to multiple Starbucks to find all of these. I love it! The next bag has the most beautiful mug with a dragonfly on it. Next is an assortment of every kind of sticky note that you can even imagine. Every shape, size, and color. It seems silly, but all of these little things just shows how well he knows me.

He gets me.

There is also a Portland Police Department t-shirt with a note that says he would rather I wear his shirt instead of my brother's, and that now I have a shirt to alternate with the USMC shirt I 'stole' from him way back when. He also gifts me a bag of fishies, because everybody needs fishies in their life. It's kind of adorable that he has adopted Ireland's name for his favorite snack food.

The final gift is a framed picture of myself and Ireland at the zoo. It was from the moment where we took a break and sat in the grass to watch the hawk demonstration on the main stage. Ireland is in my lap, and she's kissing my cheek. The smile on my face has to be one of the biggest I have ever smiled, and I am so thankful that he captured the moment.

He isn't in the picture, but part of the reason I was so happy that day was because he was with us. Even though it's only the two of us in this picture, I can't help but think of him when I look at it.

This was the day my world starting coming together and I started to love and live again. This picture makes me realize how thankful I am to have him in my life.

How did I get so lucky?

34

———————

Jonathan

With *our* album playing through my earbuds, I'm running for my life on this damn treadmill. My eyes are burning as the sweat pours off of my head and down my face. I look down and see I've already run seven miles on today's penance run.

I'm sure I am pushing harder than the doctors would like, but I don't even realize how long I've been at it. My mind is going a million miles an hour as I think about everything that Emily and I talked about last night. I'm still in shock at the way things went and the unwavering support she gave me even after my bullshit behavior.

Promising to never walk away from her again was the easiest promise I've ever made to another person or myself. My time apart from her was a misery I don't ever want to experience again. I should have let her in. I didn't, yet she still never quit on me. She texted and called every day...she left fishies on my front porch...she never gave up on me. I will spend the rest of my life doing the same for her, and proving to her that her trust and support was worth it.

I've known for a long time that I needed to talk to somebody about all the nightmares that still tend take over from time to time since losing Shell and Mom. I was in such a dark place. My nightmares didn't only come while I slept, they were always on my mind.

Finding Emily again gave me such light that I was foolish enough to think that she was the salve to all my problems; that life would be perfect just because she was in it. It's true that it's pretty damn close to perfect. But I still have shit to work through, and if it means going to a shrink so that life with Emily and Ireland can be that much better, then that's what I'll do. I could tell when I offered to go talk to somebody that she was relieved that she didn't have to ask me to go herself. I think it's been clear to everybody but me that I needed some help.

First thing this morning, I called Noah Caldwell to get the name of his shrink. I know it's helped him deal with his shooting from last year. I already have an appointment for tomorrow morning.

I haven't been medically cleared to go back to work yet, and I really shouldn't have anything to do with Emily's case, but I can't not try to help figure this shit out. No more sitting on my ass. Getting to the gym today was step two in getting my shit back together. I got my girl back, and now I need to make sure I keep her.

Offering to talk to somebody was hard, but not as hard as agreeing to slowing things down and not having 'sleepovers'. I get it, I do, but now that I have her in my life I hate to be away from her for even five minutes. I miss her when she's only in the next room so agreeing to not spend my nights with her was one of the hardest things I've ever done.

I get that she lives with her brother and she's trying to be respectful. I really do get it. It sucks, but I get it.

Right now she's at her mom's and she wants to be respectful to her as well. I know she doesn't want to confuse Ireland, but what is there to confuse her about? I love her momma, and I'm not going anywhere, so she might as well get used to me being around. We will have to have a sleepover at my place soon or I may go bat-shit crazy. It's not about the sex, I just sleep so much better with her there. I didn't have a nightmare at all the week Mick was gone. I can't say the same since the night of the wedding.

Between the sound of *Kings of Leon* in my ears, the pounding of my feet on the treadmill and my mind that won't shut off, I almost don't notice the sound of the call coming in. I look down and see that it's from an *unknown* number. I almost don't answer, but my gut tells me I should.

"Hello?"

"Officer Kelly?" says the scared voice on the other end of the line.

I instantly hit the STOP button on the treadmill, and hop off the machine and make my way to the front doors of the building. I have no idea who this is, or what they are going to say, but I know it's about my girls. I just know it is.

"Yes, this is Officer Kelly, who's this?"

"Uh sir, this is Jesse Miller. You came by my house a few weeks back. You said you were friends with Miss Jacobs?"

My heart drops to my stomach because I know this is the call we've been waiting for. I can't let him know how important it is to me so I try my best to play it cool.

"Hi Jesse, how's it going?" I try to ask casually and not like my sanity hangs on his every word.

"Uh...Officer Kelly?"

"I'm right here, Jesse, and please call me Jonathan."

"Oh okay."

"You okay, Jesse? Is everything okay with you and your brother? Miss Jacobs was real excited to see you in class yesterday. Glad you made it back to school, Jesse. That's great news."

"Yeah, it's great to be back, sir. Things are fine for me and my brother. I...uh...I called to talk about Miss Jacobs."

I think my heart might burst through my rib cage any second as I wait to hear what he has to say. I want to pull the information out of this kid's head, but I know I need to let him go at his pace.

"Okay, what's up?"

"Well, I heard that she's been getting some threats and that maybe somebody might have broken into her house?"

"Who told you that, Jesse?"

"Well, the person who says they've been doing it. Is it true?"

"It is, Jesse."

"Shit."

"Jesse, please tell me who's doing this to her," I plead to him as calmly as I can.

"I was hoping it wasn't true. Poor Miss Jacobs."

"Jesse..."

"Sir...it's my cousin...Kayla...Kayla Simmons."

"Why would she want to do this to Miss Jacobs?"

"I can't believe she would do this, but she told me all about it. After Miss Jacobs helped me, her boyfriend, Austin, wouldn't stop talking about her. He had always talked about her, but after what she did for me he kinda went off about how awesome she was. I think she's jealous of her, sir."

"Did she tell you anything else?"

"She just told me how she and Austin happened to be at the zoo when Miss Jacobs was there with her daughter. She thought it was funny to try and scare her with the picture. I guess Austin didn't see them and had no idea she had gotten the picture when he went to get food. She said she left notes at first, but then when Miss Jacobs gave Austin her number, that was when it wasn't funny anymore and she was pissed. She thinks that she and Austin are going to get married. If they break up, her chances at a happy life end and it will be all Miss Jacobs fault. I know Miss Jacobs only gave her number to Austin because she was worried about him. It's not like that, Officer...I mean, Jonathan."

"I know it's not, Jesse. Thank you so much for calling. I know it has to be hard to call when Kayla is family."

"Miss Jacobs is awesome and when Kayla told me what she did to her little girl's room, I knew I had to tell somebody. I am so sorry. I didn't know until last night. If I had known sooner I would have called, I swear."

"Don't worry about it, Jesse. You called and you have no idea how much we appreciate it. Do you mind sharing what you told me with other officers if we need you to?"

"Not at all, sir."

"Are you at school today?"

"Yes."

"Is Kayla at school today?"

"Yes, sir."

"Okay, thank you, Jesse. Now get back to class and don't say anything to anybody about any of this. Can you do that for me?"

"No problem. I haven't told anybody. Austin is gonna freak out. He has no idea and he's gonna feel so bad that any of this could have had to do with him. I'm so sorry for Miss Jacobs. Please tell her that for me?"

"I will, Jesse. Thanks for calling and I'll be in touch."

I'm not sure how I got here, but when I hang up I find myself pacing in the middle of *The Gym* parking lot. I'm still sweating and I'm filled with so much relief, anger and anxiety that I don't even know what to do with myself. I know I need to start making calls, but my brain and my body are trying to calm itself and process the information I was just given.

I bend over with my hands on my knees and breathe. I give myself two or three seconds and then run to my truck. I hop in and call Blackburn who should be sitting outside Emily's classroom right now. I tell him what's going on, and to just sit tight and not to let Emily know anything is up yet. I am ten minutes away and I need to be the person that tells her.

I call Mick next.

"What's up, Kelly?"

"Mick, we got her."

"What do you mean her?"

"Kayla Simmons. She's a student at the school and dates one of Emily's SPED students. It's all about jealousy, Mick. The kid she dates, Austin, has no idea. Her cousin is Jesse Miller. He called and told me." I know I'm rambling. I hope I'm making sense.

"This is all over something as stupid as a student being jealous over a teacher? What the fuck is wrong with kids these days?"

"I don't know, Mick, it's complete bullshit but at least we have an answer. I already called Blackburn at the school and he's notifying the principal. I'm on my way over there right now."

"Thanks, Kelly. I'll notify Detectives and we'll get somebody over to the school ASAP. I'll see you there."

I drop my phone in my cup holder and thank God that Mick is cool about me and Emily. It sure is making all of this so much easier. I'm a sweaty mess, but I don't even care right now. I just want to get to her and tell her that the nightmare is hopefully over. I know it will be hard for her to hear it's a student, but hopefully, there will be some relief as well and life can start to go back to normal.

My adrenaline hasn't calmed during the drive to the school. I grab the towel in my gym bag and try to wipe off some of the sweat, but in reality, I'm taking this time to collect myself before I talk to her. I need to be her strength; somebody she can lean on. I can't go in there all amped up. I need to be calm for her. I want to run through the front doors and into her classroom, but I know that I need to wait until her current class is over.

I make my way to her room and Blackburn is there. He quietly fills me in and tells me that Sgt. Callahan is on his way along with Detectives. Sgt. Callahan has been a friend of Emily's dad since they started on the force, and I'm sure that he's been keeping her dad up to date with what's happening. I just hope her dad doesn't show up. Emily isn't ready to see him right now if all the ignored text messages are any indication. I'm afraid that if he showed up today it might be too much for her.

There's still twenty minutes left in Emily's class, and she has no idea I'm here. I wait with Blackburn in the hall where she can't see us. By the time the bell rings, Mick, Sgt. Callahan, and Detective's Fred Wills and Matt Gilbert have arrived and are in the office with the principal. I'm glad they're in the office and not all standing here when the bell rings. I think that would overwhelm her.

The bell rings and I step aside to wait for the kids to file out. Once I see it's just Emily and Mrs. Colyer, I step inside the room. Her face lights up the moment she sees me, but falls as soon as she registers the serious look on my face. It's obvious by my appearance that I came here in a rush.

"What's wrong, Jonathan? Is Ireland okay?"

"She's fine. Everything is fine, baby," I say as I take her hand.

"Why are you here then?"

"We know who it is, Em."

"Who?" Emily and Mrs. Colyer both ask at the same time.

I look over my shoulder to make sure that there aren't any kids in the room and fill them both in on my call from Jesse earlier.

Emily has tears streaming down her face, but she isn't making a sound. Mrs. Colyer hands her some tissues and tells her to take the rest of the day and as long as she needs. As kids start to gather, she pulls herself together, and by the time Jesse enters the room you wouldn't even know that there is anything wrong. It saddens me to think that this comes from years of practice.

35

———

Emily

I have so many questions running through my head, but with the students quickly filling up the room, I know that now isn't the time. I also have so many feelings reeling through me that it's hard to keep myself in check in front of the students. I feel relief in knowing who it is and hopefully, the madness is about to end, but I also feel bad for Austin and Jesse. Jesse had to rat out his cousin, and I know that Austin is going to feel awful about this.

I can't help but feel that some of this is my fault. Did I cross a line with Austin? I don't think that I did, and I don't think he had feelings for me other than maybe a little hero worship, but now I'm so worried that I crossed a line without knowing it. I'll have to talk to him about that but now is not that time.

"Hey Miss J. Who's this?"

"Hi, Austin. This is my boyfriend, Jonathan."

"Oh, hey."

Jonathan reaches out his hand. "Nice to meet you Austin. I've heard a lot of great things about you."

"Really? Thanks, Miss J." he says as he extends his hand to Jonathan but sends a big smile full of pride in my direction.

"Of course, you're a great kid and you know that. Where's Jesse? Did he not come back today?"

"He's here, but not sure where he is right now. He must be running late."

As if on cue, Jesse enters the room. As soon as he sees Jonathan in the room he nearly comes to a complete halt, but then catches himself and continues across the room to where he usually sits with Austin.

"Hi, Miss J."

"Hey there, Jess. I know that I already told you this but it's great to see you back at school."

"Thanks," he mumbles while looking down at the ground.

Austin gets distracted by a friend and steps away. I take this moment to say a few words to Jesse.

Quietly, so only Jesse can hear I say, "Jesse, thank you so much for what you've done. I know it must have been hard. I hope you know how much I appreciate you risking trouble with your family for my daughter and me."

His face turns bright red with embarrassment. He gives me a slight nod and then sits down in his chair. This is my sign that he's heard me, but would like the conversation to be over. I respect his wishes and step away.

"Mrs. Colyer, if you don't mind, I think I will take you up on your offer and leave for the day."

"Of course. You two get out of here."

I grab my purse, my jacket and Jonathan's hand and we walk out of the classroom. The moment we exit the room, we take a couple of steps into the hallway and Jonathan squeezes my hand and pulls me to a stop.

He bends his knees to lower himself to my eye level and asks, "Baby, you okay?"

I let out a heavy sigh and look into the most beautiful pair of eyes I have ever seen. "I'm okay, just glad that this whole mess will hopefully be over soon. Besides, I have you to hold on to so I know that everything will be okay in the end."

Jonathan leans forward, and whispers in my ear. "Damn straight, baby. There's no getting rid of me. I'm here for the long haul so I'm glad you're good with it. Now, let's get out of here."

As we walk towards the front doors, we pass a set of parents that don't look too happy to be paying the school a visit. I can't help but follow them over my shoulder to see them enter the office and be greeted by Sgt. Callahan.

Jonathan leans towards me and says, "Kayla's parents you think?"

"Must be."

We cross the lot to Jonathan's truck and he helps me up and into the cab.

He takes my hand, kisses the back of it and says, "Don't go anywhere. I'll be right back."

Thinking he's running back into the school, I'm surprised when he runs around the front of the truck and then jumps into the driver's side of the cab.

"I'm back!"

He looks like a kid on Christmas morning and those dimples are on full display. There's a twinkle in his eye as he leans over the console and I know what he's going to say before he gets the words out. I don't stop him because, to be honest, I love it every time he does it.

"Gracie, I'm going to kiss you now."

And to say he kisses me is an understatement. As always, that connection that we have shoots through me and he fills me with warmth. That warmth that always comforts me all the way down to my toes. His lips tell me exactly what he wants me to know, and I can feel his love and want with every touch.

He releases my lips, leans his forehead against mine and says, "Let's go for a little field trip. What do you say? Ireland is with your mom, so let's go for a drive."

"Sure. If it will make you happy, and I get some alone time with you, then a drive it is."

We end up at the Rose Gardens and have a perfect view of Portland with Mt. Hood off in the distance. Even though it's a cold and rainy day and the mountain isn't completely visible, it's still beautiful.

Just as he shuts the truck off, he gets a text and reads the gist of it off to me.

"Mick says that Kayla got scared and confessed to the whole thing. Since she's been eighteen for the last six months, she will have some serious charges to face. To sum it up, she won't be bothering you anymore, Em."

Jonathan hops out of the truck and comes around to my side. He opens the door and takes my hand. I think he's going to take me for a walk, but instead, he opens the back door on my side.

"Get in, babe, I want to hold you in my arms, and that just won't work up front."

"Jonathan Kelly, are we parking? Are you trying to get me in the back seat to take advantage of me?" I ask in mock horror.

"Oh, Miss Jacobs, nothing would please me more, but I am not sure today is the day for that. Right now I just want to hold you and celebrate your safety and peace of mind. Now get in, baby."

I do as I'm told, and true to his word he holds me and we talk. He apologizes for not taking a shower before coming to get me, but I don't mind a sweaty, salty Jonathan at all. He doesn't try to take advantage of me. He is the perfect gentleman. I can tell he's afraid to make any moves that might push me further than he thinks I'm ready for, and this just makes me love him even more.

After a couple of hours in the back of his truck, we agree it's time to go.

Just as we're about to move to the front seat, I get a text from Austin.

AUSTIN

Miss J, I just want to say how sorry I am. I had no idea what Kayla had been doing. If I had known, I would have stopped her or told you. I hope you are okay?

MISS JACOBS

I'm fine, Austin. Thank you so much but it's not your fault.

"Poor kid. I knew he would feel bad," I sigh.

"He'll be okay, Em." Jonathan tries to assure me.

"I know he will, but I still feel bad for him. I feel like I did something somehow to cause all of this."

Jonathan opens the truck door and jumps out onto the pavement to help me out.

"All you did was care and offer support. You didn't do anything wrong, and I don't want you to dwell on it." He opens the passenger door, and as I walk in front of him to climb in he slaps me on my ass. "Now, get that sweet ass of yours in my truck!"

I don't know why, but I have the most random thought.

I let out a gasp at my thoughtlessness and ask, "Jonathan, I can't believe I never asked!"

"What are you so excited about?" He asks entertainingly confused.

"Your truck...don't you always name your trucks?"

He gives a sly little smile and says, "I do. Is that what you're so excited about?"

"Well, what's her name?" I squeal.

He throws his head back and burst out laughing.

"Well?"

"Oh baby, you are too cute." He leans in and kisses my temple. "Helen, her name is Helen."

"Helen?" I say perplexed. This is not what I expected.

"Yes, Helen. She's sexy and silver. So I went with Helen for Helen Mirren. There's no denying she's a sexy older woman; a female version of a 'silver fox'."

I can't help the fit of giggles that escapes me. He never ceases to surprise me—I think that's why it tickles me more than it should. He's strong, supportive and silly all at the same time. He's perfect. It's in this fit of laughter that I realize it's time to let him know that he doesn't need to remain a gentleman. I'm ready to be taken advantage of.

"Hey, Georgia?"

"Yes?"

"Can we go back to your place?"

He just looks at me with a smile on his face and one eyebrow raised, and I know he knows what I'm asking with my request. To confirm that he understood just what I'm implying, he grabs me by the waist, places me in my seat, stretches my seat belt around me and buckles me in. He doesn't say much on the way home, but I don't think I have ever seen him drive so fast.

Walking into Jonathan's house reminds me of the last time I was here. That day was so full of joy and passion. Jonathan did everything he could to bring back what we had in California.

That was also the first time he talked to me about Matt and his mom. He opened up to me that day, and even though in the back of my mind I knew that I belonged to him, that was the night that it became concrete. I remember being afraid to speak those three little words to him that night.

Unfortunately, it took his shooting for me to finally confess my love to him. I learned a valuable lesson sitting there in that hospital, waiting for him to wake up. That lesson was to never hold back and to always let those you love know what they mean to you. I don't plan to let any more days go by that Jonathan doesn't know how much I love him.

When we walk into the house we're greeted by a very excited Frances. I squat down and give her the attention she's looking for while Jonathan slides his truck keys onto the counter. Once I'm standing back up, he gets her attention and opens up the back door for her. He says he wants to take a quick shower and asks me to let Frances back in when she's ready.

She's an old gal, and it takes her some time, but she finally comes back to the door so I can let her in. I've just finished drying her wet paws off when I turn around and Jonathan is in front of me, already showered and dressed in clean clothes. That must have been the fastest shower in the history of all showers.

"I'm so glad to have you here again, Em," he says as he walks toward me.

Wasting no time, I take him by the hand and lead him to his bedroom. When we enter, I flip the switch for the fireplace and walk over to turn on his low lit light next to the bed, just like he did the last time I was here. I stand him next to the bed and continue to take the lead.

"Jonathan, I know you're trying to take it slow and ease back into things after our time apart."

I grab the hem of his fresh shirt and lift it over his head.

"You are being a total gentleman, and you didn't even make any moves while we 'parked' today," I add, as I kick off my flats, and then unbutton his jeans. He's barely breathing and hanging on my every word. My every move.

"I appreciate that and it means the world to me, but just because we can't have any sleepovers doesn't mean that we need to take *everything* slow."

I pull his jeans down his strong thighs and gently push him back onto the bed. He falls back but sits up on his elbows to watch the rest of the show. I pull his jeans the rest of the way down his legs and drop them to the floor. He seems to have been in a rush to get dressed because he's going commando and is now completely naked.

To see this beautiful man laid out before me is a sight to see. He is a perfect specimen, and I could study every lean muscle on his body, but we'll save that for later. He still hasn't said a word, but his eyes haven't left mine once, and I can tell he's listening intently to every word that I am saying to him.

From my standing position in front of him, I pull my shirt over my head and make sure that he's looking at me when I say, "I'm here Jonathan. I'm not going anywhere. I don't want to waste any more time away from you or hiding how I feel about you." I tell him this with all the conviction that I feel in my heart. I pull my pants off and stand before him in just my bra and panties. "I have only been in love with one person in my entire life, and that person is you. I know how lucky we are to have a second chance. I'll do whatever you need so that you know just how much I love you."

I crawl onto the bed, rest my body on top of his and kiss him with everything I have. I pour all the love that I can into this kiss so that he has no doubt how I feel about him. After a few glorious minutes, I whisper in his ear. "Make love to me, Georgia."

Without words, he spends the next few hours showing me just how much he loves, wants and needs me. I have never felt so cherished.

36

Jonathan

It's the night before Thanksgiving and I couldn't be happier.

I have my girls here with me in my hometown of Savannah. To top it all off, we're sitting in the Fanuas living room. Emily sits next to me on the love seat while Ireland snuggles up to me on my lap. She's tired from the long day of travel, and I have a feeling she's going to be asleep sooner rather than later.

I have everybody I care about in the world in one room. The only people that are missing are Devon and Gabby, but we'll chat tomorrow, and I'll spend part of Christmas with them.

Emily and Ireland seem to be a perfect fit with the Fanua clan. This doesn't surprise me at all because these two are special. They light up any room that they walk into and always seem to bring a smile to everybody's face.

I couldn't be more proud both to introduce them to my family, and to have these amazing people in my life to share with the two of them. I just wish my mom was here. She would love them both. This I know for sure.

As we all sit around and talk, I keep getting knowing smiles from Fiona and winks from Robert. I can see the joy that they have for me in their eyes. It's just as obvious to them, as it is to me, that I have found *the one.*

Emily is it for me, and this little girl slowly falling asleep in my arms brings me so many different emotions all at once. There is a fierce protectiveness that I feel for her that is different from what I feel for her mother. Knowing that the things I help Emily teach her will mold her into the person she'll grow up to be is a huge responsibility, but one that I hope Emily will continue to let me take on alongside her. She also brings me a peace I never knew children could bring.

After years of not feeling much at all, this has been a big change for me, but in only the best of ways.

Emily looks at Ireland—who has her head tucked into my neck so that I can't see her face—and mouths, "She's asleep."

Quietly, I announce to the room that it's time to put Ireland to bed. I rise from the love seat as smoothly as I can to try not to wake her.

"We'll be right back," Emily says as she gives a little wave and follows me down the hall while holding on to one of the belt loops of my jeans.

Bliss.

These simple moments with them bring me pure bliss. I know that makes me sound all girly, but I just can't think of another word to describe it.

Fiona has put Emily and Ireland in Liam's old room that now serves as a guest room. Traditional as always, Fiona has me sleeping on the fold out couch. It's not ideal, but I get it. Emily and Ireland are sharing a double bed as it is. There isn't room for me anyway. And there is still the no sleepover rule.

We haven't been perfect at sticking to this rule. Cami and Alex have both hooked us up several times over the last month, and have had Ireland over for sleepovers. Thank God for Cami and Alex!

Emily and I work together to get Ireland out of her clothes and into her adorable Thanksgiving pajamas that Mick got her.

Who would have thought that Mick Jacobs would be a part of my day to day life? If you had told me that the badass, frat brother, player that I work with, and occasionally drink with, would one day become family, I wouldn't have believed it.

It turns out he's a pretty good guy and not just the comedian, and sometimes asshole, that he lets us all see. His family comes first to him, and he has been incredibly good to Emily and Ireland. Never once has he made them feel like they are an inconvenience or in his way. He treats his mom like gold and would welcome her into his home to live with open arms if she asked. He's a good dude. He has been nothing but cool about Emily and I seeing each other.

We had one talk—shortly after Kayla was arrested—where he gave me the typical big brother lecture. He told me that her happiness comes first, and that I better not get too close if I didn't plan on this being the real deal. There were two hearts in my hands, and not just one. I assured him I was in this for the long haul and that on my part, there wouldn't be any heart-breaking going on. Since that little chat, my relationship with his sister has never been a topic of conversation.

Looking down at Ireland all tucked in with her stuffed bulldog—that she of course named Frank Junior—I can't help but smile. She is so stinking cute with those big brown eyes and those blond curls. I never knew what a button nose was until this kid came along and proved to me that they do exist. She has one and it's perfect. Right now, her cheeks are a bit rosy from the warmth of being cuddled up with me, and her hair is sticking to her sweaty little face. Perfect.

Even when she has those brief episodes where she actually

acts like a four-year-old and gets whiny, she is still perfect and stubborn just like her momma.

After she's all tucked in, I walk around the bed to Emily and pull her to me and give her a soft kiss. Much to my pleasure, this doesn't seem to be enough for her as she grabs my ass with both hands.

I love it when she gets feisty, she is sexy and adorable all wrapped up in one. She pulls me as close to her as she can get me, and she deepens the kiss. Her hands roam up my back and then back to my ass. Our kisses become fevered and frenzied and she starts to moan. She moves her hand to the front of my pants and grabs onto my rapidly hardening cock.

God, this sucks.

All I want to do is push her up against the wall and make her scream because I've made her blackout in ecstasy. But that isn't possible with Ireland a few feet away and a house full of family waiting for us in the other room.

I put my hand over her very busy one, and move it back to my ass and whisper in her ear. "Baby, we have to stop. We're gonna wake Ireland up, and I really cannot go walking out there with a rock hard dick. You aren't playing fair, Em."

She kisses me on my nose then steps away from me and says, "Okay," then walks out of the room. Leaving me there to deal with the tent I'm currently pitching, all on my own. She knew exactly what she was doing. Wicked woman.

After taking the time I need to get my shit together, I walk back out to the family room and it's happening. The damn photo albums are out, and Emily is at Fiona's side on the couch as they go through my childhood, picture by picture. Not only does Fiona have all of her family albums—that include me almost as much as her own kids—but she has all of my mom's too. Well, I guess in all actuality they're mine but wasn't ready to bring them with me when I left for Portland.

As I stand in the middle of the room with my arms crossed over my chest, Fiona and Emily both pretend I'm not in the room, but I see Emily peek up at me and try to contain her giggle that wants to break free.

From his perch on the arm of the couch Liam says, "Dude, it was just a matter of time. You should never have left them alone together. They're gonna be at this all night. Wanna beer?"

All night ends up only being about thirty minutes and Robert, Liam and I use this time to catch up and talk sports while nursing our beers. After the ladies have finished up, they join us at the kitchen table just long enough for Fiona to give out her to do list for the morning. After her marching orders have been delivered, she says her good nights since she'll be up early to put the turkey in. Robert follows on her heels, and since Kate is out with her boyfriend, that just leaves Emily, Liam, and myself.

"So, Emily, tell me something," Liam says as he leans towards her like they're planning some sort of conspiracy together.

"Liam..." I warn.

"Yes, Liam?" Emily says as she leans back in her chair with her eyebrows raised. She has a grin on her face and her arms spread out on the back of my chair and the empty one to her left. Her whole demeanor says, 'bring it on, big man'. God, I love this woman!

"So tell me the truth. How do you put up with this pretty-boy shit-head?"

Keeping a straight face, she replies. "Love and hard work, Liam...love and hard work. If I'm honest with you, I ask myself that same question every day. The only thing I can come up with is that I love him and I'm prepared for a lot of hard work."

Sitting there with my mouth hanging open she reaches a hand to my face and strokes it tenderly.

"As you said, he is very pretty, Liam. Sometimes it takes everything I have to leave the house and go out in public with him, knowing that every woman he passes by will be staring at him and thinking that they want to have his babies. It's a tough job, but somebody has to do it."

She stops and uses both hands to turn my face in Liam's direction.

"I mean look at this face, for God's sake. He just wakes up...and looks like this...every freakin' day! Do you know how much work it takes to be worthy of being seen on his arm? It's exhausting; having arm candy like this. It really is. As for him being a shit-head, do not get me started..."

Putting my arm gently around her neck, I pull Emily against me like I am going to give her a noogie. But I just kiss it instead and put an end to the bullshit that is spewing from her mouth.

"Enough already! You guys think you're pretty damn funny, don't you? Well, you aren't." Pushing Emily back a bit, I look at her and say, "You're cute, but you aren't funny. And you..." I say moving my attention to Liam. "...You aren't funny or cute, so just shut your face if you know what's good for you."

Liam stands to leave, and Emily and I stand with him.

"Whatever dude, I'll see you in the morning. You better be careful. I think I'm starting to like her more than I like you. Emily, you're good for this moron. Thanks for keeping his ass in check."

"Keeping his ass in check is my pleasure, Liam," she says as she holds her hand up. Just like they're long lost friends, he gives her the high-five she's looking for.

Emily and her damn high-fives. It should get old but it doesn't. I love that she loves them.

It's fucking adorable.

"No sneaking into her room tonight, Johnny Boy. Keep your stupid self on the couch or mom will kick your ass. You know she will," Liam snarks as he walks out the front door and shuts it behind him.

Of course, he had to leave with some smart-ass, older brother type comment. That's the way it's always been with us. Best friends and brothers to the end. To be honest, I would expect nothing less from him.

Alone for the first time all day, I take advantage of the quiet moment and pull her into my arms and capture her lips with my own. I kiss her as tenderly as I can, doing my best not to go too far, because unfortunately, Liam is right. I do have to sleep on the couch. Pulling my lips from her kills me, but it must be done.

I take her beautiful face in my hands and say, "Thank you so much for coming here and leaving your family on your first Thanksgiving home. I know it's also your first in Portland since Ireland was born. I hope you know how much it means to me."

"Jonathan, they're amazing and I'm really glad Ireland and I got to come and meet them. I still feel bad about the cost of the last-minute plane tickets though. It's way too much and I wish that I could pay you back."

"Baby, having you here with them is worth every penny. It's important that you get to know what little bit of family I have left. They're important to me. You and Ireland are important to me. It means so much to have you all together. Thank you for giving me this."

"Ah honey, thank you right back. I don't want to be anywhere else. As long as I have you and my baby girl in there, I'm right where I need to be."

It's amazing how far she's come, and how open she is with her feelings since the shooting. It feels good to know that I was the one that was able to break down her walls. That she trusts me enough to be this open and to tell me how she feels. I will never take for granted how much it means for her to give me that.

She starts to lead me down the hall and we stop outside the guest room. It feels like I am dropping her off at her parent's front door as I prepare to say goodnight to her.

She leans against the wall next to the door and whispers. "Don't I get a kiss goodnight?"

I lean in and her kiss on the cheek and whisper in her ear. "Goodnight, Gracie."

Then I let go of her hand and walk backward down the hall. She smiles and shakes her head slowly as if she finds me funny. I do catch her bringing her hand to her face where I left my kiss as she opens the bedroom door and closes it behind her.

I swear to God there is nothing better than making that woman smile. Okay, there is one other thing...but making her smile is a damn close second.

The next morning, I wake up to sounds in the kitchen. I look at the time on the cable box and it says that it's only 5:54 in the morning. I can hear Fiona humming away while she prepares the turkey, and can't be mad for being awake so early. I love the sounds of this house and the people in it.

I throw the blanket back, stretch and yawn myself awake. I take a minute to put the couch back together and then head to the kitchen to see if I can give her a hand. I plan on stealing a cup of coffee while I'm at it.

When I get to the kitchen, I see Robert is up too and pouring himself a cup. When he sees me, he hands me the full cup and then gets another for himself. We both head to the kitchen table and take a seat and a few sips before anybody says anything.

"She's a pretty great girl, Jonathan," Robert says quietly so he doesn't wake the rest of the house. He's the only real dad I've ever known, and my heart swells with pride to hear him say this.

"She is. I can't believe I found her again," I reply quietly as well.

"It's because she's your soul mate, sweetie. I knew it the moment I laid eyes on the two of you together. It was meant to be," Fiona says softly from the kitchen counter where she's stuffing the turkey.

"I know she is. She's *the one.* I knew the first moment I laid eyes on her years ago in California. I've always known. There was nobody else for me after I met her."

"What are you gonna do about it, son?" Robert asks.

"Well, she scares easily so I have to be careful. It's all happened so fast and I don't want to say too much, but I have some ideas. I love her and I love that little girl of hers. I never knew it could be like this. I know to the rest of the world this is fast, but to me, I feel like I've been waiting for years. I don't want to waste another minute. I want us to be a family, and waiting until I think she's ready is killing me. If I had my way we'd already be married, but I'm scared to even say the "M" word around her. I just don't know how she feels about marriage after what she went through with her parents."

"Then you need to talk to her and feel out the situation, son. You never know. She might just surprise you," Robert says with one of his famous winks.

"He's right. When you meet the one you were meant to be with things change and ideas you always had about how life should go fall to the wayside. When love takes over, there isn't a wrong or right timeline. Just go slow enough for her, but not so slow that it kills you. You know her better than anybody. You'll figure it out," Fiona says while working her magic on our Thanksgiving Day feast.

"Thank you both. It means a lot to me to have them here with us. I hope you know that."

"We do, son, and we're happy to have them both here too. I hope to have them around for a long time to come," Robert says and warms my heart in a way that only he can.

"After we get our list of stuff done, I was thinking I would take the girls to meet mom. What do you think?"

"Sweetheart, I think that is a beautiful idea. Why don't you leave Ireland here though? She might still be just a little too young to understand all that. Besides, it will give you and Emily some alone time. We'd be happy to watch Ireland if Emily's okay with it."

I get up, walk around the big kitchen island and give Fiona a kiss on the cheek.

"Thank you. I don't know what I would do without either of you. Liam I could do without, but you two I'll keep."

I give Fiona a big grin and Robert one of his winks back to him, then head to the bathroom to change and go for a run before the girls are up. It may be November, but the weather here this early in the morning is already around sixty. Perfect weather for a run.

When I get back, I hear the sweet voice of my little Princess coming from the kitchen. She's sitting on a stool at the breakfast bar chatting Fiona's ear off while she eats cereal in her pajamas. She is so freaking cute I can hardly stand it. This little girl has taken hold of my heart and will not let go.

She sees Fiona's eyes flicker my way. She follows her gaze and spots me and yells, "Jonafon!" She points to the shirt of her pajama's and says, "Gobble, gobble," just like her shirt says.

I kiss the top of her head and say, "Happy Thanksgiving to you too, Princess! Did you sleep well?"

"I did. Too bad you had to sleep on the couch. Mommy and I have a comfy bed and got to snuggle."

"You have no idea how jealous of you I am, sweet girl. Speaking of your momma, where is she?"

Ireland's mouth is now full of sugary goodness so Fiona interjects. "She's in the shower, honey. Can I get you anything for breakfast?"

"Sure. I'll have what she's having," I say as I take the seat next to Ireland at the breakfast bar.

I hold Emily's hand as we walk from Fiona's car towards my mom. I don't know why, but I feel nervous. I don't know if it's because I wonder if Emily will think this is all a bit strange? I mean it's not every day your boyfriend takes you to a cemetery to introduce you to his dead mother, but this is important to me for some reason. The nerves could also be because I haven't been back here in a couple of years. I have some guilt over that.

I can see her headstone some distance before we get to it, and my emotions start to swell inside of me. Sadness over the loss of my mother. Guilt for being gone so long. Pride in Emily. And joy that I get to share my happiness with the one person who wanted it for me more than anybody else.

We approach the graveside that reads:

Caroline Joy Kelly

Beloved mother, wife, sister, and friend

1965 - 2010

"I'll love you always and forever and wherever I may be."

I slow down and Emily squeezes my hand and asks. "Would you like some time by yourself first? I can go sit on that bench and you can come get me when you're ready if you want."

The love and support in her eyes are what I need to calm my racing heart.

I squeeze her hand back and say, "No, please stay. I'm kind of a mess right now and I'd like it if you stayed."

"I'd love to. Here, let's get this cleaned up a bit," she says as she releases my hand and walks towards mom's headstone. She brushes away all of the leaves and other random pieces of nature that have landed on it. I think it's her way to also give me a minute of space, even though I said I didn't want it. She knows me so well.

Once she's finished, she takes the blanket that's draped across my arm and spreads it out in front of us. She stands there with me waiting for me to make the move to sit. She's leaving this all to me, and not forcing me to do anything I'm not ready to. She lightly rubs her hand up and down my back until I take two steps forward and sit down on the blanket. Joining me, she sits next to me on my side, but turns her body so she's facing me.

The blanket that Fiona sent with us was my mom's favorite. It was a Christmas gift from me my senior year of high school. She uses her hands to flatten it so she can read it clearly, and I can see exactly when she notices the words on it.

"Every night when I was little and she tucked me into to bed, my mom would whisper it to me. It was always a whisper or said into my ear when she hugged me goodbye. I had this blanket made for her my senior year. She loved it. It was in her will that we put these words on her headstone so that every time any of us came to visit, we would remember that she still loves us wherever she may be."

"I think that's beautiful. Your mom sounds like she was a pretty amazing woman, honey."

I just nod in reply because I can't speak. I can feel the emotion taking hold of me and I am not sure that I can keep it in any longer. Emily keeps her eyes trained on mine, and I swear she reaches the deepest parts of my soul with those eyes of hers. She can see that I'm barely hanging on. She reaches over and brushes her hand through my hair. "It's okay to let it out, baby. I'm here. I'll catch you. I'm. Right. Here."

Her words are all it takes to open up the flood gates and my unshed tears begin to fall. She pulls herself closer to me and quietly holds me while I cry. Once the tears start they just won't stop. I'm no longer just crying, I'm sobbing, but she keeps holding on to me. Before I know it she has positioned us so that I'm now lying with my head in her lap and she is stroking my hair.

She doesn't say anything.

She just comforts me with her love and her touch.

"It's been so hard for me to forgive you for not telling me you were sick, mom. You knew when I was home and you didn't tell me. For the longest time I couldn't understand how you could not tell me. I heard the reasons you gave, and they were never enough. But I finally figured it out. If you had done things differently, I probably wouldn't have gone back to California. I wouldn't have met my Gracie. As much as I wish I could have been there for you, Mom, thank you so much for sending me back to California and to the love of my life."

Feeling a little stronger, I raise myself up to sit cross-legged on the blanket. Emily is facing me, but at an angle with her cheek on my shoulder, just letting me have my moment. I turn my head to look at her and she lifts her head so that her eyes meet mine, and I can see the tears that have just started to fall down her cheeks. She smiles at me and puts her head back down on my shoulder.

"Mom, I found it. That love that you always said was out

there waiting for me. I found it and I get it now. You were right, and when you know, you just know. I had to wait over five years to get her back, but she's here Mom."

Another grateful tear falls.

"And not only am I lucky enough to have found *The One,* but she has a beautiful little girl named Ireland. Emily and Ireland... they are what I've been missing, thank God they found me. You would love them both, and it really sucks that they don't get to have you in their lives. You would have been the best Grandma, and I am so sorry you didn't get to experience that."

I turn towards Emily's head on my shoulder and can't help myself when I take a small whiff. I love her smell and don't think I will ever get enough of it.

I feel her shoulders shake when she silently giggles at the move she catches me doing so often.

I have no shame when it comes to her, and don't care who knows it. Yes, I am that guy that has to sniff his girlfriend from time to time. So what?

"Mom, these girls are everything to me. They are both kind, funny and beautiful. Emily is a bit, how should I say it? Independent. She has raised Ireland on her own all these years and Mom, she has done an amazing job. She's the coolest kid I have ever met." I turn so Emily knows my next words are more for her, even if I'm directing them to my mom. "Mom, I'm doing everything I can to let Emily see that it's okay to let somebody take care of her for a change. I know she hates to lean on anybody but herself but I sure hope I can change that."

Emily places a sweet kiss to my forehead, she takes my face in her hands and those sky blue eyes of her search mine. "Jonathan, you've already broken down those walls. You have taught me to trust and to love and to let somebody else take care of me. You did that when nobody else could. I love you and I'm all in. I hope that we take care of each other for a very long time. You're *my* always and forever Jonathan."

"See Mom, she's *the one*. She loves me just like you always dreamed somebody other than you would love me. Life doesn't get much better than this, does it? The only thing missing is you. I miss you so much, Mom."

The tears are back but just tears, I'm able to keep it together this time around.

"Watching the work that Emily puts into being a single parent has given me just a glimpse of how hard it had to have been for you day in and day out taking care of me on your own. Thank you, Mom. Thank you for giving me all the love and support a kid could ever need and for taking such great care of me. I never went without, and I see now how hard you worked to make that happen for me. I love you, mom, and I miss you every day."

I move us so that we're now both lying on our backs with our faces pointed towards the sky, holding hands. No more words are spoken. Eventually, Emily rolls to her side and puts her head on my chest and her leg over mine and I pull her tight into my side. I swear this woman has done more for me and my sanity than any shrink will ever do. She gets me, and she gives me so much more than I can ever give back to her.

Friday morning, the women brave the mall and all the Black Friday shoppers while the three of us men stay home, watch football and continue to recover from our food comas from the day before. I don't know how the girls were all up and out the door at the butt crack of dawn this morning. It was like they didn't have a care in the world while we were all still sleeping.

I only know when they left because Emily came by my

make-shift bed and kissed me on the cheek and ran her hand through my hair before she left. I didn't open my eyes, but I felt it all, and I had sweet dreams for the rest of the morning.

Robert is in his recliner, Liam is hanging off of the love seat, and I'm sprawled out all over the couch when the girls come home hours later. It takes everything I have to pull my comatose ass up to a seated position to greet them. Ireland doesn't give me much choice but to wake up as she runs over to me and jumps into my lap to tell me all about her day. A day that included lots of crazy people at the mall, lots of secret shopping for Christmas presents, lunch at Romano's Macaroni Grill and her first pedicure.

She takes off her shoes and socks and shows me her adorable little pink toenails and tells me how much it tickled. She had 'so much fun'!

"Sounds like you had a great day, Princess. What's in the box?"

She jumps off my lap and grabs the box from the table. It's over half her size and looks like a little house.

"Mrs. Fanua and Kate got me an early birfday present, and it's the best! We went to *Build-A-Bear* and I got to make my own stuftie, Jonafon! I got to pick the bear, and sprinkle all her stuffing with love and then help with the machine while she got stufted. Then, I got to pick an outfit for her. Wanna see?"

"Of course I do. Let's see whatcha got?"

She's talking so fast she can barely breathe and I can't help but chuckle as she digs into the box.

I look up at the girls and they're all watching us with huge smiles on their faces. I figure out why a moment later when Ireland pulls out her stuftie. She's a pink bear with white on the bottom of all four of her paws and she's dressed in a police uniform.

Once again this little girl has me in the palm of her hand and is slowly melting my heart into a big pile of goo. I know she has Mick in her life too, but I still can't put into words how it feels to see this damn bear.

"Wow, Princess, I like her a lot. She's a police bear huh?"

"Yep, just like you and Uncle Mick. Pretty cool, right?"

"The coolest," I say mesmerized by this little girl and everything she makes me feel.

"Tell him what you named her," Emily says from across the room.

"Oooh, you'll like it, Jonafon! You know how mommy calls you Georgia after your state? Well, I named my bear Savannah after your city! Now she has a nickname like the rest of us! Do you like it?"

What in the world is happening to me right now? I think you could knock me over with a feather. This little girl and her damn bear have just rocked my world. I am completely thrown off balance over a stuffed animal that happens to be named after me, and the big brown eyes that are looking up at me for approval.

"Like it? I love it! I think that name is perfect, Princess."

She takes her bear, runs to the guest room and comes back with her stuffed Frank. She sits on the floor and starts introducing the two while she enters her own little world of make-believe.

I get up, walk over to Fiona and Kate, and thank them with hugs. They say it was nothing, and since her birthday is Tuesday and they won't get to be there, it was the least they could do. While talking to them, I feel a hand on my back as Robert steps up next to me.

"That right there son, is what it's all about. You are a lucky man, if I do say so myself."

"Don't I know it," I reply back and catch Emily's eye across the room.

She's standing there with a simple smile on her face. It's a smile that says she loves me without words. Robert couldn't be more right about me being a lucky man. The luckiest if you ask me.

"Dude, she's a ten. She's hot as hell, smart, funny, and puts up with you and your little dick. How the hell did you land her?" Liam says as we drive home from picking up lunch from Chick-fil-A.

"Man, you wish that was true. If Emily was the kiss and tell kind of girl, I'm sure she would clear that shit right up for you. But, like you said, she's a ten and therefore not that kind of girl. To answer your question though, dude, I don't fucking know how I got so lucky. Not just once, but twice. I ask myself that same thing every damn day."

I think Liam can feel the change in the conversation from shit-talking to a bit more serious as he changes his tone.

"She's the one. I can see that, man. Don't fuck it up," he says falling into big brother mode.

"I don't plan on it, but thanks for the vote of confidence and words of wisdom, old wise one."

"I'm not fucking around here, J. She is the shit, and she makes you happy. You haven't been happy in years. She's brought out the old you, and I like it. Even seeing you with Ireland is something I never thought I would see. Not that I didn't ever see you having a family, because I did, but I never would have thought your *one* would mean *two*. Those two are special, and I hope you have plans to make that shit permanent."

Liam Fanua talking about relationships and marriage is new and surprising. It takes me a second to shake it off before I can respond.

"Thanks, Liam. That means a lot especially, coming from a dog like you. I do want to make it permanent. She says she's ready, but I'm still afraid that it's moving too fast and she's not as ready as she thinks she is. I'm working on it, but I can't push too hard or too fast, ya know?"

"No, bro, I don't. Hard and fast is just how I like it, and I don't ever hear any complaints, if you know what I mean." He says as he lifts one of his eyebrows. "So no, I don't know."

"Shut up, you're such an idiot. You do know exactly what I mean, but enough about my love life. What about yours?" I deflect.

"Oh you know, nothin' serious."

"Are you seeing anybody?"

"Oh, I 'see' lots of people, but not one particular person if that's what you mean."

"So, big, bad Liam Fanua isn't ready to settle down, or just hasn't found the one?"

"I don't know if I'll ever be ready, J. There is somebody that I feel like I could give up all the others for, but she hates me and won't give me the time of day. I deserve it. I'm a player, and I played the game with one of her friends a long, long, time ago. She doesn't like what she's heard and won't come near me no matter what I do. It's my own fault, I guess," he says with a shrug of his shoulders.

"That sucks man. Sorry to hear that."

"Ah, well. It is what it is, ya know?" he says with another shrug.

"You know you could always change her mind. Do what it takes to show her what else there is to you. If she's really the one, don't give up man. Let her see that there's more to you than the bullshit you show to most of the world."

Man, he reminds me of Mick. These two men are nothing but good but they don't want the rest of the world to know. They put up this player persona so that they don't have to get too close or too real with anybody. That way when it goes bad, they can make it seem like it's no big deal. The truth of the matter is, whoever they end up with will be lucky to have them.

"Let it go, J. I have. Thanks for caring, dude, but I'm just fine with my life as it is right now. You were built for all this relationship shit, and you're good at it. You already look like the perfect husband and father, and there isn't even a ring on her finger yet. Speaking of rings...I know you know, but don't forget my mom has your mom's ring should you want to use it sometime in the near future. Just sayin'."

"How the hell did we get back to my love life, asshole? We were talking about yours."

"Hey, I was just reminding you in case it was something you had forgotten. As for my love life...well, it looks like we are plum out of time my friend," he says pulling his truck into the Fanuas driveway. Just like that, the conversation is over, and it's time to get ready to say goodbye again.

We all eat our lunch and watch as the Chick-fil-A virgins dig into their food. Emily has a classic chicken sandwich, and Ireland has nuggets but both were smart enough to get the waffle fries.

"So good," Emily says through a full mouth of fries.

"I still can't believe you don't have these in Oregon. That is a travesty," Kate says as she too shovels fries into her mouth.

"They're building one in our area, so it won't be long now. I'm gonna to need to stay away though. These fries, with this sauce, could become a serious problem."

We finish up our lunch and start to get our bags ready to go. We could have stayed until Sunday, but I thought it might be better to get home tonight. It would be nice to have a day so that Emily could do laundry, and get ready for her week, and so I wouldn't have to take a vacation day on Sunday. I'm saving all the vacation days I can at the moment. I have a plan and it's going to take some time off of work to come to fruition.

Liam is taking us to the airport, so he grabs our bags and takes them out to the truck to wait for us while the rest of the family makes their way around to each of us.

"Ireland, I had so much fun playing with you this weekend! Thanks for spending Turkey Day with us," Kate says as she lifts Ireland off the ground and into a big hug. "You be sure to take care of Savannah for me!" She says looking my way. She gives me a wink that says she was asking that little girl to take care of more than just her new stuffed bear.

"My turn! Hand her over Kate!" Mr. F exclaims next to them. I see him take her into his arms and notice Mrs. F and Emily over in the corner having a quiet conversation. I watch as Emily listens, and Fiona reaches up to pat her cheek gently then pulls her in for a hug. Once again, my heart is turning into hot liquid goo over the sight in front of me. The Fanuas acceptance of my girls into the family means more to me than they will ever know. I wish my mom was here, but this has been the best Thanksgiving ever.

"Take care of these two, Better Big Brother. They're keepers," Kate says bringing me in for a hug. Not usually too sentimental, she releases me quickly and heads over to Emily who has just let go of Mrs. F.

"Get over here, son," Mr. F orders. I obey his command and take the two steps it takes to get to him. He pulls me in for one of his epic bear hugs and says for only me to hear. "I am so proud of you, Jonathan. You are a good man, and those two little ladies are lucky to have you in their life. Take good care of them because they seem to love you just as much as you love them. It's nice to see that they've brought that light back to your eyes, son. Don't let that go."

I squeeze him a little harder and say, "Thanks, Mr. F for

everything. You're the best dad I could have ever asked for. I'm glad you like the girls because I'm hoping you'll be seeing a lot more of them, and for a very long time."

When I pull back I see tears in his big brown eyes. I look at him with confusion not sure what I said wrong.

When he sees the confused look on my face he gives my face a gentle slap and says, "I never wanted to replace your dad, son, but it warms my heart to hear you call me dad. I hope you know I love you like my own."

Now, my eyes are wet with unshed tears when I reply back to him. "I do, Mr. F. I do."

"Enough you two! Jonathan come give this old lady a kiss goodbye!" Fiona interjects.

I do as I'm told and give her a big hug and a kiss. She keeps her goodbye short and sweet. "I love you, Jonathan. Thanks for sharing your girls with us."

"Love you too, Mrs. F."

"Now get out of here, the three of you, before I get weepy!"

Heading out the door Emily takes my hand and we slowly make our way to a waiting Liam. I'm having a harder time leaving than I expected. We get Ireland in her seat, jump in and get settled while Kate and her parents stand on the porch waving goodbye until they can no longer see us. I miss them already.

It doesn't take long to arrive at the departures drop off at Hilton Head International Airport. Liam hops out and helps Emily get our bags out of the back while I get Ireland and her seat. When Ireland and I come around the back, I see Liam release Emily and then lift his hand to give her one of her famous high-fives. It means so much to me that they seem to get along. This trip has turned out better than I could have ever hoped.

Emily grabs Ireland's hand and steps away so I can say

goodbye to my brother from another mother. He gives me one of those bro handshakes that he pulls into a hug. While he gives my back a couple of slaps he says, "Miss you, man. Take care of yourself and keep going to therapy. Those girls are great. I'm happy for you, dude."

"Thanks, Liam. Miss you too. Try to stay out of trouble and fight for that girl if she's *the one*."

I take a couple steps away and turn to give one last wave. He just gives me a nod, jumps into his truck and drives off. As I turn back to grab the bags Emily is right there waiting for me. She lifts up on her toes and gives me a soft kiss. "Thanks for a great Thanksgiving, Georgia."

"Thanks for coming, Gracie. You too, Princess," I say as I look down at Ireland. She currently has a stuffed Frank under one arm and a stuffed Savannah under the other.

"Welcome, Jonafon," she says with a smile while the breeze blows her little blond curls all over her face.

Could she be any cuter?

37

Emily

"You know, every time I see one of these little boxes of raisins I can't help but feel a bit sad. Those raisins could have been grapes, and those grapes could have been wine. It's tragic really," Cami says as she opens one of the little red boxes that I have out for the kids and tosses a raisin in her mouth.

"Truth," I say back matter-of-factly as I grab my own little red box of what could have been.

My little girl is five today.

She's so excited about her birthday party that she's practically bursting at the seams. It's not anything fancy, but she couldn't be happier. In attendance today is Cami, Alex, Devon and Gabby, Mom, Mick, and just a handful of kids from Ireland's school. Jonathan is on his way and then we can, to quote Pink, "Get this party started!"

I offered to have the party this weekend, but she refused. Her birthday is the 1st of December, and I don't like to decorate for Christmas until after her birthday. I don't want her to be one of those kids that gets her birthday over-looked or all her presents wrapped in holiday paper. It's important to me that her birthday is special, and it's important to her that she doesn't miss any days of Elf On a Shelf. So a party on a late Tuesday afternoon is what she's getting.

The house is decorated with balloons and streamers and there are little gift bags and snacks for the kids. Luckily, I have Alex to take pictures. I'm glad she's here to capture all of the little moments of the day. Not only is she an amazing photographer, but it's one less thing for me to worry about.

The front door opens, and I see Jonathan bend down to pick something large and purple up with both hands, then he uses his work boot-clad foot to push the door closed.

"Jonafon!" Ireland yells and leaves her friends to run to him at full speed and hug his leg.

"Hey, Princess. Happy Birthday!"

"Thanks, Jonafon. I'm finally five!"

"No way, really? I thought you were turning thirteen?"

"Don't be silly, Jonafon. You know I'm five," she says with a giggle and runs back to her friends.

"What in the world is that? It's huge!" I ask my hot as hell, even at a five-year-old's birthday party, boyfriend.

"That's what she said!" Mick yells out from behind me.

I can't help but burst out laughing at the idiot I call my brother, but I quickly put on my mom face.

"Mick, there are little kids here. Watch it."

"What? They don't know what that means. Besides, you thought it was funny so don't even try to pretend to be mad. I see that smile you're trying to hide."

I stick my tongue out at him. "You don't have a filter do you?"

"Nope."

"I still love you. Even if you are an idiot."

Mick walks over to me and puts his big burly arm around my

neck and gives me a little noogie on the top of my head and says, "Shut it, woman!"

He loosens his grip around my neck and pulls me into a side hug and says, "You did good sis. She's a pretty cool kid."

"Ah, thanks. She gets it from your pretty cool little sister," I say as I give him a little punch to the shoulder. "Seriously, though. Thanks for letting me throw the party here and thanks for everything else. You've been so great."

"No problem, Emmers, I'm happy to have you guys here, and you know I love a party. So let's get this one going!"

He shouts that last part to the room and all the kids yell and get up and run over to him, all jumping up and down like wild animals. My big burly brother can't help but join in the fun as he jumps up and down right along with them.

I can't help but notice that as soon his jumping ends his gaze goes right back to Alex. I noticed them whispering in the kitchen earlier and his eyes seem to follow her around the room. I've always wondered if there's something between the two of them, but now I think there just might be. I've known Alex most of my life and she is stunning, so I understand why he would be interested. Let's face it. Mickey Jacobs and Alexandra Stotts would be a pretty hot couple, but I'm sure she's too smart to go there. At least I hope so.

Enough worrying about my brother's love life though, I have a party to start!

We play a few games and I make sure that somehow each of the four kids wins a prize. I debated whether it was right for the birthday girl to win a prize when she's already getting presents, but in the end, I couldn't say no to that face. I am such a pushover sometimes.

She's now opening her presents and has been equally excited over each and every gift, no matter how big or how small.

My mom got her a butterfly—she loves her butterflies like I love my dragonflies—Little Live Pets Garden Play-set. I have no idea what that is, but I'm sure I'll figure it out. Mick went way overboard. He got her an iPad and I think her head nearly exploded when she opened it. I can only assume he'd like his iPad back as well as more time with the family room TV. Cami and Alex got her clothes of course and I got her a bunch of art supplies, while Devon and Gabby gave her a huge stack of books.

There is only one gift left, and it's the big one that Jonathan brought in. He pushes it towards her, and she looks at me as if asking permission before she rips into it. My little girl is not bashful about opening gifts, and there is nothing dainty about watching her rip open a present. What there is though is the joy that I feel as I watch my little girl's face light up when she opens her gift from the man who I wish was her father. How the two of us have gotten so lucky, I will never know, but the love and happiness he brings to both of us is something I will never take for granted.

"Dude, did you make that?" I hear Mick ask from behind me.

"Yep. What do you think, Princess?"

"I love it! It has my name on it!"

"It does. Open it up and see what else you might find," he encourages her while he shows her how to open the buckles on the handmade treasure chest that he's made for her. It's painted white, and across the front of it in pink it says,

Princess Ireland

When she opens the box, her mouth drops open and she just stares for a second. Then she squeals and throws her arms around Jonathan, but she quickly lets go. She runs back to her treasure chest only to pull out princess dress after princess dress as well as shoes, tiaras, fake jewels and every accessory you can imagine. He's thought of everything and has made all of her princess dreams come true.

Surrounded by pink, purple, blue and yellow fluff she lifts her eyes to mine with a big smile and starts to say, "Mommy..."

But she doesn't finish and I don't realize why she doesn't finish her sentence until she comes up to me and pulls on my hand. I squat in front of her and she asks. "Momma, what's da matter?" She reaches her little hand up to my face and wipes away the tears I didn't even realize were falling.

"Baby girl, nothing is wrong. These are happy tears. It makes me so so happy to see you happy." Knowing I need to gather myself, I find an out and I say, "Now, how about cake?"

"Yes! Cake!" she shouts as she turns back to her friends and her treasure chest.

I stand and see Jonathan leaning against the wall watching us. He's the reason my little girl and I feel the way we do every day. He put me back together and is filling a hole in Ireland's life that she didn't even know needed to be filled.

Passing by him on my way to the kitchen I pause and kiss him on the cheek. "Thank you for her present, it's amazing."

He puts his arm around my waist and places a sweet kiss on the lips. That's all the gift I need.

I turn to leave him, but can't help myself when I turn back. Not caring who hears it say, "I love you, Georgia."

"Love you too, baby."

The party is over, and Ireland has spent the last thirty minutes trying on all of her dresses and accessories from her treasure chest. She tries each dress on, accessorizes and then goes out to the family room and shows Uncle Mick and Jonathan. She twirls, looks at herself in the full-length mirror on the back of the bathroom door and then we start again.

Now that I'm up close to the trunk that Jonathan transformed into a treasure chest fit for a princess, I see all the details on it. He's hand painted little butterflies sporadically on the trunk, and even a dragonfly here or there.

Not only did he make this gift for her, but he took the night off of work so he could spend the evening with us. Now the poor man sits in the living room with my annoying big brother while he endures a five-year old's fashion show.

It's his fault though.

He did all of this.

He had to know what he was getting himself into.

Ireland walks back into her room after showing her last dress off to the boys, and she makes a point of shutting her door.

She climbs up into my lap and says, "Momma, can I tell you what I wished for when I blowed out my candles?"

38

―――

Jonathan

Mick goes to grab us each a beer, and I hear a light knocking. Then I hear Ireland say, "Momma?"

My heart instantly starts to pound in my chest because Ireland doesn't sound happy, and she was just beaming with pride in her last princess dress. What could have happened between now and then?

As I approach her in the hallway I squat down to her level. "What's goin' on, Princess?"

"I made momma cry." She's calling Emily momma and not mommy. That's a sign that something's wrong.

"Why do you think you made her cry?"

"Well, I know I wasn't supposed to but I told her my birfday wish. I thought it would make her happy, and if she knew I was wishing for it she could wish for it too," she says so low that I can barely hear her.

She suddenly seems shy. Her tiny hands are clasped in front of her and she's looking down at them. She doesn't seem to want to look me in the eye. What in the world did she wish for that would have Emily in tears, and Ireland seem so shy?

"What did you wish for, sweetie?"

She lifts those big warm eyes up to mine. She takes a breath and blows it out so she can get one of her wild curls out of her face. She starts to speak, but stops and looks down again before she softly says, "I wished that you, me, mommy and Frances could all be a family together."

I can't breathe.

This little girl has brought me to my knees figuratively and quite literally. I've fallen forward out of my squatting position and on to my knees. I instinctively pull Ireland in for a hug, and silently thank her for what she's just given me.

I feel like Superman right now. I honestly feel like I could stop a speeding train or fly into the night's sky. It's as though Ireland's belief in me is all I need to do any of those things. My moment of elation ebbs as I remember this wish has Emily hiding in her room crying. I'm not sure how I should be taking that, but I suddenly feel a little less like I could fly.

"You aren't mad?" She asks with sad eyes and I realize I haven't verbally replied to her statement. I hate to see her looking so sad when she's made me so happy.

"No, Princess, not at all. In fact, I think that is the best wish I have ever heard. I hope you know how important you are to me Ireland. Thank you for your wish and I hope one day both of our wishes come true. Now let me go check on your momma, and you go show Uncle Mick your dress again. It's very pretty by the way," I say as I kiss on the top of her head.

"Em..." I say as I gently knock on her bedroom door. "Can I come in?"

"Yes," I hear her sniff out behind the door.

I cautiously open the door and poke my head in, unsure of what I might find. I'm a combination of nerves right now. I'm still riding high from Ireland's confession, but I'm afraid my heart is about to be trampled on by the love of my life.

I see her sitting in the middle of her bed with her back against the headboard and her knees pulled up to her chest. There is still a steady stream of tears cascading down her face. I close the door behind me. I take a seat next to her and hand her the box of tissues that I grabbed from the bathroom before I came in. Just like her, I sit against the headboard with my legs pulled into my chest and my eyes straight ahead and give her a minute before I speak.

"You okay, baby?"

"I don't know," she sniffs reaching for another tissue.

I inhale and exhale out as calmly as I can so that she can't see that I am petrified to have this conversation with her. Things have been perfect the last month and a half, but her behavior has me rattled and I'm not sure how to handle the situation. I'm the guy that always wears his heart on his sleeve though, so I can't let it linger and I just dive right in. Might as well rip off the band-aid.

"Ireland told me what she wished for and..." Emily cuts me off before I can continue as she gasps and puts her hand over her mouth.

"I am so sorry," she sobs out after removing her hand from her mouth and taking both of her hands to cover her face.

"Sorry? Why are you sorry? Because that was one of the best birthday wishes I have ever heard. Are you sorry because you don't feel the same way that Ireland does?" I don't mean to sound cold, but I can hear the sharpness to my tone as I ask the question.

Emily turns her body towards me and tucks her legs underneath herself and kneels on her knees and waits for me to turn and meet her eyes with mine.

"No, it's not that at all. I swear! Hearing her wish made me feel so sorry for her. I feel horrible that my little girl has grown up without a father and has to wish for a family. That nearly did me in. It reminded me that no matter how hard I try, my daughter still feels like she's missing something, and she's only five. A five-year-old shouldn't have to make those wishes, Jonathan."

This I get. But why do I feel like there's more to it?

"I also don't want you to feel any pressure from either one of us. I especially don't want you to want to take that next step because my daughter has you wrapped around her little finger. If we take that next step, I want it to be for the right reasons. I also don't want to get her hopes up for something that may not be in her future."

I start to protest but Emily lifts her finger to my lips and continues to explain.

"I don't mean that because I have doubts about you, Jonathan. It's myself I worry about. I have never even been in a long term relationship let alone talked about the 'M' word. What if I mess this up? What if I am just no good at this and it doesn't work out? I have no idea what I'm doing, Jonathan. I know I love you and I don't want to be with anybody else. I also know that I am in this for as long as you'll have me." She takes a breath and says, "When I look at my future, it's you I see. I'm just so scared that I am going to mess us up."

"Well, I guess it's my job to find a way to prove to you that I'm not going anywhere no matter what happens. Neither one of us are perfect, and we're both going to make mistakes. As long as we're both faithful and honest with each other, we aren't going to be able to mess us up bad enough for me to walk away from you. I would 'M' word you tonight if I thought you were ready, but you aren't and I'm okay with that. Please just remember that you can talk to me about anything. If something's bothering you or you're scared, don't hide it from me. No secrets, no lies. Just truth between us...always. Let's start with that. What do ya say?"

She nods her head and says, "I love you, Georgia. Thanks for being so patient with me."

"Whatever you need, baby. You and me. We're in this together."

39

Emily

"Merry Christmas Eve, baby," Jonathan says as he sits across from me on the floor in front of the Christmas tree; the tree that the three of us decorated together. Jonathan and I are getting some alone time as Mick takes Ireland to afternoon holiday tea at the Heathman. He really is the best brother ever. Tea was his idea, and Ireland couldn't have been more excited to get dressed up and have a date with her uncle.

"Merry Christmas Eve, handsome," I reply playfully. "So what are we going to do with hours alone with just the two of us?" I ask as I lean forward and try to devour him with my lips.

He kisses me back, but I can tell his whole heart isn't into it. "What's wrong, Georgia?"

"Uh...nothing...nothing's wrong, Em. I just wanted to give you one of your presents now while it's just you and me."

"I thought we were doing presents in the morning with Ireland?"

"We are, it's just for this one...for this one I wanted it to be just us," he says as he reaches up into the tree and pulls a thin foot-long box out from its hiding place amongst the branches. "Here you go, baby."

I swear I see him shaking as he hands it to me. I take it out of his hands as quick as I can just to end his misery. He's clearly on edge about this gift, and frankly, I'm starting to feel edgy myself.

"Open it," he says impatiently.

Under the ribbon in the center of the box is a card that says, *'Gracie'* on it. I look up at him and give him a little smile, but his face remains serious. I open the little envelope and as I start to read the card Jonathan speaks the words aloud for me.

"No regrets, Gracie. Live today like it's your last and along the way kick some ass," he leans in and whispers in my ear the next line written on the card. "I'll love you always and forever and wherever I may be. Love, Your Georgia."

I love him so much, but I'm incredibly confused and he can tell by the look on my face.

"Before you opened this, I wanted you to hear the words that you live by to remind you to live life to the fullest. I also wanted you to hear words that I live by so that you know that no matter what you say after you open this gift, I'm still here and I still love you. I'm not going anywhere, Em."

Now even more confused I just stare at the flat, thin, foot-long box in my hand. It's clearly not a ring box, and he isn't down on one knee so I couldn't be more confused.

"Just open it," he prompts me. He seems a bit more at ease, and there's finally a smile on his gorgeous face.

I wish I felt more at ease because I am scared to death.

I untie the ribbon and slide the lid off the box. Thank God there isn't any wrapping paper on it to draw this whole thing out any longer. Once the lid is off, I open the tissue paper inside and see a key and a pink dog leash. I'm not sure exactly what I am looking at, and I just keep staring at it not believing that he is asking what I think he is. He doesn't give me too long to think about the items in the box when he hops up and holds a hand out to me. He helps me to my feet, but doesn't let go of my hand.

"Before you say anything, I have a few things to show you."

He guides me to the hallway that leads to his bedroom, but he stops in front of the office door next to it. He opens the door and I cannot believe the transformation in this room. It went from a dark, messy catch all to a soft, light, comfortable living space complete with a beautiful white desk, shelves, and bookcases.

"I thought this would be a nice place for you to study and grade papers."

I walk into the middle of the room and cannot believe what I'm seeing. The shelves are partially filled with some of my favorite books, as well as framed pictures of Ireland, Jonathan and I. It finally hits me that he hasn't let me over here much the last two or three weeks.

"Is this why you've kept me away lately? You were making me an office?"

"Shhh...there's more," he says as he takes my hand and leads me across the hall to the spare bedroom aka his home gym.

He opens the door, flips on the light and steps aside. "What do you think? Do you think she'll like it?"

If I thought the office was amazing, then I was mistaken because this room...this room is fit for a princess.

"Oh my God! Jonathan! What have you done? Did you do all this yourself?" I practically screech as I turn and take in the dreamiest room that any little girl could ever hope for.

"I did, but I got some advice from your mom, Cami, Alex, and Gabby when it came to some of the decorations. But I did do it all myself."

I am so gobsmacked that I let the fact that all the girls knew about this go by. I can't take my eyes off every little detail of this room. The walls are painted a light pale green and there are light pink accents everywhere. The bed in the center of the room is what little girl's dreams are made of. It's white and covered in pink, fluffy bedding with throw pillows galore. To top it all off it has sheer white netting that hangs down on the sides of the headboard and looks like it can be pulled around the bed. There are adorable white curtains and a little white sofa with a fluffy pink rug in front of it. He also remembered to include a bean bag chair similar to the one at Mick's. There are so many other decorations and little details that I know I'm not taking it all in right now. There is just too much to look at.

My vision starts to blur from the tears pooling in my eyes. He *is* asking me what I thought he was. I turn to him to answer him, but I am shushed by the shake of his head and the kiss he places on my lips.

"One more room," he says taking my hand yet again and opening the French doors to his bedroom.

The changes to this room, are a bit more subtle, but still, they make such a difference. The room is still masculine yet soft at the same time. He's added throw pillows and blankets to the bed in feminine colors that blend perfectly with his beige bedding.

On the wall above the fireplace is a large, framed, black and white picture of me and Ireland from our day at the zoo back in October. We aren't looking at the camera, but at each other, and we both have the biggest smiles on our faces. At first glance, I already know it's my new favorite picture. On the dresser, there is a framed picture of just me and one of Jonathan and I together in Savannah.

To say I am overwhelmed with love would be an understatement.

Still holding my hand, he guides me into the main bathroom where I see my favorite lotion on the counter.

"Open the first drawer on your right."

I follow his instructions and inside are several of my favorite products, as well as hair ties like I use at home. For kicks, I open the next drawer down and find an assortment of sticky notes along with a blue and a black pen. I look at him like he is a crazy person and he just chuckles. "There's more."

"How can there be more Jonathan? You've done so much."

"Almost done, baby," he says with a subtle smile.

I walk around the huge bathroom and notice that next to the shower there is a new, big, white, fuzzy robe hanging off of a brushed pewter dragonfly hook. Below the robe are matching slippers. The robe is hanging next to the shower. A shower that is already supplied with my shampoo, conditioner, and body wash as well as a new pink loofa.

Suddenly, the weight of the key and leash in my hand hits me. "Is this my key? Are you asking me what I think you are?"

"Well, if you think that I am asking you to make my house a home then yes, you would be right. That's not just a key, Emily, I want this to be your home and Ireland's too. I want this to be *our* home."

"And the leash?" I ask as I dangle it from my fingers. For some reason all of this has me feeling confident and loved. Surprisingly I'm calm and a bit horny. It doesn't feel rushed, it just feels right.

"Well, Frances just wanted you to know that she was on board. She wants you two to move in as well. She wanted both of us to have a leash, just in case," he shrugs.

"That was awfully sweet of Frances. Tell her I thank her for her thoughtfulness," I say with a bit of a Southern drawl. I'm feeling playful and confident after receiving my gifts.

I can tell he's waiting for the other shoe to drop; for me to protest and say it's too soon.

Just as I'm about to accept his proposal—that's not a proposal—he rushes to speak before I get a chance.

With his arms wrapped around my waist and my hands around his neck he says, "Gracie, I want all of you and I want it for a lifetime. I know you may not be ready for that big final step, but I do want you...*all of you*. I want to wake up to your big messed up hair and that dreamy, sleepy smile you get when you say good morning to me. As far as your smiles go, baby, I want them all. I want your giggles and your snores."

I start to protest but he covers my mouth with his hand and continues.

"Because you do snore. Your high fives and your freckles. I want your past and your future, your fears, and your dreams. I want to make you laugh until you cry, and I want to call you mine. Forever and always, baby. I will want all of you forever and always, and I would love it if you and Ireland would make my house a home. What do you say?"

"Of course," is all I say as I take his hand and lead him out of the room. "We'll have to talk to Ireland first, but it's a yes from me, Georgia."

"Do you think she'll like her room?"

He sounds worried. How Cute.

"I'm sure she will, but we'll worry about her room another time."

I step into the office and pull my dress over my head. Revealing his early Christmas gift, I stand in front of him in my red and white lingerie that leaves little to the imagination. "We'll save the bed for later when we have more time. Right now I want to christen my new desk."

I barely get my last word out when his lips crash into mine, and he kisses me harder than he ever has before. While his lips bruise mine, and his tongue invades my mouth, his hands roam all over my body. When he reaches my ass, he finally pulls away and turns me around to find the big red bow that is tied on the back to make me look like a present. A present that is all for him.

"Good God, woman, you are perfect! I love you so much, and I can't wait to make you happy every day for the rest of your life."

He stops talking and brings his lips to my ear. He takes a little nibble before he whispers, "You look so fucking hot, baby. I can't wait to get you on top of this desk and inside of you. I am so fucking hard."

His words trigger a reaction in me that I can't control as I turn around and practically rip his shirt off of him when I pull it over his head. The moment his shirt is gone, his lips are leaving a hot trail down my neck and to my chest. I'm tearing open his pants in an almost panic to get him naked. He suddenly lifts me by the hips and places me on top of the beautiful white desk.

He leaves me on display and he takes a step back to take off the rest of his clothes when I hear him moan. It's a moan that almost sounds like a growl, and I see why when I notice where his eyes are. I don't have any panties on, and he is going to have easy access.

I think he approves.

"Fuck. You are killing me, Em."

He pulls me to the edge of the desk and drops to his knees. As soon as he hits the ground, he lifts his eyes to mine as puts two fingers inside of me and starts moving them, ever so slowly. Without taking his eyes off mine, he flicks his tongue over that spot that he knows will send me over the edge. I'm aching from the ecstasy that only he can make me feel. My back arches and I moan loudly.

I don't know if it's because of all of the emotions of the last fifteen minutes, or because it just feels that good, but I am already close. He keeps moving his fingers while he slowly tortures me with the bliss he creates with his tongue. He loves to build me up slowly so that he can watch me fall over the edge. He knows my body better than I do, and I can feel myself getting close to that edge as his fingers pick up speed and his tongue starts moving faster and stronger. His tongue stops for just a moment as he takes a small sharp bite of my bundle of nerves that are balancing on the brink. Then as soon as he does, his tongue is back working in circles while his fingers hit just the right spot.

"That's it...Oh God, Jonathan...that's it..." I feel myself pulsing around his fingers as I yell. "Yes, baby. Right there! Oh shit...baby! I'm coming! Yes!"

As soon as he feels me start to come down from my high, he does what he does best and enters me while I am still pulsing. He keeps my high going so that we can come together.

"Em...you feel so good...love to feel you come all over me."

He pulls down on the cups of my bustier so that my breasts pop out over the top. They're on full display, and this brings a small little smile to his face. He takes one in his hand while his tongue works its magic on my other hard as glass nipple. Then —because he believes in equal treatment—he switches hands and takes the other nipple into his mouth all while still keeping his steady rhythm that has me right on that edge that I never quite left.

Grabbing me by my ass he brings my body closer to his, and he lifts me off the desk. A few steps later we fall on the sofa on the other side of the room. Now he's sitting with me straddling him. He's using his hands on my ass to guide our rhythm. Our lips meet in a frenzied dance as my hands weave through his short dark hair, and I hold on for dear life as I feel myself building up again. He pulls his lips from mine, and I moan at the loss, but when he takes my nipple back in his mouth and reaches between us to use his thumb to help take me all the way again, I realize it's a loss worth taking.

"Jonathan...I'm gonna come again..."

"Not yet, baby...just hold on another minute..." he huffs as I watch him get closer to falling.

We're both right there and moments later he yells, "Now, baby! Come with me!"

His words are what I need to take me over, and when I go, he goes right along with me. The room is now quiet, except for our heavy breathing. I'm still sitting on top of him, and he is still inside me when he says, "I love you, Gracie."

I don't want to move from this spot.

I can feel all of the love, happiness, and excitement radiating off him. I can't believe he didn't know if I would say yes to moving in. But I guess if you had asked me a couple of months ago if I would have answered with a yes...I might not have believed it either.

"I love you, Georgia."

EPILOGUE
FOUR YEARS LATER…

Sitting in bed taking the rare moment I have to read one of my favorite books for the umpteenth time, I hear one of my favorite sounds; the sound of my husband arriving home from work safe and sound. I hear the door from the garage open and close. Soon after, I hear the Velcro peel open as Jonathan takes his gear off and stores it in the hall closet, as well as putting his gun in the safe.

One of the perks of being a K9 handler is that you get a take-home car to transport the dog, and therefore he can get dressed and undressed at home and not the locker room at the police department. It may not be a lot, but it's just that much more time at home with us each night.

Best of all he has a partner. It makes me feel a little bit better knowing he has a partner with him. Especially a cute, little buddy that will bite on command, and kick some ass when Jonathan needs him to.

Olaf is a sweet boy when he's not at work, but we still make sure that Ireland loves him from afar just to be safe. Jonathan let her name him when he was promoted to K9 Officer a couple years back. The second *Frozen* movie was still playing on a loop in the house, so Olaf it was.

I hear him drop something heavy like, maybe a boot, and I freeze as I listen to see if Caroline or Matty wake up. They're pretty good sleepers for nine-month olds, but when one wakes up, they both wake up. A few silent moments pass and it seems we're in the clear. Thank God. I look at the display on both of the video monitors, and they're sound asleep, at least for the time being. Putting them each in their own rooms was a hard decision, but I think it's helping them sleep through the night.

Soon, Jonathan comes sauntering into the room in just his boxer briefs—having left his dirty uniform in the laundry room on his way down the hall—and he leaps onto the bed and lays his head in my lap. He looks up at me while I rub my hands through his hair.

"How was your night, Georgia?"

"Better now that I'm home. How was yours? Is Matthew feeling better?"

"He seems to be. No fever, so I think he might just be teething."

"Was their big sister helpful tonight?"

"She was. She rocked Caroline to sleep while I tried to calm Matty. I swear I don't know what I'd do without her sometimes."

"I feel the same about you, baby," he says as he takes one of my hands from his head, kisses it and then places it on his heart.

We sit here in comfortable silence for quite some time before I follow his gaze to see that he's staring at the picture above our dresser from our wedding day. It was one of the happiest days of my life. I can never look back on our wedding without thinking about his proposal. Even four years and two more kids later, I still get butterflies in my stomach whenever I think about it.

"Happy Anniversary," I hear Jonathan say in my ear as I slowly come out of my dream-filled haze.

"Anniversary?"

"Yep, six years ago today you flipped my world upside down, and I've never been the same."

"Ah, thanks baby but what time is it? It feels like it's the middle of the night," I say on a yawn.

"It's early, sugar, but I need you to get up."

"Jonathan, it's Sunday. What is wrong with you?"

"We have to get to the airport. Our flight leaves in a couple hours so get up Sleeping Beauty!" He says as he gives me a little swat on the butt.

"Our flight? Where are we going? What about Ireland?"

"Ireland's going to be staying with your mom for a couple of days, and don't worry about where we're going. Just get up."

"What do you mean don't worry about where we're going? How can I pack if I don't even know where we are going? I didn't even say goodbye to Ireland when she went to mom's last night."

He takes me by the hand and slowly pulls me up to a sitting position.

"You can call her when we land, and I already packed a bag for you. Now get that fine ass of yours in the shower before I throw you in!"

I follow his orders and before I know it we're boarding a plane for San Diego. It's a short flight, and I spend most of it asleep on Jonathan's shoulder. I'm exhausted but Jonathan seems to have enough energy for the both of us. What is with him?

The plane lands and we collect our luggage. I did notice there is a lot of luggage for a couple of days but am too confused and tired to ask any questions. We head to the rental car check out where Jonathan has rented us a jeep to drive, and it's red. I love jeeps, especially red ones. None as much as Scarlett, but they're so much fun! Jonathan doesn't say much as he throws our bags into the back seat and then drives us off down the road.

I can tell we're headed in the direction of San Clemente, but I'm surprised when we pull up to the San Onofre Beach cottages. It hasn't changed a bit, and when Jonathan opens my door and helps me out, he gives me a little grin. But he still doesn't say a word. Just as I suspected he takes me by the hand and leads me to the same little white cabin we stayed in last time. With each step closer to our cottage, the memories start flooding my mind and my heart starts racing.

Once we're through the front door, it all comes rushing back even faster. There's a new couch and kitchen table and chairs but for the most part, it's all the same. The first thing I do is go out to our little patio to look at the view. It's still early and a little cool, but the weather is beautiful. As I turn around to head back inside, something catches my eye. On the table, just like before, there's a gift waiting there. There's a sticky note on it that says,

> Diana helped me woo you last time, so I thought I would keep with tradition.
>
> Love you, Georgia

I'm so very confused because last time we were here he bought me a Diana Gabaldon book. This package isn't a book. I set the sticky note aside and tear off the paper. Inside are the DVDs for Part 1 and Part 2 of the first season of Outlander.

Jonathan appears in the doorway to the patio and says, "I figured it might be nice to watch it together so I can see what all this 'Outlander' craziness is about. I liked Downton Abbey, so I figure I'll give Outlander a shot too. Besides, I need to see why you, Cami and Alex say this Jamie guy is so freaking great. You know how competitive I can be."

I throw my arms around him and show him my gratitude the only way I know how; with my lips because I am speechless.

He doesn't let things get too heated because he has more to show me I discover, as he takes me by the hand and guides me to the kitchen. On the counters, there are all the ingredients for s'mores and I see a Costco sized bag of fishies. He opens the fridge, and I see it's fully stocked with contents that all seem to look familiar to me. When he opens the freezer, and I can't help but laugh when I see the carton of vanilla ice cream that says Gracie on it, and the carton of chocolate that says Georgia on it.

He walks up behind me, wraps his arms around me and presses his front to my back. I shut the freezer door and say, "You really have thought of everything, haven't you?"

"Nah, I just want to make you happy. I've relived our first week together over and over again, and I just thought we could try to live a bit of it again together. I know we're in a different place now, but I thought it might be fun to bring us back to where it all began."

"I think it's a great idea. Thank you so much for the getaway. I'm excited for some alone time. Just seeing that chocolate ice cream in the freezer makes me want to start reliving some of those memories right now," I say trying to turn around in his arms to kiss him and see if we can start our trip down memory lane now.

But I am denied.

"Nope. No can do. If we get started, I won't be able to stop and I have plans for us. Why don't you go in the bathroom and change into something that you can hike in. I'll get a backpack ready."

"We're going hiking? Really?"

"Yes, we're going hiking and you'll like it. Now get moving, woman!"

He hands me my smallest bag, and I can't help but think it's weird that he insists I go into the bathroom to change, and not the bedroom. He's up to something, but so far so good, so I'm not going to question it too much.

Once I'm ready, he doesn't waste any time getting us out the door and back into the jeep.

I shouldn't be surprised, but I am when he pulls into the parking lot for the Las Ramblas Trail. I'm excited because this is the home of our first kiss, but I am dreading the hike. It nearly killed me last time, but I guess I was pregnant and probably a little more tired than usual.

He holds my hand and supplies me with water, snacks ,and conversation as we make our journey up to the flagpole at the top of the viewpoint.

Once there he grows quiet. He puts his arms around me and holds my back to his front. He rests his chin on the top of my head and gently sways us while we admire the view, and take some time to cool off and catch our breath. It's been fairly quiet on the trail today, and it's kind of nice that it's been just the two of us for the most part. It's especially nice up here with this view.

Jonathan releases his hold on me and points to the mailbox, "Look, it's still here. I wonder if our journal is still there too?"

I jump out of his arms and skip towards the box and open it up, but feel disappointed when I see a new journal inside. "Shoot, it's a new one and not ours. That would have been so cool."

"Well, I'm sure they filled it up. You better make sure you leave a note though. I'm sure we aren't the first ones here to write in the new one. You wanna go first this time?"

"Sure, let's see...here we go."

"What's the last entry say?"

"It says...Oh,My God...Jonathan..."

"What's it say, baby?" he asks again.

I turn around to face him and find him on his knee with a ring box in his hand.

"Well, read it to me."

Barely able to see through the puddle of tears forming in my eyes, I read aloud what it says in the book.

"Emily Grace Jacobs, my Gracie. I will love you always and

forever and wherever I may be. Would you please do me the honor of becoming my wife, and dancing endless dances in the dark with me? Will you marry me and make me the happiest man in the world?"

I put the journal back in the mailbox, walking back to him and join him on the ground, down on my knees. I take his precious face in my hands and give him a sweet loving kiss.

I pull back, look him in the eyes and say, "What took you so long? I've been waiting six years for you to ask me that."

I see the look of confusion and then relief color his expression. As those dimples that I love so much make an appearance, he asks. "Is that a yes?"

"Yes, it's a yes! Of course!" I yell.

"I love you so much!" He plants a big sloppy kiss on my face, puts the ring on my finger and then yells at the top of his lungs, "She said yes!"

At first, I think he's just professing his love for the world to hear—like he once said he would do as he laid in a hospital bed—but I soon realize it is much more than that.

From out of nowhere on the other side of the trail, familiar faces start popping into view. First I see Devon and Mick, followed by Liam, Kate, Cami, Gabby—and oh my God Sam and Steph!

I feel like I might be losing my mind for a minute when my mom and Ireland appear, and my baby girl starts running my way. The next faces I see belong to Robert and Fiona. Everybody I love is here, except for Alex. She's hosting a big event at home but she texted me a bit ago to check-in. Now I know why.

"What is happening? How did they all get here? Did Ireland and my mom walk the trail?"

"Mommy, I took a four-wheeler on the trail. It was so much fun! Uncle Mick isn't a very good driver though!"

"Come here, sweetheart. What are you doing here?" I say as I pick her up and swing her into my arms. I won't be able to do this much

longer, she is growing up so fast. "What are all of you doing here?" I say to the group that contains all my favorite people.

"We wanna watch you get married, mommy," my sweet girl proclaims.

I turn to look at my new fiancé to get some clarification and I think he's actually blushing. Jonathan Kelly doesn't blush. What the hell is going on?

"Baby, did you mean what you said when you said you had been waiting six years? Because I was thinking why put it off another minute? I was hoping we could get married here, tonight, on the beach where we became an us. What do you say? Too much?"

It should be too much. The old me would have run for the hills—except we're already at the top of a hill and there isn't anywhere to run.

I don't want to run.

This is where I want to be.

Looking around at all the faces of those I love the most, with Ireland in my arms—there is nothing I want more than to marry this man, here in San Clemente, where it all started.

"It sounds perfect," I say. "I can't wait to become your wife, so why not tonight?"

There are whoops and hollers all around us, and Jonathan looks beyond relieved. He reaches out for Ireland and she goes into his arms. He props her up on one side, and pulls me into his other side and kisses me on the temple.

"Jonathan?" Ireland says quietly so only the three of us can hear her, and internally I praise her for finally being able to say his name correctly.

"Yes, Princess?"

"If you marry mommy, does that mean you will be my daddy?"

Jonathan turns to me with tears pooling in his eyes and asks me without saying a word what the answer to this question will be. I answer him with a slight nod and he turns back to Ireland.

"It would be my honor to be your daddy, if you want me to be?"

"I do! I really, really do!" She says excitedly. She reaches for me and we put our three heads together with our arms around each other and she whispers. "I can't believe I'm gonna have a daddy."

"What's wrong, baby? Why are you crying?"

His voice brings me back to the present, and it's then I realize that I have tears falling down my face while I turn my wedding ring round and round my finger. I often do this while thanking the previous owner of this ring for the amazing man she brought into my world.

"I'm good, sweetie. I was just thinking back to our wedding and how happy Ireland and I both were that night. I still cannot believe you got everybody there. Not to mention every detail down to my dress and a two-week honeymoon in the Irish countryside planned without me knowing. I will never understand how I could have been so dense. How did I not notice that something was up?"

I still wonder this after all these years.

"I had a ton of help and let's just say I found lots of entertaining ways to keep you distracted. I can show you one of those ways now, if you want?"

I giggle and smack his arm.

"Some things never change."

"Not when it comes to you and me, baby. What we got is a forever thing and that ain't ever gonna change."

"I love you, Georgia."

"Love you, Gracie"

2010 Patriots Hill Mailbox Journal Entries...

Jonathan Kelly of Savannah, GA – May 24th, 2010 - I am here with the most beautiful girl I have ever met, and I am hoping she kisses me back when I kiss her in just a minute.
Wish me luck, J

Emily Jacobs of Portland, OR – May 24th, 2010 - I kissed him back (no luck needed). After that kiss, I sure would love for him to be the one to change my mind about those happily ever afters.
Wish me luck, E

YOU & ME: PART TWO PLAYLIST

Do I Wanna Know by Arctic Monkeys
Fix You by Coldplay
Back Where I Belong by Jack Savoretti
Life to Live Again by Brett Young
Lost Stars by Adam Levine
Sugar by Maroon 5
Love You More by Raccoon
The Face by Kings of Leon
Wildflowers by Tom Petty
Stressed Out by twenty one pilots
Count On Me by Bruno Mars
Roses by The Chainsmokers (feat. Rozes)
Someone Like You by Van Morrison
Can't Take My Eyes Off of You by Lauryn Hill
Brand New by Ben Rector
Make Me Like You by Gwen Stefani
Mess Is Mine by Vance Joy
Hold Me by Janine and The Mixtape
Every Other Freckle by alt-J
Break In by Halestorm

Die A Happy Man by Thomas Rhett
I'm Yours by Justine Skye (feat. Vic Mensa)
Fire and The Flood by Vance Joy
Not A Bad Thing by Justin Timberlake
You Are the Best Thing by Ray LaMontagne
Somebody by Natalie LaRose (feat. Jeremih)
Un-thinkable (I'm Ready) by Alicia Keys
By Your Side by Sade
Lost by Six60
Ain't No Sunshine by Bill Withers
The Scientist by Coldplay
Just Breathe by Pearl Jam
Nobody 'Cept You by Jack Savoretti
Parachute by Chris Stapleton
Ascension (Don't Ever Worry) by Maxwell
Special by Six60
Back Together by Jill Scott
Baby Baby Baby by Joss Stone
My Love by Justin Timberlake
Forever by Six60

You & Me: Parts 1 & 2 Combined Playlist
Listen Here:
https://spoti.fi/2OGIcKE

ACKNOWLEDGMENTS

You & Me would not be without the never ending love and support of my best friend and husband. I would have never had the courage to write this story, let alone publish it. Thank you for pushing me outside of my comfort zone, and not letting my rampant insecurities get the best of me. Whether I was excited, scared, anxious or over-joyed you always listened. You were there every step of the way. Thank you and please don't ever forget that I will *always* love you MORE.

To my kind, charming, supportive, and handsome son. Thank you for being so understanding when I was preoccupied or 'writing'. You have been more than supportive of your mom trying something new. When I told you that I was writing a romance novel—that I didn't want you to read because of some of the adult scenes—you never seemed embarrassed or acted like you wished I wouldn't. In other words, thanks for being so cool about all of this. I can't tell you how proud I am to call you my son. I love you, buddy, more than you will ever know.

Allison, where do I begin? You were the first person, besides my husband that I shared my 'little secret' with. Your unwavering support since day one means more than you will ever know. Thank you, and your boys, for all of the personal time that you sacrificed to help me with my passion project. Thank you for being just as excited as I've been with every milestone met. Here's to toasting with cake pops and high five's that burn like a mother!

Nadia, thank you. Thank you for teaching me that it was

okay to ask for help. That I couldn't do everything on my own and that I needed to delegate. I'm not sure I've mastered the whole delegation thing, but I'm working on it. Thank you for your time, creativity, talent, and expertise. Most of all thank you for putting up with me. I know that I want things how I want them, but I am insanely indecisive at the same time. I cannot even imagine how many times you wanted to strangle me. Thank you for *not* strangling me and for making everything so pretty. Most of all...thank you for your years of friendship. Love you, chica.

Angie, Tiffany, Sesha, Crystal, and Jackie – the first to read *You & Me*. Thank you for your constructive criticism, advice, encouragement and for keeping it real. You went in blind, without any kind of synopsis and just read the book. You took the time out of your busy schedules and read the story of a novice. Thank you, thank you, thank you!

To all of those official and unofficial members of the *The Black Hole*, you know who you are, thank you. You are all living proof that it really does take a village. Thank you for keeping my secret, my sanity and for still speaking to me after I asked you to share your opinion time and time again. It's not like you guys have work to do or anything, right? Thank you ladies!

Stacy, thank you for your excitement and encouragement. You aren't too bad for a little sister—I think I'll keep you. Mitch and Krista, thank you for understanding why I would want to stay back at the hotel rather than go out on the town that night in Vegas. To all my friends and family who didn't tell me I was crazy or laugh in my face when I told them I had written a book, thank you. There has not been one person in my life that has been less than supportive and I am so appreciative.

To my editor, Laura Allison. I'm sure there isn't enough cider in the world to help you recover from this job. Thank you!

To all the independent writers out there who inspired me to

take this chance, thank you. Thank you for going first so the rest of us could follow in your footsteps.

Thank you to the music that inspired me during this process. To all the artists, musicians and songwriters out there, you are awe-inspiring. How lucky you are to give people like me the 'feels' like you do. I hope you all know what a gift you truly have. I also hope everybody reading this remembers that good music is whatever is good to you. Whatever makes you feel something. Don't ever let anybody make you feel bad for the kind of music you love. There are no guilty pleasures when it comes to music.

Thank you to all the readers for taking a chance on a first timer. It means more than you will ever know.

Finally, I would like to thank our armed forces and law enforcement. Thank you for your continuous sacrifice and dedication. Most don't realize just how much of yourselves you give when you serve your country or local municipality. I also want to thank the families and loved ones of our armed forces and law enforcement. Thank you for all that you may sacrifice to support and love those that are risking their lives for ours.

WHAT TO READ NEXT

<u>Disregarded Heart</u>

A Grumpy / Sunshine, single dad contemporary romance.

The Between the Pines Series

Meet *The Crew* from Eastlyn in this series of standalone contemporary romance novels about found family.

<u>Raised On It</u>

<u>Bottle It Up</u>

Want to read Reece and Rachel's story? Sign-up for my newsletter and get their novella for FREE! <u>Click here for your copy of We Are Tonight!</u>

Blackbird

Standalone second chance contemporary romance.

The Gorgeous Duet

A steamy, suspenseful romance about breaking the rules and following your heart.

<u>Gorgeous: Book One</u>

<u>Gorgeous: Book Two</u>

The You & Me Series

Read this three-book series of sweet and sexy standalone novels filled with love, loss, secrets, and sass.

ABOUT THE AUTHOR

About the Author

Lisa Shelby is an international bestselling contemporary romance author, a self-proclaimed love geek and cake-pop addict. Born and raised in the Pacific Northwest, this is still where Lisa calls home with her husband and their dogs. When she isn't writing her next happily ever after, you can find Lisa with her husband traveling, listening to live music, and impatiently waiting for her next FaceTime call with her son, who is currently deployed with the United States Marine Corps.

Join Lisa's Reader Group: Lisa's Love Geeks
Newsletter Sign-up